THE TONGUELESS HORROR

And Other Stories

The Weird Tales of

Wyatt Blassingame

Volume One

THE TONGUELESS HORROR

And Other Stories

The Weird Tales of

Wyatt Blassingame

Volume 1

Edited and with an Introduction by

John Pelan

RAMBLE HOUSE

THE TONGUELESS HORROR—Wyatt Blassingame

This edition © 2010 by Ramble House

Cover Art © 2010 by Gavin O'Keefe

The Tongueless Horror, *Dime Mystery Magazine,* March 1934
Satan Sends a Woman, *Terror Tales,* January 1936
Song of the Dead, *Dime Mystery Magazine,* March 1935
Satan's Thirsty Ones, *Dime Mystery Magazine,* May 1938
House of Vanished Brides, *Dime Mystery Magazine,* February
    1935
Village of the Dead, *Terror Tales,* October 1934
Models for Madness, *Terror Tales,* December 1935

ISBN 13: 978-1-60543-485-8

ISBN 10: 1-60543-485-X

DANCING TUATARA PRESS #11

CONTENTS

Southern Discomfort: The Weird Tales of Wyatt Blassingame

It's a shame, but when you check standard bibliographies for information about Wyatt Blassingame you will find references to dozens of books (mostly for younger readers) on subjects ranging from the ancient Incas and the Spanish invasion to armadillos, sharks, skunks and Josef Stalin! The more complete reference works may make mention of some fictional works for the same audience, such as *Paul Bunyan Fights the Monster Plants*, which is at least in the realm of fantastic literature; and you may even see a reference to "hundreds of short stories". However, unless you're using a much more specialized guide, it's unlikely that you'll see any discussion at all of one of the most outstanding bodies of work in the annals of mystery and weird fiction. Despite writing for the top pulp markets of the time and maintaining a continuing presence by successfully switching to the more prestigious "slicks" after WWII, only a slim paperback collecting some of the exploits of Detective John Smith exists to preserve any of his genre writings.

This is a situation that we here at Dancing Tuatara Press intend to correct. While a goodly amount of Wyatt Blassingame's fiction falls outside our area, there is still a huge amount of top-drawer material that with the exception of the occasional pulp reprint hasn't seen the light of day in over sixty years. We anticipate some five volumes of his best work from the weird menace years up through the evolution of these magazines to more traditional hard-boiled mystery in the post-war years.

Born in Alabama in 1909, Wyatt Blassingame (like his contemporary John H. Knox) set off to seek his fortune and see the country via the expedient methods of hitchhiking and freight hopping. And like Knox, he found all roads led to New York and the publishing industry, where his brother Lurton was building a successful business as a literary agent. It was his brother who gave him the eminently practical advice to study the current offerings on the newsstand and write similar stories.

Whereas Wyatt Blassingame ultimately wrote (and sold) every type of genre story including horror, western, romance, detective, sports, and adventure (seemingly missing only the true confession genre), his strength was in the thriller or supernatural yarn and this was his bread and butter until the war years where his time with the Naval Air Service gave him material for several books.

Starting with "Horror in the Hold" in the December 1933 issue of *Dime Mystery* and continuing throughout the next two decades Wyatt Blassingame penned over one-hundred tales of weird detective stories and supernatural menace before making a sudden shift to work for juveniles, both fiction and non-fiction. As "Horror in the Hold" appeared in what is considered the third "weird menace" magazine to be published, Blassingame can certainly be considered among the genre's founding fathers, preceding other top writers in the genre such as John H. Knox, Arthur Leo Zagat, and even the field's acknowledged master, Arthur J. Burks.

In the 1930s, Popular Publications was well on the way to a position of dominance in the mystery and horror genres, covering every conceivable nuance of the field from traditional mystery to action-packed stories of Federal agents to the more lurid tales featured in *Dime Mystery*, *Terror Tales* and *Horror Stories*. Much of Popular Publications' success was attributable to a strict focus on a particular type of story in each publication, the exception to the rule was the venerable *Weird Tales*, subtitled "The Unique Magazine". Despite being the home to such authors as Robert E. Howard, Clark Ashton Smith, and H.P. Lovecraft, *Weird Tales* was always close to the chopping block and only marginally viable from a business standpoint.

Due to the stable of authors that went on to become household names (such as the three gentlemen mentioned previously) a sort of revisionist history became the norm in pulp collecting circles that implied that the stable of authors appearing in the "Big Three" of the weird menace genre were somehow inferior to the more literary sorts that occupied the pages of *Weird Tales* and that authors such as Burks, Knox, and Blassingame couldn't quite make the grade . . . Of course, the reality is that nothing could be further from the truth. The "Big Three" paid at least twice and frequently more than the rates offered by *Weird Tales*. Among the mainstays of the three magazines were Burks, a career military man who approached the writing business with the single-minded focus of an officer utilizing a sound strategy to conquer various markets; then there was John H. Knox, an erudite man of letters, well-known in literary circles for his poetry; and then there was Wyatt Blassingame, a consummate professional who achieved five decades of success based upon his skill at identifying the hot new markets and reliably delivering the goods. Of the three, only Burks appeared in *Weird Tales* and most of these appearances were early in his career when he was just learning his craft.

With the exception of one lone tale in *Strange Stories* in 1941 Wyatt Blassingame's work was to be found only in the better-paying markets of Popular Publications. The same held true after the war when the pulps began to slowly fade away. He targeted the best markets and throughout his career remained an author who could choose his spots.

Further essays will examine the approach that Blassingame took to the weird tale, but suffice it to say that another characteristic he shares with John H. Knox was a willingness to break the main rule in the weird menace style guide and like Knox he was easily good enough to get away with it. What rule was this that only the elite could ignore it? Quite simply, it was the utilization of a tried and true formula that was still an effective plot device some thirty years when it was the cornerstone plot element of the popular cartoon show *Scooby-Doo*. There are variations on the theme, but the central point is that the monster, demon, vampire, or what-have-you is a man in a rubber suit, who for purposes generally tied to hidden wealth or an inheritance is trying to scare the locals away. Now known as the "Scooby-Doo Ending", the denouement is generally a hurried summation of the sinister (and now foiled) plot delivered as a confession by the now captured evildoer. This was also the standard for the weird menace tales published in *Dime Mystery*, *Terror Tales*, and *Horror Stories*.

What Wyatt Blassingame and John H. Knox did on a fairly regular basis was to ignore this mandate and turn in stories that were purely fantastic in nature. It could of course be argued that using a supernatural rationale to explain amazing events in their stories was no more implausible than some of the "rational" explanations utilized by some of their contemporaries. As both authors were (with Hugh B. Cave and Arthur J. Burks) the standard bearers for the three magazines they were allowed a much greater flexibility than many of their contemporaries. This translated into a great benefit for the readers as the regular contributors stuck to the formula making the challenge to reader "how was it done?" as well as "who done it?" In the cases of Blassingame and Knox the reader also had to puzzle out whether or not mysterious forces as well as the prosaic were at work.

I was tempted to eschew my usual format for these books and present Blassingame's work in chronological order as no other writer was so synonymous with the evolution of the genre, starting at the very beginning of the weird menace genre and remaining as a leading contributor to Dime Mystery as the magazine made its shift to a less sensational type of fiction in the 1940s. When assembling a multi-volume set of a given author's work, I try to vary the content in order to make each book a "sampler", rather than a chronological presentation that almost always shows a tentativeness as the author struggles to find his/her voice early in their career, progressing to a mastery of their craft and often (sadly) diminishing quality as the author becomes bored with the material that brought about their success or they find themselves in a changing marketplace that they have failed to adapt to. There was no danger of this in assembling these collections of Wyatt Blassingame's work. As can be seen in the title story and in "Village of the Dead" he started out at a very high level and stayed there. There have been few collections that have been as enjoyable to put together for the simple reason that there was never an occasion where I felt I had to "hide" an inferior story. There were certainly some stories that I liked better than others, but there simply weren't any bad ones. It's my hope that you find this and the subsequent books as enjoyable to read as I have.

John Pelan
Midnight House
Tohatchi, NM
Summer Solstice 2010

THE
TONGUELESS
HORROR

CHAPTER ONE

A MUTILATED CHILD

JOHN HEWITT STEPPED FROM THE DOOR of the Little Italy cafe and stood flat-footed on the sidewalk before it, facing into the wind. Cold gripped the drab houses along First Avenue, the dirty deserted street. Hewitt looked with squinted gray eyes, his square, plain face expressionless.

The door of the cafe swung open again and Ed Ginnis, Hewitt's partner, came out. Without pausing, Ginnis crossed the sidewalk toward the police coupe. Hewitt watched the short, heavily-built Irishman, and frowned. The two detectives had been detailed together a week before; neither had been pleased.

Hewitt started toward the coupe, stopped short. Thinned by the whipping wind, a distant shout cracked at his ears. Ginnis took his foot from the runningboard, turned his heavy-jawed face toward the waving man who stood before an alley mouth, half a block away. Ginnis called to his partner, "What you reckon he wants?"

Hewitt squinted. It was a cloudy, gray afternoon with paper and dust swirling in the wind. "It's Father Mottole," he said.

The man at the alley mouth waved his arms and shouted. Fear made his voice strident. "Come here! Quick!"

Hewitt ducked his wide shoulders, began to run. As he ran, he put his right hand to his hip, felt his service revolver jar in its holster. Behind him he heard Ginnis' pounding footsteps.

Father Mottole was a small, slender Italian with soft black eyes and hair gray about the temples. He was not a priest, but was known affectionately in the Italian quarter as "Father" because of the innumerable charities which he financed and supervised.

His kindly, thin face was drawn now and his lips jerked spasmodically. He stared at Hewitt with round, frightened eyes then pointed into the alley with a trembling forefinger. "In there," he said. "It's in there!"

Hewitt stared into the alley. Brick walls on each side shaded the dirty pavement, made the place chill and gloomy. Orange peels and tin cans littered the concrete. Occasional barrels were piled with trash.

"It's in there," Mottole said again. His voice was a hoarse whisper.

Ginnis had stopped beside the Italian. "Okay, it's in there. But what the hell is it?"

"The child." Mottole pushed the words out with stiff lips. "I—" He stopped abruptly. Hewitt's broad shoulders tensed forward; his head twisted to one side, listening. And what he heard made him insensible to the chill of the wind.

From the gloom of the alley had come a low whimpering moan; a sobbing, choked noise like that of a tongueless beast. The moan crept through the murk of the alley, slid into the whipping wind, and faded. Hewitt lunged forward. His hard heels thudded on the concrete, jarring flat sound against the narrow walls. Behind him he heard Ginnis, the frightened muttering of Mottole repeating a prayer in Italian.

A barrel, filled with trash and with the top hoop pulled loose, was on the right of the alley. As Hewitt went toward it a new odor smeared through the stink of the garbage—a sweet and curiously sickening odor. Hewitt heard the whimpering wordless moan again as he reached the barrel. Then he stopped short, his eyes straining from their sockets.

Behind the barrel a child lay on her back. Her thin dress was ripped and torn, showing dark splotches in a dozen places, cold blue flesh in others. But it was the sight of the child's face—or of what had been her face—that made John Hewitt feel suddenly sick, that kept his big hands stiff in front of him as if frozen.

There was little blood on the child, though a black puddle was clotted beneath her head. The mouth was open and the lower lip split in three places, sagged back to show small white teeth. Strips had been cut from the cheeks, exposing raw gums. The eyes rolled white in lidless sockets. Each gash was edged with blood, as though something had been used to stop the bleeding excepting for the chin and lower lip. They were black with clotted blood and from the bottom of the gash in the left cheek a dark stream had poured to the pavement.

Muscles stiff, Hewitt knelt beside the child and started to move his shaking hands toward her shoulders. Then he stopped abruptly. His breath whistled, in chill horror through his set teeth.

Ginnis' emotionless voice jarred his ears. "What the hell's happened to the kid?"

Hewitt did not move. He knelt forward, his hands almost touching the child's shoulders, his eyes riveted on the open mouth, and when he spoke his voice sounded flat and dead. "Her tongue's been cut out!" he said. "That's why she moaned, instead of crying."

"Well, I'll be damned!" Ginnis said, and broke off abruptly. Hewitt heard the sound of his shoes shuffling on the concrete. "Where'd Father Mottole go?" Ginnis demanded.

Hewitt got to his feet without taking his eyes from the child. Evidently she had fainted some time ago, moaned unconsciously. "I don't know," Hewitt said. "I thought he followed you down the alley."

"I thought so too, but—" Ginnis stopped. From the First Avenue sidewalk came the sound of running feet. They turned into the alley, Hewitt looked up, saw Mottole racing toward them, his long black overcoat open and flapping about his legs, arms swinging awkwardly. Then, a short distance from the detectives he stopped and stood panting, speechless.

The softness had gone from his eyes, leaving them hard and black. His face was set, though his lips still jerked spasmodically. "I called a police ambulance from the cafe," he panted. "I didn't tell anybody else there about—" He stopped, his eyes avoiding the horror on the ground. Slowly he began to pull off his overcoat. He handed it to Hewitt, and said, "Wrap the child in this. I—I can't." Hewitt spread the coat on the pavement beside the girl, picked her up gently and placed her on it. She moaned as he touched her, and through his gloves he could feel the little body stiff and cold. He was tucking the sides about her when Ginnis snapped, "Well, Mottole, what were you doing in this alley? How in hell did you happen to find her?"

Hewitt got to his feet, noticed that there was blood on the forefinger of his left glove. He raised his eyes, looked at the other two men. Mottole's face was drawn and gray, but his lips had stopped twitching. "I wasn't in the alley," Mottole said. "I was passing on the sidewalk and heard—heard it. I thought perhaps it was a cat, freezing, When I came to see I found—that." He said the last word flatly.

Wind whistled, rustling paper and swirling dust and filth of the alley. A tin can, wind-driven, clanked over the pavement and into the brick wall. John Hewitt shivered inside his thick coat. Mottole's lips were blue with cold. There came the wail of a police siren on the wind. Then both wind and siren died abruptly, and the three men stood silent, staring at one another.

Mottole moved slow eyes to the bundle at his feet, crossed himself. But there was nothing religious in the harsh clack of his words.

"She was Pete Datoni's stepchild, Maria. Datoni doesn't have much money, and he never spent what he had on Maria. She played about the streets here in rags." His words grew slower, each one falling like a heavy stone. "She must have been playing along the street when someone lured her into the alley—" He stopped, his thin hands clenched hard before him.

The wail of the ambulance siren grew suddenly loud. Tires screamed on pavement. Men pounded down the alley carrying a stretcher. Hewitt said, facing Ginnis, "You go to the hospital with the child, then take Father Mottole to the station-house." He moved his head toward the Italian. "You say she was Pete Datoni's child. Where does he live?" Somebody had to tell the father. But Hewitt didn't relish the job.

"810 Tenth Street."

Hewitt nodded glumly and walked along the alley toward First Avenue.

Behind him he heard the low exclamation of horror of the ambulance men, the tongueless moan of the mutilated child.

CHAPTER TWO

HYPODERMIC FROM HELL

NUMBER 810 TENTH STREET was a squat, brick house, crouched like a hunchback, close beside the walk. The right wing of the house protruded slightly forward to shelter the low steps running up to the front door. John Hewitt went up the steps, struck the door with his gloved knuckles.

The door swung open. Hewitt stepped inside, shoulders hunched against the cold. The man pushed the door closed behind him and Hewitt turned in the gloom of the unlighted corridor to stare at a short, squarely-built Italian. The man looked curiously like the house in which he lived. Hewitt asked, "Pete Datoni?"

The man grunted assent. Hewitt flipped his coat to show the detective's badge. Datoni's eyes blinked nervously; his thick-knuckled fingers quivered in front of him. "What happened?" he asked. "Something to—my Maria?"

Hewitt went suddenly tense. His square face snapped forward. "Why?" he barked. "What do you think has happened?"

Datoni backed away, his face showing pale in the darkness. Then suddenly he was close to the detective, his big hands clutching at Hewitt's coat. "Tell me!" he said hoarsely. "Is it something to my Maria? I tried—I tried to protect her."

Hewitt looked into the man's grief-stricken face, thinking, "It's going to be harder to tell than I thought." Aloud he said, "What do you mean, you tried to protect her? Protect her from what?"

Datoni loosened Hewitt's coat. His face was pale, but composed. "I knew it," he said. He paused, added, "Come in here, and I will tell you. I—I am glad you have come."

He took two steps down the hall, turned right. Hewitt followed him into a sparsely furnished living room. There were three windows, one on a side. Near the wall was a sofa. Datoni gestured toward one of the three chairs in the room, dropped into another.

For a moment Datoni sat in the semi-darkness, head bowed, shoulders drooping. When he looked up his face was hard, determined. He began to speak slowly.

"I have been warned not to tell the police. They said I would be murdered if I did. But,"—his voice went high and his hands began to shake—"I don't care! If something has happened to my Maria, I will tell the police—everything!"

Hewitt fumbled off his glove, pulled a cigarette from his pocket and lighted it. Briefly he told of finding the child. When he had finished, Datoni sat clutching the arms of his chair, his knuckles bone white. "They said they would kill her," he said slowly. "I got my money from the bank to give them. It was all I had. I only had four hundred dollars. They wanted five thousand dollars and so they did that to—to my Maria. Now they will kill me!" His voice jumped high, cracked. "But I will tell! I will tell the police! Then let them kill me."

Hewitt leaned toward Datoni, eyes fastened on him. He said, "They won't kill you. Don't worry—we'll take care of that. Tell me who threatened the little girl."

Slowly Datoni shook his head. His jaw was shut hard, but his face was pale, hopeless. "A police guard will not help. There is no help. This—this thing—it is not human!"

A chill feeling of something unearthly, supernatural crept through John Hewitt. He leaned toward Datoni, eyes searching the man's face. "What do you mean?"

Datoni rubbed his fingers across his pale cheek. He looked at Hewitt for a moment, and an almost pathetic hope crept into his face. He said, "You—the police, I will tell. You will watch me." Then his voice broke again. "But I don't care. If it will help my little Maria they can kill me!"

"It came two days ago," Datoni went on. "There was a slow knocking on the back door. When I went, no one was there. Nothing but a paper. It said that I should get $5,000 and hold it for—for—There wasn't any name signed, just two bloody marks that looked like knife blades or scissors. It said that if I didn't get the money it, the thing, would get my Maria. I did not have the money. I got all I had to give them, but somehow they knew I did not have enough. And so . . ." His head fell on his chest.

Hewitt said, his lips curled thin and hard, "Have you got the note?"

Datoni looked at Hewitt's set, determined face. He seemed to hesitate. Then he said, "Yes. I will get them." He stood up.

Hewitt said, "Them? You've had another?"

"It came this morning. It was like the other. The knocking and nobody there." Datoni went through the door. Hewitt could hear his shoes scuff along the bare hallway.

Three minutes later he came back into the room. The pieces of paper crinkled as Hewitt opened one. Crude, scrawling writing said:

> It is too late to save your daughter, because you did not get enough money. Get $5,000—or you will be next. It is death to tell the police.

Below were two blood-colored, V-shaped marks. It looked as if the blades of a pair of scissors had been dipped in blood and held against the paper. The first warning was signed in the same way.

Hewitt folded the papers, stuffed them in his coat pocket. "I'll find the. murderer, I'll—" He stopped short.

From the rear of the house came an ominous, dull knocking. Something was beating in heavy monotones against the back door.

Hewitt's eyes jumped to Datoni. The man had dropped into his chair. His face was livid, half-turned toward the sound of the knocking. His fingers gripped the arms of the chair until his shoulders quivered.

"It's—it's the thing!" he whispered.

John Hewitt surged to his feet. His right hand jumped to his hip, came back holding the .38 police special. "Stay here!" he snapped. Stiff-kneed, on the balls of his feet, he swung out of the room, down the hallway toward the rear.

The knocking continued, a muffled, heavy beating.

The hall ended in a small, dark kitchen. Across the kitchen was the back door. As Hewitt stepped into the room the knocking thudded loud—and suddenly quit.

Hewitt hurled himself at the door, ripped it open, gun ready. Cold wind swept over a small, trash-littered yard, over bare steps, and moaned through die doorway. The steps and yard were empty.

For twenty seconds Hewitt stood motionless, his knuckles white about the pistol butt. He shook his head. It was impossible for a human to have knocked on that door, and vanished in the half second it had taken him to cross the kitchen. Yet someone, or some *thing*, had knocked and disappeared.

The gun still in his hand, Hewitt went down the steps and across the yard to the right. At the corner of the house he stopped. There were a half dozen scraggly rosebushes, bare of leaves. Beyond the rosebushes was the front sidewalk. He turned, crossed to the other side of the house. Here a high brick wall shut the place in. In the house beyond the wall Hewitt heard a baby crying. Shaking his head, Hewitt thrust the gun into the holster, turned back toward the kitchen.

Half up the steps he halted. Just inside the door was a white square of paper. He stooped, picked it up, and cursed softly. Above the bloody V of the forked knives was scrawled:

Get out of this and stay out!

Abruptly the note crushed under Hewitt's thick fingers. For a moment he frowned as he wondered how any human being could have known so quickly that he was here. Then he remembered the department coupe parked in front, and a thin smile curled his lips. So this thing that made the mark of the bloody scissors would frighten him out, would it? He stalked into the house, jabbing the note into his pocket.

As he started up the hall he saw the dark blur of Datoni. The man was crouched against the front door, making little whimpering sounds of fear. Hewitt started toward him and Datoni straightened, his eyes dark in his bloodless face. Hewitt asked, "You got a telephone?"

"Yes. But what—what was there?" Datoni moved down the hall three steps, switched on the lights.

Hewitt said, "Nothing. Just a note for me." He saw the telephone on a small table, picked it up and dialed headquarters, and asked that a detective be sent to guard Datoni. For a moment he listened, then said, "Right. I'll go over." He hung up and turned to Datoni.

"There'll be a detective here in five minutes. Then I'm going to the emergency hospital. They've found another little girl. Her tongue's been cut out and they say she can't move for some reason. Can't budge a finger. She may be connected with this. You stay here and don't go out of the house."

Fear rode high in Datoni's face, but the Italian was fighting for self-control. He said, almost to himself, "I told the police. But I am not afraid. I am not afraid!"

Hewitt heard the car stop in front a few minutes later, and opened the front door for Detective Sam Englehart. Englehart was a gaunt tall man whose bony face terminated in a wide lantern jaw.

Briefly Hewitt outlined what had happened. Then he opened the front door and stepped out. A cold wind whipped about him.

An arc light to his right threw a dull glow along the dirty street as he stepped to his coupe parked against the curb. He slid under the steering wheel and something pricked his right leg.

He sat perfectly still on the seat for a moment, his eyebrows drawn together in puzzlement. Slowly he moved his right hand along the seat to where the thing had pricked his leg. His fingers touched something small and cylindrical. For thirty seconds John Hewitt sat without moving, frozen by abject terror. Horror such as he had never known flooded his body. He knew what the thing beneath his hand was even before he snapped on the dash-light.

Strapped to the seat with black adhesive, the point raised so that it had jabbed his leg when he slid inside, was a hypodermic. The plunger was strapped to the seat and the bowl was still more than half full of a murky green liquid.

With numbed shaking fingers, Hewitt, pulled the adhesive loose, picked up the hypodermic. Very little of the fluid could have entered his body. There had been no pain except for that first tiny prick. He bent his right knee, swung the leg. Nothing seemed wrong with it—yet.

He said half aloud, "I wonder if . . ." Then he stopped, and wiped the heel of his hand along his sweat-damp brow. "It can't be! I—I didn't get much!" Still holding the hypodermic, he kicked the motor into action.

John Hewitt walked slowly from the hospital toward his parked coupe. His friend, Dr. Frank Sidney, would analyze the hypodermic contents. He had gone into another wing of the building to look at the second injured child. "The daughter of Anthony Lazelli, 1212 Second Avenue," the nurse had said.

Hewitt's face was grim as he thought of the little girl. She had lain flat on her back, her eyes staring vacantly at the ceiling. There had been a slight stain of blood about her mouth but there had been no other mark on the stiff, rigid, little body. "Her—her tongue's been cut out," the nurse had gasped. "But there's something else wrong, too. The doctors don't know what. She hasn't budged since she came here. She's paralyzed, and yet her heart's beating and her eyes reflect, but the lids won't work."

Hewitt thought of the child, and of her open eyes showing that the brain behind them was active. She knew she was maimed, knew she was dying, but she was unable to move one finger, one eyelid.

"Worse than death!" he muttered. "A living, creeping, conscious death! He stepped to the curb, pulled open the door of the coupe, stepped toward the running board.

He heard the clack of leather on steel. He staggered, flung his arms against the car, caught his balance. And then his breath froze in his body as the terrifying realization swept over him.

His right foot had struck the runningboard, but his foot had not felt the impact!

His lips apart, Hewitt looked down at his foot. He stomped it heavily on the pavement. The shoe thudded and Hewitt felt the jar in his leg.

But his foot had never known it touched the ground. His right foot was dead! For a full minute Hewitt stood there, body bent, looking at his foot. Horribly clear he saw again the girl on the hospital cot, her eyes open, her face rigid, her body utterly paralyzed.

Slowly he straightened. He whispered, can't be! Not—not totally. I only got a drop or two. It can't—" with his right hand he struck the spot on his hip where the needle had entered. The flesh was firm, alive. He tried the foot again. And again there was no feeling.

He climbed into the coupe. His mind refused to accept what had happened, struggled to find some way around the evidence. He leaned over again and tapped the foot with his fingers. He might as well have tapped the gear lever.

Fifteen minutes later he swung the coupe toward the curb, pulled the dead weight of his foot from the floor boards, pushed it against the brake. The car stopped with a jerk. He sat still then, looking at the home of the child who now lay at the emergency hospital, living, but dead.

The house was a large, square building, the top barely visible over the high brick wall that cut it off from the sidewalk. There was a wooden gate in the middle of the wall. Hewitt smiled grimly as he looked at it. Evidently Lazelli had money.

Hewitt slapped his right ankle twice with his palm. Then his mouth was a gray gash in a colorless face. The ankle was numb.

The wall offered protection from the wind as Hewitt limped through the gate and stood inside. It was dark and he could not see much. The front of the house, where lights showed from four windows, was about sixty feet away. The brick wall closed the house in on all four sides, but left ample lawns. To his right Hewitt could see the naked limbs of a maple tree. In front of him a concrete walk led to a small fountain, circled it, and went on to the steps of the house.

Hewitt's shoes clopped unevenly as he went forward.

The front door was massive with a heavy brass knocker. Hewitt lifted the knocker, rapped. Waiting, he heard a truck lumbering down Second Avenue.

The door swung open and light spilled out across the porch. A girl was holding the door and Hewitt stood, mouth half open, staring at her. She was slender and tall with jet black hair that went in little lapping curls back from a broad, pale forehead. Her face was in shadow, but Hewitt could see its perfect oval outline, the soft curve that was her mouth and the dark pools that were her eyes.

Hewitt bowed slightly, said, "Is Mr. Lazelli here?" He fingered his lapel, showing the badge.

The girl said, "Yes. Come in." She opened the door wider and Hewitt stepped over the sill. He swung his left foot first, then pulled the right, a dead weight, carefully after. The girl closed the door, looked at Hewitt, and asked, "You come to see father about . . ." She stopped, biting her lower lip with small, white teeth. Tears glistened in the corners of her eyes. ". . . About sister?" She finished.

"Yes."

The girl turned, took four steps down the hall, knocked on a closed door on her left. A man's voice asked curtly. "What is it?"

The girl pushed the door open. "Here's another detective, father," she announced and stepped back as John Hewitt walked past her into the room.

The room was poorly, barely furnished. A massive chandelier, holding only one small bulb, hung in the middle. Directly under the light was a desk and behind that a small swivel chair. Two straight chairs were drawn up in front of the desk. In them Ginnis and Father Mottole twisted around to face Hewitt as he entered the room.

Ginnis said, "Well, here you are. One by one we all get here. Me first; then Father Mottole; now you."

Hewitt didn't answer. He stood flatfooted looking at the man behind the desk. Often he had heard of Anthony Lazelli, but this was the first time he had seen the man. Reported to be one of the wealthiest Italians in the city, Lazelli was also a mystery. He seldom went outside of his walled garden, and he had the name of being a miser. Glancing at the bare floor, the frayed curtains, Hewitt had a hunch that the gossip was probably correct.

Lazelli did not get out of his chair. He leaned stooped shoulders forward, put his hands on the desk. His head was too big for his body and sat on the end of a long, scrawny neck. It was almost bald with occasional, glossy black hairs which lay flat against his skull. His mouth was pinched and dark; his eyes narrow, intense, almost mad.

The detective balanced on his right foot. He had the odd sensation that he was swinging in the air, not touching the floor at all. He swung his left leg forward, pulled his right one after it and stood with the fingers of his gloved hands on Lazelli's desk. "I'm John Hewitt," he said. "Your daughter was the—second child to be injured today, and—"

Lazelli said angrily, "I know that."

Hewitt's lips twitched in surprise. He remembered that this man had not visited the hospital to see his daughter. Now he seemed more annoyed than grieved. Hewitt remembered the grief and the terror-stricken face of Datoni, and anger made his voice brittle. "What else do you know? Who did this?"

Light flashed in Lazelli's black eyes. One corner of his pinched mouth quivered. He said, "I don't know. How should I?"

Ginnis said, "That's his story and he's sticking to it."

Mottole pointed a slim finger toward Lazelli and said softly, "There's no way you should know who injured the child. But you should go see her in the hospital. You should make some provision for her care. There are specialists who . . ."

Lazelli struck the desk with clenched fists. He shouted, "Get out of here! Don't come to my home telling me what to do! All of you! Get out!"

Hewitt's broad shoulders swayed toward Lazelli. His face was rock-hard, all sympathy for the man gone, "You may not know who did it," he growled. "But you damn well know why. How much money did those bloody scissors ask for?"

Ginnis slammed to his feet, snarling, "Bloody what?"

Lazelli squirmed in his chair, eyes darting furtively around the room. Hewitt said, "All right. How much?"

Lazelli slumped in his chair, said, 'They wanted $50,000."

Ginnis asked, "What the devil are you talking about?"

"Some extortionist who signs himself with a pair of bloody scissors or some such thing wrote Datoni asking for money. Datoni didn't have it, so they got his kid," Hewitt said. "Same thing here."

"Maybe Datoni didn't," Ginnis said, almost under his breath. Then in a rush he added, "But this guy's got plenty." He whirled on Lazelli. "Why the hell didn't you pay? Don't you care what happens to your kids?"

Lazelli sat staring at his feet. In the light of the one globe his bald head looked like a fortune teller's crystal. He said sullenly, "They wanted $50,000. I couldn't pay that much, I would have paid something, but I couldn't pay that much."

"Why didn't you tell them you couldn't pay so much?" Father Mottole asked quietly. He had folded his thin hands on the desk in front of him. "How much did you offer to pay?"

Lazelli said, "Nothing. I didn't know how to get in touch with them. They just—just left the notes."

Hewitt asked, "Have you had another, since the warning about Maria?"

"No. But I won't pay! I won't!" He sprang to his feet. His fists shook in front of him and his eyes flamed evilly. "They may kill me, but I'm not afraid. Not afraid of things I can't see! I won't pay. I—" He screamed shrilly.

John Hewitt saw the paper fluttering over his head the second Lazelli screamed. It came floating down, tilting from side to side in the still air. The paper seemed to have dropped *through* the ceiling, yet there had been no sound.

It came down between the four motionless men, flattened out on the desk top, slid to a stop. For three full seconds the men stared, still and silent. Ginnis muttered, "Well, I'll be damned!" Hewitt stood, breathing heavily through his nostrils. Without moving he read the crudely printed message below the marks made by a pair of bloody scissors:

$100,000 or your daughter Rose dies at midnight!

A long while the four men stood motionless, staring at the note.

Hewitt's brain was racing. Why had Ginnis jumped with alarm at mention of the bloody scissors? What did he know about them? And Father Mottole—why was he always on hand? Abruptly he remembered Datoni, wondered if anything had happened there since he left.

Hewitt's hand clenched hard. Death, like a strangling vine, was creeping up his leg.

Hewitt turned toward Ginnis, and said, tightly, "You stay here and look after this man. I'm going to check on Datoni now. I'll be back by midnight to help if anything happens."

Ginnis sneered. "Hell, nothin's going to happen here. Nothing would have happened"—he flung contemptuous eyes toward Lazelli—"if that buzzard thought more of his kids than his money."

With awkward, dumping steps, like a man with a new wooden leg, Hewitt pulled open the door, and stepping out into the hall, closed the door behind him.

As the door shut, Hewitt bent sharply, tapped his right calf with his finger tips. It had no feeling, and when he tried to wiggle the foot it was as if he had tried, by sitting and thinking, to move a wall. He struck his leg higher up. It was dead to the knee.

Hewitt didn't have time to be afraid. He had to work quickly now. In another four or five hours, perhaps, he would be like the child in the hospital, motionless, dead, except for a brain that functioned and eyes that stared fixedly. But wouldn't die; he hadn't got much of the fluid. Surely this paralysis would stop at the knee. If it didn't . . .

CHAPTER THREE

BULLET PROOF DEATH

HEWITT TURNED STILL IN THE HALLWAY and saw Rose Lazelli standing in a darkened doorway across from him. He stepped toward her unsteadily. She looked down at his foot; her eyebrows arched as she opened her mouth to speak. Hewitt shook his head, said, "It's nothing." He stopped close to her and looked down into eyes that were like pools of black shadows. She had been crying.

Hewitt said, "Has your father been in the house all day?"

The girl nodded. "He shuts himself up in the back. I never see him."

"Who else has been here this afternoon? In the room where they are now?"

The girl dabbed at her eyes with a small handkerchief. Even crying and grief-stricken he noticed the girl's soft beauty, the full curve of her lips, the outline of her slender body beneath the clinging dress . . . She crumpled the handkerchief in her hand and said, "Nobody except the detective who's in there now. He was there for a while before father came from the back of the house. Then, fifteen minutes ago, Father Mottole came. In the afternoon there was a peddler, trying to sell father some silks. But he didn't stay long. Father wouldn't talk to him. They were lovely things, and I—wanted—" She tried to smile, but her lips quivered. "What—what have they done to sister? I'm so frightened!"

Hewitt moved one big hand toward the girl and stopped abruptly. That living death had threatened to strike this girl at midnight. For a sickening moment Hewitt visioned her face, ripped and mangled as that of little Maria had been.

Hewitt looked at his wrist watch. 9:15. There was no need of telling the girl about the note now. He said, "There's nothing for you to worry about. I don't know how badly hurt your little sister is, but I'll find out and let you know."

The girl's hands caught Hewitt's arm. "Thank you," she said.

John Hewitt turned on the heel that had no feeling and went toward the door, and dragged himself toward the car.

At a corner drug store Hewitt stopped the coupe and went inside. His knee was stiff, dead now, and he had to walk by swinging his leg from the hip. He went inside a telephone booth, dialed the news room of the *Star,* and asked for Ralph Gill.

When he heard the reporter's voice Hewitt said, "Ralph, go through your files, find out everything you can about Pete Datoni." He spelled the name out. "Then check up on Anthony Lazelli, Ed Ginnis, and Father Mottole. Get in touch with Dr. Sidney at the Emergency Hospital, tell him I said give you the story because I don't have time. But don't break it until I let you know. I'll call you back in a little while." He hung up, called the Emergency Hospital, learned that Dr. Sidney was still in the laboratory, and asked about the girl.

"Her heart beats and respiration are both growing slower," the nurse said. "The doctors don't have much hope for her."

Hewitt said, "Thank you," and heard the nurse hang up. So, it was death at the end. Total paralysis, and then death. Hewitt rubbed the fingers of his hand through his hair. "It's got my knee," he said aloud, "but it'll stop there. It must stop there! But whether it gets me or not, I'll get it." He pushed the door of the telephone booth open and swayed outside.

A soda jerker glimpsed Hewitt's face. He stared after the detective, unconscious that the carbonated water had filled the glass and was running over.

It was difficult driving with his right leg stretched stiffly in front of him, but the traffic was light along Second Avenue. He turned east to First, and just outside of Datoni's home he cut the switch and braked the car to a halt with his left foot.

John Hewitt slipped from the coupe, and hobbled toward the squat, hunchbacked house. He went up the three brick steps, left foot first, dragging his right leg afterward, and knocked on the door.

No sound came from the inside of the house.

Why didn't Englehart open the door? He knocked again. The wind whipped away the sound, and the house was as still as if he had knocked on the door of a tomb.

Hewitt twisted the knob. The door swung open. He stepped through into a dark, silent hallway. Behind him gray light seeped through the half-open door; ahead blackness crouched like a hunted animal.

Hewitt's hand moved toward his hip and came back clenching the revolver. He moved sideways, pushed his back against the wall. He called, "Englehart! Hey Sam!" His voice rumbled down the narrow hallway, and died.

The light switch, he remembered, was near the door of the living room. He shifted his gun to his left hand, put his right hand against the wall, started toward the switch. His left foot struck the floor with a dull thud. His right shoe scraped as he dragged it forward. He swung his left foot ahead. It struck something—something soft.

Hewitt staggered, tried to jerk his right foot forward. He clawed at the wall with his right hand, swayed, pitched headlong. He struck lying across a human body.

He writhed away from the body, jerking up his gun. There was no sound excepting the echo of his movement. Tensely he pushed his right hand along the floor, touched the body and moved along an arm to the face. He jerked back his hand, gasping so that the sound stirred in the dark hallway. The man's face was a mass of blood.

John Hewitt almost screamed aloud. Every muscle in his body was taut as a bow string and his teeth scraped together.

"God!" he whispered. The darkness soaked up the word.

Hewitt put both hands on the chest of the man lying there. He drew his left leg under his body, straightened his arms, managed to get on his feet. He fumbled for the light switch and snapped it on.

In the white flood of light Hewitt saw the body of the detective, Englehart. He lay on his back, the eyes wide open and staring. The half-open mouth was a pool of blood and Hewitt knew instinctively the tongue had been cut away. There was no sign of disorder in the hall; only the body of Englehart, stark and horrible.

With stiff fingers Hewitt found the light switch of the living room and clicked it. Light jumped into the room. John Hewitt gasped.

Flat on the floor, head near the chair in which he had sat earlier, was Pete Datoni. A little splotch of blood showed above the man's temple. His, eyes were shut and his arms outflung. Hewitt went with swaying steps toward him, tried to kneel. His right knee wouldn't bend. Hewitt clutched his thigh and then the last vestige of color drained from his face. Three inches above the knee his leg was dead, unfeeling.

Hewitt put his gun in its holster, slipped to a sitting position beside Datoni. He looked at the blood-stained bump above Datoni's ear, then found the faint flutter of pulse in the man's wrist. Hewitt began to chafe the Italian's wrists.

Datoni's eyes had been open a half minute before they began to focus. He looked around dazedly, saw Hewitt and sat up. "What—what was it?" he gasped weakly.

Hewitt said, "You tell me. I came in and found you here. Englehart's in the hall—dead."

Datoni shook his head dazedly. Fear, hatred, terror, leaped into his face at once. His voice was husky. "I was sitting here. Something knocked on the door and the detective went. I heard him say, 'Hello!' Then he screamed. And . . ." Again Datoni rubbed a shaking hand across his eyes.

"And then?" Hewitt prompted.

"I jumped up and saw a man in the door—a short, thickset man. His coat lapel was turned up and there was a detective's badge on it. Then he jumped at me, and—I don't remember what happened. It couldn't have been long ago. He must have heard you, and ran."

Hewitt drew a long breath through clenched teeth. Ed Ginnis and Sam Englehart had known each other, though there had been no friendship between them. The man Datoni had seen fitted Ginnis' description. But why had Ginnis come here? Hewitt let the air from his lungs slowly.

He clutched the arm of Datoni's chair and pulled himself erect. Then half-way up he paused, muscles stiffening. The slow, heavy pounding sounded once more on the back door.

Snarling, Hewitt jerked his gun from the holster, started in a staggering, rolling run for the kitchen. Twice he tripped, caromed against the wall, but caught himself and kept going. He snapped open the kitchen door and almost fell down the low back steps.

Out in the dingy back yard a white paper, caught by the wind, skidded like a ghost. Hewitt stood still, muscles jerking, eyes big in their sockets.

The yard was empty!

Hewitt went toward the right corner of the house. He moved awkwardly, but the gun in his hand was steady. Once before he had heard this knocking, and had come to find nobody. And again there was—nothing. He should have known that, as on the other occasion, he would find nothing.

He cursed softly as he stepped around the corner of the house and saw the twisted, deformed shadows of the dwarfed rose bushes, the grayness beyond them that was First Avenue.

And then the Thing swept at him!

There was no time to see distinctly, even if the darkness had not muffled his sight. There was a sweep of purplish robes, the dull gleam of a monstrous, oversized head, long black hands, and the glint of a hypodermic.

Hewitt leaped sideways. Something touched his coat, and cloth ripped. He tried to jerk his dead leg under him, failed, and pitched into a rosebush. Thorns tore at his trousers, jabbed his flesh.

He rolled to his back, saw the monster whirl and dive toward him. Hewitt's gun roared.

The Thing stopped in its dive, staggered. The revolver jumped in Hewitt's hand, crashed again. The creature wavered, whirled abruptly, and raced toward the back of the house.

Hewitt cursed hollowly. What living thing, human or animal, could carry two .38 slugs in its chest and run at that speed? Hewitt writhed to the side of the house, pawed against it, got to his feet.

The Thing had disappeared around the rear of the building. Hewitt started after it. His dead leg hit a rosebush and he fell again. His forehead struck against the brick wall of the house. Lights burst in the darkness. He half rolled, struck the soft dirt on his side, twitched—and lay still.

John Hewitt blinked, pushed his hand against the red mist of pain before his eyes and fought his way back to consciousness. He struggled to a sitting position, tried to get up, by climbing to the side of the house. His head whirled dizzily.

Looking down, he saw his right leg stiff in front of him, his left leg slightly bent. Remembrance flooded his mind. He rolled over, put his hands flat on the ground, pulled his left leg under him, straightened his arms. Twice he fell back. Then, holding against the wall, he got to his feet. He took one step toward the back of the house, stopped, and looked at his watch. It was 11:45!

In just fifteen minutes this fiend would call at the home of Anthony Lazelli. Lazelli would not pay, and . . .

Hewitt choked as he thought of the girl with her dark eyes raised toward his, her hand soft on his arm. He started a stumbling run toward the sidewalk. No time now to go looking for Datoni.

As he stumbled along Hewitt beat his hand against his right leg. It was dead almost to the hip. He had to fight the sluggish muscles into movement.

Panting, he crawled into the department coupe, dragging his stiff right leg over the seat, leaving the door swinging. With his left foot he kicked the starter, worked the clutch. He used the hand accelerator.

The coupe raced along First Avenue, skidded into Tenth Street, screamed into First. Hewitt's hands clenched hard on the wheel. He, John Hewitt, what good would he be to protect the girl? The death that crawled up his leg had almost reached his hip. When it did he would be unable to move, except by crawling, pulling himself by his hands. How long would he be able to do that?

The coupe rocked to a halt before the brick wall that enclosed Lazelli's home. Hewitt slipped out, balanced carefully, started toward the house.

He circled the fountain, went up the walk toward the steps, his eyes jumping about the dark lawn. Not a shadow moved in the stillness. There was no sound except for the lugubrious moan of the wind, the creaking of the bare, wind stripped limbs of the maple tree.

Without pausing to knock, Hewitt pushed open the front door and stumbled. into the dimly lighted hallway. He swung the door shut.

It was then he saw the girl, standing in the door of the room where her father had been earlier. Her eyes were wide, with fear. She sighed, "Oh! It's you!" and some of the terror went out of her face.

Hewitt was breathing hard. He followed her into a side room.

"Where's your father?"

"He—he's not here. They all left just after you did." Her dark, troubled eyes moved toward Hewitt's leg, his trousers torn by the rosebushes, back to the bruise on his forehead. "You've been hurt!"

Hewitt said, "Nothing bad." He bent his left arm, looked at the wristwatch. It was 11:55. He snapped, "Quick! Call the police. Tell them to send a whole squad. And get 'em here quick!"

The girl's face blanched as she came closer to him, her lips half parted, her eyes round. "I can't call them. We've no phone."

Hewitt said, "Good God!" His hand snaked to his hip, stopped and dropped limply at his side. The gun was gone! He had left it where he had fallen. "It doesn't matter," he muttered. "I shot him before. He must have worn a steel vest. Damn those soft-nosed bullets."

Rose Lazelli caught his coat with quivering fingers. "What do you mean?"

Hewitt gripped her shoulders, twisted her toward the door. "Get out of the house quick! Call the cops and send them here." He pushed her toward the door.

The girl swayed under his hands, but her feet did not move. "Tell me," she said. "What is it?"

Hewitt swore. "The Thing that got your sister is coming here, now. It's already got me. I can't live. I'll wait for it here. You go—quick!"

The girl put her hands to his coat again. She whispered, "No. I don't want to leave you. Let's both . . ."

"We can't!" Hewitt barked. "I can hardly move." His breathing was hard, tense. "You go now—while there's time!"

Her hands tightened on his coat. "But you . . . you . . ." She stopped abruptly. Terror had returned to her eyes; her hands still clutched Hewitt's coat.

Something scraped along the floor at the rear of the house. There was an unsteady thumping. The sound moved toward the front. *Thump—thump—thump!* It was as if a man walked slowly, dragging a heavy load.

Hewitt heard the girl's wrenched gasp. Her hands seemed frozen to his coat and under them he heard the heavy pounding of his heart.

Thump! Thump! The beating, dragging sound of the steps came on. The girl turned, as though drawn by a magnet, to face the door.

The sound approached the door and paused. For one long, deathly second silence hung like a poised, menacing weight above the room. Then the sound scraped forward, closer.

The girl screamed a half strangled cry, and cowered back. Air whistled from Hewitt's lungs. In the door stood the creature which had attacked him. And in the creature's arms, the face a mass of blood, was the body of Ed Ginnis!

At the door the man dropped Ginnis. The detective hit the floor on his back, lay still. The impact jarred fresh blood from his mouth to well across his cheek and puddle on the floor.

The man stood near Ginnis' stiff body. In the dim light that came from the heavy chandelier over his head Hewitt could see that the man wore a black cloth mask in which slits had been cut for eyes. The bald, egg-shaped head was a helmet with a few painted black lines for hair. Then Hewitt saw the man's hands. Horror and revelation leaped to his eyes.

The hands were large, with blunt, strong fingers and over them thin, flesh-colored gloves had been pulled. On the inside of the first two fingers of the right hand razor-sharp knives of steel were fastened. Hewitt understood now the mystery of the tongueless bodies . . .

The man stepped farther into the room, and the girl shrank close beside Hewitt.

The man looked at her, snarled into his mask, "Where is Lazelli?"

The girl said, "I—I don't know."

Fire glinted in the black eyes behind the mask. The thick fingers dived into a pocket of the robe, came back holding a large hypodermic. A muffled voice snarled, "Where's the money? I told him I'd be here at midnight."

The girl slid along the desk toward Hewitt. Panic leapt from her large dark eyes. Hewitt felt the soft touch of her shoulder. She looked up at him, then toward the masked figure. "I—I don't know," she whimpered. "He didn't leave any with me."

The gloved hands went stiff and hard. An insane light came in the man's eyes as a snarling, wordless sound came from his throat. "All right," he said. "When I finish tonight he'll come across—if he has another chance. I—" The man pushed the hypodermic in front of him, took one step toward the girl.

Rose Lazelli caught Hewitt's left arm in both of hers. She screamed; a choked, terrified cry. Hewitt put his right hand on her arm. He said, "Quiet," and edging his body a foot from the desk, pushed the girl behind him. He told her, still looking at the masked man, "You keep behind me. When I get my hands on him, you run—out of the house, out of the grounds. Shout for help . . ."

The girl's hands tightened on Hewitt's arm. "I—I don't want to run—to leave you!" Her voice was a whisper.

The figure chuckled. He took one step closer to Hewitt, stopped and drew a revolver with his left hand. He chuckled again. "But you will not get your hands on me, my friend. And after you are dead . . ."

The man gestured with the muzzle of the gun. "Do you get out of the way," he said flatly, "and let me get at the girl; or do I shoot you first?"

CHAPTER FOUR

DEATH STRIKES HOME

JOHN HEWITT COULD FEEL THE SOFT TOUCH of the girl's body, hear her rapt breathing behind him. Muscles bulged like frozen ropes along his jaw. One bullet from the masked man's revolver—just one—and the girl would be in the grasp of those cruel knife-blades . . . There was little chance that the sound of the shot would bring help.

One sharp jab of that glittering needle into the girl's white flesh, only a second to pry open her red mouth, to clip with those steel-lined, scissor-like fingers.

The gun muzzle centered on Hewitt's belly. "If you are going to move," the man said, "move now."

Hewitt leaned his wide shoulders forward, estimated the distance between them. Not more than ten feet, but with one leg at dead anchor . . .

Hewitt said, "All right—shoot. The cops will—" He broke off short.

A heavy pounding sounded on the front door. The noise boomed through the still house.

Startled, the masked man jerked back. Hewitt grinned and leaned forward, eyes on the gun in the man's hand. "The cops," he said. "I telephoned them to come here at midnight. Now go ahead and shoot—and then try to get out."

He was praying, inside, that his bluff would work.

The gun wavered in the other's hand. Eyes were red fires behind the mask. The masked man sneered, "It's a stall; it's not the cops. It's—"

Again the front door shook under the knocking, harder this time. The sound rolled into the room where three persons stood waiting for death.

Hewitt said, "It is the cops, you fool!'

Dancing fire hardened in the other's eyes. He shifted his hand along the revolver, caught it by the barrel. He said huskily, "I've never failed, and I won't fail now. You'll die, anyway. And I'll get the girl too!"

He took one step toward John Hewitt, drawing back the gun to smash it against the detective's temple.

Slow, heavy knocks beat on the front door. Beat monotonously, endlessly.

The murderer took another step forward. The dull light from the one small bulb in the chandelier gleamed on the hypodermic needle in his left hand.

Hewitt tried to swing forward to meet the man—to give the girl a chance to run. He put his weight on his left leg, tried to move the right one.

It was dead to the hip!

The man laughed—a creeping, ghoulish sound. He swung the revolver back so that the butt was close to his temple and stepped in to smash it against John Hewitt's head.

Behind him, Hewitt heard the girl gasp sharply. Then Hewitt saw his chance. He flung his arms above his head, and his fingers clutched the chandelier. He kicked his left foot back against the desk, shoved forward. His left leg doubled under him, straightened in one smashing drive.

The masked man saw the foot driving at his face and brought the gun-butt down. Hewitt felt sharp pain flare through his leg. The foot crashed into the man's face, hurling him backward. Hewitt's fingers slipped on the chandelier and his body plunged. His head struck the floor and the room whirled dizzily.

Dull aching throbs beat through John Hewitt's left leg, but he was dimly conscious of cool hands on his face, of a warm, stirring perfume in his nostrils. Through his whole body a slow pounding ache beat sickeningly.

Conscious, Hewitt knew that he still lay where he had fallen, that he had not been out more than five or ten seconds. Rose Lazelli knelt beside him, her hands cool against his face, her dark eyes anxious.

Hewitt tried to rise, but his right leg lay stiff. He snapped, "What—what about that killer?" He tried again to get up. Hot pain flamed through his left leg.

The girl looked beyond Hewitt, then back to the detective's drawn face. "He fell on his hypodermic," she said. "He hasn't moved since."

Again the knocking jarred through the house. "Is it really the police?" the girl asked. Her fingers moved softly across Hewitt's forehead. She slipped her left arm under his shoulders, helped him to a sitting position, let him lean against the desk.

Hewitt said, "I don't think so. Go see."

The girl went out of the room. Hewitt looked across the bare floor at the sprawled man who had made the mark of the bloody scissors.

His right hand was under his hip. His masked head lay twisted to one side. Hewitt laughed harshly, without humor. "Well," he said aloud. "We killed each other. But you went first."

Steps sounded in the hall and he looked toward the door. Dr. Frank Sidney came into the room. He had a black physician's bag in his right hand. Behind him came Rose Lazelli.

"Thank God I found you!" Sidney panted. "Can you still move?"

Hewitt said, "A little, but my right leg's dead."

Sidney flung his bag on the desk above Hewitt's head, talked as he fumbled in it. "I found what was in that green fluid—by luck, mainly. Deadly as hell," he said cheerfully, "a poison only recently discovered, and based in tetra-ethyl lead. I happened to have been doing some research on it at the hospital lately, but we never knew what effect it would have on a human being before. There's an antidote, all right, if you get it in time."

Sidney, a hypodermic in his hand, knelt beside Hewitt, jerked up the detective's left trouser leg. Hewitt winced. Sidney said, "Something hit you an awful wallop on the leg; may have broken it." He jabbed the needle into the flesh.

Rose Lazelli stood behind the doctor, watching every move. When the doctor had made an injection in each leg, Hewitt said, "This lady's the sister of the little girl at the hospital. How's the youngster?"

Sidney grinned. "Doing splendidly," he said. "I gave her an antidote before I left." He turned, looked at the masked body sprawled on the floor. "Who's this?"

Hewitt said, "He's the man that's been spreading the green fluid, and he's got a dose in himself . . . His name is Pete Datoni."

Sidney knelt beside the body, rolled it over. He opened the shirt, grunted. "A steel vest," he said. "And with two big dents in it." He picked up the man's wrist, stripped back the glove, felt the pulse. "Dead already," he muttered. "Got too big a dose."

Sidney stripped the mask from the man's face, and Datoni's swarthy head bumped on the floor. Sidney said, holding the mask in his hands, "Well, I'll be damned! Datoni—why, it was his little girl who was tortured! You don't mean . . .?"

Hewitt grunted. "The first child we found was his stepchild. Datoni doesn't have any money, but he said the extortionist asked him for five thousand dollars. Nobody would try to get money from a man who didn't have it. And there was a lot of knocking on his door with nobody there. That was an electric bell on the chair arm. I rang it by mistake, but didn't realize it until too late. Besides, I don't think even he would have tried to keep this date at exactly the right time if he had known cops might be waiting for him. And he was the only suspect who didn't know that both Ginnis and I had seen his note saying he'd come at midnight. He must have come here earlier, disguised as a peddler, and stuck the note to the ceiling. Impressive—but he didn't know that we'd be here when it fell. That flair of his for being impressive is what got him in trouble.

"After I left here Ginnis most likely decided he'd find out what he could from Datoni, and went over. I stopped on the way and Ginnis got there first. He may have stumbled on something, or Datoni may have been afraid he wouldn't leave in time for him to pay his midnight call. So the Italian stuck him full of that fluid, as he did Sam Englehart. He had just done it when I came in, so he knocked himself on the head, waiting for a chance to get me. He almost did."

The full lips of the girl trembled slightly. "When you came in I was afraid you had been—seriously hurt."

Looking at the perfect oval of the girl's face Hewitt said, "Doc, how long before I'll be up and around?"

"Not long, unless your left leg is broken. I'll take you to the hospital, make an X-ray."

The girl flushed under Hewitt's steady gaze. Looking at her, Hewitt said, "I can't have a broken leg. There are things I want to be doing."

The girl looked up, smiled. "If your leg is broken," she said, "may I come and see you in the hospital, do something to repay what you've done for me?"

Hewitt caught a slow breath. "Doc," he asked, "can you break my leg?"

SATAN SENDS A WOMAN

CHAPTER ONE

DEATH'S SWAMP

"There are different kinds of courage," Ed Roland said. "A mad bull elephant will charge almost anything on earth, and will run from a mouse. Smiling, a woman can face death through childbirth, and will scream at a tiny sound in the dark. There is nothing on God's earth that is totally without fear."

His voice had an odd, strained sound, but at the same time it rang as though those sentences had been repeating themselves over and over in his brain for years. I stopped the julep halfway to my lips and looked at him. Once more the feeling, half fear, half amazement, that I always experienced when I saw him, came over me.

He was sitting on the top step of the porch. His feet were drawn up close to his haunches, his arms were akimbo; he looked like a spider, with his long arms and legs reaching out from a small, round body. There was something about his face, too, which had always reminded me of a spider, hideous, with large, round eyes that are impossible to describe. Looking at him I always got the impression that once he had been a big man, perfectly built, perhaps handsome. But God knows he was ugly enough when I knew him.

Perhaps it was the way he looked, as much as the thing he said, that made me stop the julep, elbow half bent. The moonlight, sliding past the eaves of the house, barely touched him. The small, flower-covered yard was liquid silver in its light, and dark pines loomed up tall and slender, to lean their wide-flung arms on the shoulders of heaven. Beyond them the gulf of Mexico was as placid as a blue mirror with a glittering silver frame of sand.

"What do you mean, there are different kinds of courage, Ed?" I asked. "You sound as though there were a story behind it."

"You might call it a story; I've never known." He sat there for a long time looking like some huge spider backed against the porch. I took a pull on the julep, burying my nose deep in the mint.

"I'll tell you," he said. "Maybe you'll call it a story. All I know is—it happened." After a moment he began to talk.

It was a man called Paul Jenkins who first said that about "kinds of courage." I had never seen him when I got the note asking me to come to his hotel room in Mobile. The note sounded interesting, and I went.

"I know you've got courage," Jenkins told me after we had talked a few minutes. "But there are different lands of courage. I know you are not afraid of bullets and knives, but how about other things? How about swamps where two or three inches of water covers everything, and below the water the mud is without bottom? How about snakes, thousands of them? And how about—?" He paused, his mouth open and a queer, frightened look in his eyes.

I said, "All right, how about it?" I had never been afraid of anything and didn't think I could be. It may sound funny to hear me say that, when you see the way I appear now. But at that time I didn't look like this. I was handsome enough then to get into trouble with women wherever I went, and that was the main reason I was listening to this man's proposition. I was involved with a married woman in Mobile, and was ready to get out. I hadn't met her husband and didn't want to, because she was rather well placed in the city and a scandal would have hurt. So I said, "All right, what do you think I might be afraid of?"

Jenkins licked his lips. "There's probably nothing worse in Death's Swamp than the bogs and snakes. But nobody goes far in there—and comes out. Persons around the edges are superstitious. Perhaps the whole story is superstition, but anyway I'm willing to pay you a thousand dollars to find out."

"For a thousand dollars I'll bring you back a ghost," I said. "Spill it."

Well, maybe you know already the legend of which Jenkins spoke. A ship, carrying a fortune in pearls, was supposed to have been wrecked on the far side of the swamp, about five years ago. There was no way to reach the place except through the swamp, because a boat coming in from the gulf would be caught and wrecked, as this one had been. Nobody was certain, however, for every person on the wrecked ship had vanished. Legend said that a few had gone to investigate, but none ever came back.

"A sailor who claimed to have seen the hulk of the ship from the gulf gave me the location," Jenkins confided. "I'll give you a thousand to investigate. If the ship's really there, and you find the pearls, we'll split. If the ship's not there, the thousand's yours."

"What if it's there?" I asked, "How do you know I won't take the pearls and skip? We never saw one another until an hour ago. What's your guarantee?"

He was a big man with a square, hard mouth, and when he grinned there was something savage about it. "How do I think I know you might be willing to try this?" he asked. "I've investigated you for weeks, and I'll gamble on your word to play fair."

"Okay," I said. "Now where is this place?"

Two days later, without saying anything to Ann Bentley, I left Mobile, the thousand dollars already in my pocket.

I had forgot what Jenkins had said about different kinds of courage until twilight started settling heavily around me. I had been in the swamp since sunrise and knew I should be getting close to the gulf shore. Above the trees light was still in the sky, but the swamp was dark with a heavy, almost tangible gloom. It wasn't black, but there was a sort of murky greyness that pushed vision back against my eyes. Long, coiling vines came suddenly to strike against my face, and I knew that snakes would give no more warning than the vines. I could hear them in the water, only a few inches from me sometimes, as I poled the flat bottomed boat, and now and then I caught the glimmer of white that meant a cottonmouth moccasin had bared its fangs. The pole sank into the bottomless stuff below the water with each stroke, and my wrists and shoulders ached from tearing it out.

It was then that those words about kinds of courage came back to me and I began to understand what Jenkins had meant. I wasn't afraid, yet there was a feeling inside me that had never been there before: a kernel of dread that might burst open at any moment and loose its tendrils around my heart. I knew that it wasn't the snakes or the quicksand that put that feeling inside me. Dangers of that kind had been meat and drink to me for years. It was something else, something in the gloom and in the very feeling of the place.

"Maybe I ought to tell myself a ghost story," I joked to myself, grinning. I forgot the feeling for awhile, and began to wonder what Ann Bentley would do when she learned I had left Mobile. Probably storm about the house for a half hour or so, then find herself another lover. "Her husband will get back in time to look after the next one," I thought, and laughed.

It was the amazing loudness of the laughter that shocked me, stiffened every muscle in my body and made my hands jerk tightly around the boat pole. "What the hell?" I said aloud. "There's—" I stopped, mouth open, listening to the tremendous boom of my words.

All at once there was an indescribable coldness along my spine. I knew I hadn't laughed or spoken any louder than usual. It was the absolute, utter stillness of the swamp which had magnified the sounds!

If you have ever been very deep in a cave without lights, you know how the darkness can become so thick that it is like a black, living thing against your face; you *feel* as well as see it. That's the way the silence of the swamp had become; a terrific, furious soundlessness that made my eardrums ache almost to bursting as they strained for some noise. But there was nothing—except that terrible silence that was louder than thunder.

You have no idea how many sounds there are in the air until suddenly they are all gone. You don't hear the crickets, or the frogs, the whisper of wind in the trees, the almost noiseless, multitudinous noises of the swamp that mingle into one low, unnoticed murmur. Then when they are all gone, the silence becomes so sudden that you can almost *hear* it . . .

I was leaning forward on the boat seat, the pole held across my body with both hands, my eyes straining into the grey-black murk of the swamp. I wasn't breathing at that moment and I don't think my heart was beating, or I should have heard its heavy pounding thud. Then I saw the eyes . . .!

They were more than fifty feet away, and yet the glare of them was so intense I had the impression they were almost on me, that they were the eyes of some monstrous animal crouched only a yard off, ready to spring. I tried to cry out, but the words stuck in my throat, hurting. Perhaps it was the pain that brought full consciousness back to me and shook off the terror.

I put the boat pole across the gunwale, very softly, still leaning forward and watching the motionless eyes. With my right hand I found the rifle between my feet, lifted it. I was beginning to smile, crookedly, half ashamed of the terror which I had felt. After all, I thought, they are only the eyes of an animal. At this range I can't miss, even if it comes charging. I snapped off the safety catch, brought the gun to my shoulder.

But I didn't shoot. I can't tell you why. Perhaps the eyes kept me from it, for when I began to study them carefully they didn't seem to belong to any creature I had ever seen. A panther's eyes, reflected in the dark, are terrible, but there is no word for those which blazed at me. They were a furious, hellish red, perfectly round, large and unblinking. They were like two red holes scooped in the darkness; like two red hot coals that had burned everything away from them and were floating in nothingness. In them was an expression of inconceivable lust and hunger.

The rifle at my shoulder, I sat motionless, staring, unconscious now even of the silence that stormed against my ears.

Then, with the suddenness of light, the eyes were gone. For a moment that seemed so long I thought my lungs would burst, because I didn't breathe during it, the silence held. And when the eerie sound came I reeled back in the boat as from a blow, hands shaking, almost dropping the rifle. It was the soft and hideously beautiful laughter of a woman!

There wasn't any mirth in that laughter. Instead there was the same hungry lust that had been in the eyes, a lust that froze the marrow inside my spine.

Life began to return to the swamp then. Far off a frog croaked and the sound was warm and sweet to my ears. Another answered him, and then a cricket set up its lazy humming. I almost cried out in joy without understanding why.

With the blood flowing through my veins again, my brain began to work, I laughed harshly, cursed myself for a damn fool. It was just a night bird that made the noise, I thought. The eyes—those of some damned animal. Why I didn't shoot it, I don't know. I could have carried it back to Jenkins and told him that it was his ghost. I lit the gasoline lantern in the bottom of the boat, looked at my compass and began to push ahead again. In another mile or two I should reach the coast . . .

But somehow I couldn't forget those eyes, and all at once the full significance of their ghastly glare struck me. "Good God!" I said aloud. "Even the eyes of a cat have to reflect some tiny bit of light before they'll glow. There wasn't any light back there—no light at all!"

My brain quit working then, frozen on that thought: they couldn't have been the eyes of a panther or any natural animal at all! Then, what kind of *thing* was it?

I cursed myself for a damn fool, took a long drink from one of the bottles I had brought with me. The liquor burned the dryness from my throat and lay like a warm pool in my stomach, radiating golden lines of heat. "Hell, I'm getting jittery as an old woman," I said, stuck the pole deep in the mud and sent the boat shooting forward. "I take this job because I claim to be afraid of nothing, and the first time I see an animal's eyes in the dark I get chilblains." I began to think of Ann Bentley again and the way she would act when she found that I had left Mobile.

But somehow I couldn't keep my mind on her. The picture of those eyes would come before me time and again, round and hellishly red, unblinking, with that wild, hungry lust burning in them.

I thought, too, of that eerie laugh in which had sounded the sadistic, terrible joy of hell. Like the daughter of Satan, I thought, then tried to laugh at my own imagination.

Jenkins had been right about "kinds of courage." There was no natural man or beast that, given a rifle and cartridges, I feared. Yet I couldn't forget the look on Jenkins' face when he had spoken of this swamp and the thing that kept men from coming out of it alive.

I came to the end of the swamp almost suddenly. The boat bumped against a few grass hillocks, and then there was no more water. The trees ended, and beyond a slight rise I could hear the unending murmur of the gulf. Taking my knapsack and bedroll, lantern and rifle, I left the boat and walked down to the wide, sandy beach. There was no moon, and when the waves broke they made little glimmering white threads that vanished sharply.

Using the lantern I found driftwood and built a fire where the beach rose into a low bank covered with sea-grape plants. I scrambled eggs, fried bacon and flapjacks, hunger pushing out all thought of the fear that had touched me. But after I had eaten, the feeling came back. Once more I found myself thinking of those eyes and the laugh and the furious, un-explainable silence which had gripped the swamp.

No matter how I tried, I couldn't shrug the feeling off. "Hell," I thought to myself, "there's no need of sitting here all night acting like a baby, I'll get some sleep, and in the morning I'll find whether or not there's any wreck hereabouts."

I began to spread out my bedroll. In the firelight I could see that my hands were shaking. I had never been afraid before, and I had been in some tough spots; so I couldn't understand the feeling which was in me now, the weird, cold shadow of something as ineluctable as death—and more gruesome. All the veins in my body were getting stiff, taut, the muscles contracting upon themselves as though preparing for some hurricane of terror about to strike.

I had spread the bedroll beside the fire and was sitting down to take off my shoes when the first of it broke, with a low, growing sound that came above the unending mutter of the gulf. Someone was running down the beach, madly, blindly, falling, staggering erect, coming on again.

I twisted from the bedroll, caught up the rifle, and with two steps I was beyond the light of the fire, crouched in the darkness.

The thing ran madly. I could hear it fall, claw at the sand until it was on its feet again, then come on. I could hear its breathing, labored, agony-torn. Finally it plunged into the circle of light, and stopped.

I had the rifle under my armpit, and when I saw the creature I almost fired as I staggered up, reeling backward, my brain screaming at me that it couldn't be human. Then, the firelight full on its face, I knew that it was only a man, hideous and horribly deformed. I stepped forward, holding the rifle ready.

In the second or two before I entered the range of the firelight, I saw him clearly. His head was too big for his body and his hair fell in wild, tangled masses to his great shoulders. A scar slanted downward across his forehead, closing one eye and twisting the right corner of his mouth into a hideous grimace. One leg, shorter than the other, was curiously bent, which explained why he had fallen so often.

The man saw me as I stepped into the firelight. His mouth jerked open in one wild, horrific scream, as thin and fierce as the breaking of a violin string. He lunged through the fire, scattering the burning wood, flinging red sparks high into the air, coming straight toward me. "Stop!" I yelled. "Stop or I'll shoot!"

He screamed again, lunged the last step and hit the muzzle of my rifle with his chest. I don't know why I didn't shoot. Perhaps it was the wild, terrible look in his eyes; perhaps it was because he so obviously didn't mean to harm me. Instead he stood, pushing his chest hard against the rifle muzzle, the scream still thin and terrible in his throat

I went backward a step, keeping the butt of the rifle tucked under my armpit, my finger curled around the trigger. The slow, creeping terror that I couldn't understand began to crawl through my veins again. There was fear in this man's ugly face, and yet he did not sense the fact that I had almost killed him. If he wasn't afraid of death, then what in God's name . . .?

"Damn it," I said huskily. "What's wrong with you? Who are you?"

He lunged at me again, caught the rifle with his left hand and pushed the muzzle against his chest. "Kill me!" he screamed. "Kill me! Kill me! For God's sake, kill me quick before she comes!"

Terror and unbelief must have drugged me then, for my only emotion was a dull stupor through which I gazed at the man, my mouth hanging open, my eyes wide. I was accustomed to men unafraid of death. I had seen men fight for life and die grinning. But never before had I seen a man pleading for death, with wild, unspeakable dread blazing in his face. I didn't speak; I couldn't ask him any questions; I just stood looking at him, dazed, stupefied.

"Kill me!" He screamed again, jerking the rifle until I thought the muzzle must crack his ribs. "In the name of God, kill me before she comes!"

"Before *she* comes? What the hell do you mean?"

His voice plunged down to a whisper and his twisted face became a sickly yellow, as though he knew that already he had made too much noise, and it was too late. "She's already done in your boat. I tried to get away in it, but she'd wrecked it. She'll be here in a moment. Please!" His voice went high and shrill again. "Kill me, *now!*" He tried to paw for the trigger, but I jerked away.

"Damn you," I said. "What are you talking about? Who is 'she'?"

"Desis!" He hissed the name. "The daughter of hell. I don't know who she is. But she's killed them all. Eaten them! And she'll get me if you don't kill me. Please!"

It was evident this man was mad. I'd seen crazy men before, but somehow I couldn't accept this explanation. The words I used weren't what I should have spoken to calm a man gone insane. "Desis," I snorted. "What the hell are you talking about? That's a type of water spider, poisonous I believe, but I'm not certain."

The man's face went more yellow than ever. The eye across which the scar ran turned into a black hole of horror while the other blazed at me. The crooked mouth jerked so that saliva drooled down across his chin. "I don't know," he sighed. "Maybe she's a spider. Maybe she ain't, but she's hell's—" His whisper stopped sharply, and a silence that was almost titanic smashed against my ears.

It wasn't more than a second that we stood there. Time seemed to have died, while the surf rolled on, slushing over the beach.

Abruptly the man lunged at me and his scream was like thunder torn into one thin, agonizing sheet. *"Kill me! Oh God! Kill me now!"* His left hand pulled the rifle barrel to his chest, his right hand fought for the trigger.

I tore the gun away from him, and the motion hurled him sideways, out of the circle of light from the fire. I heard the frantic crunch of his feet on the sand, heard one explosive, whimpering curse. Gradually the silence that was like an utter and absolute darkness shut down on me, soaking up the sound of his running. Then he was gone into the night. I stood almost at the edge of the firelight, rigid, mouth open, unbreathing, eyes wide and peering across the scattered fire into the darkness.

All at once, utterly without sound, she was there!

The scattered fire made only a pale, thin radiance which touched on the darkness and vanished. She stood at the very edge of the light, her eyes downcast so that I could see only the pale shadow of her lids. Her face was more beautiful than a human being's should be—softly oval with the wide, shadowed eyes that I couldn't see because of the long lashes, a skin that was almost golden and glowing with health, a wide, sensuous mouth. Her hair fell to her waist in a heavy silver cascade that seemed to stir gently though there was no wind. She wore a short skirt made of one piece of cloth tucked about her waist.

The first shock of seeing her was like a blow in the chest knocking the air from me, stopping my heart for a moment. Even in that first instant I began to feel the desire for her tingling through my body, making my blood go hot and jerky in my veins. But I knew also that something was wrong, horribly wrong, though I didn't know what it was . . .

"Hello," I said finally, inanely. "Where did you come from?"

"I've been here a long time," she said without raising her eyes to look at me. Watching her, that sense of dread came cold and creepy through me, but the sheer power of her beauty drowned out reason. Abruptly she said, "Won't you put some more wood on the fire? I'm cold."

"Surely." I gathered the sticks the crazy man had scattered, piled them together and put on more wood. The flames began to crackle, the red and gold light of the fire grew brighter. "How's that?" I asked and stood up.

She nodded gratefully, knelt, stretched her hands out to the blaze. The movement stirred the thick, silver hair that was like a mantle about her, and I saw for the first time that she wore no clothes above the waist. Her breasts were high and round, delicately shaped and small.

There was no understanding the passion that burst in me then, shook me like a leaf and stopped the breath in my throat. It was a flame crashing down on me, enveloping my whole body. And with it came, stronger than ever, that uncanny sense of terror.

If she felt shy because of her lack of clothes, she made no move to indicate it. She just knelt there, hands out to the fire that sent flickering shadows across her breasts, eyes downcast.

I became aware of the curious quality of her hair. Its thick, silver sheen seemed to dance in the firelight, as though every strand of it were alive and separate from the others, moving with the gentle undulations of a spider web rocking in the wind. There was something curious, something gruesomely attractive about that hair. I wanted to reach out and touch it, see if each strand were as thin and soft as the spider web it resembled. But when I thought of touching it, a cold shudder shook me.

"It's very good to have a fire," she said, and smiled. Her lips were large and blood-red, but they didn't part with the smile, and I couldn't see her teeth. She had never raised her eyes so that I could look into them. I began to wonder what color they were and why she avoided my gaze.

"I thought this beach was totally deserted," I said, "but it's almost as crowded as Fifth Avenue at Forty-Second Street. First some idiot comes whooping along here, and now a very beautiful lady."

"Do you think I'm beautiful?" There was something alluring, inviting about her tone, but still she didn't look at me. She didn't have to, for there was no doubting what she meant. With three steps I reached her side of the fire, and during each of those steps horror and passion warred inside me.

"I've never seen anyone so lovely," I murmured, kneeling beside her. My heart was like a rock against my ribs and my mouth was open, fighting for air. My hands trembled as I rested them on my thighs, fighting to keep from throwing my arms around her, crushing her hard against me, my fingers tight against the warm flesh of her shoulders, my mouth hungry against hers. Yet all the while that cold, inexplicable fear writhed inside me.

She turned slightly, her curious hair twisting in the firelight, showing the high mounds of her breasts. One hand came forward slowly, touched on mine, then closed around my fingers. "I've been on this beach a long time," she whispered. "There's been no one here except that—that hideous crazy man. I'm so glad that you've come."

I swayed toward her, my left hand sliding along the warm skin of her forearm. She still had her eyes downcast. Perhaps that was what stopped me; perhaps it was the way her hair had moved, seeming to reach out hungrily for me like a spider web ready to tangle itself about an insect. Anyway I paused, trying to breathe against the fear and passion that stormed inside me.

"Look," I said huskily, "look at me. Raise your eyes. I want to see them."

"Why see my eyes?" Her other hand came out to touch me, and the movement bared both breasts. "You don't want to see my eyes."

She pulled me toward her, and as I responded she lay backward on the sand. After that, it happened in one tremendous bursting flare of horror when I had lunged toward her. Then, my mouth almost against hers, my head blocking the light from her face, I saw her eyes . . .

They were the round, hellishly red and terrible eyes of the swamp!

Blind with terror I hurled myself away from her. And at that instant my fingers brushed lightly on her hair.

The tiny threads jumped like living things, wrapped themselves around my fingers and half jerked me backward. They had the sleek, tenuous feeling of spider webs and were strong as steel wire. I sent a scream slashing into the stillness, and hurled myself forward in one terrific effort. The clinging hair tore skin from my fingers but pulled loose, and I went hurtling through the darkness, blind with terror, falling, clawing erect, and plunging up the bank and through the sea-grapes. There was only one flaming idea in my brain then: to get away!

Almost suddenly I hit the edge of the swamp, plunged knee deep into muck and water before I could stop. I heard the hissing of a snake, the slither of a body across slime. My feet began to bog deeper. Twisting, I managed to fling myself flat, catch tufts of grass and pull myself from the swamp. Then I began to look about for the boat. I knew I had left it within twenty yards of this place

—and I raced up and down the edge of the swamp, sobbing and cursing the darkness.

Reason came back to me slowly. The boat simply wasn't here, although this was the place I had left it. Then I remembered the words of the man who had wanted to die: "She's already destroyed your boat. I tried to get away in it, but she'd ruined it."

I stood dead still, hands clenched at my sides, mouth open, un-breathing. I was trapped with this woman and the man who wanted to die rather than face her!

CHAPTER THREE

HEADLESS DEATH

IT WAS FIVE MINUTES LATER that I regained control of my muscles and brain. By that time I was half a mile away from the place I had camped, the fire hidden by a curve in the beach. I had run until I felt exhausted, and crouched now on hands and knees almost at the water's edge. As my breathing grew more normal my brain began to function again, to battle at the terror which had gripped it. I tried to find some explanation for the things that had happened.

"The man was crazy," I told myself. "I could see that in his eyes. The woman evidently got trapped when some boat sank nearby, or maybe I'm on the wrong beach and she lives around here somewhere." But I thought of her eyes and shuddered.

I tried to convince myself that it was the firelight which had made them so red and hideous. "And her hair—anybody's hair might have got tangled around my fingers, at a time like that. There was nothing strange about her hair." But even then I knew I was lying. No woman had hair as finespun as a spider web and strong as steel. The way it tangled around my fingers was like a web around a fly, like a spider . . .

I tried to stop thinking then, but I couldn't. "She looked like a spider," I said half aloud. "There was something about her whole feeing, her long, slender legs and arms, her small body . . ."

I stood erect, trying to laugh at that, and the sound hurt my throat. "Imagine thinking that *she* looked like a spider," I said. "Why great damn! That was the prettiest woman I ever looked at. I was a fool for jumping up and running, just because her eyes burned redly in the firelight. She'll probably never give me another chance after that fool act, but tomorrow I'll find her and try."

I made no attempt to explain to myself why I didn't want to find her again that night. I knew, though I wouldn't admit it, that I never wanted to see her again—and I knew, too, that I *would* see her, that I could not escape, because she was as unavoidable as death. She *was* death . . .

"Hell," I said, and laughed again, huskily. "I'm the man who told Jenkins I was afraid of nothing. Now I've let an idiot and a damn good-looking woman frighten me almost out of my wits." I began to walk along the beach, away from the place I had left her.

Some two hundred yards farther, the shore line began to rise into a cliff, and near its base I found a cave. There's not much tide along that part of the gulf, and as well as I could tell the whole cave was above the high water mark. Taking matches from a moisture-tight pack, I began to search the place.

It was fairly long and about ten yards wide with a smooth, sandy floor. Some thirty feet in, the cave bent sharply to the right. "If I build a fire near the back," I thought, "no one outside can see it." Then I cursed myself for a coward, but it was near the back that I built the fire.

The warmth and the light flickering over the sand gave me courage. I told myself that it was a damn good thing none of my old friends had seen me during the last two hours, or they would never speak to me again: Bill Race and John Burdett who had fought in Chinese and South American revolutions with me, Ed Fuller who had gone with me into a part of Africa where no other white men had ever been; those fellows wouldn't have believed that fear could make a screaming coward of me, as it had done.

With courage running warm in my veins again, I stood up and began to look around me. The floor of the cave was as flat as a table, the sand white and fine. My fire was built against the right wall, the light flickering high up, but not touching the ceiling. Around me, on every side, the dark shadows crouched like some huge animal ready to spring.

I stopped, picked up a handful of the fine sand and let it slide through my fingers. I took a stick, one end of which was burning well, and began to examine the cave more closely.

It's strange how in pitch darkness things brought into a small light seem larger and more vivid than normally, while the light itself appears tiny and lost in the enveloping blackness. The sand seemed abnormally bright under the torch, the little flecks of coral in the cave walls glittered like rubies. But I had the impression that the darkness had swallowed me, that I was lost in the bowels of eternal night and would never find my way back to the fire. I laughed at the sensation, and managed to throw it off. I was still laughing when my right foot struck something that made a dull, crunching sound, and looking down I saw the skeleton.

I felt as though a fist had struck me hard in the pit of my stomach. I reeled backward, the torchlight dancing crazily along the wall. Half the blaze went out, a plume of smoke drifted upward and the darkness rushed in closer to me. Then I checked myself, said, "Damn!" and held the stick carefully until the blaze was bright again. After all, I had seen plenty of skeletons. That wasn't the sort of thing to frighten me.

Holding the stick so that the light fell dearly over the bones, I knelt and examined them. In the cave where no light touched them they had never bleached, but were a moldy grey. All the bones were in perfect order as though the man had died here.

Then I noticed that the head was gone!

"Well I'll be damned," I said. "I wonder what carried that off." I leaned over to examine the spine more closely. There were small, chiseled places around it, so that it came to a point like a sharpened pencil. I put out my right hand and touched them.

All at once, as though the touch had shown me beyond doubt, I knew! I didn't move because I couldn't even breathe, and my heart slammed once against my ribs and stopped. *For the marks round that spinal column had been made by human teeth!*

Somehow I shook myself out of the terror which had frozen me, stood up. After all, I had no way of knowing how those marks were made. There were thousands of crabs along the beach. Perhaps they had done it. I swung the light, paused, and stepped forward. There, not three yards from the skeleton, was the skull, its eyeless sockets peering up into the red glow of the torch.

And just beyond the skull was another body, the head missing!

I found three skeletons, all with the heads gone and those peculiar marks around the tops of the spinal cords. Then I went back to the fire, put on more sticks and sat huddled close beside it I tried to keep my mind fastened on the blaze and the warmth of it against my face and hands. Hell, I was accustomed to skeletons. I'd seen men die in a dozen countries.

Suddenly I was thinking of the woman, of her eyes blazing at me as my mouth came close to hers. There had been the living fires of hell in those eyes. And I remembered the mad man saying, "She's killed them all! Eaten them!" I thought of the wild sound of his voice pleading for death, and the sobbing curse with which he had plunged into the darkness before the girl's approach.

He had said her name was Desis. That was a type of water spider—and the female spider kills the male, after mating, by biting
off his head!

"Good God!" I whispered, staring into the darkness where the
headless skeletons lay.

I lunged to my feet. I'd spend the night on the beach under the
stars, but not here in this cavern of the dead. Not here where in the
pitch darkness beyond the fire . . . I had taken one step toward the
cave mouth when I heard it! The whispered crunch of feet in the
sand!

I had the weird impression that the blackness around me had
closed in, holding me like a strait jacket so that I couldn't move. I
wanted to run, to hurl myself madly toward those creeping steps,
meet whoever was coming and have it over with. But I couldn't
budge, and the only motion of which I was conscious was my eyes
swelling larger and larger in their sockets until they ached, while
my eardrums strained to catch the grating of every grain of sand
moved by those feet

Closer, closer, so that the sound swelled in the darkness and I
could tell the difference between heel and toe, the feet came on.
They were just beyond the bend of the cave. Then the madman
stepped into the circle of light!

The force in my throat burst then, not into a shriek but into the
wild, hysterical laughter of relief. That horrible cachinnation jab-
bered and banged against the walls of the cave, rolled in furious,
insane torrents into the darkness.

The idiot stood watching with his one good eye, while his scar-
twisted mouth seemed to leer sympathetically. Finally, when my
laughter had choked to a gurgle and I was on my knees beside the
fire, he said: "So you thought I was Desis and you wouldn't be
able to escape this time. No wonder you was glad to see me."

"Listen," I said. "Who in God's name are you? And who is
she? How did you get here? What's happening here?"

"You don't know?" The eyeless socket peered at me like one of
the skulls in the dark; the twisted mouth bent only on one side
when he spoke.

"How in the devil could I know? A man in Mobile paid me to
learn if a ship had wrecked here five years ago carrying pearls. I
came across the swamp in a boat and got here tonight. That's all I
know."

His mouth twisted in that hideous, one sided fashion. "I'm the last livin' one outa that ship's crew. Soma the others are around you." He gestured toward the dark where the skeletons lay. "She loved them, and killed them, and ate them."

I lunged half erect, shouting, "You're lying, lying! She couldn't have done that." Then, the words choking in my throat, I asked, "Who is she?"

His mouth twisted again. "Howda I know? She was here when I came. She says her name's Desis, and you say that's a spider. Maybe she is; maybe she's the daughter of hell. I thought at first she was just a cannibal woman. But she ain't human. I know that now!"

I had been thinking these very things, letting them grow on me until I was half mad with superstition and fear. But when he put them into words it acted like cold water on me, and I began to fight again against the terror. I told myself that I was letting fear run away with me; that I had to keep a cool head, and think. But it was damned hard sitting there in that dark cave, with the firelight bringing out all the horror of the face across from me. I dug my fingers into my thighs, pulled every muscle in my body stiff.

"Listen," I said. "All this is a lot of tommyrot. Desis may be unusual, but she's human. There's no need for two men to be afraid of any woman."

He leaned toward me, the firelight running in a red flame along the scar that twisted his face. "You oughta know," he said. "You barely touched her, but from where I was hid I saw you jump and yell. You was damn lucky to get away. None of the others ever did. She loved them, and then she'd bite into their necks and then—" His face convulsed horribly.

"Why didn't she bite you?" I shouted at him. "What are you doing here?"

"I asked you to kill me," He began to pant now, like a dog. "I want you to do it now. When we got wrecked here I had a broke leg. That's why one of 'em's bent like it is, so I can't run well. And my face was all cut up, too. I woulda died, but she saved me. She's been waiting for me to get well enough so she—she can—" He choked.

Without warning he was on his knees, reaching toward me and his voice had taken on that high, thin pleading. "You gotta kill me! Now! She'll take me soon! I'm not brave like the others! I don't wanta have her love, in spite of what she'll do to me afterwards!"

"I can't kill you. I left my gun back there."

"Do it with your hands," he whispered. "With a stick. Anything."

"Goddammit!" I said. "If you're so anxious to die, why don't you do it yourself? Why don't you go out into that swamp, or swim out into the gulf. There are moccasins on one side of this place and barracuda on the other. They'd get you."

"No. They won't touch you after—after she has."

"You're crazy!" Then, suddenly I remembered the sound of that snake slithering away from me when I ran into the swamp. A cottonmouth moccasin is more likely to strike than run, but this one . . .

"You could die in the swamp, anyway," I suggested at last. "You could swim out and drown. Why don't you do that?"

"I don't know. I wanta die and yet—somehow I can't. Maybe it's because she won't let me. I tried to drown, but I couldn't right off, and then she came and got me. I tried goin' in the swamp, and she pulled me outa there too. Somehow I can't kill myself. I want you to do it."

I shook my head, swallowing hard. "I think you are crazy," I said. "I think I'm crazy, too, and that this whole night's some kind of dream. But crazy or not, I'm going to get out of it, and I'll get you out, too. I've been in tight places before, without turning yellow—and I'm not going to do it this time." I stopped talking, feeling the man's eyes on me.

He knew, and I knew, that I *was* afraid, horribly afraid, and trying to bolster my courage with words.

With early morning sunlight pouring down across the beach, I felt almost normal again. The knowledge that I was marooned on this narrow strip of coast stuck in the back of my head, but that was the sort of danger I was accustomed to and didn't fear. I had no doubt that I could escape in some way. With the sun warm against my skin, the fantastic terror of the night before seemed almost absurd.

From the beach at the mouth of the cave I could see, a half mile to the west, a black hulk protruding from the water. It was about a quarter of a mile from shore, and the way in which waves piled up there indicated a reef.

"Is that the wrecked boat?" I asked the one-eyed man, pointing.

His lips twitched, the old fear came back in his face, "That's her. She hit there five years ago and rolled part way over. That's her stem stickin' outa the water."

"Where are those pearls I was told about? Tell me where they are; I'll help you get out of here."

I never expected him to tell me. I didn't really believe in the story of the pearls, and wouldn't have expected him to tell me about them if they did exist. But he said quickly, fear growing in his face: "They're still on board, in that cabin, aft. But you can't get them."

I was suddenly tense, staring at him. Then the pearls were real! Within a half mile of me there was a fortune, for the taking. My breath began to come shallow and quick. "Why in hell can't I get them? I can reach that cabin some way."

The man's leathery, sunburned skin had turned a sickly yellow. He whispered, "You can reach the cabin but you—you can't get out again. Some of the others tried it. They none of 'em got out. Desis"—his voice slipped down to where it was barely audible— "she got all of 'em who went there."

His words would have frightened me the night before; they sent a strange, eerie tingling along my spine even now. But in the bright sunlight things looked differently. I was ashamed of the terror I had felt because of a woman, and I was determined to prove to myself that I had conquered fear. Besides, well—I was thinking of that fortune, mine for the taking, and the lust of it had got in my blood stronger than fright. I could almost feel the pearls between my fingers, and a wild procession of the things money could buy trooped through my imagination.

"Listen," I said, "I'm going out there and get those pearls. If you've lied to me about them, I'm coming back and answer that prayer to kill you."

A hopeless, pitiful look was in the man's distorted face. "You'll go out," he said. "Maybe you'll find the pearls. But you ain't comin' back."

"I'm coming back—with the pearls." I began to walk up the beach, almost running in my eagerness.

He stumbled after me, caught at my hand, jerked me around. "Don't go!" he screamed. "Don't go! Kill me first. Please, *Please!*" He went down on his knees, arms around my legs, keeping up that wild, frantic pleading.

Fear struck back at me, dank and cold as a black fog rising in my stomach, closing dreadfully about my heart and lungs. The man was insane, I told myself desperately. If he really wanted to die, he would have managed to kill himself.

Then I thought of the skeletons lying in the dark cave and of the marks like human teeth that pointed their spinal columns.

"You said Desis was a kind of water spider," he gasped, clinging to me. "You can't dodge her in the water. Others tried it who could swim good. She'll get you out there!"

In that moment, if I could have had the flat-bottomed boat I would have gone blindly, frantically away without caring in which direction I poled, as long as the hellish spot was behind me.

But I didn't have the boat, and after a moment the sunshine took effect again. The horror evaporated from me, my heart began to beat normally again. Once more the thought of those pearls, and the wealth they would bring, was a hot lust in my veins. Perhaps I should say that I thought of Jenkins and my duty to him for sending me here, but I didn't. All I thought of was what my half of the fortune would amount to.

I slammed my hand against the cripple's chest, hurled him away from me. "Those pearls damn sure better be there," I said, turning and beginning to run along the beach.

Behind me I heard him sobbing. Then his voice raised in a high, thin shriek. "You said that name meant a water spider. In the water you can't—" My own curses drowned out the rest.

From that time on things happened so swiftly, plunging so straight down to their gruesome finish, that I had the impression of falling from some immense height, hurtling headlong, whirling over and over without the slightest ability to control myself, through clouds of horror and misery and hell.

Even as I was running along the beach, I knew that if I paused the fear would overcome me and I would turn back; so I kept going. At a point opposite the hulk of the small ship I stripped myself down to my shorts, then ran into the water, began to swim.

I swam to the ship and around it once, then tread water, looking at it. She was a small, two-masted schooner which had hit the reef hard, running almost entirely over it. She was all under water except her stern which protruded some eight feet, barnacle encrusted, above the waves.

I went close, took a long breath and dived. The water was glass-clear, and once below the surface there was not much surf. I found that the hatch leading into her stern was open, then I came up for air. "It shouldn't be any trouble to go through that hatch and find the cabin and the pearls," I reasoned. "I can get air where she sticks above the water."

Sodden, eerie apprehension struck me. I didn't want to go into that ship! I didn't want the pearls! I wanted to turn and swim for shore, with a wild, explosive speed that would take me there faster than thought. The fear of the ship, of the darkness beneath it, and the things I might find in that darkness chilled me even more than the water I swam in. I knew that in another moment I would turn for shore; and so, frantically, I dived. Once under the water I got control of my nerves and muscles again, but the fear didn't leave me entirely.

I didn't have to go deep, yet the temperature of the water seemed to change sharply, becoming colder and colder. It was fairly bright at first, only the shadow of the ship being dark. I could see the hatch easily, and using the breast stroke and kicking scissors fashion, I went through it.

The light changed swiftly now, dulling to a thick, heavy murk in which it was almost impossible to see. I cursed myself for being without the underwater torch which I had brought from Mobile. I almost turned back, but I knew that once away from this ship I would never have the nerve to return, I forced myself to swim on.

Feeling along the bulwark I found a cabin door, looked through. It was too dark here to see anything, so I pushed away, let myself float upward. My head struck wood, and I felt along it until I came to an opening. Glancing upward I was conscious of grey-light. I struck down with both hands, felt my body rising.

Something tapped my forehead lightly, swayed, and slipped along my face. It was sleek and hard and cold. At first I thought it was a fish. Then I felt it along the whole side of my face, and I *knew!*

I tried to scream, my mouth wide open and bubbles bursting out to roll past my ears with a sound like exploding shells. I thrashed the water, fighting to get out of there, but struggling blindly without any sense of direction.

For the thing which had touched on my face was a human bone!

Abruptly my head broke water. Tiny threads of mote-filled radiance made a grey gloom in the place, and I knew I was in the elevated stem cabin of the ship, the sunlight filtering between cracked planking. What had been the bottom of the 'tween deck sloped very gently down into the water, I crawled up on it, looked about and saw a built-in bunk where lay another of those headless skeletons!

There was a pile of blankets at one corner, an overturned table near the water's edge, a chair tilted back against the left bulwark. But I wasn't conscious of seeing those things. My eyes were on the blankets, straining against the gloom, swelling until they ached in their sockets. My mouth was open, twitching, but I made no sound.

Piled among the blankets were three disordered skeletons—*and the skull of each one had been severed from the spine!*

I went toward them, the way a bird may go toward a snake which has hypnotized it. I was half crouched, my fingers extended in front of me were both reaching for the bones. I already knew the way those skulls had been displaced, yet I could not keep myself from examining them, from the thought of what I would see . . .

Slowly, my whole body trembling, I knelt, reaching out for the bones. But I never touched them, or if I did I can't remember. For it was in that second, hand extended, that I saw the pearls.

There was a great pile of them resting on the rotting blanket beside one of the skeletons, a bony hand of which seemed almost to cup them in fleshless fingers. For one moment I gazed at them, dazed and unbelieving, then shouting with hysterical joy, I scooped them up and almost buried my face in them. There must have been at least fifty—each absolutely alike—about pea-sized, and even in the dull gloom I could see the pink glow of them that was more delicate than a flower. I had a fortune in my two hands, a fortune beyond estimation.

I stood up, laughing, head thrown back and chest shaking. I had almost turned back with this wealth at my finger tips, because I was afraid of a woman. After the bone had touched my face under water it was blind fear which had sent me bursting into this treasure. "Afraid of a bone caught between two planks under water," I shouted. Tilting my cupped palms, I rocked the pearls back and forth, listening to the tinkle of them.

Gradually, my eyes still watching the pearls, I felt *her!*

I didn't look up, because at first I wasn't sure she was there. I wasn't sure of anything except a slow-growing fear that crawled like some black and ghostly fungus through my body, coiling with sickening pressure about my intestines, slipping up toward heart and lungs.

There had not been any sound in this place except the noise I made and the eternal lapping of water against the planks around me. There was a new tenseness, a strange tangible lack of other sound in the air, which made the water seem hungry and lustful and hideous.

My hands shook and the muscles in the back of my neck stiffened as I heard her voice saying, "Do you think the pearls are pretty? I hoped you would come for them."

I staggered backward on the sloping floor, cowered there, still holding the pearls in front of me, and looked at her.

She was in the water just beyond the point where the deck slid into it. Her breasts were half visible, the tawny golden flesh looking exotically white against the gloom. Her face was as beautiful as some savage orchid that lures life into death by its beauty. She made no attempt to hide her eyes now, and I could see the red, hellish flame of them, the unbearable, terrific glare that was like hot coals from hell pushed against my own eyeballs.

I must have stared into those eyes a full minute before I was able to shift my gaze, to notice her hair. It lay in a long, heavy silver mass that fell about the sides of her face and floated on the water. And although her breasts and shoulders glimmered wetly the water seemed never to have touched her hair! It was like a mass of silver spider webs, widespun and waiting for their victims.

"Aren't you glad to see me? You ran away last night." Without any evident motion she came closer to the edge of the deck, her breasts lifting higher from the water.

Mingling with the terror that had frozen me, passion came, slow and tremendous. I could feel it starting low in my body, heating my already taut muscles, setting a flame to lapping at my heart. With the desire came an overwhelming, furious terror that made me fight the desire more than I had ever fought fear; that set my whole body to trembling so that one of the pearls dropped from my shaking hands and rolled along the deck. "I knew you would come for the pearls," she said. "I want you to have them, but"—with one graceful movement she was out of the water and standing, entirely nude—startling—and amazingly beautiful, on the edge of the deck—"you can have the pearls later," she whispered. "I've been here so long alone." She held her hands out to me.

Desire burned out the fear inside me then. One white wave of flame seemed to sear my body to burn the woman's beauty into my soul as I went reeling toward her, mouth open with a quick intake of breath, desiring nothing but her body. It was unconsciously that I clung to the pearls.

"Take me—!" Her whisper throbbed in the narrow space as she came swiftly nearer. Her eyes blazed with passion, and her lips were pulled back wide from her teeth. One tiny stream of sunlight caught her face then, held it so for a split second, as if in the light of a torch.

For the first tune I saw her teeth! They glittered white, long and needle sharp as those of a barracuda! Teeth that could sever a man's skull from his spine!

I must have screamed, for there was a splitting cacophony tearing at my eardrums, a shriek that drowned out the tinkling fall of the scattered pearls. With one terrific lunge I avoided her outstretched hands, leaped for the water. My foot skidded on the deck and I fell hard, rolled, clawed at the wood, then dived. In that half second while I was in the air, while my scream still shuddered through the place, I heard Desis laugh. It was the low and hideously confident laughter of the swamp.

And even as my hands found the underwater opening through which I had come, I heard the small sound she made in diving after me.

I'm a good swimmer, and with terror lashing me I must have gone swiftly. "I'll make it!" I thought. "I'll make it!" A dull light showed up ahead, and I knew that I was almost free of the ship. At that moment I felt her hand on my foot.

Desperately I tore free, struck out again. But now her arms closed around my waist, pulling me down. I twisted toward her, doubling my fists. In the dim light I could see her face just below mine, feel her naked breasts flattened hard against me. I uttered a gasping, choked curse—and swung a powerful right at her jaw.

But my fist never landed. Something jerked it back, held it and when I tried to strike with the left hand, it too was tied against my side. And then I went mad! It was her hair that had tangled around me, the way a spider web wraps about a fly!

I weighed a hundred and seventy and was in good condition. Madness added to my strength, and I fought as a sane human being could not fight. My whole body writhed and twisted, every muscle in me strained and tore in a cyclonic effort to break free of the woman's hair. But it was no use.

The fight went out of me. There was a grey twilight world under the water, and I was conscious of Desis pressed against me, of every voluptuous curve of her naked body and the sleek feel of her hair about my shoulders. There was no emotion in me except a dull desire for her, and my head tilted down toward her lips.

I must have lain quietly for some time after regaining consciousness, because when I first moved, and looked about me, most of my strength had returned. And with it had returned the passion and fear. But I knew, even from that first moment, that the passion would win this time and I was doomed.

I was lying far enough inside the cave for the darkness to merge with the sunlight reflected from the mouth into a dull semi-lucent greyness. Beside me, her body unbelievably alluring, was Desis, a few strands of her silver hair coiled around my shoulders. The rest was massed like a great pillow of spiderwebs below her head.

I moved, almost unconsciously, and the hair tightened, holding me beside her. She raised her head and smiled at me. "You almost drowned by acting so foolish. I had a hard time saving you."

For a moment her red eyes blazed lustfully into mine, sending mingled terror and passion boiling through my veins again, setting my muscles to twitching.

"Am I so ugly you'd rather drown than love me?" Her hand touched gently against my shoulder.

I knew what would happen if I loved her. I had seen the skeletons without heads. I'd heard the wild cry of the cripple, "She's killed them all! Eaten them!" I no longer doubted. I knew that he had told the truth, and I knew that once I had loved her I would be only one more moldering skeleton within the cave.

I fought, so help me God, I fought against the desire for her. But from the first I knew I couldn't win. She wasn't human, and the lust she stirred in a man was beyond human enduring.

"Am I so ugly?" she whispered again, both hands on my shoulders pulling me toward her. The white, pointed teeth gleamed between her lips, hungry and trembling; her red eyes burned like fire into mine. I rocked toward her; then, fighting with every muscle in my body, I stopped, though I could make no effort to pull away.

"You're not ugly," I panted. "You are beautiful, damnably, inhumanly beautiful." The words ached in my throat as I fought then out.

"Then why? Why do you not take me?" She kept pulling me gently toward her, and her hands seemed to burn into my flesh.

"It's because you'll kill me!" I was panting like a dog and my whole body hurt with wanting her. "You'll bite into my throat, take my blood. You did it to the others. You'll kill me, too!"

"Yes." She almost hissed the words, and the red lips trembled around her teeth; her eyes blazed. "But don't you want me-enough for that?"

I don't know how I managed it, but I made one last, terrific effort to pull away from her. Somehow every muscle in my body seemed to explode, in one furious backward lunge. I came to my knees, thought I was away!

Then the strands of hair that were like steel cords tightened around my shoulders and I was jerked back against her; and with the touch of her flesh, all resistance went out of me. I caught her fiercely against my chest. There was a bursting flame of wild passion that enveloped us, and through which I could not see. I heard her cry out, moan, but I could not see her because of the fire coming in with one last great wave, leaping into a final burst—then going completely.

It was in that moment of utter emptiness that her teeth found my throat! I felt the parting of the skin, the hot spurt of blood and her lips against me. I went insane, screaming, trying to jerk up my fists and strike at her. But her hair tied me, and then there was no strength left in my muscles to struggle.

I have never remembered the beginning of the cry; perhaps I didn't hear it. But all at once, just over my shoulder, a man was bellowing, "By God this is how you should die, how I wanted to kill you! And now . . . !"

I managed to twist my head, feeling Desis's lips let go their suction grip on my throat, hearing the short gasp of fear that she made. And then I saw the man standing above me, saw the knife rip downward. I rolled to one side, still tangled in those few strands of Desis's hair.

How it happened after that, I can't say exactly. The knife ripped at my shoulder, sliced through the restraining hair. Somehow I was on my feet, staring into the face of Jenkins, the man who had sent me to this place. He swung up the knife, came toward me slowly.

"You didn't know," he panted, "that I was Ann Bentley's husband. You didn't know that I sent you here so that I could kill you, without anyone learning of it. Even here you find a woman, but I'll—"

I turned and ran. Behind me I heard the short, terrible scream of Ann Bentley's husband—and then there was silence.

I found the boat in which he had come, and I left in it. I didn't look for clothes; I went just as I was. If you'll look in the Mobile papers for October some eight years ago, you'll find an account of the capture of a naked madman. But I wasn't insane. I just made the mistake of trying to tell the truth.

~ ~ ~ ~ ~

Ed Roland stopped talking. He was still sitting with his back against the post, his long spider-like legs drawn up under him, arms wrapped around his knees. For a moment I looked at him.

"Are you trying to get me to believe that?" I asked at last.

He said, "No, I didn't think you would believe it. But it happened."

"You're crazy," I told him. "The only thing which could have happened is that Jenkins, or Bentley—or whoever his name was—sent you to that place in order to kill you, planted the man and woman there to frighten you first. But there's no sense to that, and it wouldn't explain the woman's eyes and a lot of things."

"No," Ed Roland said calmly. "It wouldn't explain those things. It wouldn't explain why Ann Bentley's husband never came back to Mobile. And it wouldn't explain this . . ." He stood up, pulled open his shirt collar and stepped toward me.

A great circular scar such as teeth might make twisted one side of Ed Roland's throat.

SONG OF
THE DEAD

CHAPTER ONE

DEADLY DOGGEREL

YOU MAY SAY I'M CRAZY, but it you look at me you won't laugh while you say it. You will turn away from me, shutting your eyes tightly, shaking your head in an effort to forget. It's not that I'm deformed, and my face is not hideous. But you will see in my eyes some shadow of the things I have seen—and you will want to forget.

For me there is no forgetting, and it is not a pretty thing to live as I do, remembering the things which I must remember, and knowing already the misery which death holds for me. It is not a pretty thing to look into the mirror of a morning and see in your own eyes the things which I have seen in mine, the things which you may turn away from, clenching your teeth.

We first saw Saba Island from St. Martin's. We had anchored in what goes for a harbor and rowed into the little Dutch town of Phillipsburg. Our schooner was the only vessel in the harbor and looking back at it we could see the Caribbean stretch blue and purple to where a big rock formation rose like a tall blue cone, badly rumpled on one side, out of the sea. Silver clouds hid the top of the cone. Mary Wayne nodded and asked, "What island is that?"

There were several Negroes standing around gaping at us the way they do at strangers. I pointed toward the cloud-topped island and repeated Mary's question.

"Dot's Saba," one of them answered.

"Saba." Mary spoke the word slowly. "I never heard of it."

"It's on the chart," John Wayne said. "That's all I know."

Carl Hammer said, "I've heard about it. It's Dutch. Not many persons live there; it's just an extinct volcano sticking out of the sea. Practically nobody ever touches there."

Behind us the Negroes made a little shuffling noise and began to whisper among themselves. I turned toward them. "What sort of place is Saba?" I asked.

They continued to shuffle uneasily. At last one said, "You sail-ors?"

"We're sailing that schooner," I answered.

The Negro said, "Sailors don't go 'shore in Saba."

John Wayne's triangular shaped, blond eyebrows went up. "Why?"

"Well, they—they . . ." The Negro hesitated.

"They scared of Bill Wales," another of them blurted suddenly.

That was all we could get out of them, that sailors were afraid of Bill Wales. But the place sounded interesting and we decided to go.

Reaching Saba, we found Fort Bay, the only anchorage, wasn't really a bay at all. The whole island rises sheer out of the water and the Bay was merely a place where it was possible to drag a small boat ashore. We could see a pathway leading up the moun-tain, circling along the edge of a deep gorge. There was one small house at the foot of the path, but no sign of life. "The other houses must be hidden back in the mountain somewhere," Mary said.

We anchored about a hundred and fifty yards off shore. There was an unusually heavy swell and the schooner dipped and rolled. Hammer and Wayne had gone forward to lower our one boat, when I saw the man on the shore. He was standing almost at the water's edge looking out at us. I can't explain it, but the instant I saw him I knew that something was wrong. I felt as if the wind had suddenly turned colder and I shivered.

At first I couldn't tell what there was strange about him. He seemed to be dressed in blue denim work clothes such as sailors or the natives on the islands often wear. It was too far to see his face, yet looking at him I found myself swallowing hard and my lips working. The sun was still an hour high, hot and intense. It made the water a glittering blue and where it lashed about the rocky shore the foam was startlingly white. I hardly noticed these things, however, looking at the man.

And then, all at once, I knew what was wrong with him. *I could see straight through him!* He was standing there looking out at us, and yet I had the impression I could see the rocks directly behind him. It was like a thick mist which has body and substance but which you can look through and on the other side of which you can see things.

Mary's heels made a clicking sound on the deck behind me and I turned quickly. "Come here," I said. "Look!"

She stared at me and began to smile. "What's the trouble? Seen a ghost?"

"I don't know. You look." I turned and pointed toward the shore where the man had been. He was gone.

Mary said, "I don't see anything but a lot of rocks. I don't even see how we're going to get ashore."

I took a deep breath, searching the shore. The man might have ducked behind one of the rocks or he might have reached the little house by running, but where he had stood there was only warm sunlight. "It must have been some trick of light and shadow that made him look that way," I thought.

"All right," John Wayne called. "You two come forward if you're going to the isle of Saba."

Pete, the Negro cook, was standing amidships as we went toward the small boat. "Would you like to go ashore and climb that mountain?" Mary asked him.

He said, "No ma'am. Hit looks too steep fer me."

Mary laughed. "Well, you can guard the schooner," she said. I helped her over the side and followed her into the small boat with Carl Hammer and John Wayne.

It was a strange crew we had on the *Sink or Swim,* our dilapidated old two-masted schooner. I had often wondered how John Wayne, Carl Hammer and I ever got together and just what the common bond was that made us such close friends. We didn't have much in common except a desire to ramble; yet for five years we had been together almost constantly and any one of us would have gladly gone through hell for the other two.

Hammer—it was an odd trick we had of calling each other by the last name—was an artist whose pictures brought him in just enough money to let him keep moving. They were strange pictures, going deep into metaphysics, and the man himself was strange. He was thin and dark, with glittering black eyes, sharp features, a thin mouth and long, slim fingers that moved quickly and nervously. Sometimes when he was painting one of those strange, physic pictures of his the light in his black eyes wasn't human. Wayne and I had often said his mind was set on a hair trigger and he was likely to go crazy very suddenly, breaking the way a stretched cord may break.

John Wayne was the biggest man in the group. Tall, heavy shouldered and blond, sunburned but with a slight redness to his nose caused by almost constant attention to the bottle, he was one of the best-natured men I have ever known. And one of the most worthless, from the world's point of view. He had never done a day's work in his life, except on hunting and fishing trips and things of that sort. There had never been any need for him to work otherwise. He had several million dollars, I don't think he knew exactly how much. He was the man who had actually bought the *Sink or Swim,* though Hammer and I had contributed and had insisted, therefore, on the ship being a cheap one. You would have known Wayne anywhere because he always had a bottle in one hand—or very close to it—and a big grin on his face.

Mary was Wayne's sister and the one thing I had ever cared enough about to try for—and the one thing which always had seemed utterly impossible of attainment. She had been very much in love with some fellow in New York and he'd thrown her over just before we left for the West Indies. She'd been pretty badly broken up about it and Wayne had suggested we bring her along.

I had never understood how anybody could help but be in love with her. She wasn't tall, but she gave that impression until you were close to her. She was slim, with high, round breasts and a waist that curved as delicately as a flower into full thighs, and her legs were long and slim and well turned. Her hair was almost as blond as her brother's but with a trace of gold in it. Here eyes were wide set and very blue. Her mouth was a little too big to be classical, but to me it had always seemed the perfect mouth for kissing, though I had never kissed it.

Carl Hammer often said there was only one more worthless man in the world than John Wayne, and that was I. I had been left enough income to live on if I lived cheaply, so I spent my life moving from one cheap part of the world to another.

There you have the four of us who rowed ashore. Hammer was at the tiller, Wayne and I at the oars. He had to slide right in between two boulders to the small, rocky beach, but we made it.

I still had my back to the shore when I saw that strange look come over Hammer's face. Without asking, I knew what he had seen. His black eyes had suddenly grown very wide in his lean face. His thin, dark lips had parted. For a moment he stopped breathing; then over the beat of the surf I heard the air hiss through his nostrils. I believe he could see, even then, with that almost mystic power of his, what was coming. During that long minute ho sat in the stern and stared, he must have recognized the thing at which he was looking.

Wayne noticed the expression on his face and said, "What the hell, Hammer? What the hell?" He went over the side then, without waiting for an answer, and began to tug the boat onto the shore. The surf was heavy and I should have gone to help him, but for some reason I couldn't.

I had shipped the oars and I began to turn slowly. The muscles in my neck seemed very cold. I heard Wayne's voice, sounding far away. "Damn it, get out and give me a hand."

Then I was looking at the shore and at the man standing there. As I looked he moved, caught the prow of the boat and tugged. I knew that he was the same man I had seen from the ship. He was tall, in his early thirties, and very sunburned; yet under the darkness of his skin there was a strange pallor. It was the shade of thin brown paper held up to the sun. I thought, suddenly, of a well-embalmed corpse and of the pallor beneath the paint on its cheeks. I had got the impression of seeing through the man when I looked at him from the ship, but now, while he kept moving and tugging at the boat, I lost that impression. In that first moment I saw nothing strange about him except the color of his skin. His face was dirty and with little wrinkles around the corners of his eyes as if from looking into the sun. He wore an old cap so that I couldn't see the color of his hair and with his face half turned I couldn't look into his eyes.

I went over the side then and helped them tug the boat onto the shore. Mary clambered out, threw back her head and looked up at the mountain which towered over us. Hammer was still sitting in the stern, staring at the man, but his breathing was more natural. Slowly he came forward and got out.

Wayne turned toward the man who had helped him beach the boat. "Where's the town?" he asked.

The man kept moving, stepping from rock to rock and back again, yet he did it with a slow calmness that did not seem at all nervous. I wondered then why he kept moving. As he stepped from one rock to another he nodded toward the path which led upward. "Up the hill about half a mile," he said. He talked with a distinctly English accent.

From directly behind me Hammer spoke. His voice was breathless, rapid. "What's your name?"

The man turned quickly and looked at Hammer. When he did I saw his eyes and instinctively I stepped to one side. His eyes were like those of a fish, an utterly lifeless blue. Like those of a corpse,

I thought. And in the second that he stood motionless, staring at Hammer, I once more had the weird impression that I was looking through a figure made of mist and that directly beyond it I could see the rocks of the shore.

Then the man moved sideways, calmly. He grinned and said, "My name's Bill—just Bill—to sailors like yourselves."

Wayne said, "Well Bill, we'll find the town if we go right up this path?"

"I'll show you," Bill said. "Got nothing else to do myself." He turned and started up the path.

Wayne made a quick duck into the prow of the rowboat and pulled out a bottle of red wine. "It looks like a long climb to go thirsty." he said. He started up the mountain. Mary went next and I followed her. Where the path was wide enough I stepped up beside her. Carl Hammer brought up the rear.

I was thinking that the name Bill on this island should have some special significance, but I couldn't remember what. I kept staring at the man, wondering what had given me the impression of seeing *through* him, but now he was moving steadily up the mountain and most of the time both Mary and Wayne stood between us. Watching the liquid movement of Mary's white linen skirt across her hips I forgot about the man called Bill . . .

We had climbed for nearly ten minutes when Bill began to hum. The sun was low now, but it was still hot and the climb and the heat had the rest of us panting heavily; yet there was no hint of exhaustion in Bill's breathing. After a moment his humming changed to a low singing. At first I couldn't understand what he was singing, then, as his voice grew louder, I began to catch the words.

> *"Oh, the first man died in a fall from the cliff,*
> *And the second one died the same.*
> *And the third man went to a watery grave.*
> *And the woman died from shame."*

It had the swing of a sea chantey and he sang the same lines over and over, his voice gradually getting louder. We kept climbing.

The path rose sharply, clinging to the canyon wall. On our right the sheer drop grew deeper and deeper. The mountain above us was matted with big rocks, a thick wide-bladed grass I had never seen before, and mango trees. Small goats wandered about among the rocks and bleated mournfully. I noticed that when we came near one he would whirl, stare at us for a moment and then go bounding away in terror.

"It's odd," I said to Mary. "Those goats shouldn't be that wild."

Behind us Hammer said, "It's not us they stare at. It's Bill." His voice sounded strange.

We both turned to look at him and it was in that second that it happened. Bill's voice had risen high and booming on the final line, *"And the woman died from shame."* As he had started the stanza again his tone changed, dropped and took on a weird tenseness, *"Oh the first man died in a fall from the cliff."* That one line and no more. His voice went out as sharply as a light and left a silence thick as darkness.

Wayne made a choked, half-screaming sound. "You—you—" Mary and I were spinning to look at him.

He was at the very edge of the cliff, reeling backward. The bottle of wine was held stiffly in front of him as if to guard himself from the thing he had seen. His eyes were bulging, his mouth twisted with incredulous fear. His left hand was chest high, and shaking. I couldn't see Bill and I thought that he must have rounded the sharp curve ahead.

The whole thing happened in a half second. Wayne went reeling backward while the three of us stared, spellbound. Then his left foot went over the cliff's edge and he toppled. Mary screamed, "John!" and leaped. I went past her in a rush.

It was too late. Wayne was falling, his face still upward—and I could see the fear-twisted mouth, the bulging eyes. Then he was out of sight below the brink of the cliff. I heard the crash of underbrush, the sickening thud as his body struck. There was a rattling, rumbling sound as rocks and body tumbled downward.

I was still kneeling at the edge of the cliff, my right hand stretched out over it helplessly and Mary was standing close behind me, body rigid, face blank with amazement, when Carl Hammer passed us. He reached the bend in the path moving fast, and ripped around it. I heard the skid of his shoes as he stopped.

He came back just as I was getting slowly to my feet. Mary was still motionless, looking out over the canyon where Wayne had fallen. Hammer said dully, "Bill Wales has vanished."

CHAPTER TWO

"THE FIRST MAN DIED
IN A FALL FROM THE CLIFF"

"The dead call the dying
And finger at the doors."
—Housman

I LOOKED AT HIM BLANKLY. "Who?" I asked.

He said, "Bill Wales." His voice sounded hopeless, beaten.

Even then I didn't remember. Perhaps I would have, had not Mary suddenly begun to sob. I caught her quickly in my arms. "Don't worry," I said, knowing even at the moment how foolish I sounded.

I turned to Hammer. "We've got to get him, quick!"

Hammer nodded, but his black eyes held that wild, spiritual look I had seen in them when he was painting. I don't believe he knew exactly what I said.

The cliff was too steep where Wayne had fallen for us to go over. We had to run back a hundred yards or more, then work our way down gradually. It was hard going, but we found Wayne lying half between a huge stone and a mango tree. He was on his back, his face bleeding from two long gashes and a bad bruise on his right cheek. He still held the neck of the broken bottle in his right hand.

When I knelt beside him I saw that his eyes were wide open and he was still breathing. He recognized me and tried to grin, but there was more than pain twisting his mouth. There was fear and a dull groping for understanding. His voice was a whisper. "He never touched me. He was just there and then—then I—I was afraid. But he never touched—"

"That's all right," I said. "You just keep steady. You'll be all right. You'll be—"

I had to stop. I was about to cry. I wasn't ashamed but I didn't want Wayne to see me.

Hammer and I made a stretcher of our linen coats and our shirts, using a couple of limbs we tore from the mango trees. As we worked I could see Hammer's thin lips twisting, see him blinking his dark eyes to keep back the tears; for one look at Wayne had shown us both that he was badly injured. The mystic, frightened expression had gone from Hammer's face, though he must have known then what lay in store for him and how utterly impossible it was to avoid.

It wasn't easy to carry Wayne up the cliff side. Before we reached the path we heard the excited voices, the pounding of shoes.

"Mary must have gone to the village for help," Hammer said.

From the cot Wayne whispered, "I'm hurting deep in my belly. I'd sure like a drink." He paused, then the whispering started again. "He never touched me, just—"

"Don't talk, fellow," I said. "Just take it easy."

"I'd like a drink."

"You damned sot," Hammer said. There was a little sob in his voice.

Then, all at once, men were around us and helping us lift the stretcher to the path, and carrying it up the mountain to a little village cuddled in what must have been the crater of an old volcano. A doctor had cut Wayne's clothes from him and set a broken leg and several ribs and put him to bed in the small government hospital. There weren't any other patients.

Wayne was still under the ether and Mary was sitting beside the cot, her thin brown hands holding one of his, her blond head bowed, when the doctor called Hammer and me outside. The doctor was a Negro, the only doctor on the island but his work had seemed very competent. Now he looked from Hammer to me.

"Well?" I asked.

The doctor spoke softly. "He may come through. There's a chance, but a small one. He'll have to be kept very quiet. Any exertion . . ." he made a short gesture.

"We'll keep him still," Hammer said.

The doctor hesitated. His very white teeth slid out over his lower lip. "While he was under the ether he kept saying, 'He never touched me. He just turned around and—I was afraid.' I think you two had best come down to the police station and explain how this happened."

"We'll come," Hammer said. That strange look was in his black eyes again and his dark lips were very thin across his teeth.

We finished our report. There wasn't much we could say. The Brigadier, as they call the chief of the five-man police force, was a sleek, very black Negro. He stood beside his desk looking at us and we looked at him. Almost suddenly Carl Hammer said, "Tell us about Bill Wales."

No surprise showed on the Brigadier's face. Instead there was an abrupt show of fear. Then the muscles about his mouth tightened, leaving no emotion at all.

"It's a very old story around here," he said. He spoke crisply and very precisely as if conscious of his office and that he should speak correctly. He kept his face masklike; so calm it gave me the impression he was afraid to be natural lest belief should show in his eyes.

"Bill Wales," the Brigadier said, "was supposed to be an English sailor marooned on Saba years ago. His ship had stayed here for awhile and he'd married one of the native girls. The captain took Bill's girl and left him here. The next few ships that came— only one every six months or so in those days—were low on water or food, couldn't get any on this island and refused to take him. He went crazy and died swearing he'd kill every sailor and every sailor's sweetheart that landed here."

"And has he—" Hammer's voice was slow, deliberate—"kept his vow?"

The Brigadier looked nervous. "Of course I—I don't believe the story. But sailors *are* afraid of this island. A number of them have been killed accidentally here. The natives claim that if Bill Wales fails to kill them the first time, he comes back and makes good. The local boatmen always keep a cross in the back of their rowboats, claim it keeps Wales from going with them out to the ships. And—and—" The muscle's around the Negro's mouth relaxed, trembled for one moment, then froze hard again. He tried to smile. "And it's true that as long as sailors stay ashore they keep meeting accidents. Of course, the walks around here are dangerous, if one is not used to them."

We thanked him and left. Once outside the building I said, "That was a swell story he told," and laughed.

Hammer looked at me without speaking and the laughter died in my throat. His face was like that of a man who looks at certain death and watches it coming toward him.

We ate supper at the little hospital and afterward all three of us sat around Wayne's bed. He was conscious now and suffering terribly. Whenever he caught one of us looking at him he tried to grin, but at other times there was a strange, drawn expression on his face. Not pain exactly, but bewilderment and something very close to fear. It was the same look that had been on his face when we reached him at the foot of the cliff. I kept remembering the thing he had said: "He never touched me. He just turned and I—I was afraid."

And I kept wondering what had happened to our guide. He'd never shown up, and our description had been too vague for the Brigadier to tell who he might be.

Mary got up from her chair beside the bed and tiptoed to a small window. "There's a moon just over the mountain-top," she said.

I didn't say anything and in the silence I could hear Hammer's breathing. It wasn't natural and I turned to look at him. He was leaning forward, black eyes glittering, head cocked to one side.

"Listen," he said. The word quivered in the room.

I said, "I don't hear anything."

Hammer didn't make a sound but his thin lips were moving, framing the words, "If he fails, he comes back and makes good."

Wayne stirred on the bed then, and we all turned to look at him. His head was raised, his shoulders almost off the pillow. At first he seemed to be listening, but slowly his face changed. The corners of his mouth began to tremble, his eyes to dilate. Even as I looked beads of sweat started to break out on his forehead.

"God!" he whispered. *"It's him!"*

Mary came toward him with a rush. "John! John!" she was saying. "Lie still! What is it, John?"

Wayne whispered again, *"It's him."* His whole life seemed to go into those words.

And then I heard it, still soft and barely audible, drifting in with the breeze through the open window. At first there was only the tune, the rhythm of the sea chantey. Then I began to catch an occasional word. *" . . . first . . . died . . . second . . . went to a watery grave."*

I didn't move when I first heard those words. They were like cold iron bands around my chest, stopping my lungs. I just sat there and I could see my hands tightening around the arms of the chair. All at once I knew that I was afraid.

I shook myself then and stood up quickly. "I'm acting like a kid," I thought, "getting afraid of stories."

Mary had her arms about Wayne now, her fingers on his mouth, but he was saying, "You'll *have* to leave the island. You'll have to!"

"Be quiet," Mary said. "Just lie still . . ." She stopped, her head raised, her eyes growing wide. She too had heard the song.

"I'll go see that fellow," I muttered. I turned toward the door. Not until I reached the small porch did I realize that Hammer and Mary were following me.

Moonlight flooded softly over the village, showing the small white houses and their red roofs like dim shadows. We could see the stone walls that separated most of the houses, low and dark. A breadfruit tree made a rustling sound in the wind.

"Oh the first man died in a fall from the cliff."

The line rang loud, clear. There was something horribly vicious about the sound, something undefinable yet deadly, the way there is in the burr of a rattlesnake. But there was more than that in these words. They weren't earthly.

Then I saw the man who had called himself Bill. He was standing just beyond the left corner of the stone wall around the hospital. He was dressed as he had been in the afternoon, the cap pulled down over his temples, the ragged blue overalls. His head was thrown back, bathed in moonlight, mouth open as he sang. And even now I could see the strange pallor of his face, and his eyes, as utterly lifeless as those of a fish, showed palely blue. Even at that second I wondered why I could see his eyes so plainly by the moonlight.

"The second man died the same."

The words broke, each as clear and distinct as a glass ball. They hammered at my ears with a terrible meaningfulness. They jerked at my nerves, sent fear and anger flooding through me.

"The third man went to a watery grave."

The man had never moved, but stood, head thrown back, singing. And even then I had the weird impression that I was looking *through* him and seeing the moonlight spilling over the ground beyond.

"Oh God!" Mary cried. "Stop him! Stop him!"

"I'll stop him," I said. I didn't know then why I was so angry or why I was so afraid, but I went off the porch with a rush and down the path toward the gate. Behind me I heard Hammer and Mary running.

"And the woman died from shame!"

I went through the gate moving fast, stumbled where the path dropped to the sidewalk, caught myself and whirled toward the left.

I took three steps, still running, before I could stop. My eyes were getting big in my face. I could feel the eyelids stretching. Perhaps I had stopped breathing altogether. I took one long step and reached the corner of the wall.

The man had vanished!

There was no sound for a long time—utterly no sound in the whole world. Even the moonlight had taken on a stiff frigidity. It lay on the leaves of the breadfruit tree, stiff and cold. The little white hospital with its red roof seemed frozen, taut, waiting for something to happen.

After a long while I heard breathing behind me and turned. Mary and Hammer were standing at the end of the stone wall, staring at the place where the man had been. And in Mary's face was reflected the look I had seen in Hammer's. Her hair seemed as white as the moonlight, as white as her cheeks, and very still.

Then suddenly she moved. "Oh God!" she said. "John! Alone . . .!" She was turning even as she spoke.

We heard the voice before she could finish turning, before she could take one step. It wasn't the booming voice that had sung the other lines. It was low and tense. It was clear, hideously clear, yet it was little more than a whisper.

"Oh the first man died in a fall from the cliff."

That one line and no more. Not even a ghost moved in this world of death.

Something made a jarring noise inside the hospital. Mary and Hammer were running along the walk toward the gate. I was jumping the wall, in the air, striking the ground, running. The porch boomed under my steps, the door banged. I stopped just inside the room where John Wayne lay.

I never heard Mary and Hammer come up behind me. I don't know if Mary cried out at first; but before she reached him, moving slowly, stiffly, she knew he was dead. He lay there beside the bed, his body bent in a half circle, the sheets tangled about him and his face turned upward with the eyes wide, the mouth open, fear showing in every stiffening muscle. Carl Hammer knew it and I knew it. We stood in the door motionless, watching.

After a minute Mary knelt beside him, began to sob, very quietly. I went and put my arms around her and lifted her up and carried her out of the room. Hammer must have gone for the doctor, for he came soon and gave Mary a sedative and got her to sleep.

It was the fall from the bed, he said, which had killed John Wayne.

We buried Wayne at sea the next day. He'd always said, the big, good-natured grin showing on his face, that he wanted to be buried at sea. He liked liquid and he wanted to spend eternity in it.

We rowed out in the small boat, Mary sitting beside the body, a priest in the stern. Before we reached the schooner we could see Pete, the Negro cook, standing at the rail. We told him Wayne had fallen from a cliff accidentally. Then we upped anchor, sailed out about a quarter of the way to St. Eustatius and slid the body overboard. We went back and dropped anchor off Fort Bay.

Hammer and I were forward, ready to lower the small boat and row the priest ashore when I said, "I'm going to wander around that island for awhile. I'm going to find the fellow that does the singing."

Both the priest and Hammer turned swiftly to look at me. Hammer said, "You fool."

The priest was a small man with a face all angles and lean, wrinkled fingers. For a moment the fingers twisted the crucifix about his neck. He said slowly, "I advise you to leave the island—without coming ashore."

"And you believe that legend?" I demanded scornfully.

The priest looked down at the deck and his wrinkled fingers kept twisting the beads, toying with the cross. Almost suddenly he looked up.

"If I didn't believe in a life after death, I wouldn't be a priest," he said simply. "All religion is founded on an after-life. Man has believed in it from the dawn of history. The Bible has innumerable references to 'The Spirit' of a departed person, and that can be only what we call a ghost today. A number of your scientists believe also. There are things which they can't explain otherwise. Conan Doyle always believed. The German physicist Von Berunth came to that belief after years of study. Your own Dr. Tillingham in California, probably the greatest of American scientists, has recently come to believe in the life after death."

I made a grunting sound and gestured with both hands as if I thought the man a fool. And yet there was a cold hollow deep in my chest. I couldn't believe that the man we had seen was the ghost of Bill Wales, and yet . . . How else was one to explain what had happened? I think that even then the awful certainty was forming itself in my brain, but I had laughed at the idea for so many years that now it was almost impossible to believe.

Hammer spoke then, his voice bitterly contemptuous. "You don't believe in spirits because you don't understand them. It's like saying there can't be a radio because you can't understand how it works. And you don't understand because you've never tried, you've never thought. You were told once that what you call a 'ghost' could not be, and you've shut your mind to any other belief, closed your eyes against the evidence which every day of your life piles up around you. It's only those of us who study, who face the problem . . ." He was looking now as I had seen him look while painting, the muscles in his dark face grown taut, his lips thin across white teeth, his black eyes glittering as though they saw a thing great and awful beyond human vision.

Seeing him made fear crawl along my back. The muscles in my throat began to tighten. But even then I wouldn't believe. *There weren't any ghosts!* I shut my mind on that idea, tightly, refused to look beyond. Sometimes now, gazing into the mirror, seeing the thing that is reflected there and remembering that moment while I still had a chance to escape, I feel like tearing my own throat. But I did not know then what was to happen.

"You're both crazy," I said. "I'm going ashore and find the man that killed Wayne."

Part of the life went out of Carl Hammer then. He raised his right hand with its thin, long fingers halfway to my arm, stopped. His lips twitched. "All right," he said. "If you're going, I'll go along."

We dropped the boat over, helped the priest in, followed him. We were halfway to the shore when, looking back, I saw that Mary had come up from the cabin and was standing in the cockpit. The Negro cook was on the deck amidships, gazing out after us.

I didn't have any idea where to look for the man who bellowed a sea chantey before death struck. I had an eerie feeling that he would come looking for me and the thought made my heart contract. But Hammer and I followed the priest all the way up to the Bottom, the misnamed little village situated 800 feet up that rocky mountain-side, without anything happening.

It was late afternoon by then. We told the priest good-bye. "Maybe we better start back now," I said to Hammer. "We don't want to leave Mary alone too long."

Hammer nodded, but he didn't speak. I don't believe he could have spoken at that moment. The skin on his face was as taut as parchment and wet with perspiration. I could see a vein beating in his throat. His mouth was thin, but the left corner kept twitching. All at once I remembered what Wayne used to say as he watched Hammer painting: "That man has a hair trigger brain. He'll go off it some day."

There wasn't anybody along the narrow winding steps that lead down to the sea. The sun was out of sight below the mountain, but the tops of the cliffs were white gold. Goats bleated from above and below us. The path went downward, one edge against the cliff, the other sometimes above a gradual slope, sometimes bordered by a sheer drop of two hundred feet or more. The wind had died and there was no sound except for the mournful cry of the goats.

It may have been the twilight, it may have been the silence, it may have been some premonition of the thing which was about to happen that made me feel the way I did. With each step toward the point where Wayne had fallen, the feeling grew on me. I was having to draw my breath consciously and the effort hurt my throat and lungs. It was hot and it was hard exercise going down that precipitous path; but the sweat that broke out on my shoulders was cold.

All at once I noticed that the goats were not bleating any more. There was no sound except the scuff of our shoes as we went downward. I had several Dutch quarter-gilders in my pocket and in the silence I could hear them clinking as I walked. Ahead of me Carl Hammer was moving stiff-kneed. He seemed to force each leg the way a man does who is wading upstream. His back was rigid, head high. His long fingers were held stiffly at his side and I saw a bead of sweat slide from one to make a dark spot on the ground.

And then I heard it!

CHAPTER THREE

"AND THE SECOND MAN DIED THE SAME"

IT WAS VERY SOFT AT FIRST, more a stirring of the wind than a whispering of leaves, not as loud as the murmur of the sea heard from far away, or the notes of a death march dying into thick twilight.

It seemed to me that Carl Hammer's body grew more stiff than ever. His fingers seemed to get longer and more rigid at his side. The motion of his legs was heavier, pushing through the thick current of fear which flowed about him. But he did not hesitate, did not look around.

The sound grew slowly, becoming more distinct as the wind puffs and fades and puffs again, coming more strongly each time until the hurricane strikes. Hardly knowing that I did so I glanced to the left of the path. It dropped away for a hundred feet or more, straight down.

"We must be near the spot where Wayne fell." I heard the words without knowing I had spoken them. Hammer did not pause, did not look around.

The tune was very distinct now. It seemed to keep an eerie, death-march time with the crunching of our steps. I didn't hear the words, but I knew them.

"Hammer," I said. "Hammer!" I stopped. It couldn't have been long since I first heard the sound and yet it seemed like years that I had walked straight toward it, moving like a somnambulist without realizing I was walking.

Carl Hammer kept going, moving with that awkward motion like pushing his way through water or against a heavy wind. "Hammer," I said again. He kept going and never turned his head.

"Carl Hammer!" I screamed the words.

He hesitated, swayed as though drunk. The fingers at his side were clenched. Veins stood high on them and the knuckles showed white. Little muscles jerked in his wrist. Then he stepped forward again.

Ahead of us the song was a booming volley, sweeping down on us, crashing about our ears.

"And the woman died from shame!"

Then came the silence. It seemed to creep on cold and brittle feet through eternity. It froze me standing there on the brink between life and death, standing there motionless and watching the man ahead of me.

There was a sharp bend in the path. Hammer went toward it. He was there when I remembered.

It was here that Wayne had plunged over!

"Hammer!" I screamed.

He took two more short, awkward steps. They brought him to the curve and half around it.

"And the second man died the same!"

Even before it happened I knew then there was no stopping it; I knew that a power beyond life, beyond the touch of a human being, had control of us, was closing about us. I knew that one of us would die quickly, for that last line been as tense and low and soft as the hiss of a snake.

Carl Hammer was half around the curve when he stopped. For one half second he stood there. Then he reeled. His hands, stiff and clawlike, came up in front of his chest. He staggered backward.

"Hammer!" In the silence that had followed the last line my cry boomed like a gun. And with the boom, Hammer turned.

He came like a fury, black hair slithering back from a lean face and eyes that were crackling madness above a dark and twisted mouth where teeth gleamed white. He came snarling, the breath husking in his nostrils, saliva drooling from his mouth. He came head first, lean shoulders driving—a man who had forced himself to the edge of death, going first to take the place of the friend who followed, but whose nerves had broken at the last step, flinging him backward and insane.

I threw up my hands and he crashed into me. We went over, hard. It seemed that we fell a long time and all that while through utter silence. Then we struck the path.

The breath jumped from my lungs and I heard Carl Hammer sob. I was teetering, rolling; my legs were swinging out into space and my fingers were clawing at the path while I hung there, almost like a bird who has stopped, wings outspread and motionless for a long second. Then I heard Hammer sob again, far away and below me; and I was pulling myself back on the path when I heard the crash of his body. There was the tinkling of rocks, the rustle of stilling leaves after the body passed through, and then there was silence.

I lay on my back on the path and did not move. High above me I could see the broad gold beam of the sunlight. It was like a clear river, flowing deep and strong. It touched the mountain-top and soaked it in warmth and flowed around it without movement, without ever a ripple.

Far off a goat bleated lugubriously.

I got to my feet then. My hands were grimy from clawing at the path and one fingernail was broken. It hurt but the pain seemed totally removed from my body. It was as if I were watching some-one else nursing a broken fingernail, knowing that it hurt them, but unmoved, unsympathetic.

I went to the curve in the path and looked around it. The steps led twistingly downward. A ragged cliff on the left stuck out far enough to hide the sea.

During the whole time that I struggled down to Carl Hammer's body I was in that dazed, almost unconscious condition. It was seeing him lying there, one leg bent under him, the bone sticking out through his linen trousers, the bone unbearably clean and white, whiter than the linen through which it stuck, that brought feeling back to me. I didn't cry, yet there were tears sliding from my eyes. I kept trying to get the lump out of my throat and I began to curse, slowly, completely. Letting each word stand on my tongue, mouthing the full harshness of it, letting it fall slowly be-fore I said the next one, I cursed myself.

Carl Hammer had known all the while what was coming. He had tried to tell me, but I had refused to listen. And then, because he had known, he had come ashore with me and had walked to his death ahead of me, standing between me and the thing which no human being could fight.

After awhile I got the body up in my arms. There was blood on it and the blood felt clammy on my arms. I fought my way through the brush and the cactus trying to shield his body with my own, remembering always how he had shielded me and that the gesture I was making now was only absurd, yet forcing myself to do it, cursing at the pain of the thorns and cactus.

The sun was down when I reached Fort Bay, but in the east there was a flaming rose of piled clouds. I made my way through the big rocks to the water's edge and stopped. The rowboat was gone. Looking out to the anchored schooner I could see the shadow of the boat bobbing at its side.

"Oh God!" I said aloud. "He couldn't—couldn't—" I swallowed hard,

"And the woman died from shame."

The line stabbed suddenly through my mind.

Still holding Hammer's body in my arms I began to shout, "Pete! Pete! Mary!" A shadow moved on the deck. It was the Negro cook.

"Bring me that boat!" I yelled.

For a moment he didn't answer. Then I heard his voice, soft in the twilight. "Boat?"

"You're damn' right, the boat!" I shouted. "It's tied forward."

He went to the rail, looked over. Then he went forward and climbed over and into the boat.

There's always a heavy surf around Saba, probably the roughest seas in the West Indies. I don't know how Pete ever got the boat ashore by himself. I didn't watch. I stretched Hammer out on the ground, straightened his leg as best I could, covered his face with my coat. Then I began to wash the blood from myself—I didn't want to frighten Mary any worse than need be. But I did these things almost unconsciously, for my brain was clamped cold with fear. Who had rowed that boat out to the ship?

I tried to think of something else, knowing that guessing would do me no good. But I couldn't shake the thought from my mind. Mary couldn't have swum ashore and rowed back. Who had carried the boat out to the schooner? And why?

I heard the boat grate on the beach and looked up. Pete had gone over in water waist deep and, waiting until a wave came in, heaved the boat higher. He came up on the rock and turned toward me. All at once he noticed Hammer's body. He stopped and even in the twilight I could see his eyes growing wider, the whites seeming to spread across his face.

"What—what dat?" he asked.

"Mr. Hammer fell over the cliff," I said.

Pete began to stammer, to ask questions, but I stopped him. "Who rowed the boat out to the schooner?" I asked.

The words seemed to come to him slowly and far apart. As he listened his mouth dripped open; the pupils of his eyes contracted until they were invisible in the rolling whites. "I ain't goin' back on dat ship," he said at last. "Naw Sur, not yit. I—I'se goin' where dere's folks."

He began to back away from me, up the path. I watched him go without speaking. It didn't seem important to me then, For a long moment nothing seemed important. And then, abruptly, I thought of Mary.

She was on the schooner—alone or—with Bill Wales!

I caught Hammer's body in my arms, carried it to the boat and put it in. I shoved the boat off and began to row. It's strange that I didn't capsize in that sea. I don't even remember the passage. But I remember tying the boat to the schooner. Then I was crawling over the rail with Hammer's body in my arms.

It was dark now. Just over the sea to the east the sky was growing white and gold from the rising moon, but now I could hardly see the length of the deck, the dark shadow of the boat-house and the cockpit. I laid Hammer on the deck and went aft. There was no sound except the lap of the water against the schooner, the dull echo of the surf booming on the rocky shore. No light came up from the cabin into the cockpit.

I stood on the deck for a long minute, gazing down into the darkness, scarcely breathing. My heart ached against my ribs. I could feel a nerve twitching at the right corner of my mouth. On the seat of the cockpit I could see the pale blur of a box of writing paper. Evidently Mary had been there during the afternoon.

I hadn't thought much of Mary during the last twenty-four hours. I had believed Wayne's death an accident and since Hammer's sudden madness and death I had been too shocked to think. But now the fall significance of the song which rang as a death knell came to me.

"The third man went to a watery grave,
"And the woman died from shame."

Standing there, looking down into the silent darkness of the cockpit, seeing the black square of doorway which led into the cabin, those words kept beating through my mind.

I was the third man, and Mary . . .

CHAPTER FOUR

"AND THE WOMAN . . ."

MY FISTS KNOTTED SUDDENLY and I jerked a great breath into my lungs. By God! I wouldn't go down without fighting. Nothing would touch Mary until—My fingers relaxed and the breath slid in a sickening gasp from my nostrils. Fighting—how could I fight this thing? It had killed twice without ever touching its victim. At last I knew what I was facing, *and I knew that no human being could hope to withstand it.*

How long I stood beside the dark cockpit I don't know, but with each moment I grew more afraid. There was only darkness and silence in the cabin. Suppose I called to Mary and she didn't answer. Where would she be? What would have happened to her? What horrible thing . . .

And then I couldn't stand it any longer. I heard my voice calling out, calling frantically, "Mary? Mary!"

For a long while there was nothing. The water lapping against the schooner took on an awful roaring. My breath congealed in my nostrils. And then, "What is it, Tom?"

"Thank God!" I said aloud.

I went down into the cabin with a rush. I flicked a match across the doorsill, lit a storm lantern, and turned. Mary was sitting on the edge of Wayne's bunk. Her hands were folded in her lap, fingers motionless. Her hair was golden in the light and hung very still around cheeks as pale as those of a corpse. Her blue eyes were wide and large, and in them an expression which took the joy out of seeing her. It was as if she were looking into the face of death and waiting, waiting quietly, knowing absolutely there was no escape.

"Mary," I said. I found myself wondering if it had already happened. Had she—but I put the thought from my mind.

Her voice was like her face, emotionless, dead. "He killed Carl like he did Wayne. I saw him."

I made a gasping sound, then stiffened my muscles. "Where did you see him? On the ship?"

She shook her head slowly. "No. I didn't see Bill Wales. I saw Carl fall from the cliff."

"But—but Mary . . ." I was close to her now, kneeling in front of her, holding her folded hands. "How did you get ashore?" At the same time I could feel hope coming up through my chest, spreading out like a soft flame. That meant she was the person who had rowed the boat out to the schooner.

"I didn't go ashore," Mary said. "I was trying to write a letter, sitting in the cockpit. I saw it from there."

My hands tightened savagely about hers. "You *couldn't* have seen it from the ship. There's a cliff in the way, and—"

"I saw it," Mary said. "I was in the cockpit. I just—just saw it. I knew just when it happened."

I didn't say anything. I had heard of persons who had visions of things which happened miles away. It did not seem strange to me now. Nothing seemed impossible any more.

But one thought did keep growing in my mind: if Mary had not rowed the boat out to the schooner someone else had. And the only other person . . .

I stood up. Mary did not move. She sat with her hands folded, looking off into space. I took the storm lantern from its bracket and made a slow circuit of the cabin. Nothing there. I went into the small cabin where Mary stayed, found nothing. I searched all the ship below-decks that I could reach from the cockpit. Everything was exactly as it had been.

Leaving the lantern with Mary, I went on deck,

The moon had swung up out of the sea now. It was a silver bubble and a shimmering path led from it to the schooner. The water was a rolling blackness where now and then white foam glimmered and vanished as the wind whipped the top from a wave. On the port side Saba rose in a great, dark shadow into the sky.

What I intended to do if I found Bill Wales, I didn't know. But somehow it seemed that I had to find him. Perhaps I thought I could do something which would help Mary to escape; I don't know. But I went toward the forward hatch, intending to enter it. I had the tarpaulin off when I stopped, rigid, staring.

I was on the starboard side of the hatch, looking out across the empty deck to the port rail. The deck showed clearly in the moonlight and little shadows rippled up and down it as the schooner rocked.

I was looking at the spot where I had placed Carl Hammer's body—and it was gone!

It was a long time before I began to laugh, a half crazy, guttural laughter. Carl Hammer had gone overboard, without a Christian burial; and he had believed in a hereafter . . .

"There was only one before," I said, and my voice had a ringing, insane note, "but now there're two." I kept holding to the edge of the uncovered hatch and laughing. The sound grew higher, wilder, madder. My shoulders began to shake. Madness clawed through me and burst out with the laughter.

"Tom! Tom!" Mary was calling to me from the cockpit.

My hands tightened on the hatch. I jerked at it, shook it and shook myself. The laughter choked in my throat.

"Steady," I said to myself. "Steady. You've got to help Mary." I turned and went aft, conscious of the fingernails biting into my palms, the pain from the one I had broken.

Mary was standing in the cockpit. The moonlight made her hair and cheeks seem very white and her eyes were dark pools of shadow. "I have never seen her quite so beautiful," I thought. "And soon . . ."

"What—what was that laughing, Tom?" she asked.

I dropped into the cockpit beside her, put my arms around her. It was the first time I had ever held her that way except when dancing. Her body was warm and firm. "It was me," I said. "I think I—I was going crazy."

She pulled away just enough to tilt back her head and look at me. She smiled, a pitifully brave smile with her lips trembling. "You can't do that," she said. "I had given up for awhile, but we can't. Carl and—" a shadow of pain came in her eyes before she said her brother's name "—and John wouldn't want us to give up. They fought it out."

I pulled her close, held her there, her breasts flattened against my chest. I had loved this woman for five years and never held her this way until now, and now . . . Her hair brushed softly against my chin and mouth. "We won't give up," I said. "I'll get you out of this some way. There's got to be a way. Got to be!"

After a few minutes we went back into the cabin, sat side by side on what had been Wayne's bunk. I rested elbows on knees, hands clenched in front, head bowed, thinking. There had to be some way. If I could only be certain whether or not the thing was on board. If I could get him ashore . . . But Mary couldn't sail the schooner alone. If I could get her ashore, and sail off, carrying the thing with me . . .

"The third man went to a watery grave."

That was the line he'd sung and I was the third man. Well, I wasn't afraid of drowning, if I could save Mary. When the Brigadier had told us the story he'd said the local boatmen never left shore without a cross in the back of their boats.

All at once I sat up straight and stiff. That was it! I'd row Mary ashore, forcing the thing to stay on the ship. Then I'd come back and sail away. If I drowned, why . . .

"What is it, Tom?" Mary asked.

"I'm going to get you out of this," I said. "Listen—"

And then, as if in answer to the word I'd spoken, I heard the sound. In the half second after I said, "Listen," and paused to draw a breath, there was no noise except the lap of the water against the wooden hull of the schooner. But before I could speak again the sound came.

It came softly, gently, like the very lapping of the water, like waves striking one after another against the side of the ship, each coming a little faster and a little harder than the one before and yet maintaining a perfect rhythm, a growing cadence. The sound started in silence and yet it was a visible, audible silence like a current of water revolving slowly, and it grew louder as the current grew, whirling up, up until it crashed and roared about us.

"Oh the first man died in a fall from the cliff,
And the second man died the same.
The third man went to a watery grave—"

The sound boomed and whirled around us like a giant wave, filling the cabin, coming from nowhere and everywhere. Mary and I turned, slowly, like puppets on a string, until we faced the companionway to the cockpit. The light of the storm lantern spilled out into the darkness and faded. I got to my feet. *"And the woman died from shame."*

There was a silence in which the world died. Mary and I had stopped breathing. I believe the water quit lapping against the ship. My ears were aching for some tiny sound, screaming into the silence.

And then, standing in the light of the companionway, motionless and grinning horribly, was Bill Wales. And beyond him, *straight through him,* I could see the light spilling out into the darkness of the cockpit, and fading.

It seemed an eternity that no one spoke, no one moved. And in that long silence I could feel myself plunging downward, downward. I was like a man falling from a cliff, living aeons of time in the seconds that it takes him to reach the bottom, waiting for the next line of Bill Wales' song, powerless to move.

"And the third man . . ." Destruction whirled up. I thought of Wayne, seeing it coming.

"Went to a watery . . ."

Something moved in the light that slid through Bill Wales body, some shadow that at first I could not believe. The last line of Wales' song was never uttered. It was jerked from his mouth. He whirled, crouched and snarling. He stepped backward into the full glow of the light.

The shadow in the cockpit moved again. It was a man, but I could see *through* him as I had seen through Wales; and then the light was on him as he stood in the doorway, and I was looking at the blood-smeared face of Carl Hammer.

"Now there are two of them," I said half aloud. On the bunk Mary did not move.

Bill Wales quit snarling and for a long while there was no movement in the cabin. Then he began to laugh, softly. It was a quiet laugh, but terrible in its quietness. If ever there was a sound of absolute confidence, it rang in that cabin.

Still laughing, Bill Wales stepped toward the cabin door, his eyes—which showed no mirth, no light, no life—fixed on Hammer's bloody face. There was no sound in the cabin except the laughter,

Wales was very near him when Hammer stepped backward. Wales followed, laughing. The light from the storm lamp fell on his face, the lifeless blue eyes, the twisted mouth. And then he had passed through the door and he was only a shadow among shadows, and that shadow moved again and vanished.

From the deck overhead the laughter kept flowing, softly, horribly. It glided forward and toward the starboard. It grew fainter, more distant, but not for one instant did it lose that note of dreadful certainty.

Then there was only silence.

Slowly, my muscles feeling cold and sluggish, I turned my head until I was looking at Mary. She still sat on the edge of the bunk and her hands were still folded in her lap. Her mouth was slightly open, her eyes open, but when I saw them I shuddered and turned away.

It had been very quiet in the cabin for perhaps a minute when the idea came to me. Bill Wales was not on the ship now. If we left there might be no way for him to follow! I plunged down into our small engine-room, started the auxiliary. I don't know how I ever got the anchor up alone, but I did. Then I sprinted back to the wheel in the cockpit, set a course for St. Kitts, lashed the wheel and went back into the cabin.

Mary sat as I had left her, mouth open, eyes staring. I don't think she'd moved at all. I felt sick when I went toward her. I took her hand and said gently, "Come out in the cockpit, darling. It's cooler there."

She didn't answer. She just quivered and sat still.

I bit my lip. It wasn't easy to look at her, remembering how beautiful she'd been a few hours before. I said, "They've gone now. There's nothing to be afraid of."

"No," she said. "They haven't gone." There was no hope, no emotion in her voice. It was as cold and certain as death.

"They have gone!" I said. "They have gone!" I think I screamed the words.

"No," she repeated. But she let me lead her out to the cockpit. I pushed out of her way the box of letter paper she'd left, and she sat down.

The schooner was running before the wind and making good time. There was a big swell and she ran up the waves and dropped down the far side of them. The wake trailed behind, pale and greenish in the moonlight.

"You'll feel better soon," I told Mary.

But she only answered, in that bleak, dead voice, "No, they haven't gone."

I opened my mouth to scream at her, to say they had gone, they had gone and would never come back, but I didn't speak. It was her face in the moonlight that stopped me first. The light was falling cold and clear and soft into the cockpit. Her mouth was slightly open, her eyes open and blank. She looked exactly as she had when I turned to her in the cabin.

And then I saw the difference. I was standing at the wheel, hands clenched around it, or I would have fallen. I wanted to run and I couldn't. Every muscle in my body was motionless with cold.

Crawling through the night, shivering cold and soft and horrible, was the laughter. It took me a long time to raise my eyes. The moonlight came down strong on the deck. Bill Wales was standing near the forward mast. Between us, straight and motionless, was Carl Hammer.

"Look in the cabin," Wales called.

"Look in the cabin." His voice was part of the pounding of the sea. It was in the trade wind that ruffled my hair and it came with the throb of the motor throughout the schooner; it was the blood that beat hard in my temples.

But I did not look in the cabin. I can't bring myself to that, though I know what I should find there. I have sat here in the cockpit, writing on the paper that Mary left. It must already have happened, then, before I got to the ship. But not till just now did she—

My muscles keep jerking me toward the cabin, but I won't go. I don't want to look at Mary, yet at times my eyes turn toward her and I am unable to stop them. And then I see her mouth, still open, her eyes still staring; and I see her blonde hair her face, hair which the trade wind does not ruffle. And straight through her I see the edge of the cockpit.

THE HOUSE OF VANISHED BRIDES

CHAPTER ONE

THE HOUSE THAT MOVED

I DID NOT WANT TO LEAVE JANE and she did not want me to go. She stood on the porch of the little bungalow which the evening before we'd rented, on the mountain outside San Juan, and her strange green eyes held mystery, desire and even something of fear as they watched me backing down the steps. Almost I turned and went back; my lips opened to say, "I can't leave you. Put on your hat and come with me." But that was foolish, I knew. She had to unpack, make the cottage livable; and I had to go into town for supplies. With an effort I forced my gaze from the haunting beauty of her strange green eyes, and turned and ran down the path.

Once in San Juan I placed an order for the necessary supplies, secured a week-old copy of *The New York Times,* then waited impatiently for the bus. Somehow, even then, I was worried, as if the horror that was to come had thrown a black and numbing shadow over my heart.

The bus finally came, but instead of relief my impatience mounted as we left the little Porto Rican city behind. When I got off the bus on the country road I found myself running up the mountain path. It was with a conscious effort that I checked my pace, forced myself to look appreciatively at the palm and banana trees which lined the path and at the occasional clumps of that big-leaved plant called sea grape.

I passed the hut of the native from whom I'd bought chickens the night before and noticed his two children playing naked in the yard. I waved to them, increased my pace.

I kept expecting that around the next bend I'd come on the house Jane and I had rented, but each time I found only thick trees and vines hemming in the way. Without conscious volition I found myself running again, running fast. "Hell," I panted, "it's a damn sight farther up than it is down."

Two minutes later my brow was wrinkled, my eyes squinted. It seemed that I had come much farther than usual, but still there was no sign of the house. I pulled out my watch. 6:05. I hadn't noticed the time when I left the bus, but I must have been walking for twenty minutes. The sun was almost gone and great masses of blue and saffron and silver clouds were piling up between the sea and sky.

Then I saw a turn ahead and said aloud, "Ah, there it is." I lengthened my stride. Then seconds brought me to the corner and a few steps took me around it.

I stopped as though I had struck a brick wall. My mouth must have dropped open for later I noticed that my tongue was moving back and forth across my upper lip. My eyes moved slowly in their sockets. My brain at first refused to believe.

Palm and thorn trees crowded against the path, reaching out long hands as if to choke it. And thirty feet ahead the road ended in a thick clump of tropical undergrowth. There was no sign of the house and it was impossible to go forward without chopping my way with a machete!

I must have stood there for a half minute, dazed and unbelieving. I was so sure that I had taken the right road that the possibility of error did not occur to me at first. When it did, I cursed myself for a blundering fool, turned and went back the way I had come. Yet even then I seemed to feel the shadow of horror.

When I reached the native hut and knew that this was the right road and that the house in which I had left my wife no longer stood near it a feeling of terror was already shaking through me. I kept telling myself that a house could not vanish, could not walk off into space. This had to be the wrong road! I went on downhill until I reached the point where I had left the bus.

I knew then there had been no mistake.

But my brain still refused to believe. Perhaps I had walked past the house without noticing it. It was almost hidden by vines and bushes. Certainly I would find it this time. I started up the hill again.

At the hut I stopped and asked the children for their father. They only stared at me big-eyed and refused to answer. Perhaps they didn't understand my Spanish, but there seemed to be something else in their eyes. I remembered then the way the man had looked when I tried to tell him of taking the next house up the mountain.

I pushed on up the hill and the feeling of terror grew in me as I went. This *was* the road! I knew it was the road. And around the next corner I would find the house. It had to be there!

But curve after curve slid behind my long, frantic strides. And there was no house. I came once more to where the road ended in the blank impenetrable wall of tropic growth.

Panic shook me then. I turned and went racing a hundred yards down the mountain. Stopping, I shouted Jane's name, ripping the word over and over from my throat. The sound boomed out into the thickness of late twilight, and faded. In the silence that followed I heard a lizard scuttle across the grassy path.

For a few minutes I must have been half crazy. My mind whirled furiously, battering itself against the enormity of the thing which had happened, finding it impossible to believe. A whole house couldn't disappear! It couldn't have slid into the sea without leaving some sign.

And yet it had vanished. And Jane, my wife, had vanished with it.

"It was her eyes," I said aloud. "Her eyes." I stood with hands clenched listening at the word I had spoken, which even to me seemed to have no meaning, and to the silence of late afternoon that followed them. Then a low wind came rustling down the mountain and the fronds of a coconut palm beside the road made an eerie, grating sound.

For a long moment I did not speak again, did not move, though utter panic shook through my body. My mind was dazed, blank, yet inside it fear was a hideous and crawling thing.

A voice said, "It was her eyes." I knew it was my voice, though as yet I hardly knew what I meant. I no longer felt that I should turn and run madly from the place where I stood, for there was no way to turn, no way to run. I just stood there feeling the cold sweat breaking on my forehead, the hollow, unbelieving emptiness of my mind and that ineluctable, all-consuming fear crowding like the blade wings of the night about me. And I heard my own voice saying, repeating, over and over, "It was her eyes. Her eyes."

It had all begun so gradually I could not remember the first signs. I had watched the change too constantly to see it, the way a person may watch children grow without seeing the actual development. I had felt more than seen the strangeness which had come into Jane's face after her illness. Then there had been old Dr. Parsons looking at her through his thick-lensed glasses and saying, "You'll be as well as ever in a few more months, Even your eyes will be back to their pretty blue again. But you'll have to be careful. No shocks, no worry. They might prove fatal, You should take a vacation; go down into the Indies or to Mexico."

She hadn't wanted to go, but I had insisted. I didn't want to take any chances with the girl I'd married, so short a while before. I loved her so much that the idea of harm coming to her stopped my breathing like death.

There had been the way the persons on the boat looked at her, starting suddenly and gasping, "Her eyes . . ." without realizing they had spoke aloud. Leaning against the rail on the boat deck I had overheard two of them talking. "That's Mrs. Reynolds," one had said. "I never saw a woman like her."

"It's her eyes," the other man had said His voice had held a husky, almost frightened note. "They are like green fire. And contrasted against her red hair and that milk-white skin, they—they—well, they take your breath away; they make your blood start boiling."

"She's been ill. That's what made her eyes turn green and made her skin as white as it is. I asked her. She's going to Porto Rico to recuperate."

And then there had been Dr. Jose Espaldo in San Juan. His black eyes had brightened when he looked at Jane; the thin hawk line of his brows had contracted. A handsome man with the dark arrogance of the Spaniard and young to have gained the reputation he had. It was he who had advised us to move out of the hotel and take a home in the mountains. "You'll get the benefit of the trade winds there even more than at the hotel," he had said, "and the altitude is better for Mrs. Reynolds. She can't afford any nervous shocks or worries of any sort." He'd mentioned a couple of renting agencies from whom we might be able to get a place.

The agency had been on the *Calle José de Jesus Tizó* beyond the Plaza. It was back in one of those wide, dirty courts that you reach through a narrow passage. When we saw the door a man was standing in front of it. We started toward him and Jane said, "I hope their houses are cleaner than the office court."

The man must have overheard her, for as we reached him he bowed and said in English, "It ees something I can do, *Señor?*" He was a tall, thin man with straight black hair, but there was something about his face—perhaps it was the rather flat nose—which suggested Negro blood.

I said, "We want to rent a small home somewhere near San Juan, on the coast but with some elevation." I saw the puzzled look in his eyes and I made an upward gesture with both hands.

"In the mountains, high up, understand? But near the sea, the ocean."

He smiled then. *"Si.* I have what *Señor* and—" He bowed toward Jane, smiling. But as his eyes met hers, the smile vanished. His body stiffened, his lips jerked slightly apart. Then he caught himself and went on. But his eyes kept twitching back to hers. "I have thee house *la Señora* will like."

Without taking us back into the office he led to way to the street and his automobile, drove us up the mountain. We had liked the house at once, isolated though it was, and had rented it. And now the house had vanished—and Jane, my wife, had vanished with it.

I came back from the period of fierce, detailed memory to find I was standing flat-footed, breathing heavily, staring with dull, blank eyes at the wall of the mountain on my left, the blue black of the sea below me on the right. The sun was gone now. The clouds about the horizon were changing from saffron and purple to silver and grey. Twilight beat thick, dusk-colored wings about the mountain, and in the narrow path it was almost dark.

Again I heard myself saying aloud, "It was her eyes."

Everybody had stared at them, been fascinated by them. Old Dr. Parsons had said their color was merely the result of Jane's illness, but was he right? There was something weird, something more than human about that strange and furious green.

After a moment I shrugged. My hands had been clenched so hard that the muscles in my wrists ached and the nails had made deep, purplish lines in my palms. I said aloud, "I can't go crazy this way. I've got to figure out something to do. This *has* to be the wrong road, or . . ." My voice trailed away. I was on the right road, and the house *had* vanished.

The wind rustled the fronds of a coconut palm again. I took a deep breath. It would soon be dark. I had to do something quickly! But what?

In that instant there came from behind me a sudden burst of sound, of crackling limbs and rustling leaves! A voice shouting, *"Señor! Señor!"* I whirled, shoulders half crouched, jaw muscles rigid, fingers stiff in front of me.

The man half fell into the path. He stumbled almost into the underbrush on the far side before he caught himself. I saw that he was a squat mulatto wearing overalls. His heavy, painful breathing was audible as he turned to face me, and even in the semi-darkness I recognized the man from whom I had bought the chickens.

He started toward me, reeling, and I could see that his whole face was twisted with agony and terror. *"Señor,"* he whispered. The word was a living, aching thing wrenched from the pain within his chest. I couldn't answer, but stood there dazed, watching him.

He came two steps closer. His mouth was working and suddenly words burst from it in a twisted torrent of sound that I could not understand.

I said, *"Habla mas despacio."*

He stopped talking then and I could see the muscles of his face work as he tried to overcome the pain and terror which prevented him from obeying my order to speak slowly. His mouth opened, closed, then opened again. I was leaning toward him, unbreathing, waiting.

He said, *"Si."* He got no farther. Blood came in a dark storm from his open lips, gushing across his chin, spilling on the torn overall tops. He swayed, plunged forward. My muscles moved with cold slowness as I tried to catch him, and failed. He struck flat on his face, rolled over on his back, arms outspread, and lay still. For five seconds the thick blood bubbled from his mouth, it ran down across his cheeks and throat.

I knelt beside the body without touching it. There was no need to feel for the pulse. The man was dead from a hemorrhage of some kind.

Then, looking at the distorted shape of his chest, visible through the torn clothing, I went sick at my stomach.

Great welts showed on the dark flesh. Something had circled the man's chest and crushed it, cracking ribs, probably rupturing the lungs.

Then I was on my feet, staring wide-eyed into the gathering darkness. Blood hammered at my temples and cold fear took the breath from my nostrils. For this man could not have run far with his chest crushed, Whatever had killed him was nearby!

My eyes strained in their sockets as I stared at the point where he had entered the path. In the gloom there was nothing but the black wall of vegetation, the rise of the mountain-side. In that moment even the wind seemed to hang paused, the invisible movement of twilight to halt. All the world was cold and terrified, waiting . . .

Far down the mountain a *coqui,* the little whistling frog so common in Porto Rico, began his two-noted serenade. The sound hung quivering in the heavy dusk; it was an almost cheerful noise, and the blood began to beat once more through my veins.

I said aloud, "Perhaps it was a python killed him." I almost laughed, but the sound was harsh and choking. I knew there were practically no snakes in Porto Rico, certainly no pythons. Yet what else could have crushed this man's chest, and done it within less than a hundred yards of where I stood?

I can't describe exactly the things that happened then. It seemed like some weird, fantastic nightmare beating batlike wings at my brain, driving me mad, swelling my blood with terror until it almost burst from my veins. Perhaps there was sound which I could not hear because of the fear which gripped me, but it seemed that the whole thing took place in a titanic vacuum of silence and madness.

It was in that dead silence that the thing stepped into the path. One moment there was nothing but the dusk, the blue-black sky above the downward sloping earth and the sea on one side, the mountain on the other. Then *it* slithered like some giant and bodiless shadow into the dusk.

I think part of my mind broke when that thing came into the road. Already my nerves had stretched to the breaking point. My mind had hammered at unbelievable things and fallen back beaten. I couldn't understand how the house had disappeared. The thought of what had happened to Jane had sent half-mad terror leaping through my body. Then the peasant had died terrifically at my feet. And now this *thing!*

It came toward me slowly. It was monstrous, towering in the darkness, and even while it was only a vague shadow I knew that it was hideous and evil—and I knew that in its touch was death . . .

It wasn't more than fifteen feet away when my mind broke into action, and my eyes in one terrific second recognized the thing at which I was staring. It was a man, yet more beast than human. A full seven feet high with the gigantic arms and shoulders of an ape, arms capable of crushing a man's chest! He wore a pair of tattered trousers and no shirt. The dark ocher of the skin showed three-quarters Negro blood, some Spanish. And the face was the face of a nightmare. It was long and thin as that of a wolf. The lips were wide, pulled back from great white teeth. Saliva drooled from his open mouth and ran across his chin. His hair was coal black and hung almost to his shoulders.

It moved again, coming toward me. The motion was awkward, muscle-bound. Great ropes seemed to slide under his skin as he moved. His hands reached out for me.

My nerves broke then. I don't think I am a coward, but there is a limit to my courage and I'd reached it. There was nothing but mad and unreasoning terror in my mind as I whirled.

I heard him grunt sharply, heard the thud of his feet on the ground as he dived after me. I went down the path like a dark wind, blind instinct keeping me from plunging into the brush on either side. Terror was a scourge across my back. My legs seemed to move with aching slowness, yet I must have been going at almost superhuman speed.

There was a light in the peasant's cabin. It drove some of the sheer madness from my brain, and still running I glanced behind me. There only the darkness of early night, and silence.

I stopped and looked back up the mountain, breathing heavily. I began to feel ashamed of the terror which had sent me rushing away from the giant, leaving the murdered body of the peasant behind. But a new fear was growing in me now.

Did that hideous giant have any connection with the disappearance of the house—and Jane? Had the thing which killed the peasant also murdered her? If not, where was she?

"I've got to find her," I said aloud. "Got to find her!"

I took two steps up the mountain, and stopped. I'd already searched that path and found no trace of her. If the giant had captured her, what good would I be alone, unarmed, even if I could find her? I turned and started at a run toward the bus line and San Juan.

CHAPTER TWO

THE MAN WHO WAS NOT

THE DETECTIVE WAS NAMED RAMON DIAZ and was short, stocky, and nearly bald. He spoke fair English and had been assigned to pay attention to my excited shouting. Now he looked at me out of black, squint eyes, and I knew before he spoke that he thought I was crazy. "Just where you say this house ees?"

I explained again. His eyes squinted more than ever, his mouth turned up at the left corner. He tapped the desk with blunt fingers. "I never hear of a house en that place." He sounded as if he would prefer to tell me to get the hell out of there and on my way to an asylum.

I had both hands on the edge of his desk and I shook it so hard an ink bottle almost overturned. "Damn it! I know it was there. I spent the night in it."

The twist of Diaz' lip increased. "Who was the rent company?"

I told him and he finally got the manager on the phone. After a brief conversation in Spanish the detective hung up. "He says he never heard of such a house, has rent nothing to Americans the past week."

"Get him on the phone again," I said. "Find out who the agent was and we'll go see him." I described the agent to him. I was still gripping the edge of the desk and my nails were white from the pressure, yet my muscles felt weak and sick. I had to find Jane! Had to! Why, good God, by this time . . .

Diaz spoke briefly over the phone. When he hung up the curl was gone from his lip. His eyes had begun to glitter. "He never had an agent who look this way, he never know of one, and you never enter his office."

"But—" I said.

Diaz said, "What you after? You crazy?" His stocky shoulders leaned forward and I thought for a moment that he was going to grab the handcuffs which lay on the desk and reach for me.

"No," I said slowly, "I'm not crazy." The words sounded strange, and for a moment the eerie thought hit me that perhaps I was crazy. Perhaps I had never rented a house, never had a wife who meant more than life and death to me, a wife whose eyes were a strange and terrible green beneath her red hair.

I wiped my right hand across my eyes. The whole thing did sound mad, but I *knew* what had happened. I had to find Jane, and yet—I found myself shaking, clenching the desk to stop the cold, hollow trembling of my body.

Diaz, watching me sharply, said, "What ees it?" And I answered, "Nothing—nothing at all." For I could not tell him I'd just seen myself declared insane, wandering for a lifetime over the hills of this island looking for a house which had disappeared—a house and a woman with green eyes.

I said, "You'll come out and see about the man who was killed?"

Diaz nodded. *"If* he was killed."

I did not talk during the ride to the peasant's home. There were too many thoughts crowding through my brain. What had happened to Jane? Was she still alive? Doctors had said that shock or worry might prove fatal.

There was one dim light showing in the little hut where I had bought the chickens. Diaz stopped the car, got out. I followed him along the path, stood behind him as he knocked on the door. It was a woman who answered, thin, gaunt, old. Diaz spoke with her for several minutes in Spanish. At last he said, *"Gracias,"* and turned slowly to face me. Behind him the door clicked shut, cutting off the light.

I took two steps backward into the shimmer of the half moon which silvered the dirty yard, Diaz followed, moving slowly. His left hand was in his coat pocket, his right hand near his chest. I knew there was an automatic hung under his left arm.

"Well, what did she say?"

Diaz stood motionless a half step from me. I could see the glint of his eyes. "She said there has never been any house up the hill. Her husband told her of selling some chickens to a crazy man who talk about such a house, but there was none."

Again that cold wave of fear flowed out of my spine toward my brain, but I shook my head viciously. I was not crazy! Jane had disappeared from this mountainside, and by God! I was going to find her.

Diaz' left hand came halfway out of his pocket. I saw the glint of moonlight on steel. Handcuffs. He said slowly, "I don't know if you are crazy or if it ees some joke. But we go back to the jail, find out." He held the handcuffs toward me. "You will put these on."

My fists had knotted now, shoulders half forward. If they got me in jail, charged with being a lunatic, it might be days before I got out. And I had to find Jane! I said, "No. I'm not going to put those on."

Diaz' face changed in the flickering of a second. His mouth jerked back in a snarl. His eyes almost vanished behind squinted lids. He said, *"Caramba!"* His right hand dived under his coat.

I had been waiting for that and I moved quickly. My left foot went forward, my left hand came up and caught his right wrist. I swung my right fist, hard. It made a dull crack as it landed and Diaz' head snapped back. I shoved with my left and let go. Whirling then, I leaped for the road.

I sensed the blast of the gun a split second before I heard it, and flung myself far to the right. The bullet made a whispered scream as it passed my ear. Then I was around a bend in the road. Behind me the gun crashed twice and the bullets tore through the leaves over my head. I went around another curve, skidded to a halt and fought my way through the underbrush on the left. About twenty feet from the road and below it I stopped, hidden in black shadows.

Diaz made no attempt to find me. Three or four minutes later I heard the car's motor. Another half minute and it had faded into nothingness, headed toward San Juan.

For a long while I stayed where I was, thinking, and once more than strange fear of the unnatural, of the thing I could not understand, began to come over me. I had to find Jane, and yet . . . I felt certain the giant had played some part in her disappearance. Unarmed, I would be a toy in his hands. And where could I hunt for Jane, anyway? In the jungle . . .?

There was another fear in me too, and try as I would I couldn't shake it off. Had I really seen that monster in the twilight? Had I really had a wife and a house here? A house couldn't vanish into nothingness. It could never have been built without someone knowing it. Was I crazy, after all? Perhaps I was still searching on the wrong road.

I stood up suddenly. If I could find the man who had rented me this place, I'd make him explain. Climbing back to the road, I turned toward San Juan.

I walked all the way, afraid to ride the bus. Diaz had probably reported and the police would be looking for me.

When I reached the *Calle José de Jesus Tizó* it was after midnight and few lights were showing. The office of the San Juan renting company was dark. I had hoped the manager's name would be printed on the door and I would be able to learn his address from a phone book. But the door showed only the name of the company.

"All right," I said, half aloud. My jaws were set and the words came muffled through clenched teeth. "Dr Jose Espaldo sent me here. He should know the manager's name." I started the long walk toward the doctor's home in Santurce.

Dr. Espaldo answered my ring himself. He was wearing a dark wine-colored dressing-gown over his pajamas. His black hair was tousled, but the glittering eyes over the hawk nose were undimmed by sleep. I stepped past him into the hall and he shut the door, then turned. "What is the trouble?"

I told him. As I talked I saw the same change come in his eyes that had shown in those of the detective.

In spite of me, my voice went high and shrill. "I want to see the manager of the company, see what he looks like. I know that house was there—and—and now it's gone. And Jane's gone with it! The man who rented us the house was standing outside the door. He—"

Espaldo leaned forward. "Are you certain he came out of the office? It might have been one of the doors nearby."

"By God!" I said. I stood up quickly, lips pulled thin across my teeth. "I hadn't thought of that. Thanks." I turned and went out of the house.

It was a fifteen-minute walk back into San Juan. Near the Notre Dame convent I found a loose board on a fence. I pulled it off, split it by hammering against the curb. Carrying a piece about four feet long and nearly three, inches wide, I started for the *Calle José de Jesus Tizó.*

I had to circle the *Plaza de Cristobal Colon* to keep from meeting a policeman, but I reached the narrow, trash-filled court on the *Calle Tizó* without being seen. The moon had gone down now, and no light from the street reached this place. It was almost pitch dark and I had to strike a match to make out the words, *San Juan Renting Agency,* painted on a door.

It was very still in the court, and hot. Not a breath of wind moved through the darkness, not a sound except the scrape of my heels on the stone flooring. Sweat stood out on my forehead and the backs of my hands. I wrinkled my nose against the odor of decaying vegetables and trash.

The match burned my fingers and I dropped it, struck another. The yellow light flared up to show a dark blot in the wall ahead of me. I moved toward it. Far off somewhere an automobile horn blew twice, and stopped.

A narrow passage led back to a small door. The match in my left hand, the club in my right, I entered the passage. The light flickered over the door as I held the match close.

The glass panel was filthy. Cobwebs hung from the low sill. In the dust of the corridor there was a mass of tracks, some of bare feet, some of shoes. They might have been made by persons from the court who had wandered in here.

Then I noticed a heel-print near the door. I took a long breath and went down on my knees. The match flickered out and darkness wiped away all sight and sound and motion.

I found another match and struck it. There was a slight scraping sound as it rubbed the stone floor. The light flickered high, then guttered suddenly and almost went out. I felt hot air brush at my face.

Somewhere in the darkness a thing had moved!

There was utterly no sound. Even my own breathing had stopped. Yet I had *felt* something move. And all at once, though I saw nothing but the burning match and my hand, and the circle of light in the darkness, I knew what it was.

The match wavered, then burned high again. The light flickered along the stones, reached the doorsill. The door was open!

It seemed a long while that my gaze moved upward though it must all have happened in a half second. My left hand seemed sluggish, creeping, as I raised the match. And then the light flamed higher and I saw him staring down at me.

It was the giant killer of the mountain!

"Great God!" I said aloud.

That sense of infinite slowness continued. It seemed that I knelt there staring up into the hideously twisted face of the giant for hours. The match was quivering in my left hand and it made the shadows dance across his face and I could see the fire glinting in his eyes. His big hands came up out of darkness into the light, moving with the same slow, unending reluctance. They came toward me.

The feeling of slowness snapped like a string drawn too tight. I flung myself up and backward. The club in my right hand swung high. The match went out.

The giant was only a great shadow as he lunged, a wave of darkness without features or limits. I sucked one sharp breath into my lungs and brought down the club.

The great shadow crashed over me, hurling me backward, wrapping itself about me. I felt distinctly the jar of my head striking the wall. Then the wave of blackness seemed to sweep over my mind.

CHAPTER THREE

THE TUNNEL OF CRAWLING DEATH

DARK AND RESTLESS OCEAN tossed my body gently, swayed it up and down. But the sound it made was not like the slushing of waves. It was a whining, purring noise. There was a throbbing pain inside my head and the sound made the pain worse.

Some time must have passed before my brain cleared, and even then I didn't realize what was happening. The first sensations were weird and terrifying. Fear struck me suddenly, making me conscious of a cold, sweat-smeared body. That body was bent, hanging head down from its waist. And it was moving jerkily through an eternity of pitch darkness! I wanted to scream, but it was hard to breathe and something kept bouncing into my chest.

A long white cone stabbed the darkness, I saw it glint on damp and glistening blackness. Something swayed and jerked. The light went out and a wall of darkness swept at my eyes again.

Gradually then I came to realize what was happening, though the white cone had flickered twice more before I understood fully. I was being carried on the shoulders of the giant along a tunnel of some sort.

I began to wriggle slowly, first my hands, then my feet. They were untied but the giant held my ankles and wrists in a grasp that was as sure as iron hoops.

The cone of light stabbed out through the dark. The tunnel was sloping downward more sharply now and growing narrow. It seemed to bend to the right.

We reached the curve and the light swept around it, showing two dark holes in the jagged rock wall. Some of the pain had gone out of my head and my brain was working better. We were almost around the corner when I saw my chance. A large rock stuck out from the right wall. The giant's shoulder would almost touch it as we passed—my feet would be very close! The muscles in my legs grew hard, but I did not move.

The giant kept the light burning. It spotted the protruding rock, then swayed away from it. We were only half a step away. The giant shifted his grip on my wrists slightly, in order to move the flash. My feet were opposite the rock.

Every muscle in my body lashed out in that single effort. I jerked upward with both hands. The giant clutched at them and as he did his body went closer to the right wall. My feet touched the rock and I shoved, straightening knees and hips in one vicious effort.

Just what happened I don't know. I felt my body skid along the giant's shoulders, felt his arms clutching at me. The cone of light went spinning as the flashlight dropped. The white finger flickered across a dark tunnel leading off to the left. Then I was falling, free of the giant. The flashlight struck the ground and went out. On back and shoulders I landed in pitch darkness, went rolling away.

Somehow I came to my feet, arms widespread on each side of me, touching nothing. Three yards away I could hear the giant's heavy breathing, hear the faint movement of his body, the scrape of a shoe on earth. The darkness was like a wet blanket tied across my eyes, but I knew that he was swinging his arms about in search of me. And I knew the meaning of his heavy breathing. It was like the panting of a blood-hungry wolf. He wouldn't carry me, alive, on his shoulders any more. Anger was a snarled sound in his breathing. If those sweeping hands found me—*it was death!*

I didn't move. Fear stopped even the breath in my lungs. If I made one sound and he heard me . . .

There was the scrape of a shoe almost against mine. A hand struck my shoulder.

Terror was a scourge whipping my body into blind and furious action. I made a gasping sound and flung myself backwards, arms still outstretched. My right hand touched stone, slid off into space. I remembered the tunnel leading off to the side.

The giant was muttering now, a sound almost like laughter. I heard him move toward me, slowly. I whirled and leaped toward the opening my hand had found. I pawed at the wall. Then I was stumbling blindly, furiously through the darkness. Time and again I staggered, ran hard into the wall, beat out with my hands until I found space and plunged on.

All at once I realized that the giant was not chasing me. I stopped and stood listening in that well of eternal darkness. The sound of my own breathing was loud and husky.

Then there was another sound. It came through the darkness slowly at first, crawling like a hideous spider. Gradually it swelled in tone, though muffled by the twisting stone walls. *Somewhere back in the tunnel the giant was laughing!*

After a moment the laughter stopped and the giant's voice, heavy with a Spanish accent, boomed along the narrow tunnel. "Till you come back, I wait here. *If* you come back."

I've never been much afraid of things I could see and put my hands on and fight, but standing in that cave I knew unmitigated terror. I had to struggle against my muscles to keep them steady. To turn back would mean the giant and death. There was no escaping him. To go ahead meant—what? The hideous certainty in his laugh . . .

But I couldn't stand still forever. Reaching in my pocket I found a match and struck it. It showed the damp walls of the narrow tunnel, the rock floor. Beyond the circle of light something made a rustling sound.

Slowly, always holding a burning match in front of me I began to move along the cavern. But I hadn't gone over a hundred yards when I realized that only three matches were left in my pocket.

I tried to save those matches for an emergency; yet every moment of darkness seemed fraught with terror and danger. I was afraid to crawl lest my hands should touch a poisonous insect, afraid to walk upright lest I stumble into some bottomless pit. Once the passage seemed to end and I struck a match to find my way around a sharp curve. The flame ate swiftly down the wood. I stumbled and the match went out.

At that moment I heard sound ahead!

It came faintly at first, and I held the air in my lungs for a long while, listening. It was like a vague shadow moving through the dark tunnel, a dark wind rustling the darkness.

I struck a match and went ahead as fast as I could. When the match burned out I stopped. There was only one left now.

The sound had grown more distinct. It was a low, aching moan. But it wasn't human. No human being could make a sound with the infinite mystery and pain that came rolling through the darkness in vague, uncertain whispers. It was like some gigantic, prehistoric beast sobbing out its last breaths beyond miles of rock-walled caves. It was horrible, that sound in the darkness. My flesh was cold and prickly. The muscles of my throat were swollen so that I could scarcely breathe.

I fought my nerves to stillness. "I've got to go ahead," I whispered. "I've got to get out of here, get a gun or a knife, something. Then I've got to come back and find Jane."

The sound grew slightly louder as I pushed through the darkness. It came in low, intermittent moans that slobbered off into silence like a deep-drawn breath, and came again. And now there was something new in the air, a new odor. I wrinkled my nose. A smell of salt . . .

I moved forward, listening at the sound. Realizing that it came from somewhere far below me. I didn't know what it was. I knew instinctively that it was terrible, yet I had to go toward it. My nerves were drawn taut as bowstrings.

Something slithered in the darkness. A wet, slimy thing brushed across my shoe and touched my leg. I made one choked scream and leaped sideways.

And then I was falling, plunging straight down, hurtling through black and endless space!

CHAPTER FOUR

UNDER THE SEA

I TRIED TO SCREAM, AND COULDN'T. The blackness was a bottomless eternity through which I went whirling down. Sound thundered and rolled about my ears, and in the sound and the darkness was a frigid terror beyond comprehension.

I must have hit flat on my back and the jar was like falling on solid rock. My brain was paralyzed with fear, and I struck madly about me, not knowing what had happened. It was the strangling salt water in me that brought realization.

The water was all about me, over me. How far I had sunk I didn't know. My eyes were wide open and the salt stung them, but I couldn't see. I flung my arms about, thrashing the water. Frantically I tried to breathe, sucking in water, strangling. Then I felt cold air against my face.

I tread water, coughed and cleared my lungs. It was so dark I couldn't even see the water in which I swam. Which way to turn, I had no idea.

Finally I started to swim, trying to keep in a straight line. My left hand slapped rock and I sighed with relief. Once on ground there was some chance, but in this water . . . I slid my hand along the rock, trying to find the top. It rose sheer as far as I could reach.

My nerves almost broke then, but I bit my lips until the blood came and the pain helped control the terror. I had to get out of here, had to find Jane.

I managed to shed my shoes and wet clothes. It made swimming easier. Then I began to make my way along the wall.

Something brushed against my bare leg and electric fear shot through me. I knew that the water around Porto Rico was infested with shark and barracuda. The smaller, more vicious barracuda were particularly numerous here. A man might fight a shark, but he stood no chance against barracuda. They struck with the speed of light, ripped the flesh and whirled to strike again. The shark could sometimes be frightened away, but never the barracuda.

For a long minute I remained almost motionless, barely treading water. The fish, or whatever the thing which had touched me, did not come back. I began my circle of the wall once more.

It was some time before I became conscious of the tug of the current. As I moved along the wall to the right it became more and more noticeable. It began to pull at me, moving me more rapidly. Then I felt its downward tug. It made me fight to keep on the surface.

For a half minute I tread water. My breathing was deep and heavy. My body was cold, but the coldness didn't come from the sea. For I knew now there was only one chance left—to dive with the current and try to follow it to open sea.

I took a deep breath and dived.

I must have been five feet or more below the surface when my hands touched the rock wall again. I kept going down, feeling along the side. The current was strong here and it moved me swiftly without much effort on my part. I realized that the tide must be going out.

My hands found an edge of the wall, moved downward—and touched nothing! I took a half stroke forward, swung my-arms about. On both sides my hand touched the wall. The current had carried me inside a passage. There was no going back!

I began to swim forward then, moving with the current. My lungs were already aching and my ears had begun to hurt. Now and then my hands or shoulders struck the roof.

I couldn't stay down any longer! I'd die . . . die . . .

Well, it didn't matter. If I had to die, I'd go. I'd breathe in water and stop this aching in my lungs. It didn't matter if I died, except—

There was something in the water! It was grey. God! It was light!

I don't remember those next few seconds, only the aching, eternal pain of them. Then I was half floating, half treading water, and sucking deep breaths into tortured lungs. It must have been a full minute before I began to notice things.

I was at the foot of a high cliff. The morning sun was a half hour high. The water was vividly blue and when it washed against the cliff white spray jumped and fell backward. Fifty yards to my right the cliff came down to low rocks that thrust out into the water. I could climb out there. Wearily I began to swim.

My head was strangely fight and clear. It seemed to float on the water in contrast to the heavy, dragging pain in my body, Thoughts ran through my mind in queer, vividly bright geometrical processions the way they pass through the brain of an opium smoker. When I raised my head from the water the mountainside was more like a picture than actuality, and I knew I had seen that same picture before, but from a different angle. I had seen it from above, from the porch of the home which had disappeared with my wife! And in my strangely clear brain I could see Jane's face, the red hair, the pale cheeks, and the green eyes. They were hypnotic, almost terrifying eyes and in them was a sensual appeal that was inexplicable, and irresistible. They were eyes that would make men follow her, women hate and envy and sell their souls to be like her.

Somehow I knew then that I might find Jane still living, and how I would find her, but I knew also that my chances of rescuing her were very small and that by now she might prefer death. "It was her eyes," I said. The words sounded small and meaningless against the murmur of the sea.

For minutes I lay on the beach, gasping for breath, letting strength return to me. At last I got up, stood for a moment and looked down at myself. I was wearing only a pair of dripping white shorts. I had to follow the beach for two hundred yards before I found a path inland. I picked a cautious, barefooted way along the path for five minutes. Then I reached a small road and recognized it as the one which I had searched the night before.

It wouldn't do to go back to the city in this condition. The police were already looking for me. They would never believe now that I was not insane. If I were going to save Jane it had to be a lone game. I turned uphill.

There were three naked children playing in front of the peasant's cabin when I rounded a corner of the road and saw it forty feet away. Even as I saw them the oldest, a boy about six, looked up.

I was watching him and I didn't notice the other children, but abruptly one of them screamed. The sound jangled high and shrill and it sent the oldest boy into a spasm of action. He whirled and leaped for the cabin. The three children reached the door at the same time, pawed and fought their way through.

I stood gazing at the empty doorway. My throat and lips were dry. Again the idea came to me that perhaps I was mad. There was something nightmarish and inhuman about the whole thing. Those green eyes . . .

I licked my lips and tasted the salt that still clung to them. *That* was real enough. I swallowed at the lump in my throat, went toward the house.

At the door I paused and raised my right hand to knock, but my knuckles never touched the sill. The door was open and on the far side of the room I could see the children and their mother. They were all crouched close against the wall, staring at me. Their eyes showed stark terror and the left corner of the woman's mouth was jerking. I knew it would be no use to try to explain my visit. I probably couldn't make my Spanish understood, but she wouldn't believe me anyway. A man who claimed to live in a house where there was no house, and who claimed the house vanished, a man who was wanted by the police for insanity, was certainly crazy. It would do no good to explain.

I stepped through the door into the room. The woman and her children never moved. Their breathing was like the low whispering of fear. I did not glance at them as I searched for and found an old pair of shoes and trousers. In the corner was a huge, swordlike machete and I was grinning crookedly when I picked it up. I'd counted on finding that machete. The natives used them in the cane-fields and almost every peasant had one. I turned and went out of the door and up the path,

Around the first corner I stopped, put on the trousers and shoes.

A few minutes walking and I came to a bend in the path that made me stop, mouth pulled straight, eyes squinting. On the right tulip and kinip trees almost screened the mountain. On the left the road fell away sharply so that I looked down on the thin, spidery leaves of flamboyant trees, and farther down was the rocky shoreline and the sea. It was around this bend that the house had sat, its back against the cliff.

I reached the bend, took two long steps, and halted. The tulip and kinip trees gave way here to the squatty, broad-leafed sea grape. I'd never seen it this far from the shore, for it generally grew in sand along the beach. A bougainvillea vine made the sunlight burst into flame with its purple flower.

It took longer than I had expected to find the tunnel. The cliff behind—the spot where the house had sat seemed solid enough. It must have been a hundred yards to the left that I found the small mouth of a cave hardly big enough for a man to enter upright. I stood with my body flat against the rock wall, head twisted so that

I peered into the dark gut of the earth. Grey light filtered in for a few yards, and thickened into pitch. There was utterly no sound.

I turned and took a long breath. My eyes seemed to strain as I looked at the sunlight and the green mountain and the blue sea. It might be the last time I would look at these things. The muscles of my jaw were aching as I swung and stepped through the cave mouth.

CHAPTER FIVE

WHEN BARRACUDA FED

IT WAS COLD IN THE CAVE yet sweat continued to break out on my back and shoulders. The drops slid downward, feeling like crawling tarantulas. The dark air hurt my swollen throat muscles as I sucked in long breaths. The blackness was like a great wall crashing down on me, crushing out my sight.

The path wound and twisted. Time and again I bumped into the wall with my bare shoulder. I had no way of knowing this was the right tunnel, no way of knowing what horror might find me there in the dark. But I kept inching forward.

Then I heard sound and stopped, listening. It was a low, slobbering, chanting noise that crawled through the darkness, getting higher and higher, then breaking, whimpering into silence. And after a moment it came again.

It wasn't the sea this time. It was human—*and inhuman.* There was pain and terror and a weird, barbaric joy in the sound, though yet it was no more than a whisper in the darkness.

All at once, then, I knew I had reached the end of my hunt. I was glad—and I was afraid. I shut my jaw teeth hard. My fist tightened around the machete. Inching my left foot ahead of me, I moved forward.

Light came into the passage gradually. I couldn't see the walls of the tunnel two feet away, yet I knew that somewhere there was light because there was a grey mistiness in the dark. It brightened as I went forward. The sound had grown louder. It was a chant of some sort and its tempo was increasing; it was growing wilder, more terrible and barbaric.

I knew that only women could make that sound—women half mad with lust and passion and terror and pain, that curious and terrible mingling of emotions which only women can blend into one furious whole. I remembered, suddenly, the ancient Porto Rico, the cruel, aristocratic Spaniards surrounded by and gradually mixing with and becoming part of their own slaves, the Negroes with the jungle superstitions and fears and their elemental, voodoo passions, the Indians with their fierce, untamed lusts—all mixed into one and all running in one sensuous current through that wild chant. Even as I stood there in the dark I was sick at the thing I imagined. And Jane . . . "Oh God!" I whispered aloud. On tiptoe I slid forward.

The end of the passage came without warning. I stood just inside, close against the right wall, and peered out into the great lighted vault of the cave. It was a weird, primeval light, flickering and dancing, thick with coiling smoke from the torches about the stone walls.

I didn't cry out, didn't make any sound as I looked into that light. I was almost sick at my stomach as if I had seen some hideous and fearful thing, but the blood was quickening in my veins, growing hot, making the muscles deep in my stomach grow taut and quivery. I felt as though I were taking part in some perverted and sickening, yet furiously passionate and terrible love affair. I wanted to turn away in shame—and I wanted to enter the cave.

The house which Jane and I had rented stood on the right of the cave; yet it was not the same house. Gone was the simple whiteness of its front porch and walls, the low straight lines of the tropic bungalow. It was some exotic, primitive hut where a Circe changed men into swine and where love was a bestial and mysterious incantation. Along the porch and down the steps and out into the center of the cave women knelt or writhed and twisted. They were naked except for their hair and for loincloths of green-gold and scarlet that were sickeningly wrought. It was the women who chanted.

In the middle of the cave the floor dropped away to what looked like a river, though I couldn't see clearly from where I stood. On the far side was a couchlike throne worked in the shape of lovers in embrace. I was staring at it, feeling that strange sensation of shame and desire when the chanting stopped and silence rolled like thunder through the vault.

My eyes moved back until they found the front steps of the house and saw the thing coming down them. It was the giant, but he didn't look like a human being. He was costumed like a beast and it was like a beast that he went down the file of women. I don't remember the things that happened then—though even now, months later, occasionally I awake, half sitting up in bed and shivering, a part of that vision horribly smashed against my mind. I remember the whimpered screams, the animal cries.

I must have turned away, for all at once I realized there were no more cries. I looked back into the vault with its smoky, weaving light—and my heart quit beating, my blood became shivering ice.

For there was another man beside the giant in the center of the vault, and near the dark line, which looked like the brink of a river. I must have stared at him for two full seconds before I recognized Dr. Jose Espaldo. In his right hand was a long coiled whip. And beside the doctor was Jane!

Like the others she was naked except for the terrible scarlet about her loins. In the smoky light her hair was a red and gold torrent about her shoulders and her flesh glowed with the iridescent whiteness of a moonflower. I could see the slight rise and fall of her breasts. Her eyes were wide open and furiously green.

For a long moment the tableau held while I stared, unable to move. Then I saw Jane's eyes fasten on the couch made in the likeness of entwined lovers. She swayed slightly forward.

It looked for a moment as if she were going to fall. I remembered the warning of old Dr. Parsons: *"Any strain might prove fatal."*

The thing that had held me motionless snapped. I hurtled from the mouth of the tunnel, drove straight across the cave toward Jane, Dr. Espaldo and the giant. My right hand swung the machete high overhead.

Even as Jane fell, the doctor lunged for her. He was on his knees beside her when the giant saw me and shouted. The doctor looked up. Under the paint that was on it, his face went white. He leaped up and backwards. I drove straight at him, my mind a dead blank of rage.

The giant swung out to the left, ready to tackle me as I passed. My eyes shifted to him, I pivoted to meet his charge—and the machete was snatched from my hand! The giant's voice rose in a shout of triumph.

I tried to swerve again, away from him this time, but my own speed tripped me. As I fell, my mind so dark with despair that I did not feel myself hit the stone floor, I saw the satanic exultation on Dr. Espaldo's face; saw the long, uncoiled whip in his hand, the lash wound around my machete.

Then the giant was on me. His fingers closed around my throat. The room floated upward like a giant balloon, the women swimming in it like fish in some transparent water. Far away I saw green eyes, filled with a furious and consuming lust . . .

I returned to consciousness filled with a great lassitude and indifference. For a while the cave swam hazily before my throbbing gaze, then settled slowly, as a building rocked by an earthquake quiets itself in still quivering air.

Near me I saw one of the women, her body swaying with anticipation. My eyes followed slowly upward from her twitching hips to her face, hard and cruel and burning with eagerness. In her right hand she held a short whip.

My eyes moved with labored and indifferent slowness along the line of women. They formed a snake's track around the cave, each holding in her right hand a whip. And each woman was staring fiercely ahead, her body twitching with the eagerness of sadistic anticipation.

Finally my eyes reached the end of the line. It ended at the foot of that couch. And on that couch lay Jane!

She was bound there, her arms above her head. She was looking at the line of women with their whips, and upon her face, in those green and maddening eyes, was a look of greedy longing. She was waiting anxiously for the signal which would release those women to take their dreadful and insensate pleasure with her!

My eyes shifted a trifle, and I saw the doctor upon one side of the couch near the head, the giant upon the other side. The two of them were chanting in Spanish, the words and tune rising and whipping the women with horrible meaning.

My mind cleared, and I recognized all this, yet somehow I did not care. My body was worn with continual struggle.

For hours I had fought against madness, darkness, the sea, the giant, to find my wife and rescue her. I had failed. There was no more hope now. I was tied securely. And if I had not been, I had arrived too late. That look in Jane's green eyes . . . She wanted those women released. She had descended into hell; I had followed her; and I could not bring her back.

The chant reached its high point, broke off sharply. Dr. Espaldo's arm rose and fell. The first women in the line cried out sharply, like a hungry dog, and leaped forward. Her short whip rose, fell. It struck across the smooth whiteness of my wife's belly, leaving a red trail like a snake.

Then Jane screamed.

It was not a scream of desire, but of unutterable fear and shame and hatred. The pain of that blow had released the spell Dr. Espaldo had cast upon her. Her white face rolled, her green eyes saw me. And in them burned suddenly hope and trust and a cry for help.

The whip in the hands of the woman at the couch rose and fell. Jane cried out again, twisted away from the agony. Leaning forward over her, the giant and Espaldo seemed carved from dark stones brought from hell.

My body was suddenly convulsed with new strength. I seemed to shoot upward from the pit of despair in which I had been. I felt my muscles knot and writhe against their bonds. Jane wanted me, needed me.

Ten feet away from me lay the machete I had brought into the cave. Rolling like a dervish, I reached it. Jane's screams beat upon my ears, drove me on. At the same time her writhing agony held the gaze of Espaldo and the giant. Holding the handle of the machete braced with my heels, I sawed the bonds of my wrists against the heavy blade.

Work as I might, it seemed my hands hardly moved, though blood from a cut made them slimy. Then I was free. With a swift blow I sliced the rope around my ankles, rolled to my feet.

The doctor was on the side of the couch toward me. I drove at him. He screamed and dove backward, flinging up his arms. The heavy blade landed on his right forearm, went clean through. I spun, sliced the rope which held Jane on my side of the couch. Then I leaned over her, cut the other rope.

The blade twisted, tore out of my hand. I saw the machete glimmer in the firelight and fall where the giant's swinging blow had knocked it. From the corner of my eye I saw the doctor, his face livid with pain and rage, try to draw a revolver with his left hand. I leapt. My charging body struck his and we both went over.

What followed then happened in a half second, too fast for me to realize it clearly. Still falling, I saw that we were on the bank of an underground river. I could see the black water five feet below, see silver shadows swirl in it. Then I was clawing at the bank, holding on, and Dr. Espaldo was plunging down.

As he fell his scream was a wild, tearing sound in the room. And even in that second I knew he was not screaming from the pain of his amputated hand. *He was screaming in fear!*

His body struck the water with a splash, went under. White shadows whirled and struck and a darker stain arose to the surface. Once the doctor's face came into the air and he tried to scream, but most of his cheek and one eye had been torn away and the sound was only a gurgle. He went under again. I knew then that the pool was full of barracuda.

There was a sound behind me and I whirled. The women, except for Jane, had vanished. Beside her, holding the machete and laughing, was the giant.

"When they do not agree," he said, "we drop them into thee water. The doctor like to see if thee barracuda or thee shark would finish first when one went to each."

I twisted my head and looked at the water. It was either an underground river or an inlet from the sea such as the one into which I had fallen. Across the middle there was a screen of some sort. On one side a black dorsal fin slid through the water above a dark shadow nearly twelve feet long. On the other side smaller fish swirled and twisted.

I heard the giant move and I whirled. He tossed the knife behind him. It clanged as it hit the floor. He looked at me, laughing that softly hideous laughter of confidence. "You will not swim from here."

Then he lunged.

My hands came up, caught his right wrist. I went over backward, bringing up my feet. Handicapped by his costume, his movements were slow and my feet caught him full in the belly. I heaved.

It seemed a long time that his body was in the air above me. Then it was falling and I tried to release the wrist. But the giant's fingers were clawing at mine now!

There was a terrific jerk at my arm. The giant yelled. Then I was on the edge of the river, rolling, falling. I heard the giant strike the water. Cold wetness swept over me.

I kept my eyes open even as I went under. It was salt water and very clear. I was near the screen, the giant on the other side. In that same flicking instant I saw a barracuda strike, rip flesh bare, and knew that I had fallen with the shark. I rolled and saw the dark shadow of him.

He circled me slowly, swimming very near the surface. I beat the water with my arms and yelled, knowing that some sharks can be frightened. This one continued to circle. I went backward until I touched the bank. It was five feet above the water and there was no chance to get out without help. And I was afraid to take my eyes from the shark.

Then, suddenly, Jane was shouting over my head and holding down the machete. As my fingers closed on it, the shark came at me. I planted the machete the way a bull-fighter places his sword, used the force of the oncoming shark to fling my body away. His belly turned up as his great weight struck the machete.

I felt myself flung through the water with terrific force, but my eyes stayed open. Before them the blade of the machete vanished swiftly, as if the white belly of the shark had swallowed it. The water was suddenly red with blood, and it was not mine. Then Jane was holding a loincloth over the edge of the pool. I seized it and was climbing out, sobbing like a child.

All the ramifications of Dr. Espaldo's activities were never completely cleared up, though the police did find the man who had claimed to be the renting agent. He was really the captain of the ship which carried the girls to Buenos Aires, New York and other cities. He had been warned by the doctor and had been waiting for us outside the renting agency to appear as though he were just coming out.

The doctor was a power in the white slave traffic, though he made money in other ways. Many of the women were patients originally, a good many of them young brides, and through the cautious use of drugs Espaldo gained complete control over them, forced them to find other girls without families who might be slipped from the country and never missed. He had played on the native superstitions, which was easy, for many of the girls were taken from the lower classes—and he had built up an elaborate religious cult. When the girls had gone too far to back out he sent them by shiploads to be sold like slaves.

When he'd seen Jane's green eyes he had realized that she would be invaluable in the religious ceremony. There was something hypnotic about her eyes, and many women would have given their souls to have them. He'd made her take some part in a ceremony before I arrived. She never told me exactly what, and I never asked because the mere recollection of the thing set her quivering with horror.

The house and what looked like the solid wall of the cliff were set on a revolving stage like those in a theater—and I believe that the house, as it was when we first saw it, played some part in the ceremony. Perhaps the change which came over it represented the change in the women themselves. I think Jane knew, but she never said. Perhaps it had been used to trap other well-to-do women as the doctor had used it to catch Jane. But if so, there were no records to indicate it.

We never found out why the peasant had been killed. It's probable that he chanced to see the house as it revolved back into the earth and was killed by the giant in the fight that followed. It's certain that a number of women had been fed to the shark and barracuda. "When they do not agree . . ." the giant had said.

I don't know the exact horrors to which they had to agree, and I am glad I don't. Now and then I start up from my sleep, shaken awake by the vision of the thing I saw there in the cave as the beastlike giant went down that row of naked women. I look at Jane sleeping beside me then, and . . .

Sometimes she awakens, panting heavily. I wonder what dream has been in her mind.

SATAN'S THIRSTY ONES

CHAPTER ONE

DEMON OUT OF THE NIGHT

"YOU TALK A LOT about brave men and heroes," McGruder said. "Your brave men are generally fools, and the difference between a hero and a coward may be the direction he's facing at the moment danger comes."

We asked what he meant.

"Real terror." he said, "striking suddenly and without warning, stultifies the mind. The reaction is instinctive, reflexive—you try to escape. I'll give you an example.

"When I was about twelve or thirteen I had to spend a night alone in a farm house. It was when I was first reading Robert Louis Stevenson and my dreams were full of Alan Breck and wild flights through the heather and John Silver flinging his crutch. And in the middle of the night I woke up and saw a man's head and shoulders framed in the window. He had a knife in his mouth. For a while I couldn't move; I just lay there, propped up on an elbow staring at him. I wanted to run and I couldn't. I would have remained except that the muscles in my jaw were locked. And then finally I got out of bed, staggering, and ran—*toward* the man. He turned out to be nothing but my shirt and cap on the back of a chair with the moonlight falling over them. That's not the point. The point is that I went toward the man rather than away from him. Not because I was brave but because I was afraid; so afraid that I had to take the quickest method of finding relief, and it was quicker to run toward him, get the whole thing over with, than to run the other way and be chased through the dark house."

"I saw that happen during the war," Andrews told us. "A man in my company went mad with fear. He ran toward the enemy instead of away. They gave him a medal."

"But that sort of thing is the rare accident," I said. "If there is a moment in which to think, then real courage has a chance."

We argued the point for a while without McGruder taking any part in the discussion. He sat with his big head tilted forward, his eyes veiled with thought. And finally, still with that half-dreaming look upon his face, he began to talk. We listened, politely at first, and then with more than politeness.

This fellow I'm going to tell about (McGruder said) was young, twenty or thereabouts. He was still in school. And he was in love. You've got to remember those points because things couldn't have happened as they did otherwise. A young man in love is more than half insane to begin with; and then add to this—blinding, maddening terror.

He was a pleasant, likeable fellow, rather small. There was nothing unusual about him, nothing that gave him an advantage in the things that happened. Even his name was ordinary enough. It was Andy Parker.

The terror, or the beginning of it, came without warning. He had gone walking one night with Mary Carlyle and they had climbed the mountain that overlooks the little college town where they were both going to school. They sat on a rock and looked down over the dark sweep of trees to where the lights of the town, far below, made little winking crosses.

He was in love in the way only a very young man ever is, and he felt the desperate, aching need to tell her, to show how much he did love her. He wanted to reach up and tear down the stars and pile them in her lap; he wanted to say the things that John Keats must have felt like a hot pain inside his heart, to use words for her that no man had ever used before.

And she—she wanted to talk about Bruce Adams.

"I can't understand why he left so suddenly," she said. She was pretty, the only child of wealthy parents, and rather spoiled. She wasn't accustomed to having men run out on her. "I saw him the afternoon before he disappeared—that was Friday, two weeks ago."

Parker said he wished it had been ten years ago, but he said it to himself.

"There was something wrong that afternoon," Mary said. "He quarreled about everything, said his head hurt him, and then he just walked off. And nobody's seen him since."

"It couldn't be something had happened to his brain," Parker said. "Not *his* brain."

"He had plenty of sense," Mary said angrily. "Just because a man plays football you think—"

"Listen," Parker said, "if you're an All American halfback, have a face like Robert Taylor and a body like a double edition of Jack Dempsey, you don't need brains."

He finally persuaded her to forget Bruce Adams. She was really very fond of Andy, almost in love with him, though the very fierceness of his devotion frightened her at times. He told her how much he loved her, told her in a dozen different ways while time flowed sweetly through the dark trees around them. A full moon climbed above the mountain's top, making everything ebony and liquid silver.

They were busy talking about themselves, though there really wasn't much talking, and they didn't hear the voices until the other couple had got close to them. Mary raised her head from Parker's shoulder and peered down over the rock's edge.

They heard twigs crack, a girl laugh softly, a man's voice. The red eye of a cigarette showed for a moment through the trees. "If they want to sit on this rock," Parker said in a half-whisper, "they can't do it. The place is occupied."

"Who is it?" Mary asked.

He listened. The voices were nearby but subdued. "I don't know," he said.

There was a small clearing below the rock with moonlight half filling it and shadows black upon the other side. While they watched, the couple came into the moonlight below them. The girl was one of Mary's sorority sisters and Mary opened her mouth to call. Parker put his fingers across her lips. He didn't want company.

And in that instant it happened.

A figure hurtled out of the darkness upon the couple below them, and the sight of that figure was like a shell bursting in Parker's mind, stunning him with sheer disbelief. Perhaps Mary screamed, but he didn't hear her. For the thing below him was not human, thought it had the general shape of a man. It was almost seven feet tall with monstrous, hulking shoulders, but even so its head was too large for the body. It was the size of a basketball, the hair matted and wild. The forehead rolled in a heavy crease over the eyes. The mouth showed as a black hole in the bearded, bestial face. Its right hand was raised and the moonlight played like quicksilver on the blade of a long hunting knife.

The couple below the rock had no time to defend themselves. The knife lashed down, buried to the hilt in the chest of the boy.

And then the monster screamed, a wild terrible cry like that of a horse in pain; but there was more than pain in the cry; there was a hunting, hungry sound. The creature jerked the knife from the boy's chest and a dark gush of blood followed. Unbelievably the boy stayed on his feet, and stepped toward the monster, swinging both hands. The creature made no attempt to dodge but stood there, taking the blows and making a kind of gurgling, laughing sound. And then it drove the knife into the boy's stomach and ripped upward.

The rest of that night was only a crazed and distorted memory to Andy Parker. He and Mary crouched on the rock, looking downward, unbreathing, unmoving, clinging to one another without being conscious that they touched. In the moonlit amphitheater below them the creature went about its business. The girl had fainted, and the giant leaned over her, the knife still in his hand and blood dripping from the blade to fall upon the girl's face. But he did not strike. He chuckled and pawed the girl's body with his left hand. It was a misshapen, horrible hand, the fingers swelling to blunt knobs at the tips. Then he turned away from her and crouching then at the edge of moonlight and shadow he began to pile small twigs together.

There was no chance for the two on the rock to escape without being heard. They huddled together in the shadows, and they heard the tiny crackle of fire and saw red and yellow light play up across the face of the thing below them. And then it moved away from the fire it had built to the corpse of the boy, and stooped, back to them, and went to work with the knife, its great hulk shutting off the view of its movements. But when it straightened they saw the formless flopping thing in its left hand.

Mary Carlyle screamed. She leaped upright, her face mad and blank, and flung herself from the lock and began to run. Parker cried out without knowing what he said, and plunged after her.

They ran blindly, insanely, following only the natural pull of the mountainside. And behind them came the monster! Thorns sliced at their hands and faces, ripped clothes and the flesh underneath, but they felt only the white hot lash of terror.

And then, somehow, they were at the edge of the town, and Mary was lying flat in the street, sobbing, with Parker crouched beside her. The lights of an automobile played over them and there were voices and a crowd gathering.

CHAPTER TWO

THE CREATURE IN THE MINE

YOU MAY SAY THAT ANDY PARKER was not very heroic that night, and you'd be telling the truth. But remember, he never wanted to be a hero. He was just a normal, average youngster. He didn't reason out that it would be suicide to attack the creature. Parker weighed around one hundred and thirty, and he knew his limitations. And it never entered his head to do the obvious thing—keep hidden until the thing chased Mary out of sight, and then escape himself. He saw the girl that he loved running, and he ran with her.

The story they told set the town on its ear. For an hour or so persons believed them mad and refused to credit anything they said. But they persisted, and finally a group went back up the mountain to investigate. There was a local policeman in the bunch, Dr. Drake and Professor Hendricks of the faculty, and a couple of boys from Parker's fraternity house. They had an assortment of weapons. Parker carried a twenty gauge shotgun loaded with birdshot.

"What are you going to do with that birdshot?" Hendricks asked. "Pink this monster of yours on the wing?" He was a lean, sardonic man, eternally driven by the lash of ambition. He was not popular with his students. He complained that they were all morons, that the school was not properly equipped, that the trustees resented any liberal thought on the part of faculty members. But he came near to being a genius at chemical engineering, though his talents ran more toward laboratory work than practical application.

"If there's anything up here," the policeman said—he sounded as though he didn't believe it—"you should have brought a gun like this one." He slapped the .45 at his hip.

"If I have to shoot," Parker said, "I want to hit what I aim at. I couldn't hit the ground with one of those cannons." He was afraid, furiously afraid, and trying not to show it, the way a man does in the company of other men.

Charlie Craton said, *"If* there's anything up here, I want my feet in good shape. You can have the guns."

Dr. Drake was quiet, stolid as usual, willing to let developments prove themselves. "We'll see," he said. "Where was this spot, Parker?"

"Over to the left." He was wondering now if the whole thing had not been a nightmare. He remembered it as one remembers a dream: vivid flashes with blank gaps between them. It was incredible, impossible. And then close ahead of them they saw the dying glow of a fire. "There," Parker said. He could scarcely get the word through his throat. "Right there."

The group pulled tight together. There was no joking now. The policeman's flashlight stabbed out ahead of them. And then Charlie Craton yelled. "Oh my God!" and reeled backward, his face a sickly white in the gloom.

The corpse of the boy lay at the edge of the clearing—or what was left of it lay there. The policeman turned the round beam of his flashlight full upon it; then the light shuddered away, leaving the body barely visible, a dark blot against the earth, and in the rear of the group there was the sound of somebody being sick.

"What—what did it do to him?"

Nobody answered. They stood there without speaking. Far up the mountainside a night bird called eerily,

Dr. Drake said, "Let me have the light." He took it and swung the beam back to the body. He stepped forward and knelt. They watched only the dark hulk of his back and shoulders, grateful they could not see the thing before him.

He stood up and turned, moving the light. They could not see his face; his voice seemed to come out of nothingness. "The body has been rather crudely—butchered. Some parts are missing. He must have carried away those portions he wanted."

"But what for?" the cop asked. "What in God's name did he want them for?"

"I told you," Parker said. "I told you I saw him start toward the fire."

"You mean he was going to—cook . . .?"

"Yes."

"Geezus!" the cop said. "Geezus!"

In the rear of the group the same boy was sick again.

Professor Hendricks said, "There's no sign of the girl."

"None," the doctor said. "He must have carried her with him."

"We got to have dogs," the cop said. "We'll never find him on this mountain without dogs. Somebody's got to get them."

"I'm going whichever way the most people go with the most guns," Charlie Craton said. "This is one time the gregarious impulse is strong with the Cratons."

"Huh?" the cop said.

"I'll go," Hendricks said. "Where are the dogs?"

"Just telephone the prison and they'll bring 'em. The rest of us will wait here."

"All right." Hendricks turned and vanished into the darkness. They heard the sound of his shoes for a while. Then there was silence.

Charlie Craton said, "And he claims other folks are crazy."

The dogs growled and backed away from the scent on the ground. The deputy had to urge them ahead and they went slowly, without straining at the leashes, the hair on their necks raised stiff. "I never seen them act this way before," the deputy said. "They—they act—scared."

The policeman asked, "What they got to be scared of? How can they know anything?"

"They can tell by smelling," the deputy said. "Dogs are funny that way. They know quicker than a man when there's something—unnatural."

"So now the monster's a ghost," Charlie Craton said.

The deputy said. "If you're so damn smart why don't you get out there and track him with your nose?"

"I got a cold," Charlie said. The group moved along in silence except for the whining of the dogs. And then Charlie Craton spoke in a voice that Parker scarcely recognized. There was nothing jesting or satirical about it. He said to the deputy, "I wasn't trying to kid you. That's just my natural way of talking. I want to know: can dogs really tell if the thing they smell is—is superhuman?"

"I don't know. That's what folks say." One of the dogs whined and looked backward and the beam of a light caught his eyes They shone blood-red. "Go on," the deputy said. "Go on, boy."

The trail wound up the mountainside, the country growing wilder as they went. Huge boulders jabbed savagely from the earth and trees clung to the small pockets of dirt between the rocks.

The dogs began to whine again, a thin, keening sound, and the deputy said, "We're getting close. God! I wish the damn dogs would bark. That whining is awful to listen to."

Professor Hendricks said, "Ah-h . . ." They thought he was going to add something else, but he didn't. The group pulled closer together. Lights flashed outward in every direction.

The black side of a cliff rose ahead of them. The dogs pulled straight up to it. A light slid along the cliff face, showed the round, gaping maw of a cave. The dogs whined and went into the cave, the deputy pulling back on them now, stopping them, saying sharply, "Hey! Wait, wait!" and holding them until the rest of the group stood around him. "He's in there somewhere," the deputy said.

Dr. Drake cleared his throat a couple of times. Hendricks said, "Let's find him." They began to move along a tunnel-like passage which sloped downward gradually.

It was narrow here and the men could walk only two or three abreast. They jostled into position, Parker beside the deputy, just behind the dogs. He had the shotgun tucked under his right arm, and in his left hand was the deputy's flashlight. As they went downward the air took on a stale, heavy odor, the darkness crowded in upon them with that terrible thickness that comes only underneath the surface of the earth. Parker found that he was breathing heavily and his hands were clammy with sweat. He had to wipe them time and again upon his clothes.

The flashlight beam reached out and touched a bend in the tunnel. Beyond, the darkness brooded, waiting. They went forward slowly, but was a sharp turn and they couldn't see around it. The dogs went first, then Parker and the deputy.

The dogs yelped and crowded back upon them. Parker felt his heart wrenched upward from it's place. His throat constricted on a cry.

"My God!" the deputy whispered. "Oh my God!"

The cave ended in a widening room. To the left were the ashes of a fire, recently extinguished, and there were slabs of meat beside it, and beyond them lay the girl, her dress torn, her blonde hair pillowed under the blank white face. But it was not these things that Parker and the deputy saw first.

It was the monster!

He was less than ten feet away, crouched far over, animal-like, his hands with those curious knobbed fingers reaching almost to the floor, his gigantic, misshapen head thrust forward into the glare of the light. There was blood smeared across the matted beard around his mouth, and saliva mingled with it and drooled down across his chin. His eyes glittered like those of some beast, wild and insane.

For an instant that was death-long the tableau held. Then the creature's head moved slowly and he was looking at Parker, squinting against the light. And in those insane eyes recognition flamed! He screamed, plunging past the dogs and past the deputy—straight at Parker. The knife was in his right hand, raised to strike!

Terror held Parker motionless, rigid as a statue watching the monster come at him. Then the frozen moment broke and he was raising the gun. But one of the dogs had crowded back against the barrel. He couldn't get it up in time. The madman struck!

Parker never heard the shot. He was staggering backward, fighting with the gun, raising his left hand instinctively to protect himself. And then, moments later, he realized that the knife had not reached him. The creature lay at his feet with blood running from a thin bullet crease across his head. Behind Parker, Dr. Drake said, "I think I shot just in time."

The cop and the doctor looked at the girl. She wasn't dead. Drake said, only unconscious. And the creature wasn't dead either. They were tying his hands and feet when Charlie Craton yelled, "Hey! Look who it is! Look!"

"Who?"

"It's our lost All American! It's Bruce Adams!"

"He recognized Parker," Hendricks said. "He tried to murder him!"

The girl had regained consciousness. She began to scream, one long cry after another, high and flat, without meaning, without even terror in the sound.

CHAPTER THREE

A TOWN GOES MAD

FINDING BRUCE ADAMS was a nine-day sensation. He was confined to the local hospital and examined by every doctor in the state, but they couldn't say definitely what was wrong with him, what had changed him from a handsome man into a monster. Some form of elephantitis, they said; a suddenly overactive pituitary gland. They said all sorts of things.

The girl that he had captured never regained her sanity. But almost overnight her bones began to grow, her head got huge, knobs formed at the ends of her fingers and toes, hair began to grow on her body. The doctors watched these things, but there wasn't much they could learn. Only one thing was obvious: that she was in horrible pain. Then she attacked one of the hospital nurses and tried to kill her with hands and teeth.

The doctors wondered if it could be a contagious disease that she had contracted from Bruce Adams. They attended her with that strange sort of fatalism that I sometimes think doctors use for courage. They wondered which one of them would be next.

But the next victim wasn't a doctor; it wasn't anybody that had even talked to Bruce Adams or to the girl that he had captured that night. It was a big, hulking boy in the agricultural school. They didn't know at first that anything had happened to him. He simply vanished as Bruce Adams had done. And then a child picking blackberries on the mountain disappeared, then another, and the boys who had been with him told of seeing an ape, a hideous giant of some kind, carry him off. He was hunted down. He attacked the men who caught him and was killed. Friends said that just before he disappeared he had complained of headaches and been very irritable.

Then another student vanished. He killed a girl on the campus one night and was seen as he fled through the backyards. They couldn't find him even with the dogs. He remained at large.

You can imagine the terror that gripped the whole town by the throat. Women stayed locked in their houses. Men walked in the middle of the streets to guard against surprise attacks, and they went armed. No one knew where the madness would strike next, or what caused it. Persons fled the town by the score, but several of them were stricken elsewhere; so running away seemed to do little good. And soon the town was quarantined. Those who remained were forbidden to go.

A fear that verged on madness ate into the persons in the town. The only warnings the disease, or whatever it was, seemed to give were headaches and ragged tempers. These complaints, common enough at any time, were aggravated now by strain and terror— and a person noticing either in himself was likely to believe that the end had come.

A girl walked out of a picture show on the main street and found that her head was hurting. It had ached often enough after using her eyes, but she forgot that. She stood very still with blood-less knuckles pressed against her temples. Her mouth was open, the lips pulled white against her teeth. The boy with her said, "Ann! Ann, what . . .?" She fell in a huddle on the street; she bit at her lips until they bled; she frothed at the mouth. They took her to the hospital. There was nothing wrong with her except eye-strain and fear. But her brain never recovered from that fear.

A man complained about the food his wife served him for supper. She said she had been working all day mending clothes and tending the baby and there had been no time for fancy cooking. The baby began to cry and the sound got on his nerves, frayed by his day's work. He yelled at his wife, "I wish to God I had never met you!" He stared at her, realizing what he had said. The very fury of his outburst left him weak. He imagined that his head hurt. He went to his room and wrote a note saying that he believed he was going mad. He was afraid he would murder his own wife and child. He put a gun against his temple and pulled the trigger. It was terror that murdered him, for in actuality he was as well as he had ever been in his life.

A half dozen boys sat about the living room of Parker's fraternity house. They tried to talk about the prospects for next year's foot-ball team, tried to pretend they were casual about what was happening around them, but in the eyes of each one there was a slow, cold terror. Occasionally one would begin a sentence and stop in the middle, staring off into space. But they kept up the show of courage—all except one. Tom Wilkie stood in front of a window, biting at his fingernails. His face was bloodless, his hands trembled.

Parker asked, "What the hell's wrong with you, Tom?"

Wilkie started. He was a tall, rather sleekly handsome boy who had quite a reputation with girls. His successes were helped out by the Packard roadster he drove and his income of nearly two hundred a week. He said, "I—I—nothing's wrong." He grinned, but it was a sickly attempt.

Another boy said, "He's been like that for the last couple of hours."

"For God's sake try and look less like a funeral!" one said. "We've all got as much to be afraid of as you have."

Wilkie jerked upright, both hands clinched beside his face. "Leave me alone!" he shouted. "What have y'all got to be afraid of? It's only . . ." He choked, turning suddenly toward the wall and resting his head upon it.

"What do you mean?" Parker asked. "You mean that you . . .?"

It was then that Charlie Craton came bursting through the door. "Well, gentlemen," he said, "I've solved it! I know the cause and I regret to say, I know there isn't any cure."

Craton stood there leering at them. He was a thin, sharp-faced young man with a high forehead and black hair brushed straight back from it. He was one of these men with a photographic memory and an insatiable thirst for information. He remembered everything that he read and he read constantly. He could tell you how many baths there were in Rome, and the height of Mt. Everest, and the income tax scale for corporations. But he had a twisted sense of humor and you never knew when he was serious and when he was mocking his audience. Now he looked at them with his sharp, black eyes glittering and said, "I know what's causing this plague of madness. And I know what makes the poor devils ache for human flesh!"

They did not speak. They stood there, rigid, looking at him.

"I was in the library," he said. "I found an interesting bit of local history."

He waited, and Parker said, "Well, go on."

"It seems that about three hundred years ago there was a family of Indians who lived where this town is now. It was a wild, outlaw family made up of monsters and freaks. The neighboring Indians weren't cannibals, but this particular family was. They preyed on the neighbors. They lived for years in caves up in the mountain, lived off the flesh of neighboring tribes. Generation after generation grew up, all monsters. But finally the tribes got together and hunted them down and killed them. But not before a curse was put on this place." He stopped and stood looking at them with that half grin, half leer on his face.

Parker said, "Bosh!"

"Maybe," Charlie Craton said. "But no Indians ever lived here after that. There are several histories that will tell you how they shunned this place. Early travelers speak of it."

"Indian superstition," Parker said. Craton said softly, "You think so? In 1784 a priest came into the country. He was probably the first white man to reach this town and he changed into a cannibalistic monster! Twelve years later a party of white hunters reached here. One of them became unrecognizable. His head got double its size. He killed one of the party. The others left. Look!" He dropped on the table three volumes of the same book. It was like him to slip every volume out of the library; he didn't want anybody else stumbling on his story.

It was a little known but authentic history—and the story was there! They crowded about it, reading it. Tom Wilkie held a volume with both hands, clutching it until his fingernails whitened. There was a frantic, almost crazy light in his eyes as he read, a kind of furious hope. He whirled on Charlie Craton. "You mean—you mean, really—it's because of something that happened all those hundreds of years ago?"

"Stranger things have happened," Craton said. "Smart men don't scoff at the supernatural any more. In the East, in a land older than ours, religion is founded on reincarnation. Our own religion teaches eternal life for the spirit: if that is true, why can't the spirit return and inhabit a new body? It can! And the wisest men admit—"

"Nuts!" Parker said. He was getting angry without quite realizing why. He rubbed a hand across his forehead and found it was damp with sweat.

Wilkie had Craton by the lapels of his coat. "Then—then it's not done by somebody here! Nobody could . . ."

"If it comes from so far back," Parker demanded, "why hasn't it happened around school before?"

"This town's no older than the school," Craton said, "They were both founded just fifteen years ago. That's not long."

The telephone rang in the back hallway. A freshman answered and yelled, "Andy, it's for you."

He was still half angry when he answered the phone, muttering to himself, angry, he thought, because deep inside his heart he was tempted to believe the story that Charlie Craton had found. A great many intelligent men believed in the supernatural. Doctors and scientists were constantly finding data they could explain in no other way.

And then he heard Dr. Drake's calm, professional voice over the wire. "I thought I ought to call you, Parker. I'm out at the hospital. There's been a little trouble here."

"Yes, sir?"

"Bruce Adams escaped."

At first the significance of what the doctor had said didn't strike home. Then Drake's voice jarred in the receiver again. "You know how he tried to kill you there in the cave; probably jealous of you before he went mad, and after that . . . He's been talking about you and about Mary Carlyle. The cops will be looking . . ."

Parker never heard the last of the sentence. His fingers got stiff and the receiver slid through them. He had a vision of the mad giant he had seen upon the mountain, saw him lunging, knife raised, striking. And in the picture he saw Mary Carlyle's face, the soft curve of her body. And all at once he had turned and was running. He did not stop to think that he would be of little help; that his presence might even add to her danger. His thinking processes were a little confused now; there was a pain under his skull.

Early warm dusk was thickening over the campus and when he reached Mary's sorority house Parker was sweating, breathing hard. The girls had finished their meal and gone upstairs. The living room was empty. Parker stopped on the stairway, shouting up it, "Mary! Mary!"

Above him a girl called, "She's not here, Andy. I think she's on the sun porch."

He did not answer. He turned, staggering slightly, across the living room to the small, closed-in sun parlor the girls generally used for their courting. He knocked and flung the door open and went in.

From across the small room the monster that had been Bruce Adams stared at him! A long instant they stood there looking at one another. And then the giant screamed, that furious hungry cry. His knobbed fingers clutched a huge metal flowerpot and swung it above his head.

CHAPTER FOUR

THE INSANE DEATH

INSTINCT HURLED PARKER BACKWARD. He grabbed a table, swung it between them. The giant crashed into it, whirled it ahead of him; and Parker, leaping backward, slipped at the same instant. The table struck him across the waist and he went down under it. The giant screamed. He hurled the great metal bowl with a force that should have crushed Parker's head like a dropped egg had it reached its mark.

As it was, Parker's frantic roll saved him. He threw the table from him, and got to his hands and knees. The house was full of screams, doors banging, running steps, but through and above it all he could hear the snarling of the creature beside him. The monster drew back his foot and kicked at Parker's head the way he had once kicked at a football. Parker saw it coming, saw the foot moving with seeming slowness toward his face. He tried to duck.

It caught him on the shoulder, lifted him clear of the floor and smashed him against the wall. He went down in a huddle. He ached to move and couldn't. His muscles were like thick syrup, unable to bring his body erect. And still snarling, the monster came toward him.

Parker never fully realized what happened. The kitchen door had banged open and the negro cook stood there, a loaf of bread in one hand, the bread knife in the other. She stood there for full slow seconds, her mouth open, her face turning a sickly liver color. Then she screamed and in blind terror hurled both the knife and the bread. They struck the giant and dropped to the floor. He whirled, saw the knife and the negro. He picked up the knife and plunged at her. Then she was gone, out of the back door and into the night, with the madman after her.

Somehow Parker got to his feet. Dazedly he staggered into the sun parlor. It was empty, one big window standing open, the screen ripped out. In the swing was a copy of *Thorndike's Psy-*

chology with Mary Carlyle's name on the flyleaf. But Mary was gone.

Girls were pouring into the room now, hysterical, screaming, wanting to know what had happened. Men were coming through the front door.

Parker grabbed one of the girls by the shoulders. It was Mary's roommate though he scarcely recognized her. "Where is she?" he cried. "Where is she?"

The girl was sobbing with fear and excitement. Probably she didn't understand what he said. But suddenly anger flowed through him and he shook her, slapped her across the mouth. "Where is Mary?" he yelled.

The girl was suddenly quiet. Even one in the room was quiet, staring at Parker. He swayed and put one hand to his forehead. His head hurt like hell. "I'm going to find her," he said. He turned and went out.

No one touched him; no one came near him.

The door closed and for a long while the room was icy still. Then a girl said, "It's got Andy. He's gone—mad!"

Parker did not hear her. He was outside reeling along the walk, half running, not knowing at first where he wanted to go. And then, all at once, there was purpose in his face. "By God!" he whispered. "It might be . . ."

He found Tom Wilkie in his room at the fraternity house. He caught the tall, handsome boy by the chest, slammed him against the wall. "Tell me!" he yelled. "Tell me about it!"

Wilkie's face went white. "What—what are you talking about?"

"You said tonight that you were the only one who had anything to fear! Then when Charlie claimed all this was caused by men who died three hundred years ago you weren't frightened, you were glad! Why?"

"I—I don't know what you mean. I—"

Parker struck him. Wilkie was two inches taller than Parker, twenty pounds heavier. A few hours before, he could have licked Andy Parker without much trouble, but now the sheer insane fury of the smaller man frightened him. "All right!" he said. "I—it's not much. I got a letter threatening me, saying I had already been given the germs that cause this and unless I paid forty thousand dollars I'd be allowed to die. If I paid the money I'd get an anti-dote."

"Did you pay it?"

"I couldn't get that much. I couldn't! My old man left my money in a trust fund and I've spent every penny as I got it. I couldn't pay it."

"You got only the one letter."

"That's all."

"No other messages."

"None. But the letter said if I went to the police, told anybody . . ."

"Where is it?"

"But if the police find out, I—"

Parker hit him again. "Give me that letter!"

Wilkie looked at the mad white face and suddenly there was a new terror in his eyes. "All right," he whispered. "I'll get it. I—" He pulled away from Parker, edging along the wall, his mouth working. His hands shook as he opened a dresser drawer, pawed under clothes and brought out a folded paper. He handed it to Parker without coming close to him. "That's it," he said.

Parker snatched the paper, opened it. The paper was blank.

He jumped at Wilkie again, grabbing him by the shirt. "Damn you!" he yelled. "I want that letter, quick."

"That's it. I gave it—" then he too was looking at the paper, his eyes getting large, his mouth working. A thin stream of saliva drooled down across his chin. "It's blank," he whispered. "There's nothing on it!"

"Where's the right one?"

"That's it. I know it is! I hid it and I kept this room locked. I know that's it—but the writing's—gone."

Parker tilted the paper to the light. It was totally blank, no trace of writing anywhere. But the water-mark showed, and suddenly he had turned and was out of the loom running.

In Charlie Craton's desk he found paper that matched. But Craton was gone. "He went out the back door," someone told Parker. "Said he was going to the library, but . . ."

Parker paused on the back step, the twenty gauge shotgun in his hands. A half moon rode high in the sky, tearing its way through thick, tattered clouds. And a mile away, dark against the heavens, rose Black Mountain. Andy Parker began to run.

He did not try to follow a trail up the mountainside. And yet he went swiftly and directly toward the spot that he wanted. Perhaps with his mind clouded by pain, a kind of animal instinct rose in him to guide him; perhaps it was the reincarnation of the savage, a new being taking possession of him: a rediscovered knowledge that had been his hundreds of years before. Anyway he went upward without conscious thought, driving headlong over country he had not traveled before as instinctively as a homing pigeon.

Dark clouds had massed over the moon now. Thunder rolled off to the west, low and deep like a distant earthquake. Perhaps he had some eerie ability to see dimly in the dark; it seemed that way although he was never to remember, never to recall clearly any of the things that happened that night. He was beyond memory though he didn't know it then.

And finally he stood almost at the top of the mountain. The moon broke through clouds and for an instant pale light washed over the blank face of a cliff and the round maw of a cave that tunneled into it. And Parker made the whimpering sound of a dog that nears the end of his trail. He plunged into the cave.

Here the darkness was like a physical force thrusting itself against his eyeballs, jamming black ramrods into his brain. The sound of his breathing seemed to be magnified by the overhanging walls, to grow into a dull roar and hammer back against him.

He stumbled and became confused in the utter darkness. He groped on hands and knees then until he found a stick. It was of fat pine and when he struck a match to it the blaze caught and made a sputtering sound and threw wavering red and yellow light out upon the cave walls. They were damp and fungus splotched. Queer pale lichen hung from the ceiling.

He must have made a strange picture as he went deeper into the earth. His hair was matted with sweat. There was a cut across his forehead made by some tree limb and blood trickled down into one eye. He held the torch high with his left hand and the light seemed to flow backward into darkness as he walked. The shotgun was in his right hand, and the barrel burned blood-colored and ebony under the light.

Close ahead he saw the turn in the cave where the darkness waited for him. He went slowly now, crouched over, holding the shotgun with its butt between his hip and elbow, the stock resting along his forearm, his finger on the trigger. He turned the curve and came into the large end room of the cave.

At first he saw nothing at all. His light, reaching out and lapping against the darkness, did not touch the wall. He took one, two, three steps ahead. And then he saw the dim white shape crouched upon the floor ahead of him.

Almost he fired. His finger twitched at the trigger, taking up all the slack. And then he heard the gagged cry, and his own voice came hoarsely, "Mary!" He went down on his hands and knees beside her.

She was tied and gagged, though the bonds were not tight. It was the fear in her face, the half mad appeal of it, that turned his legs to numb useless sticks. He did not make a move to untie her. He began to pant, catching his breath in deep gulps. His head seemed to be expanding, swelling until it threatened to burst. His gaze rolled over the girl, wild, fearful, uncertain of what he demanded from her. And the light, flaming up against his face, showed it clearly. Against her gag the girl screamed. She flung herself away from Parker and back against the cave wall.

Behind him an animal shrieked, furious and terrible. Parker spun, coming half erect, swinging the gun, bringing the light high. For a moment the blaze wavered, then reached outward.

Ten feet away stood the monster that had been Bruce Adams. His eyes glittered like those of a beast. His huge head was thrust forward. In his right hand he held the breadknife and there was a dark stain upon its blade. He screamed again and lunged forward.

Andy Parker fired, squeezing both triggers of the double barrel gun together. The leaden shot took the monster full in the chest, stopped him, hurled him backward. But he did not fall. He braced, wavering, shaking himself. And then he came forward again, still holding the knife. Parker dropped the torch. It struck the ground, went black for an instant, then burned up again dimly. With both hands Parker swung the gun butt at the monster's head.

It never landed. The creature reached up and clutched it with his left hand and tore it from Parker's grasp. He hurled it behind him. And laughing deep in his throat, his whole chest one gaping wound, he came on again. There was no dodging him now, no chance to escape. In the pale light Parker could see the glistening wetness of the knife blade.

A figure materialized behind the monster as though out of the air itself. There was a swish and the thud of a gun butt landing with terrific force. The creature doubled in the middle and went down, the knife underneath it. From the semi-darkness Professor Hendricks' sardonic voice said, "It seems I was just in time."

He came forward, holding what was left of the gun: it had broken across the stock. When he picked up the torch it began to burn more brightly and he held it close to Parker's face. He said, "Just take it easy, fellow, and we'll get you down to the hospital in no time. I think you can be cured all right."

He untied Mary and was straightening when they heard the sound of voices coming along the cave. Hendricks' lean face twisted in a bitter sort of smile. "They are too close," he said. "It won't do any good to bluff. They've got me."

McGruder stopped and looked around at us. "Well," he said, "that's the story."

We stared at him. "You mean that this Professor was causing all that trouble?" Andrews asked.

"No. He'd had very little to do with it. The real cause was the same that had changed that original Indian family into monsters, and had occasionally changed other persons during the course of time."

"What are you talking about?" I asked.

"The water supply. There was a mineral in the earth, a combination of minerals, rather, that broke loose into water under the earth only rarely; you know how the earth remains steady for years and then without warning there's a quake. In that same way these minerals now and then got into the underground streams and from them into the valley's water supply. When it did, it attacked the pituitary gland, caused the bones to start growing again, even though the ends had hardened. That's what made the heads bulge, the fingers and toes bulb at the ends."

"But if it was in the water why didn't it affect everybody?"

"Because some persons are better able to resist it," he said. "Every child in a classroom may be exposed to measles and only four or five contract it. In the old days when a plague struck a town practically the entire population would be exposed, but the percentage of victims would vary."

"What about the cannibalistic urge, the tendency of the victim to hide?" Andrews said.

McGruder hesitated before he answered. "They claimed that was part of the disease; that the pain of the expanding skull drove men crazy and made them want to hide, that the excess of secretion of the glands made persons crave meat and the insane brain furnished the tendency toward cannibalism. That's what they claimed, but I don't believe them."

"What do you believe?"

Again he looked at us before answering. "Have you ever seen a hurt animal?" he asked. "Even a lap dog with a broken leg wants to hide until the pain is over. It's the instinct of the animal, of the savage. Well, you'll laugh probably, but I keep thinking of the story Charlie Craton discovered, of the savages who lived there three hundred years before and who cursed the valley with a reincarnation of their own souls."

We didn't laugh. After a moment I said, "And Professor Hendricks, what did he have to do with it?"

"He had discovered the trouble with the water supply. And once he knew that, he was certain that any new victims could be cured. But like I told you, he was a man of very fierce ambition. He was almost a genius at his work, and he knew it; but the laboratory the college furnished him didn't meet his needs. He thought he was being held back from great discoveries by lack of equipment."

"'So—?" I asked.

"So he determined to make use of the disease and get the money he needed. He tried to frighten Tom Wilkie into paying (he wrote the ransom notes in an invisible ink of his own discovery that left absolutely no trace and consequently could never be used as evidence against him); but Wilkie wasn't able to pay. Hendricks thought he had simply failed to frighten Wilkie enough, so he decided that he would try a real kidnapping, telling the parents that the victim would be given the disease unless they paid. He chose Mary Carlyle because her family was wealthy. He never planned to harm her in any way."

"But why the cave?"

"He needed a place to hide her. He didn't know, of course, that Bruce Adams would escape and return there. And since persons generally thought the trouble was contagious, the spot where Adams had stayed was shunned like the plague itself. When Adams escaped, first Parker, then other persons, decided that he would go back to the cave. Hendricks was there when Parker came; he had come to feed Mary. She had been kept in the dark and didn't know who had kidnapped her. Perhaps he could have escaped, certainly he could have tried, after Adams turned up. But he didn't. He stayed and saved Parker's life."

"What did they do to him?"

"Nothing very much. They were too glad to have somebody discover the cause of the plague and a cure for it. Then Mary Carlyle didn't prosecute. After he had saved Andy's life and hers, she felt he had paid his debt."

"How about the paper the note was written on?" I asked. "You said he found some like it in Charlie Craton's room."

"It was the type of paper furnished some of the departments by the school. Charlie was a grader for one of the instructors and he'd helped himself to a bit of the paper."

For the last few minutes I had been trying to recall news stories of years before. I said, "I remember something about all that. But I didn't think the boy's name was Parker. I thought it was—" I saw the expression on McGruder's face and I stopped. "I can't remember what if was." I said.

A door opened and Mrs. McGruder came into the room. Andrews said, "Hello, Mary. Your husband has been telling us a story. Quite a story."

McGruder turned quickly, moving that big, awkward head of his in the strange way he had. Then he smiled and stood up. "That's the end of the story," he said "How about a drink?"

VILLAGE OF
THE DEAD

CHAPTER ONE

TOWN WITHOUT PITY

THE TRAIN PULLED RAPIDLY AWAY from the shack-like station. Standing alone on the narrow platform, Ann Meadows watched the lighted windows glide past while a feeling of distaste and loneliness grew upon her. Then the train was gone into the creeping, dusky twilight.

She should be happy, Ann thought, not nervous and half afraid, for she was coming home for the first time in five years. But it wasn't the sort of homecoming of which she had dreamed. Tom wasn't with her, and her sister's letter with its almost hysterical note and the strange invitation to stay away . . .

Footsteps padded on the platform and Ann turned quickly. A man in his middle fifties, his white hair almost a halo above his round, kindly face, was coming toward her, smiling. But as Ann ran toward him, her hands outstretched, she saw that his smile was tense, unnatural.

Bob Wilson's blue eyes twinkled as he looked at her, but there was a strained note in the cordiality of his greeting. "Gracious, child," he said, "when I saw you last you were seventeen and afraid to leave home. And now you come back prettier than ever with that red hair of yours. And a renowned pianist with a concert in Town Hall had all the New York papers raving about you. I was afraid you wouldn't speak to persons in the home town." He caught his words then, stopped short as if afraid of what he might say. Almost under his breath he added, "There aren't many persons left to speak to . . ."

Ann's lingers tightened convulsively. "What—what's happening at home?" she demanded, "Marie's letter was so—so strange. Asking me not to come home, saying that everybody was leaving town. That's why I came so quickly. Is there—anything wrong? Is Dad . . .?"

Robert Wilson shook his white head. Ann had known him since she was a child, had gone to him with her troubles as everyone in the little town of Livingston had done. Now the old man's face was gray in the twilight. "I don't know what's wrong with the town," he said softly, "but nothing's happened to your father. Yet I wish you—you had done like Marie told you and stayed away."

Ann Meadows felt a weird, unreasoning fear crawl like a scaly thing along her slim legs and up her spine, as she watched the old man's face working, felt his fingers tremble against hers. He said, "Your sister told me you were coming on the train and asked me to meet you. She wants me to—to drive you over to York for the night, persuade you to go back to the city tomorrow. Won't you?" he finished with an eager, almost plaintive light in his eyes.

For a moment Ann stood looking at him and feeling that strange fear deep in her breast. Then she thought of her father, of his square, broad face and high brow. And of her sister Edith, who was two years older than Ann and who had been paralyzed since an accident five years before. That was one reason Ann had wanted to bring Tom Adams with her. He was a young doctor, but his reputation was growing, and Marie, Ann's younger sister, had written that the local doctor said it would mean death to move Edith at all.

"Won't you go over to York for the night?" the old banker asked again.

Ann squared her slim shoulders, raised her small, oval chin defiantly. "I don't know why all of you are trying to run me away, Mr. Bob, but I'm going home. I'm going to see what's the trouble."

The old man's hands quivered against hers. "I told Marie you'd say that. But we both hoped . . ." Fear was coming into his face, but he shook it off and tried to smile. "I'll get your bags," he said,

The gravel road lay through flat, piney woods country. The noise of the motor, the whir of the tires on gravel, were the only sounds as they started the five-mile ride to Livingston. The banker drove slowly and Ann smiled as she remembered how cautious the old man had always been. A little suspicious of automobiles even yet, she thought.

"There've been strange things happening in Livingston for the past two weeks," Wilson said. "Perhaps you'll think I'm crazy. Maybe we're all crazy." He paused, added, "You remember those half-breeds that live along the edge of Crazy Man's Swamp?"

"Yes." Everyone in Livingston knew the stories, but few persons ever saw one of the swamp-dwellers. Ann didn't remember having seen but one. Years ago when she was squirrel hunting in

Crazy Man's Swamp with her father, she had heard something behind her and suddenly turning, gazed into the most hideous and abnormal face she had ever seen. It was a long, dark face with a twisted mouth. Close-set black eyes and black hair above an unbelievably narrow forehead. She had screamed and the man had vanished into the swamp the way a partridge can dive into brown sage and disappear.

Her father had told her about the people then. Two hundred years ago Spanish soldiers had deserted, married into a group of degenerate Creek Indians. Since then they had lived in the same swamp, doing a little farming around its edges, fishing, hunting. Countless intermarriages, malaria and other diseases had reduced the entire group to a large family of half-wits. A psychologist had come here once to study them, but he hadn't been able to learn much. They were a sullen, lonely people. Many persons in Livingston claimed that they murdered and scalped persons caught in the swamp as the Indians had done years ago. Others said they were harmless. There was a small wagon road that led to their village, but nobody ever went there, and they practically never came out of the swamp.

"What about them?" Ann asked.

The old man stirred restlessly in his seat and the car moved more slowly than ever. He said, "Well, about a month ago, some of them began to come to town. Persons saw them slipping around fences and down back streets. They never said anything to anybody, but they kept coming, more and more of them, slipping in and then out again. What they were after I don't know. And then—" The old man swallowed harshly—"then things started happening to the townspeople."

Ann was leaning toward him. Her hands were clenched in her lap and her eyes wide. "What things?" she asked.

"There were just rumors at first. Persons claiming they heard noises and saw things. Then one afternoon two weeks ago old John Perkins appeared suddenly in the middle of Main Street. He had blood all over his face and he was running, staggering like he was drunk. Everybody saw him, but he just kept running until he got right in front of Doctor McGruder's office. Then he pitched over on his face.

"I was at home, but Dan McGruder called me. He said Perkins had all his ribs cracked, but had died of poison of some kind. Dan said he was coming right out to see me. Several persons saw him leave his office. He—he—" The old man stopped.

"Yes." Again the girl whispered unconsciously.

"He never got to my house. He just disappeared. Old Mrs. Calloway claimed she saw him two nights later slipping along Jenkins Alley, but by that time everybody in town was seeing things. Two other persons had died. Ben Larkin is the town marshal now. He can't find anything. Those half-breeds kept showing up and everybody got to saying they were causing the trouble."

"But Mr. Bob . . ." Horror and incredulity were in the girl's voice. "Why—why don't they call out the National Guard or something?"

The old man turned his face toward her for a moment, then looked back at the road. "Maybe you've forgotten how folks do things in this part of the country," he said. "We've always been able to take care of ourselves. I—I did suggest getting help but Ben Larkin jumped on me. Said as long as he was town marshal we didn't need any troops. Folks all seemed to think that way for awhile, but things kept getting worse. The half-breeds kept showing up and the idea that some kind of ghosts were at work got around. It sounds foolish, but—but just about everybody has left town."

Darkness had set in now and from far off to the right came the eerie chirping of crickets, the mournful cry of a whippoorwill. The white lights of the car jabbed through the night, touched on the decaying timbers of a short bridge. Beyond the bridge Ann could see a white blur, and knew it was the sign marking the Livingston town limits.

"I know it's absurd," the old man said. "But—but it happened. And everybody's running away now. There—"

The car rattled over the rickety bridge, drowning out his words. Ann was unconsciously reading the lettering on the town limits' marker.

They were across the bridge and abreast of the sign when the thing happened in one wild, terrifying second.

Ann Meadows saw the sign directly beside the car and in the same instant heard the blasting, rending explosion, felt the car shiver under the impact. Flame leaped. Window and windshield smashed in a shower of flying glass. The car staggered, reeled toward the shallow ditch on the right, plunged into it. Ann was flung forward, her head cracking against the instrument panel. The world spun in a blaze of light and darkness . . .

The laughter sounded far away and detached. A dark, reeling blindness gripped Ann's eyes and brain. Then she heard the laughter again, closer and hideous with evil and ugly hunger. She fought to steady her spinning brain. Her eyes came open, slowly, slowly, with lights and round, dark spots dancing before them.

The laughter rumbled in her ears and sent terror surging through her. She tried to scream, but the muscles of her throat were contracted and there was no sound.

The dashlight on the car was still burning. Ann's head was hanging forward, almost touching the dashboard. She realized these things dimly, but objects still swam before her eyes. Then into the swimming circle came a dirty, clawlike hand holding a piece of jagged, knife-edged glass. The hand moved toward her throat, reaching underneath her chin, the glass gripped, ready to slash.

In a wild surge of terror, a cry broke from Ann's throat. She flung herself back against the seat, her scream a furious thing leaping into the night.

The seat stopped her backward movement. She saw not only the hand, but the wrist and forearm now as they moved the glass toward her throat.

A white light burst soundlessly, flooding the car with brilliance for one second. Ann Meadows crumpled in a faint.

Something wet and slimy striking Ann's face brought wild fear and consciousness surging through her brain. She heard herself scream, heard the sound beat like wings against her ears. She tried to spring erect and run, but something held her, pushed her back.

"That's all right, Miss Meadows," a voice said. "Jest take it easy, take it easy. You ain't hurt much."

Ann's eyes flew open then, but unconscious terror was still jerking at her limbs, fluttering her eyelids. In the darkness she did not recognize the man leaning through the window of the car, holding his hands on her shoulders. He said again, "Now jest take it easy, Miss Meadows."

Then she recognized the lean, sallow face, the blond eyebrows and colorless eyes of Ben Larkin, the town marshal. She remembered him as a man of about thirty, but now the dashlight showed deep wrinkles in his sallow skin and there were dark lines under his eyes.

The wild terror had gone out of Ann now, but her body felt weak. Her knees trembled and her voice quivered when she asked, "Who—who was that laughing—that reached for me with the glass?"

The wrinkles deepened in Larkin's face and the lines under his eyes seemed to tighten. He opened his mouth, shut it. After a moment he said, "Musta been that idiot Lem Prune I seen running away from here when I drove up. One of them half-breeds from down in Crazy Man's Swamp. But you jest set still while I look at old man Wilson."

Ann remembered Bob Wilson now and turning saw him leaning forward over the steering wheel, his face twisted toward her. From a bruise on his forehead a narrow stream of blood was running down into his left eyebrow.

She caught his shoulders, pulled him back against the seat. "Mr. Bob," she whispered. "Mr. Bob."

The old man stirred. His eyes blinked open but did not focus. He put a shaking hand up to his blood-stained forehead.

Larkin asked, "You hurt bad, Mr. Wilson?"

The banker moved his head slowly, blinked again. At last he said, "Hello Larkin." He twisted in the seat, saw Ann. "Child," he asked anxiously, "are you hurt?"

Abruptly Ann realized that she had a headache from the blow against the dashboard, but she said, "No, sir. How're you?" She opened the car door and stepped out into the ditch. Her knees quivered and she had to grip the door to keep from falling.

Larkin helped the old man out, made sure there were no broken bones. Strength was returning to Ann's legs now, but her head still ached. Larkin asked, "What happened? How come you-all run in the ditch?"

Wilson shook his white head. "I don't know. We had just come across the bridge when something seemed to blow up. My head must have hit the windshield and I don't remember anything else."

Ann heard her voice saying in a hushed, frightened whisper which she could not believe was hers, "It happened just as we passed the city limits sign. It was like something had been waiting there, just inside the town, to keep us from entering."

Both men stared at her for a moment. Larkin said, "I'll take you-all on into town in my car, since a wheel's broke on yores, Mr. Wilson, I reckon Miss Meadows will be wanting to see her folks."

Few lights showed as they rode down the main street. There was a dull glow from behind the door of the big white home where Wilson had lived alone since the death of his wife several years before. One or two other lights showed, but most of the houses were dark and deserted.

"I reckon after the folks hear about this," Larkin said, "there won't be *nobody* left round here."

The old banker's voice was brittle when he answered, "I'll be here, alive or dead. I been running this bank for fifteen years and the only time it shut down was when Roosevelt closed all of them. Every other bank in the country failed, but I kept mine open. And I don't mean to shut it now."

CHAPTER TWO

DEATH'S FOOTSTEPS

THERE WERE TWO BEDS in the large, high-ceilinged room. On the one nearest the windows, her face white as the pillows on which she rested, was a girl. Her hair was long and chestnut-colored and lay in a soft mass about her face.

Ann Meadows felt a queer tightening of her throat as she came into the room and looked at her invalid sister. She said, "Edith, dear!" and ran toward the bed.

Edith Meadows turned her head slightly and her pale lips smiled. But under the cover her body was as motionless as wood. Then Ann was kissing her and kneeling beside the bed. "I heard you in the front hall," Edith said, "and thought you'd never come in here."

Ann said, "We were telling Mr. Bob Wilson good night. He brought me home."

"I know," Edith said. "Dad is—is—"

Ann pushed away from the bed, gripping the cover with taut fingers. "Where—where is he?" She turned to look at her younger sister standing in the middle of the room.

Marie Meadows said, "Aw, he's just out for a little while. He'll be in here soon. He should be back now." Marie was a tall girl, well built, with hair the soft auburn color of Ann's. She was pretty, but her face had a harder look than Ann's and her mouth was straight and thin.

Beyond Marie stood Dorothy Harkins. She was small, plump, with a round face, round eyes, and close-cropped brown hair around her small head. Before Edith Meadows had been injured, she and Dorothy had been close college friends. When Dorothy's father had lost his fortune in the 1929 crash and committed suicide, the girl had come to live with the Meadows. Now she said, "Mr. Meadows told me he would be back for dinner." She looked at Ann, smiled slightly. "You know there aren't any servants any more. All the Negroes have left town."

"*All* of them?"

"Every darn one," Marie said. "Been gone two weeks now."

Ann felt the cool touch of Edith's fingers and turned to look at the girl on the bed. "Didn't Marie write you not to come?" Edith asked. "She promised me she would."

The cold, empty hollow formed in Ann's breast again, but she said, "You shouldn't try to keep me away when there's trouble. I want to be with the family."

"But you shouldn't be here now. None of you should." Edith put her fingers against Ann's lips when her sister tried to interrupt. Her pale face was deadly serious and in the brown eyes a fire was burning. Her voice was scarcely above a whisper, but vibrant, heavy with emotion. "Marie and Dorothy thought I was foolish at first. They still try to pretend. But they know I'm right. Just lying here all day a person *feels* things that other human beings don't. And I *know* you can't stop what's happening here. You can't! It'll kill you all if you don't go. Please. Leave me, there's—"

"Hush! Hush!" Ann said. She put her hand on her sister's mouth. "Don't talk like that. We're going to have you well soon. Tom Adams, you know, the boy I wrote you about, the one I'm going to marry, will be down tomorrow if not tonight. I came as soon as I got Marie's letter, but I left a note for Tom."

The girl on the bed tightened her fingers about Ann's. "Listen," she said. "You're in love. You've got everything to live for. Please leave. Go back to Tom. If you don't—" She stopped, her head half raised from the pillow, her face taut, listening. There was a dead silence in the room, through which Ann could hear the ticking of the little radium-faced alarm-clock on the dresser.

Edith said, "That must be Marie's friend coming up the walk. He's staggering like he was drunk."

"If I could hear as well as you—" Marie began. The expression on Edith's face stopped her. "What is it?" she asked.

"That's not a drunk. It's—It's—"

They all heard the sound then. Two quick bumps on the front steps. Silence. A dragging foot.

Every person in the room was facing the door into the hallway. Dorothy Harkins moved deeper into the room and stood close beside Marie.

The sounds came again. The person was on the porch now, cross-
ing it. The steps were irregular, jerky. A heavy *bump, bump. A*
long pause. The sounds took on an eerie, unreasoning significance.
They hammered at Ann's ears, at her brain. She found herself
leaning forward, waiting for each new step, her heart beating and
pausing with the sounds.

There was a scratching sound at the front door. A wavering,
scraping noise that ceased abruptly. The lock on the door clicked.

Then the steps were coming down the hall, wearing, irregular,
dragging along the floor. Twice the unseen person fell heavily
against the wall, dragged himself erect again and came on. Almost
unconsciously Ann stood close against the bed, between her invalid sister and the door. She could feel Edith's thin, cold fingers
gripping her left hand. She heard her own breathing, harsh under
her eardrums. Her eyes, were straining in their sockets, swelling,
staring at the dark frame of the doorway.

The steps thudded. Stopped. Came on again.

Dorothy Harkins screamed, a high, flat cry. Marie Meadows
choked, "Oh God!" Ann staggered back against the bed, almost
fell, and stood there wavering. Her eyes were aching in sheer disbelief. Her heart was a cold lump of horror deep in her stomach.

Framed in the light of the doorway was her father. He was a big
man and his shoulders, swaying low in front of him like those of
an ape, almost touched the sills. His broad, square face was a mass
of blood and torn flesh out of which his eyes showed like dulled
lights. His big jaw hung crazily to one side, pulling his mouth
open. Arm saw that his big hands were bloody and in that long,
horrible moment one drop slid from his forefinger with infinite
reluctance, to fall with a dull thud upon the floor.

Then Ann was running toward him, pushing her sister out of
the way, crying aloud, "Dad! Dad!"

She stopped two feet distant, unable to fight herself closer to
the hideous thing that had been her father. Behind her she heard
Dorothy Harkins sobbing hysterically.

The big man's face moved, contorted itself behind its bloody
mask. The jaw wagged slightly and from the blood-filled mouth
came an unintelligible mumbling.

Arm jerked herself a half step closer. She put her hands on his
coat. "Dad!" It was the only word she could say.

The big jaw wagged again and the face twisted in torture. Ann
rocked, clinging to her father, all but fainting. She knew that he
was trying to talk and that his broken jaw and blood-filled mouth

made words impossible. She managed to say, "Come over here; sit down." Mark was beside her now, reaching out for her father's arm.

Light flared in the man's eyes. Ann realized that her father *had* to speak, had to tell them what had happened to him—to warn them.

For now *he* knew the thing which terrified the village!

He leaned forward, opened his month and spilled bloody saliva on the floor. He raised his head but the words were still muffled on his tongue. Twice he tried, his face twisting in agony. *"Geuu buer . . ."* The sound trailed off into nothing.

The man seemed to draw himself together, collect every muscle in his great body. The fight in his eyes flamed.

Pulling himself away from the hands of his daughters he turned toward the writing desk. His bloody right hand pawed in front of him. He took two steps, stopped. For a moment he wavered, then fell over on his face.

For the next half hour Ann Meadows moved in a dream. Her body felt cold from the sheer horror of her father's death, and a chilling fear enveloped her like a fog. This whole thing was incredible, fantastic. It sounded like some weird folk-tale that had been handed down from generation to generation, growing more monstrous with each repetition. It was unbelievable—yet it was happening before her very eyes.

She hardly heard her voice as she called Old Bob Wilson and Larkin, the marshal. Larkin had just come back from inspecting the place where the wreck had occurred, and had found nothing suspicious. He told her this before she was able to tell about her father. Then she had gone back into the room where her father lay and had sat on the bed with Edith while Marie called Sam Mason, the undertaker.

She thought dimly, sitting there holding her sister's frail hands in hers, that at last Sam Mason would come inside their home. But her father wouldn't know it now. For years Marie and Sam had been in love. Wayne Meadows had opposed them both because Mason was ten years older than Marie and because he drank too heavily.

Edith Meadow's cool hands quivered as they gripped her sister's. She whispered, "Ann, you and Marie and Dorothy must leave here. You'll die if you stay here! I've been lying here, thinking about this thing. Invalids get to know things, just lying and thinking. And I know it'll kill us all, one at a time. One—"

"Hush," Ann said. "We'll be—" She stopped, thinking about her father and unable to say the last word. But she wasn't going to leave her sister here to die, trapped by some monster that nobody knew. When Tom Adams came . . .

But suppose he—suppose the same thing that had happened to her father . . . "Oh God!" she said aloud.

Steps sounded on the front porch, in the hall. She sat there, mouth half open, face bloodless and drawn as the men came into the room. There was Bob Wilson, his round, old face full of fear and determination and sorrow. The sleepless lines in Larkins' sallow face were deeper than ever.

And then Sam Mason came into the room and Marie went to him quickly. Mason was a short, heavily built and dark-haired man. He had a full, pleasant face that was drawn now with deep lines about the mouth and eyes. His nose seemed swollen and red and there were red lines in the whites of his eyes. He wavered slightly as he walked, and the odor of liquor came into the room with him. He was carrying a folding stretcher and Ann thought dully that all his assistants must have fled the town, leaving the terrible work of the last few days to him alone.

Dully through the mist of pain and grief, Ann heard Mason ask if the body should be buried or changed to ashes in the crematory. He framed the question so that it favored cremation, and when Marie turned toward her, Ann nodded dully. She thought it was odd that so small a town should have a crematory. It hadn't before . . .

Wilson crossed the room, his head twisted slightly to one side. His thin white hands reached out, caught the hands of Ann and her sister. Ann heard the old man's cracked, kindly voice and the sound was comforting though she was too dazed to heed the words. She kept her face turned from the thing on the floor, not wanting to see her father's body removed.

And then, without warning, laughter struck like a foul knife at Ann's eardrums, jarred at her brain!

For a moment she could not move, but sat frozen in terror, cold sweat oozing from her body, muscles jerking but helpless to answer the call of her brain. Then her head moved, slowly. Even before her eyes reached the window she knew what she was going to see. Every sound inside the room except the laughter had died; even the ticking of the clock, it seemed to Ann, had ceased and there was no movement in all the world but the slow turning of her head and no sound but the horrible, cackling laughter.

The same laughter she had heard after the wreck.

Her eyes found the window. Beyond it she saw the hideous face, leering at her. Black straggly hair hung over a narrow forehead. Close-set eyes glared madly, and below them was a twisted red mouth. She had seen such a face once before. She had been a child, squirrel hunting with her father, and—

Dorothy Harkins screamed shrilly.

Behind her Ben Larkin's voice boomed, "It's Lem Prune!" Larkin's shoes banged as he raced down the hall toward the front door and Sam Mason's steps beat an unsteady chorus.

The man beyond the window was standing with his head flung back, mouth open, laughing the wild, maniacal laughter of the insane. The sound flung high, clicked short. The face seemed to fade back into the darkness of the night—and vanish.

In the stillness that followed Edith's voice sounded loud. "You'll leave, Ann. You and Dorothy and Marie. You'll die— you'll *have* to die if you stay here."

Wilson said, "I—I think she's right. The three of you take my car tonight and drive to York. I'll take care of Edith." He tried to smile, but his thin lips quivered. "I bounced her on my knee twenty years ago; so I ought to be able to look after her now."

Ann hesitated. Marie and Dorothy Harkins watched her. Their lives, her life, might depend on what she said. Then she saw the bloody body of her father stretched on the floor. She turned to the old banker.

"No. I'm going to stay with Edith. Father—" Her voice caught. "Father wouldn't have left, and I'm going to stay, find out . . ." Her voice trailed off and she swallowed hard. "Let Marie and Dorothy take the car," she said. "No need we should all stay."

Marie said flatly, "If you stay, I'm staying."

Ann could hear the quaver in Dorothy's voice though the girl fought to keep it steady. "After all these years with you, if you think I'm going to run away when you're in trouble . . ." She began to sob, and Ann heard the clip of her heels as she turned away.

From outside the window came the sound of voices. Three minutes later Mason and Larkin came back into the room. "We couldn't find him," Mason said.

The town marshal's voice was gaunt. "By God! I'll get him if I have to chase him through—" He glanced at the girls, caught himself and said—"through hell and high water."

It was ten minutes after eleven. The three men had all promised to come by again early in the morning. Dorothy and Marie were sleeping in the next room. Ann, her silk pajamas molding themselves around the soft, full curves of her body, stood straight and slim, looking down at her invalid sister. She felt cold and hollow and sick with grief. There was fear also, a gnawing and unmentionable fear of this thing that struck without warning and that left in its wake no track but death. She tried to shrug off the fear and leaning down kissed her sister's thin, pale lips.

Straightening, she cut off the light. Soft moonlight glimmered through the screened window to touch on Edith's bed. Her own bed was a white blur farther back in the shadows. She went to it, eased her slim body under the covers. Beneath the pillow she could feel the lump formed by the tiny automatic Tom had given her a year ago.

The soft ticking of the clock filled the room with a murmuring current of sound. She thought of her father, as he had been five years ago. Kind, smiling, understanding . . . A sob choked in her throat.

There was a low wind blowing. She could hear it in the sweetgum tree outside and in the flutter of the curtains at the window. Once, years ago, she had climbed that tree and couldn't get down. Her father . . . she rolled over, buried her face in the pillow and began to cry quietly.

The covers quivered over her body, but gradually their motion ceased. Ann's breathing became more regular, less labored. The clock on the dresser kept beating out its little double-noted tune. The three-quarters moon was swinging downward and the light slid from Edith's bed to huddle in a milky pool near the screened window.

Somewhere, off toward Crazy Man's Swamp, an owl hooted. On the outskirts of the village a dog began to bay at the moon . . .

Ann realized suddenly that she was wide awake. She was lying on her side, her eyes straining open, staring into darkness. There was the chanting of the clock's endless ticking and her eyes, moving slowly, fearfully, found its face. The radium dial showed spectral in the darkness.

It was exactly midnight.

As suddenly as she had awakened Ann knew that she was afraid, horribly afraid. There was no sound except the ticking of the clock, but there was *feeling*. In an uncanny, inexplicable way Ann *felt* the eyes staring into the room before she turned her head, before she heard the tearing sound against the window-sill.

Near the edge of the village the dog began to howl again, and in that moment of bone-chilling terror, when she lay stiff and unable to move, she remembered the stories that Negroes told of a dog howling at the moon. A sign of death.

The tearing sound came from the window-sill again, a bare whisper of noise, yet in the stillness she heard it. She was turning her head when she heard Edith's breathing. It was a harsh, catchy sound.

The girl was awake, and frightened.

Ann's eyes found the window as her right hand started groping toward the pillow and the small automatic beneath it. Then her hand jerked, her body turned to ice, a sob burst in her throat.

In the pool of moonlight beyond the open window was a man. His face was slightly turned, twisted sideways in an awkward position when Ann first saw him. He was sliding his hand and the long knife which it held through a hole cut in the screen. And less than two feet from the window, unable to move on her bed, was Edith Meadows.

As the sob burst involuntarily from Ann's throat the man jerked his head about, stared into the darkness of the room. Ann saw his face then. It was full, square, with deep lines about the eyes and mouth. The nose was large, swollen.

In that first shocked moment Ann could not remember where she had seen this face before . . . Then she knew that it was Dr. McGregor, the man who had disappeared. Yet it wasn't his face—or it was changed.

Breath whistled from her nostrils. McGregor and Sam Mason had always looked alike . . .

CHAPTER THREE

MADMEN PLAY

ANN'S HAND FLASHED UNDER THE PILLOW, came out holding the automatic. She saw the man beyond the window swing the knife high. Her finger tightened on the trigger and the little gun made a blasting sound.

The man leaped backward, jerked his hand out through the screen. Ann knew she had missed. Tom had always joked about her shooting.

She flung back the cover, struck the floor with her bare feet. Twisting around her sister's bed, she reached the window. Dark in the moonlight, a man was racing across the lawn toward the distant, serrated wall of trees that marked Crazy Man's Swamp.

She stabbed the gun through the hole in the screen, fired twice. The man kept running. There was a cornfield beyond the lawn. The man raced into the corn and vanished.

"What—what's happened?" It was Marie crying frantically from the next room.

Ann did not answer. She was down on her knees beside her sister's bed, whispering, terrified, "Edith, Edith! Are you all right?"

Edith Meadows' eyes were wide, almost glazed. Her lips were parted and her breathing harsh. After a moment she said, "Yes. I— he frightened me, but I'm all right."

The door of the room swung open and against the light from the other room Ann saw Marie and Dorothy Harkins framed in the sill, holding tightly to each other. "Nobody's hurt," Ann said. "Come on in." She heard Edith's breathing under the sound of her words and a wild idea flashed in her mind. Ann said huskily, "Edith—you saw the man before I did. Why didn't you scream?"

Edith Meadows turned her head away. There were tears on her cheeks. Ann could scarcely speak when she asked, "You—you wanted him to kill you?"

Edith whispered, "I thought then you would leave, save yourself. I'm going to die anyway."

"Oh God!" Ann dropped on the bed beside her sister, arms holding her tight.

Marie and Dorothy had come close to the bed. Without warning Dorothy cried, "Look! Look!" She jabbed a finger toward the window.

Ann came to her feet, spun to face the window, still gripping the automatic. At first she saw nothing but the empty window, the torn screen with the moonlight white beyond. "Look!" Dorothy cried again. "Near the corn!"

A man was racing across the lawn toward the house. He was squat, heavy set, and carried something big in his hand. The thing seemed heavy, and he wavered a bit as he sprinted.

Ann pulled up the gun, waiting, her heart hammering high in her throat, fear shaking at the muscles of her arm. She mustn't miss this time! The man came running head on. Ann's finger began to tighten about the trigger.

Something struck at the *gun,* knocking it to one side. Ann swung, saw that Marie was gripping her wrist. She cried, "Don't! Don't! That's Sam!"

The man had swerved and was running toward the front of the house. Marie threw up the screen, called, "Sam! This way."

Sam Mason jerked to a halt, spun and came back to the window. He was carrying a gun in his right hand, a gallon jug in his left. He asked between heavy, panting breaths, "What's happened? I heard—shots. Came running."

Ann explained, but as she talked she stared into the face of Sam Mason. It wasn't the same face which had showed in the window, but there was a resemblance. It must have been McGregor, she thought. She turned to Edith. "Did you know who it was?" she asked.

The girl on the bed hesitated. "It—it looked like Dr. McGregor. But there was something that didn't look like him. I reckon it was, though. I was too frightened to see clearly."

Mason said, "I been down in the swamp getting a little liquor. They're still bootlegging in this state you know, Ann. I—I need quite a bit to keep going like I have been these—"

Ann thought of her father and her teeth closed on her lower lip. Mason saw her and clipped his words short. He stood there, spraddle-legged, holding the jug and gun. His broad face turned slowly to look squarely into Marie's eyes as she leaned across the window-sill toward hint. He said, "I'll be up all night, and'll come by here every now and then . . . make sure there's no more trouble.

But tomorrow we're leaving here, you and I. There's no need that everybody should be killed . . ."

He turned on his heel and went toward the front of the house.

Dr. Thomas Adams sent his big coupe bounding over the narrow, bumpy road. His headlights spotted dark mud-holes, a wagon-track, and farther ahead where the lights widened they touched on dark trees parked close on either side. Giant oak and cypress towering overhead made the road a narrow chasm of blackness. A myriad lightning bugs glimmered white and gold, vanishing and reappearing among the trees. Far off in the swamp a bullfrog hoarsed and another answered in basso. Somewhere an owl hooted.

Adams' wide, pleasant mouth was pulled hard across white teeth. His wide-set brown eyes, looking oddly dark under his blond hair, kept steady on the road ahead. His long, slender surgeon's fingers held the wheel easily despite the pull of the mud-holes, the jerk of the ruts.

He had been driving all day and the muscles in his back and shoulders ached. Now, within thirty miles of Ann Meadows' home, he'd lost his way, got on this confounded swamp track. It was just a little after midnight now. He'd be seeing Ann soon, find out what she meant by that note. Thinking of the girl and her copper-colored hair, he smiled. Lord! He loved that woman.

Ahead of him a light wavered dully, like a fire built near the road. Then he saw another beyond the first. There was an opening in the trees, and through it he saw figures moving about the fires. Whoever it was, he'd stop, find out how far it was to Livingston and if this mud track went there . . .

He was within a hundred yards of the fires when he saw a number of small wooden shacks built back from the road on a high knoll in the swamp. "Well, I'll be damned," he said aloud. Why would anybody want to live out here? Perhaps these were the persons Ann had told him about once. Half-breeds, half-wits or something. He'd like to see these people. A worthwhile psychology study. If they had any white blood it was a wonder malaria hadn't killed them.

Then he heard the chanting. It came through the night, drowning the low song of his motor, drowning the croak of the bullfrogs. Several fires burned in the small yards before the shacks and about one of the fires a crowd was gathered. They were chanting, a weird, eerie, singsong cry that rose and fell like the chirping of crickets. But in it there was one note, hideous, continuous, filling the whole chant to overflowing, throbbing.

The horrible, age-old sound of unreasoning fear.

Dr. Adams stopped his car and got out. The houses were more than a hundred feet away, and every person in the group had his back to the road. Men, women, children, clustering about something in one thick, terrified knot.

Adams reached back, took the heavy Colt automatic from the pocket of the car. Foolish to think that he might need it—yet there was something about that chant, something about those persons. He hesitated, wondering if he should drive on without asking the way. But they must be the inbred half-wits and he wanted a close look at them. Not often would a doctor find people like these. He started picking his way toward the group.

It must have been a person on the far side who saw Adams. He was within thirty feet when there was one high, shrill cry, a word he did not understand. The whole group spun like puppets on a string and he stopped dead in his tracks, staring into faces the like of which he had never seen before.

His first impression was that he had wandered into another Jukes or Kallikak family, one of the groups that psychologists study to prove how insanity and feeble-mindedness may be inherited. But there was more than feeble-mindedness in the snarling, half savage faces which he saw. There was lust, and hate, and a primitive, unnamable fear. The firelight blazed clear on the black hair, and close-set eyes of one of the men and Adams noted the little muscle jerking under the right eye, the way the bony hands kept twitching. A dope addict. And in the same moment he wondered how these poverty-stricken people got dope. Perhaps something they manufactured from swamp herbs. He sniffed. "Smells like an autopsy room," he thought.

Adams was surprised at the harshness of his voice when he asked, "Can you tell me how far to Livingston? I got lost and—" The words clogged in his throat and he went back a half step as he saw the thing on the ground beyond the fringe of men and women.

He checked himself, went forward at a half run. "I'm a doctor," he said, pushing one of the men out of the way.

But there was no need to kneel beside the man on the ground. One glimpse showed him the fellow was dead, had been for more than a week. He lay sprawled beside the fire, face up. And his half decayed face was still marked with purplish, coagulated blood as though he had died of a hemorrhage. His hands were bloody, fingers bent clawlike, and his chest had a flat, deflated look as though some gigantic arms had crushed his ribs. The body was smeared with blood and dirt, had evidently been dragged around the yard. From it arose a nauseous, sickening stench.

Adams looked up and saw that half the crowd had vanished like shadows. There had been no sound and yet only half a dozen men remained. One of them was twitching nervously at his trouser top and Adams saw the gleam of a bone-handled knife.

"What happened to this fellow?" Adams asked.

The men were silent, some of them backing away, the others sidling closer. They were beginning to circle him and he took one long step toward the road. One of the men said, "He . . . he's dead."

The doctor's head jerked, stopped. No need to get angry. The man was only a half-wit and death would mean nothing to him. Adams turned toward another, repeated his question. The man stared back at him, sullenly, blankly.

Adams looked at the body on the ground again. Judging by what was left of his clothes the fellow had not been one of these morons. Perhaps he had been murdered. It would do little good to report to the police in the next town. By that time these idiots might have hidden the body, destroyed it altogether. Best to take it with him he decided.

He raised his eyes to one of the men, said, "I'm a doctor and I'm taking this body with me." He bent broad shoulders, clutched the collar of the dead man's coat.

The little group broke like a sudden clap of thunder. Adams heard a man snarl, spun as two of them launched at him. A knife gleamed red in the firelight Adams leaped away from the man with the knife, squarely into the other. His left fist jarred on the man's chin, flinging him backwards. His right hand came from his coat pocket, holding the automatic.

A body crashed into the middle of his back, driving him forward, straight down at the fire. He twisted sharply to his right, caught one sucking breath as the fire rushed up at him, as he struck at the very edge of it. He heard the crackling of the wood and flame, saw red sparks leap and whirl. The man who had dived against him had fallen squarely into the fire!

With a furious, howling shriek the man leaped to his feet, smoke and flame streaming from his ragged clothes. Like a bull of Hannibal, trailing fire he tore through the group, hurling them right and left. An odor of burning flesh and cloth hung thick in the air behind him.

During the moment when the other half-breeds stared spellbound at their burning fellow, Tom Adams rolled away from the fire and came to his feet holding the automatic. The muzzle centered on the five men still clustered near the body.

"Listen, damn you . . ." he said harshly. "I'm taking this dead man away with me. To the police."

Two of the men began to back away. Two stood hesitantly, mouths open, faces blank, dazed. The other made a whimpering, insane noise in his throat, took one quick step forward and dived straight at the automatic.

Tom Adams went back a step before the madman's rush. His finger was tense about the trigger, but he did not pull. He wasn't the police and to shoot a man, even a crazy man, was murder. The idiot was almost on him when he swung the gun out to the right, then hard against the half-wit's temple. But he had struck too late and the man's shoulder crashed into his knees, pitching him forward.

Like a pack of hounds the others came at him, snarling, crying, shouting. Knives glowed red and yellow in the firelight.

Adams saw a hand swing up, then down. A knife-blade plunged at him. He swung his gun, heard the clang of steel on steel. Fire ripped across the flesh of his left arm. He lashed out with his feet, felt them thud hard against shinbones. Then three men crashed down and he was buried under a wave of bodies.

A gun roared twice, close at hand. One of the men above Adams seemed to jump straight into the air. A voice roared, "Goddam it! Stand up and then don't move!" There was the crack of a fist on bone.

Adams flung the last man from him, rolled to his knees, stared squarely into the black muzzle of a .45 revolver and into the sallow, lined face of the man behind it. "Drop yore gun," the man said.

Adams let the gun slide from his fingers, got slowly to his feet. The moron he had hit with his automatic, and another, lay unconscious. The others stood cowering in the firelight

The man with the gun turned his slow glance from Adams to the body on the ground. Abruptly he stiffened. His sallow face drained of blood, leaving the dark circles under his eyes like lines painted on a mask.

"Great God!" he said aloud. "That's old John Perkins! He was burned in the crematory a week ago!"

CHAPTER FOUR

LEM PRUNE CALLS

THE MOON HAD GONE DOWN beyond the dark line of trees that marked the edge of Crazy Man's Swamp, and the room where Ann Meadows and her invalid sister slept was a pool of black shadows. With the approach of dawn the wind had freshened and grown cool. It rustled the drying leaves of the sweet-gum, jarred gently against the window which Ann had closed against a return of the midnight visitor.

In the room where the sisters slept the sound of a dog howling was muted by the closed windows. On the dresser the small alarm-clock ticked its monotonous song. The breathing of the girls was hushed, slow. The bed made a tiny, creaking sound as Ann turned slightly.

Through the silence came noise marching in heavy, ominous beats. *Boom. Boom. Boom.* The sound struck through the thin mist of sleep which held the girls, brought Ann erect and quivering in her bed, snapped open the pale eyelids of her sister. In the next room Dorothy Harkins made a short, frightened cry.

Boom. Boom. Boom.

Ann whispered, "It's somebody at the door."

Lights snapped on in the next room and she saw Dorothy and Marie coming toward her. "Who is it?" they asked.

Ann reached up, turned on the light over her bed. Edith lay with her pale face turned toward Ann, her large dark eyes open and staring. To comfort her sister Ann said with a diffidence she didn't feel, "How do I know who it is? I'll go see."

Boom. Boom. Boom. Heavy and unhurried, the sound struck through the house again,

"Take your gun," Edith whispered.

Ann slid from the bed, stuck her feet into a pair of purple mules. Reaching under the pillow she pulled out the small gun and turned toward the hall. Her slippers made clacking sounds in the stillness.

In the hall Ann turned on the light. It was probably that drunken undertaker, she thought, wanting to make certain they were all right and frightening them to death in doing it. But she mustn't be afraid of a knocking at the door. This was no time to be pulling any Lady Macbeth stuff.

She reached the front door and without unlocking it called out, "Who is it?" There was something tight and hard in her breast

"Ben Larkin, ma'am. The marshal."

Some of the fright went out of her at the sound of the voice. But why . . .? "Oh, all right, Ben," she said, and turned the key in the lock.

The light from the house spilled out in a bright rectangle across the porch. There were two men, one back near the shadows, one just outside the door. She saw the blond hair, the lean, good-natured face.

"Oh, Tom!" The tight thing in her breast broke and the words leaped from her lips. With them she threw herself into the man's arms. "I'm so glad. So glad!"

Tom Adams gently pushed her head from his chest, leaned down and kissed her. She could feel his hand cool against the flesh of her back, the roughness of his coat against the tops of her breasts. For the first time she remembered that she was wearing only a pair of silk pajamas. But she didn't care. It was good to have Tom here at last, someone on whose shoulder she could cry, someone to share the responsibility with her.

With his arm still around her, Adams turned toward the man on the porch. "Well, Larkins," he smiled, "you'll believe now that I'm Miss Meadows' fiancé?" Ann liked the way he smiled, the bare glimpse of even white teeth showing below his full upper lip.

Larkin said, "Yes sir. I—"

Ann looked up to the lean, sallow-laced marshal. "Why Ben," she said. "What—?"

Larkin grinned a taut, nervous smile. "Well ma'am, I told you I'd catch that prowlin' half-breed Lem Prune, the one we seen lookin' in yore window. So I went out to Swamp Town and I found Mr. Adams—I mean Dr. Adams." He tried to smile again but there was no humor in the faded, heavy-lidded eyes. "He was havin' a fight with a bunch of them half-breeds, and—well . . . I didn't know who he was, and . . ."

Adams said, "Oh forget it. I don't blame you for picking me up. I owe you a lot of gratitude. They'd probably have killed me if you hadn't come."

Ann could feel the hard thing in her breast growing again. The terrible strain. The weird menace. This thing that killed and left no track. Had she gotten Tom into it? Was he too going to be murdered like her father? Wasn't there anything . . .? She said aloud, "Oh God! No! No!"

The doctor spun to face her. "What do you mean, Ann? What's the trouble?"

Ann buried her face against his chest. "Nothing," she whispered. "But you'll leave town—now? Get in your car *now.* You can't stay here. *You mustn't.*"

He pushed her away from him, looked hard into her face. "Keep quiet," he said harshly. "You know I'm not going to leave you now. I've got to stick—as your doctor," he added smiling.

Larkin shifted restlessly in the light. He looked down at his feet and when he raised his face it was grayer than ever.

"At that town," he said, "was old John Perkins. He was one of the first to die. Sam Mason buried him in the new crematory a week ago."

Adams kept his arm about Ann, turned his head towards Larkin. "I suggest, Marshal, that you get some sleep. That's professional advice. You need it. You look as if you hadn't slept in two weeks and your nerves are going to crack if you don't get some rest."

Strength came into Larkin's drawn face, He said, "Thanks, Doc. But I'm the marshal here and long as this stuff is goin' on I ain't got time for sleep." He turned and stalked across the porch into darkness.

For a moment Ann stood there, her head close against Adam's chest, feeling his hand against her back, the pressure of his coat against her breasts. She said, "Come on, Tom. You've got to meet my sisters, and Dorothy."

"At this time of the night?"

"We—we haven't slept much. They're awake now."

Adams' arm tightened about her shoulders. "You poor kid," he said. "Larkin told me."

Morning sunlight lay with the warm gold of autumn along the dusty street. Tom Adams, up for an early walk after a sleepless night, turned left, toward what appeared to be the center of the little village. The houses on both sides of the street were closed, shutters pulled tight. The day was usually well started in towns this size by eight o'clock, but now there was no sight of human life in Livingston. On one of the porches a dog was standing, his head cocked to one side, puzzled. Off to the right an unmilked cow mooed in pain.

After two blocks Adams reached the six stores of the village. Their doors were closed. Beyond them was what appeared to be a small bank. The doctor went toward it, stopped in surprise.

The bank doors were wide open, and from the inside came the sound of voices. He reached the bank, went in. Morning sunlight flooded through the open door. Inside were two men. One was a cherubic-faced old man with white hair and kindly blue eyes. In those eyes now was a worried, frightened look as he turned toward Adams.

The other was a squat, powerfully built man with a red nose and red lines spider-webbed in his eyes. He had evidently had a great deal of liquor and little sleep. He raised a pint bottle toward Adams as he came in, said, "Welcome to the Village of the Dead, stranger. It's a great town for undertakers."

Adams introduced himself. Both men had heard of him from the Meadows. "Ann told me last night you were coming," the banker said.

Adams looked at the old man, said, "It seems funny to see your bank open when nothing else in town is."

Mason took a pull from his bottle, offered it to Adams. "Oh yes, something else is," he said. "My undertaking shop. I'm doing a damn sight more work than the bank."

Adams said nothing but his mind was racing. Ann had told him of Dr. McGregor looking into her window last night, told him of the doctor's resemblance to Mason. He wanted to recognize Mc-Gregor if he saw him.

Wilson was saying slowly, "You are Miss Ann's fiancé and should have some influence with her. Somebody tried to kill her sister Edith last night. Maybe he would have killed all the others. But I wish you'd get the girls to leave. If Edith can't be moved, I'd be glad to look after her. But the others . . . There's no need . . ." He paused, half embarrassed.

"But why—what's back of this?" Adams asked. "What can anybody gain by it?"

The banker shook his white head, said miserably, "I don't know."

"I'll see that the girls leave," Adams said. "'But I'm going to stay here with Edith. I examined her last night—to move her now would kill her. The recent shocks have weakened her. She needs a doctor, but—I'll see that the others leave."

He went out then, strode back toward the Meadows home.

Some time later, Adams was forced to admit to himself that the task of convincing the Meadows girls was more difficult than he had expected. Ann wanted the others to go, but refused to leave Edith herself. Marie would not go without Ann.

In the meantime, while he had been away, Dorothy Harkins had gone out to find the undertaker or the banker, to get one of them to milk a cow before lunch. Hours had passed now and the girl had not returned. Tension was growing in the house. The strain showed in the face of every person; it crept into the very atmosphere, like a bow stretching until it must break.

Adams had searched the town for Dorothy. There was no sign of her. The marshal too had disappeared. Neither Wilson nor Mason had seen the girl.

Now Adams sat facing the three sisters, taking up the old argument again. Edith joined with him. Her voice was low but steady. "Dorothy's gone, disappeared," she said. "She wouldn't run away. The thing has her. It'll get you all if you stay. I wish—"

She stopped when the sound of knocking on the back door jarred through the room.

Adams stood up. "I'll see who it is," he said, and went out of the room.

He pushed open the back door, and stopped. His right hand jumped toward his coat pocket. His breath made a whistling sound through his teeth as he looked into the evil, half-witted face of the man before him. For a moment he thought it was one of the group he had seen last night, then knew differently. But it was the face that Ann had described to him—that of Lem Prune, the man for whom Larkin was searching.

The idiot was babbling in a broken, half-Indian dialect. "You come, come with me." He stabbed out nervous fingers, plucked at Adams' coat. The doctor noted the twitching of the man's mouth and hands. Another dope addict.

"You come. You come," Prune kept saying. He began to tug on Adams' coat.

Adams said, "All right." If he could keep this man in sight, he could turn him over to the town marshal. Perhaps then the mystery behind these horrors would be cleared. The whole thing sounded mad, insane. He had known insane men to be monstrously clever in ways. And yet . . .

The idiot kept saying, "You come. Come with me." He had Adams by the hand now, leading him across the wide back yard, past the garage. There was a rickety fence separating this lot and the yard of the deserted house which faced the only other street in the small town. They climbed the fence and went toward the empty house.

The idiot went straight ahead, bent on reaching some unknown point. He kept pulling on the doctor's hand, hurrying him. Adams could feel his heart hammering under his ribs. There was something satanic, something monstrous about the half-wit and about the way he drove forward, head lowered, shoulders swaying. Adams began to hold back, to look about him nervously. "Where are we going?" he asked.

"You come," Prune said. They had reached the back of the house and began to walk beside it toward the front. They were a step short of the front corner when Prune said again, "You come." He turned suddenly, caught Adams' hand in both of his, and jerked.

The doctor was snatched forward, almost off his feet. "What the hell?" he snapped.

From behind the corner of the house a dark figure surged forward abruptly. Adams, spinning, caught one glimpse of a falling hand, a blackjack, a square, masklike face with a large nose. He flung himself sideways, jerking the gun from his pocket. In the split instant the name, "Dr. McGregor," burst in his brain. Then the blackjack landed.

The face was wiped out by a blanket of darkness. Dully Adams felt the thud of his body striking the ground . . .

CHAPTER FIVE

OUT OF THE SWAMP

THROUGH A FIERCELY REVOLVING SEA of blackness Tom Adams felt his body go swinging. Then after a while it began to move more slowly, and in the distance red and white lights began to glitter. Even before he was completely conscious his professional brain told him that he was coming out from under the influence of chloroform.

The red died out of the glittering lights and the white began to grow steady, driving away the darkness. He felt a little sick at his stomach and once he thought he was going to vomit After a time he began to see things around him, and to hear.

He was in a small, shack-like room, bare of furniture. He lay flat on the floor, hands tied behind him, ankles bound together. His gun, of course, was gone. There was one small, paneless window in the room and through it he could see sunlight and the tops of pine and cypress trees. One of the planks on the sill had been torn loose at one end and hung swaying. He decided he must be somewhere in the swamp.

Lem Prune was sitting on the floor near Adams' feet. His red mouth was curled in an ugly smile and when he saw that the doctor's eyes were open he began to laugh. He leaned toward Adams, thrusting his face within inches of the doctor's—and Adams could smell the sweet, sickly odor of dope.

"You're goin' to die. Die, die, die." Prune began to chant the word, laughing constantly.

As Adams' brain cleared fear began to take hold of his body. Who was the man who had knocked him on the head? The missing doctor? And why had he done it? Did he mean to . . . He remembered the way the week-old corpse had looked with blood still smeared on its rotting features. Sickness struck at him, adding to the nausea of the chloroform.

The idiot began to laugh more loudly.

"You're goin' to die," he chanted. "You're goin' to burn, burn, burn."

Adams rolled over, struggled to a halt sitting position. Sweat was breaking out on his forehead and there was a cold lump in his chest. "Burn?" he husked.

The idiot chanted, "Burn. You're goin' to burn." As he talked his mouth kept twitching and he rocked back and forth, eyes half closed. The dope had fingers deep in his system, Adams noted, but was beginning to wear off. In another hour, unless he got more, there was little telling what the man might do. Adams had seen dope addicts go completely insane. Some sat and cried like babies. He had seen one stamp the life from another with his feet.

Adams forced his voice to be steady. "How am I going to be burned? Why?"

The idiot ran a tongue over his dirty lips, said, "He'll burn you. Ashes. Nothin' but ashes. That's what you'll be." He began to laugh again.

Adams felt the muscles jerk along his back. "He? Who's he?"

The idiot kept laughing.

For a moment Adams lay there, breathing harshly through clenched teeth. How could he be burned into ashes, or was that merely the gibberish of a madman? In a crematorium . . . But why had he been brought here? To wait until dark so that he could be slipped into the funeral home?

Adams flung the thought from his mind. The thing to do now was to get free. Questioning Prune gained nothing. Evidently the madman did not intend to tell who his master was, if he himself knew. The missing doctor? How otherwise did these people who couldn't buy food get dope?

Tom Adams began to try his bonds, straining slowly against them and keeping his eyes on Prune. The ropes held firm, biting into his wrists when he tugged. He felt sick in his chest, hopeless. He'd never pull loose from these things. The twitching of Prune's mouth was growing and the swaying of his body became broken, jerky. He'd have to have another shot soon, the doctor knew . . .

Adams looked out of the window again. The sun was white and gold on the tree-tops, but around the window were heavy shadows. It must be late afternoon. Whoever was holding him here would probably return soon after dark. He had to get free now, or . . . His teeth made a grating sound as he clenched them, braced himself and strained at the ropes. Lem Prune snarled and lunged forward.

His open right hand struck Adams' face with a sound like gunfire, popping the doctor's head to one side. "Loose, huh? Loose!" Prune shrilled.

The half-wit's right hand drove to his belt on the left side, came back holding a big, bone-handled knife. The point stabbed at Adams' side in a rough gesture, went through the coat and into flesh. Adams rolled away, feeling a slow trickle of blood along his ribs.

Prune squatted, staring at Adams with squinted, fiery eyes. The doctor lay, breathing heavily, mind racing, fear cold along his back. It would be death to keep trying to free himself. If the half-wit stabbed that hard in warning he would kill at the next effort. And the dope was dying out of the man, leaving him angry, insane, and with a knife in his hand.

Adams swallowed twice at the hard lump in his throat. He said, keeping his voice steady, "You want more dope? Powder?" He sniffed, as if taking the white opiate.

Prune's body jerked taut. His eyes were wide and red and his mouth hung open. He grunted, "Huh? Huh?"

"Dope," Adams said, and sniffed again. "I'm a doctor. I've got plenty."

The red eyes flamed. The maniac began to edge toward him, still squatting, his left hand touching the floor, right hand holding the knife. "Gimme," he whined. "I want it. Gimme."

"Not here," Adams said. "I haven't got it here. Turn me loose and I'll get it." He jerked at his wrists, nodded toward his ankles.

The sagging mouth of the maniac drew tight. Lust, fury and wild desire were in the red eyes. "Now," he said. "Gimme now." His right wrist was hooked, muscles hard. The blade of the knife touched the floor as he moved, making a low scraping sound.

Adams knew that he had made the wrong attempt. The idiot would never believe he didn't have the dope with him. Instead of turning him loose, the madman would kill him while he was tied, then try to find the powder on him.

Sweat was cracking from his body. His lungs ached and his eyes bulged as he watched the madman edge toward him. Adams tried once more, but the muscles of his throat all but choked back his voice. "It's not here. Turn me loose and I'll go get it."

Lem Prune's voice had changed from a whine to a snarl. "No," he said. "I take it now." The forearm began to bend, the knife to rise from the floor. He was squatting now, his knees almost against Adams' hips.

The doctor sucked one long breath through hard lips. There was just one chance. A poor one, but a chance . . . "All right," he said. "It's in my pocket, This one . . ." He jerked his head toward the side away from the idiot. "Reach in and get it."

Prune grinned. He was panting like a dog and his eyes were a-squint again. He leaned forward, reaching out with his left hand across the doctor's body. His shoulders, then his waist, were over Adams as his hand curved toward the pocket.

Tom Adams flung his back against the floor, hard. Both knees came up with a rush. There was a thudding sound and Prune's breath wheezed from his mouth as the knees drove deep into his groin. The blow lifted him from the floor, flung him over on his back. The knife skidded harshly across the room. Prune's breath was an agonized gasp.

Adams rolled furiously to his knees, but his hands were bound behind him and he went over on his head. He swirled, pivoted on his left hip while his eyes flashed about the room for the knife. He saw it, six feet to the rights wriggled to his knees and dived. He heard his trousers rip on the jagged floor, felt the skin tear from his knees, but the knife was close by. He squirmed, twisting his back to the blade, caught it up with his hands.

Prune was lying balled in a knot ten feet away, groaning, his hands wrapped around his belly. But even as Adams fumbled with the knife the half-breed began to straighten his body, twisting until he faced the doctor. Then the pain in his face gave way to an immense and terrible rage. Whimpering, he lunged to his feet, staggered and clutched at his belly again.

Adams had twisted his wrists until the bones seemed ready to snap. The blade of the knife was against the ropes, but when he tried to work it back and forth he could not keep the steel pressed down. Prune was erect now, glaring around the room. His eyes reached the window-sill where the plank hung loose at one end. He dived for it.

Adams could feel the rope giving now, twitching along his wrists as he sawed. The muscles in his arms ached, the bones in his hands seemed to be breaking. Sweat stood in cold beads all over his body. His eyes bulged from his head as he watched the maniac swing around, hands gripping the plank he had ripped from the window.

The madman took one step forward, swung the plank back. It made a swishing sound in the air. He held it there for one long moment, his red eyes glaring. Adams balanced himself on his knees, waiting. The hands clutching the knife were motionless-now. No time to saw at the ropes.

The board swung.

Adams flung himself backwards and to the right. Wind whipped his face and his eyes blinked as the heavy plank ripped past, less than an inch above his nose. He hit rolling, came to his knees. His wrists were arched furiously again, sawing at the ropes.

The swing had carried Prune off balance, spun him half around. He caught himself, turned back to face Adams. At the same moment the ropes around the doctor's wrists parted.

Prune flung the board up, whipped it down hard. Adams was off balance and his roll to the right was slow. He barely had time to jerk up his left shoulder before the blow landed.

It caught him full on the shoulder, bowling him over, smashing paralyzing pain through his left arm. But he clung to the knife with his right hand. He hit the floor on his right side, knees doubled under him. One sweep of the knife slashed the rope about his ankles.

Prune had swung back the board again, straight over his head now to smash it down on Adams' skull. He rocked back on his heels, balancing, muscles bulging in his arms. He started the board down, fast.

Adams was on his knees. He saw the board start, saw there was no time to dodge right or left. He went straight forward, under the sweeping plank.

His shoulder struck Prune's shins, knocking them from under him like ninepins. Both men came to the floor with a crash. The plank tore loose from Prune's hands. The idiot made a snarling sound, sprang half erect, then launched himself like a mad dog at Adams' throat.

For a man who, three years before, had been intercollegiate light heavyweight boxing champion, the rest was simple. Adams dropped the knife, brought up his right fist in a short uppercut. The blow cracked when it landed and it turned Lem Prune over backward. He hit the floor and lay still.

For ten seconds Adams stood breathing heavily. He took off his coat, examined his shoulder. It was a bad bruise, but nothing else. There was a welt across his biceps where a knife had grazed from the night before. The place on his ribs where Prune had pricked him in warning had already stopped bleeding. Adams grinned wryly. Close shaves, all of them. That luck couldn't hold out forever.

Taking off his tie and belt he bound Prune, gagged him with a handkerchief. He took the knife and stuck it under his trousers, stepped to the door of the hut and pushed it open.

The shack was on a heavily wooded knoll which sloped down to boggy swampland. Through the swamp a wagon-trail wound from knoll to knoll. A wagon and a pair of moth-eaten mules stood nearby. The trees shut out the direct rays of the sun, making semi-twilight in the place. Nearly sundown, Adams decided.

For three full minutes he stood there, thinking. After dark the person back of this whole foul business would probably return. If Adams stayed, he might capture the fellow, solve all the mysteries of who and why and how. But the man would probably be armed. He might bring more of these dope-eating half-wits with him. And Adams had only the bone-handled knife.

Ann Meadows, where was she all this time? With no one there to look after her, what might have happened? Adams sucked a deep breath through parted lips. It couldn't be far to the town. He should be able to make it, see that Ann was safe, and be back here before dark. He wondered if Dorothy Harkins had been found . . .

It was farther than he had thought.

At times his feet sank up to the ankles in bog that sucked at him, tired him with every step he took. There was still a slight pain in his head from the blow and his stomach was weak from the chloroform they had given him.

It took someone who knew his business to administer chloroform: too much would easily kill a man. Adams thought again of the missing doctor, grinned crookedly. Whoever had given him that crack on the head hadn't cared whether he was killed or not. It had been only a matter of a few hours anyway.

Muscles corded along Tom Adams' jaw and his chin pushed forward. He'd find what lay back of this now—and by God! he'd settle it. Even if he and Ann and her sisters were to escape from the thing now, they'd never be able to have peace and happiness while this mystery, this dread of the unknown, hung over them. It *had* to be settled, and, damn it! he meant to do the settling.

It was sundown when he finally came out of the swamp and saw the house-tops of the village half a mile away. His muscles ached with fatigue and his feet felt heavy. His eyes sagged from lack of sleep, but his lips were hard, his jaw thrust forward.

He returned to Ann Meadows' home by slipping across the deserted back street and up to the back door. He meant to leave again without seeing anyone but Ann. He didn't know the monster who had originated this reign of terror, and until he did know he trusted no one.

He went across the back porch quietly, moving on the balls of his feet. He tugged on the door, found it locked. The windows also were locked. He whistled the soft, three-noted whistle that Ann knew.

A moment later the door burst open and she had her arms around him. Her brown eyes were wide with relief. "Where have you been?" she cried softly.

He pulled her inside the kitchen, kissed her. He outlined briefly what had happened. "I'm going back there," he said, "and I don't want anybody to know I've been here."

"Mr. Bob Wilson is here now," she said. "We called him when you didn't come back because we were afraid. Oh, Tom!" She pulled him close to her again.

"I'll be all right," he said, and patted her shoulder reassuringly. He added, "If there's another gun in the house beside that little one I gave you, I'd like to borrow it."

"There's a twenty-two rifle upstairs, and a shotgun."

"Get me the rifle. It'll shoot more times and farther."

"All right." She paused. There was fear in her eyes when she said, "Tom, why do you suppose Dr. McGregor is doing this?"

"Are you sure it's McGregor?"

"I—I don't know. The man in the window last night looked like him. But—he looked like Mason, too, and it couldn't have been Sam. Didn't you say it was McGregor who struck you?"

Tom Adams shook his head. "No," he said. "I've never seen McGregor and I didn't get to see much of the fellow who bumped me. Just a glimpse. He looked like what you had told me of the doctor—but he looked like he had on make-up, or some disguise."

"His face did look . . . painted!" Her voice went slow, hesitant. "Do you suppose it might have been—Sam, made up to look like McGregor?" Then she shook her head, harshly. "No! It couldn't. Why would he do this?"

"Your father didn't like him?"

"No-o-o. But—" Her words cut short. A wild, throat-tearing shriek had sounded from the bedroom! A cry in which terror and despair and surprise conglomerated in one high, flat wail. There was the soft, rapid tattoo of bare feet in the hall.

Both Ann Meadows and Adams swung to face the kitchen door. With his left hand Adams pushed the girl behind him, while his right hand dug the knife from his trouser-top. He held it, waiting, eyes fastened on the door. His heart and lungs seemed suspended.

The sound of the feet came with a surging rush. The kitchen door burst open. There, framed in the long hallway, was Edith Meadows, who had not taken a step for five years!

CHAPTER SIX

TERROR KILLS

"OH, GOD!" ANN SOBBED.

The girl in the doorway started toward them. Her face was as white as porcelain, save for two vivid spots of red in her checks and the dark pools of her eyes. Her lips were open and all but transparent over her teeth. She whispered, terror shaking her voice, "Oh, I know. His head twists . . ." She swayed, caught herself.

Tom Adams leaped forward, dropping the knife to clatter on the floor. Before he reached her the girl said, "I know. It's—" The words choked in her throat. She pitched headlong.

Adams caught her, went down on his knees, holding her cradled in his right arm. He snapped at Ann, "Get my bag! Quick! The adrenalin!" His left hand went in the throat of the girl's lace nightgown, down to her small left breast. Before Ann returned with the bag he knew he had no use for it. The girl was dead.

Footsteps sounded in the hall. Adams looked up to see Wilson's white head showing above the auburn hair of Marie Meadows as both stared at him, wide eyed, open mouthed. Marie began suddenly to cry. She came forward, swaying, and dropped beside her sister. "Edith . . . Edith . . ." she whispered.

Adams lay the girl gently on the floor, stood up. There was a hard question in his eyes when he looked at the old banker. Wilson said huskily, "I was standing by the window, talking to both of them. Suddenly she looked past me and screamed."

"What was outside?"

"I don't know. I turned to her when she screamed, and then I saw her jump out of bed. It surprised me so that I followed her to the door without looking."

"Damn!" Adams said. He ducked, scooped the knife from the floor, turned and went out of the door on the run. There was nothing in the bade yard and he cut to the left, his tousled blond hair blowing as he sprinted.

There was a wide, empty lawn on this side, the tall sweet-gum tree just outside the bedroom window. A brown, autumn-tinged leaf swirled down from it as Adams raced toward the front of the house.

He went around the corner, running fast. And stopped. A squat, heavy-built man was staggering up the front steps. Adams' hand tightened on the knife and he leaped forward as he recognized Sam Mason.

The undertaker heard him, turned and stood swaying on the top step. His hand moved clumsily but quickly to his coat pocket, came out holding a gun. Amazement and surprise flashed on his face.

"Stay where you are," he said. The words were thick from liquor but the hand was steady on the gun.

Adams stopped. A knife wasn't much good against a gun, not at this range. His body was tensed forward, weight on his toes.

"You just come from around the side of the house?" he asked.

Mason didn't answer, but a puzzled look was growing on his face. "Who're you?" he said. "I meet you somewhere?"

Adams grinned crookedly. "At the bank this morning. I'm Ann Meadows' fiancé."

"Oh, yeah. My future brother-in-law, huh?" He put the gun back in his pocket, said apologetically, "I've been drinking pretty heavy these days. Lot of work for an undertaker, you know, and my memory's not so good."

Adams went toward him, the knife seemingly forgotten in his hand. "Did you come from around the corner of the house?" he asked again. "Or see anybody?"

The drunk said, "You."

Adams cursed under his breath. Was Mason the person Edith Meadows had seen outside the window? If not, who was it? Where had he gone? He couldn't have vanished . . . but if it wasn't Mason then he *had* vanished.

Adams took the undertaker by the arm, held him while he explained what had happened, watching his face at every word. Surprise, sorrow, a tinge of fear crossed the man's face. That was all. Acting? Perhaps . . . What could Mason or any man hope to gain by spreading wholesale murder and terror? . . . Inside the house again, Adams once more examined the dead girl. He had known cases before where a great nervous shock had cured paralysis, sometimes permanently. But in this case the shock and the exertion had been too great and had killed instead of cured. He stood up, went back into the bedroom where the others were gathered.

Mason was holding Marie Meadows by the wrist, saying, "You've got to leave now. I'm taking you to York. I'll come back then, and—" He stopped. Looking at Ann, he said, "You come with us if you want."

Ann hesitated. She saw Adams in the door and went toward him, hands out, her face a mask of grief. Near the window, Bob Wilson stood with his white head bowed. Two tears had slipped from his faded blue eyes.

Adams stood flat-footed, hands gripping each side of the door. His lips were thin, nostrils distended with heavy breathing. If Mason was the fiend behind this, Ann certainly wasn't driving away with him. If Mason were innocent, it would be best to have him take her to safety. Personally, he was staying and fighting this matter through to the end. There had to be a reason, and by God! he meant to find it.

Ann settled the matter for him. "I'm going to stay here," she said huskily, "until . . ."

Abruptly the thought came to Adams. If Mason were guilty, there might be evidence at his home—or more likely, at the funeral home. It was empty now. And while he'd be gone, it wasn't likely that Mason would try anything here, with three persons to watch him.

Adams said aloud, "I think I know where to find Dorothy Harkins. If you will all wait here a little while, I'll be back." To Ann he said, "Will you get me that rifle now?"

Ann held to him. "Where are you going . . .?"

Adams gently pulled free. "I'll be back," he said.

The Mason funeral home was an oblong, stucco building with the sedate, solid front of most funeral houses. A lighter-colored extension at the rear showed where the crematorium had recently been added.

The front door swung open at Adams' touch and he went in without pausing. He crossed the thick-carpeted reception room, the chapel where services were held. He was at the door of the long corridor leading to the offices and working rooms at the rear, when he heard the sound. It tied him motionless, head pushed forward and cocked to one side, listening. The butt of the rifle was tucked into his right armpit.

The sound came again. The rasp of a drawer being pulled open, a man's grunt of satisfaction.

Adams started forward, quietly. He kept the rifle at ready, finger on the trigger. The sound had come from the rear of the building, where the crematorium and the new offices were cut off by a curtain.

He pushed past the curtain, saw light spilling across the gloomy hallway from a doorway on his right. He heard papers rustle, the sound of footsteps. Adams kept close to the left side of the hall until he reached a point where he could see inside the room. It was the crematory room. On the left wall he could see the end of the plant, the square door through which the caskets might be shoved to the heat.

He took another step, saw a table and chair in the middle of the room. Against the far wall was a low, rubber-wheeled carrier for coffins. The man was evidently working near the door on the right, out of Adams' sight.

The doctor took one more step forward. It brought him full into the yellow rectangle of light.

Inside the room Ben Larkin, the town marshal, was bending over a small office-desk. The top was littered with papers and Larkin was shuffling through them awkwardly, his sallow, lined face held close. He did not see the man outside and in the quiet Adams could hear the rustle of the papers as Larkin moved them.

Adams lowered the rifle, took one step into the room, letting his heels thud. "Hello, Marshal," he said.

Larkin leaped like a frightened cat. His right hand dropped a long envelope, flashed to his hip, swung up the big forty-five. His shoulders swooped low; his lips parted.

"How the hell—?" There was a dazed, surprised look on his face that faded quickly. "Whatta you want?" he asked.

Adams hesitated. He was a stranger in this town and country folk were suspicious of strangers. And why was Larkin so surprised to see him? Had he believed him to be tied up in the swamp? Adams lied, "I saw you come over not so long ago and followed. I wanted to see you."

"Yeah?" Larkin said. "What about?"

"About these damn killings, this whole horrible mess." He began to pace the floor as though nervous, his eyes darting about. He wanted to see as much as he could.

"What about 'em?" Larkin asked. He tried to make the words sound harsh, but Adams caught the strain in the man's voice. His nerves were cracking. Born in the lower middle class, the constable had been raised on stories of Negro superstition, though as a white man, he denied their truth. Now a combination of eerie happenings, a lack of sleep, and a constant fear for his own life was breaking down the man's resistance. He'd go to pieces soon.

Adams was near the desk now. He stooped, carelessly picked up a sheet of paper from the floor. His eyes flicked over the page. The second sheet, evidently, of a government report. He saw the words, "oil on sandy land is—"

Larkin jumped forward, snatched the paper from Adams. His face was purple with anger. "Why the hell you lookin' at other folks' mail?" he snapped.

Adams' lips curled back and words rose to his throat, but he stopped them. If he angered Larkin now, it might cause trouble, serious trouble. And a new idea had come to him. Unless the missing doctor was the man back of all this killing and terror, the criminal would not return to the shack in the swamp. Every other person in the town had learned that Adams had escaped. But why not bring Lem Prune to the criminal, let him identify the man who gave him dope?

He said to Larkin, "I was just picking it up," and tossed the paper on the desk. "I think I'll go on back to the Meadows'." The rifle cradled under his arm, he went out. Larkin glared after him . . .

CHAPTER SEVEN

THE GIRL IN THE SWAMP

THE THREE-QUARTERS MOON had swung up into the sky, but a tinge of sunlight remained in the west. Tom Adams set out on a long-legged trot for the point where he had left Crazy Man's Swamp. As he ran, the last faint sunset glow died and darkness came out of the swamp to meet and mingle with the pale moonlight.

He pushed steadily through the swamp, flicking occasional bushes out of the way with the rifle butt. The knife stuck in his trousers handicapped his movements slightly and he shifted its position, kept going. Already the lightning-bugs were out in myriads, weaving webs of silver and gold light that twinkled and vanished.

When first he heard the voices ahead he thought it was some night-sound of the swamp, but then it came again, and he paused, listening. Abruptly the hideous, jarring laughter of the idiot Lem Prune struck at his ears. The sound came from directly ahead—from the shack. But he had left Prune gagged.

The idiot laughed again, someone else joining with him this time. And then a woman's voice whimpered through the darkness in a soft, hopeless cry of pleading and despair.

Tom Adams sucked a wild, agonized breath into his lungs? Ann . . .? He shook his head, cursed through clenched teeth. He plunged forward, rifle ready.

The voices came clearer as he started up the low knoll to the shack. From the window came a dull, flickering light. He heard the girl whimpering now, a low, almost continuous moaning. Laughter and jabbering, insane voices. The unceasing, confused babble of half-wits.

Adams reached the open window, moving with long, cautious strides. His knuckles were white about the rifle, his fingers curled hard around the trigger. He could feel his breath move like a hard, frosted thing from his lungs to his nostrils. He stopped it, held it soundless while he peered in the window.

The breath wheezed from him, a sigh of mingled relief and furious anger.

The room was a lurid flickering of yellow and red and black from the smoky pine torch stuck in the window-sill. There were two men in the room: Lem Prune and another half-breed whose face and even the ragged overalls he wore resembled Prune's. On her knees near the far wall was Dorothy Harkins.

Her short black hair was in wild confusion about her face, in which fear and pain and horror had mingled to wipe out all coherent expression; so that now she crouched on hands and knees, moaning like an animal. The clothing had been ripped from her body and bits of it were scattered about the shack. Adams could see the lurid glow of firelight on the flesh of her throat and breast. Something had scratched her right cheek, leaving a narrow thread of blood. Two large welts showed red upon her shoulders.

Hatred flamed through Adams then, a hatred as bitter and intense as if he had at last found the murderer of Ann's father. Both Prune and the other half-breed had their backs to the door, looking at the girl and laughing. In his hand Prune held the belt which Adams had used to bind him, and as the doctor watched he swung the belt high, whacked it across the girl's back! A bloody streak showed where the blow fell. The girl moaned softly, but did not try to move, There was utter helplessness and despair in her position.

Adams went forward with a rush, but before he could reach the door the second half-breed had moved. Laughing insanely, he leaned down, caught Dorothy's bobbed hair and jerked her head erect. The firelight glowed on the girl's round breasts, on the curved flatness of her stomach. Prune lashed out with the bolt again, full across her breasts. The girl cried out in agony.

Adams burst through the door shouting, "Damn it! Take your hands off that girl and keep 'em up! Both of you!"

The two men whirled like frightened cats. Prune flung the belt away as he spun. A mad hatred blazed in his eyes, turned to fear when he saw the gun. Both began to cringe backward, simpering.

The girl kept sobbing, her head sunk on her breasts again. All hope of escape had long since gone from her and she knelt there, her mind drowned by the horror of what had happened, thinking only that this was another half-breed come to molest her.

Adams was breathing heavily, his finger twitching against the trigger. For the moment a wild impulse to kill these beasts burned him. He shook his head fiercely. He had to take Prune back to the village, use him to help solve this mystery. He'd take the other also. Much better to let the law settle with them. His eyes flickered to the girl and he said gently, "Dorothy. Dorothy Harkins."

The girl quit whimpering but did not raise her head, Adams could see the muscles in her shoulders and in her plump legs tightening, as though the words had stirred some memory in her and she was fighting to understand. "Dorothy," he said. "I'm Tom Adams. Ann's friend. I'm going to take you home."

She raised her head then, her eyes big and wild in her face. For a moment she stared uncomprehending. Then suddenly she swayed forward, buried her face in her arms and began to sob. Adams nodded grimly. Crying was good for her.

The two half-breeds were crouched in the corner. Their eyes caught the light of the burning pine torch and glowed like the eyes of wolves. Their faces seemed to twist and weave in the smoky light. Adams could see the bone handle of a knife above the second one's belt.

"Pull that knife out," he said, "and slide it along the floor, over this way. Easy." The muzzle of the rifle swung to cover the man's chest. The half-breed did as Adams told him, and the doctor picked the knife from the floor, stuck it beside the other one.

The girl's sobs were quieter now. "Can you walk?" he asked her. "We've got to take these fellows with us, so I can't carry you."

She raised her head and the tears in her eyes glittered in the firelight. "Yes," she whispered. "I—I can walk." She got to her feet weakly, holding against the wall.

Adams said, "Slip on that dress. It's not too badly torn." And when she had finished, he added, "We've got to tie these fellows' wrists so they'll be a little safer, and we'll halter them together so they can't run away." His eyes found the belt and tie with which he had bound Prune. He nodded toward them, told Dorothy, "Pick those up and tie them while I keep 'em covered." He looked at Prune, jerked his head. "Come out in the middle of the room."

The girl picked up the bits of clothing while Prune edged forward. His mouth was open and there were white flecks of foam about the corners of his lips. His face was dirty, his black hair tangled. He looked like a dog gone mad as he came, half crouched, his breath making a whistling sound. He paused in the middle of the floor.

The girl had started toward him, but her eyes were on Adams in the doorway. Tears were still trickling down her face and the torn dress had fallen from her right shoulder. Then, in the tear-dimmed eyes, light flamed abruptly, terror. She screamed, flung both hands up, pointing toward Adams.

The doctor whirled, leaping inside the room. The movement was not fast enough. A man struck him full in the back. Their legs tangled and they smashed to the floor. Adams caught a glimpse of a snarling idiot's face, of a knife-blade glittering. He released the rifle, stabbed up his right hand, felt the thud of the wrist bringing the knife down.

Even before the other two men had crossed the room to bury him under a rolling, tossing mass of flesh, he knew what had happened. As silently as the animals they lived with, another half-breed had slipped upon him. Only the girl's warning had saved him from a knife in the back. Now, as he struggled furiously, his right hand gripping the other's wrist, he shouted, "Run, Dorothy! Get out of here!"

He felt knees driving against his legs, bruising him. A fist crashed into the top of his head. In their fury the three men were handicapping one another. But the knife-blade was three inches from Adams' cheek, bearing down. Every muscle in his body ached as he tried to hold it off. His body creaked from the strain and sweat leaped from his pores. The wrist began to grow slippery in his fingers. He fought frantically to hold it.

A knee jarred into Adams' hip. His feet beat the floor as he tried to roll, but legs were tangled with his own. Fists hammered at his ribs, at the side of his face. If the men had not been fools, he thought wildly, they would have picked up the rifle and killed him. But in their half-witted anger they thought only of their hands and knives.

One of the knives in his trousers sliced at Adams' stomach as he tried to roll, but he managed to get his left hand under the man on top, grip a bone handle. He jerked the weapon out, slashed wildly. A man screamed.

At the same instant the wrist slipped from his right hand. He snapped his head to one side, felt fire rip across his cheek. Warm blood spewed over his face.

Adams struck with the knife again and a man howled, jumped from the doctor's legs. The half-breed's knife flashed high again, paused for the downward stroke. A hand tightened on Adams' left wrist.

With one terrific movement the doctor got his feet under him, heaved. His body went skidding across the floor. The idiot's knife came down, missed. Then Adams was struggling to his feet, back against the wall, blood pouring from his sliced cheek.

Prune and the late-comer were facing him, between him and the door. The other half-breed was on his knees, both blood-stained hands gripping his ribs low on the left side. Dorothy Harkins had gone.

Adams' eyes flickered. If he could get the rifle . . . But it lay at Prune's feet, and as the idiot took a half step forward, his toe kicked it. He looked down now, yelled in joy, and ducked for it.

It was Adams' last chance and he didn't hesitate. He launched his body straight at the idiot with the knife and the open door beyond. His right arm was as stiff as the blade he held in front of him, driving like a halfback ready to stiff-arm.

The idiot's arm flashed up. His knife was blood-smeared and foul in the shifting light. But Adams came straight on and the breed's nerve broke. He flung himself to one side, snarling. Adams went out the door and into darkness like a rock from a catapult.

He twisted to the right, away from the trail. If Dorothy had gone that way he didn't want them to catch her. The moon had come higher and the house and the tops of the knoll were washed in light. Forty feet away were the dank swamp and the black shadows of the trees. Adams raced for them.

Behind him he heard the idiots shouting. The rifle cracked and a bullet whined past his ear. He flung himself sideways in midstride. His foot caught in a trailing vine and he pitched ten feet through the air, struck rolling. The idiots shouted and came pounding after him, thinking the bullet had struck home.

Then Adams was on his feet, driving into the darkness of the swamp. Mud had sucked at his feet, slowed him down. Prune screamed in fury and the rifle cracked twice; but Adams was blotted out by the shadows and the bullets went wide. The half-breeds came racing after him.

He turned sharply to the right, trying to move silently. He slipped, fell with a splash into slimy, inch-deep water. But Prune and his companion were plunging into the swamp and did not hear.

Adams kept heading toward the rising moon, but without the wagon-trail the going was hard. Time and again he sank in mud above his ankles and once plunged waist-deep into stinking water and slime.

It took him more than an hour to get out of the swamp. He had lost his coat. His shirt and trousers were mud-caked and tattered. Blood and slime had made his face into a mask of horror. Weariness was like a drug in his muscles and his feet dragged as he moved them forward.

He came out of the cornfield and started across the wide lawn of Ann's house. Lights showed from several windows, but the house was as quiet as death. He could see the dark shadow of the sweet-gum tree like a blot of ink against the white.

Even when he reached the tree and turned toward the front of the house, he heard no sound except the wet sloshing of his shoes, the scraping of the muddy trousers as he walked. There would naturally be quiet, he thought. This was not a time for laughter and talking.

Then he noticed that Mason's automobile was no longer parked in front of the house. He paused for a moment, swaying on weary legs. Had the undertaker persuaded Marie to leave town with him? Had he taken Ann?

Abruptly fear thrust its cold fingers into his chest. The mud cracked on his lids as his eyes grew wide. The utter silence of the house took on a new and terrible meaning. The quiet seemed to grow, to take on weight and crowd about him, thrusting at his eardrums. Slowly, his breath heavy in his nostrils, he went toward the steps and up them to the front door.

The door was open and beyond the hall showed brightly lighted—and empty.

Tom Adams' nerves broke for a moment and he went down the corridor with a rush. "Ann!" he shouted. "Ann!" The words boomed through the house, drowning the thud of his mud-coated shoes, echoing along the hall and up the dark stair-well.

He reached the bedroom and stood there, gripping the doorsill with blood-coated hands, staring at the empty room. "Ann," he whispered. The word stirred tiny waves of sound that lapped out into stillness, and faded.

He turned and went rushing from room to room, shouting. In the kitchen where she had fallen, lay the dead girl. He and the corpse of Edith Meadows were alone.

Two persons had died in this house—Edith Meadows and her father. Now Ann had disappeared. If she, too . . . All his efforts, all his fighting and wounds had amounted to nothing. This monster, this demon had won in the end.

He didn't *know,* of course, that this Thing had carried Ann away. And yet . . . "It's nerves," Adams said harshly. "If I were one of my patients, I'd say take a rest." But his laugh was without humor.

He went back to the bedroom, staggering with fear and the weariness which had descended on him again. There was not even a note. But against the right wall was an overturned chair. And on one leg of the chair was a small bloodstain. He leaned closer, staring, his breath frozen.

The blood was fresh.

The silence of the house came like thick-packed, black cotton about his ears, about his body, holding him motionless, as still as the corpse two rooms beyond. Across his muddy forehead one slow drop of sweat trickled, growing bigger, mud-colored.

It was a strain to raise his hand to wipe away the perspiration. As the bloody fingers moved upward he saw that they were quivering. He stopped the hand, chest high, tried to force it to steadiness. The fingers kept quivering and he cursed aloud.

So—he had lost. The monster had won, and this was Ann's blood upon the chair. She had been killed. He would go next. Another victim to the creature that could kill and vanish. Well, if Ann was dead, he didn't care . . .

Then . . . he had turned and was running toward the front of the house before the thought had become clearly conscious in his mind. He never took time to put it into words, even mentally. Before his eyes had flashed a vision of Ann; and his right hand had suddenly felt warm as though he was touching that crematory door . . .

The three or four street lights which the town boasted were not burning tonight but the moonlight made a dull white river of the dusty street. Once he thought it was odd that this street should be so dusty and that little white clouds should flutter around his feet as he ran, when only a mile away Crazy Man's Swamp was full of water and muck. Then he had rounded the corner into the rear street of the village and was racing down it toward the Mason Funeral Home. It was less than a block away.

Two men came from a house on the right, shouting. One of them was pointing wildly, the other raising a rifle. Tom Adams whirled toward the trees lining the left side of the street, the house beyond the narrow walk. He leaped sideways, running, twisting, dodging. Breath was like a hot iron in his nostrils. He wondered how well the idiot could shoot.

He heard the whine of the bullet so close that he jerked his head even as he heard the report of the gun. Then he was into the shadows, hurtling for the protection of the deserted house beyond. The gun cracked three times, fast. A bullet glanced from one of the trees, went wailing out into the night.

CHAPTER EIGHT

INTO THE CREMATORY

As Adams raced toward the back of the house, he heard the half-breeds start after him, still shouting. He reached the rear, cut to the right. Thirty yards ahead was the dull tan outline of the funeral home.

No light showed from the windows of the funeral parlors and evidently the building had no rear door. Behind, the idiots were still searching for him. His lungs felt swollen as thought they would burst against his ribs, and the race had started blood flowing from his cheek again. He could feel it dripping onto his shoulder. He was too weak to fight now. If the half-breeds caught him it would mean death. And if he entered this home of death, unarmed except for a knife—if the monster behind these killings, the man who had doped and bribed the halfwitted village were here—what then . . .?

He stood there while the jaws of hell closed on him from both directions.

Abruptly he heard Prune scream, and knew that the man had seen him. He leaped along the side of the funeral home toward the front, crouching low, hidden now by the shadows. He heard the swish of grass as the breeds came rushing toward him.

Adams saw that he couldn't make the front without being seen. Three feet ahead was an open window, shoulder high. He leaped for it, slapped his bloody hands on the sill, and throwing the last ounce of his strength into the effort, flung himself up. His knees hooked on the sill and he balanced there for one second, staring into the darkened room.

Behind him, Prune shouted again. A rifle cracked and the bullet struck like a hot pin in Adams' left arm. He swayed forward.

Across the room and corridor beyond a door burst open. Light fell out into the hallway, almost to the open door of the room into which Adams was crawling. He saw the dark figure of a man framed its the doorway, saw the gun in his hand. And he saw the lighted room beyond the man—the crematory room!

In that room Ann Meadows, her clothes half torn from her body, her long auburn hair wild about her face, was tied to a chair!

Then the man saw him framed in the window of the darkened room, swung up the gun.

Tom Adams dived forward and to his right. He heard the pistol thunder, the smack of a rifle-bullet striking the window-sill while he was still in the air. He hit the floor with a boom, rolled farther to the right, out of range of the hall and window.

For a moment he knelt there, regaining his breath, eyes jerking from doorway to window. Evidently the fire from inside had frightened the breeds, for they made no sound. The doorway remained empty and Tom Adams grinned a blood-caked, crooked smile. Whoever had tied Ann didn't know whether or not he had a gun and was afraid to come in the room after him. Adams began to crawl toward the doorway, silently.

Outside in the hall he could hear the man's expectant breathing—like some animal waiting at the mouth of his lair.

He was near the door when he heard the first move. The soft *tup tup* of stealthy walking. Then came the clunk of wood on wood from the room across the hall, and what might have been a muffled cry.

His face flat against the floor so that a man watching would look over him, Tom Adams peered around the door-sill. His jaw sagged open at what he saw.

In the room directly across the hall old Bob Wilson, his white hair tousled over his head, a gun in his right hand, was trying to drag Ann from her chair. He was keeping his eyes on the doorway, and, using only one hand, seemed unable to move the girl. She jerked away and half fell from the chair.

"All right!" the old man snapped the words aloud. "You're going in the fire unconscious." He swung the gun up over her head.

Tom Adams never heard the curse that broke from his lips. He came to his feet in a surge, but had to round the door and stumbled. His wounded left arm struck the sill. Then he was leaping across the hall at the banker, shoulders low, head forward,

Wilson heard him strike the door, swung the gun around. Adams saw the black muzzle straight in front, but there was no chance to dodge. He dived. Flame leaped. The gun roared.

A star-shell exploded on Adams' skull and the world was a blaze of light that went out suddenly.

He never felt himself strike the floor, though he never totally lost consciousness. Through the blackness where lights sparkled came strange words. "Well, you've seen *him* die. Right through the head. Now both of you in the crematory and there'll be no trace of you." Then there was another sound: footsteps beating. More voices, cursing, shouting.

Finally Tom Adams fought his eyes open, fought the blackness from under his skull. Wilson, the gun still gripped in his hand, was standing before Ann Meadows. The girl's head was flung back, her eyes wide and rolling. To one side of her were the two half-breeds.

Wilson was gesturing toward the open door of the crematory. "Throw those two in." he snapped. "Then we'll talk."

Lem Prune shook his head. "Not the girl. Want her."

"Uh-huh," his companion said. "Other girl got 'way. Want this one." He took one step toward Ann, punched her in the breast with his forefinger and began to laugh. The girl tried to jump away from him and as she tottered on the edge of the chair, the breed put his arm around her, pulled her back.

Wilson caught him by the shoulder, snatched him around. "You can't have her!" he yelled. He pointed at the crematorium with the gun, said, "Throw her in there."

The breed kept his arm around Ann. His hand began to feel along the flesh of her throat, downward. His breathing was harsh. Prune asked, "Throw 'em in there, you give more powder?"

"Damn you," Wilson snapped. "I haven't got any more. I told you that."

The words seemed to strike the halfwit's brain slowly, soaking in. His eyes began to glitter; his mouth was open and Adams could see his tongue licking at his lips.

The other man was still holding the girl, laughing at her struggles, his right hand crawling down her breast. He kept gloating eyes on Ann, but his words were for Wilson. "Want the girl. We keep her, throw in the man for you."

Wilson swung the gun toward him. "Damn it! You'll throw them both in, or—" He stopped, staring at the expression on the half-breed's face.

The man had taken his hand from Ann's breast. He was half crouched, glaring at the old banker. Saliva drooled from his snarling mouth. "Gonna keep the girl," he husked. "Maybe kill you, but keep her."

Wilson went a step backward before the threat of the madman's eyes. His finger twitched at the trigger of the gun as he hesitated. Lem Prune was moving toward him, slowly.

"All right," Wilson said. "You can have her. But throw in this fellow." He nodded at Adams lying helpless on the floor, his face a mass of blood.

With a quick cry the half-wit jumped back to the girl. Ann screamed against her gag as he began to paw at her, running his filthy hands over her body. Adams fought his weakened muscles, tried to crawl erect, but his legs barely twitched.

Wilson was saying to Lem Prune, "Throw the man in that door. Quick!"

"You gimme powder then?" The idiot was breathing rapidly. His tongue licked across dry lips.

"Throw him in," Wilson said.

The half-wit moved slowly. He bent, put the rifle on the floor. He slid his arms under Adams' neck and knees. The doctor struck at the man's face, cursing hoarsely. The blow was feeble and Prune laughed shortly. He picked Adams from the floor, took one step toward the crematory door.

Despair, fury, terror, surged like a black wave through Adams' body. Three seconds to live. And then, Oh God! to burn . . . He tried to fight, but the idiot held him like a baby.

Then a desperation-born idea came to him as in a dream. He heard his voice without knowing the words it was going to speak. "Wilson's not going to give you any more dope—more powder. He hasn't any more. I have it all."

Prune stopped. Still holding Adams in his arms, he turned toward Wilson. "You got powder? Show me."

Wilson's face flushed red with anger under his white hair. "Damn it!" he snapped. "I told you there was no more. Now or ever!"

The whole thing broke like thunder. Before Wilson could swing his gun, Lem Prune had dropped Adams, launched his body straight at the banker. He smashed into the old man, driving him back toward the crematory, battering at his face.

Adams struck the floor not more than five feet from the rifle. His head spun dizzily, and he was conscious that his left arm worked slowly, painfully. He heard the roar of Wilson's gun, but did not turn. Every fiber in his body was bent on reaching the rifle. He lunged, rolled, fought toward it.

The half-breed who held the girl heard him, whirled. His dark hand whipped to his waist, came up holding his knife. He jerked it high, dived at Adams.

Adams made one last roll, caught up the rifle. The twenty-two spat once, twice. Two small holes popped in the breed's shirt, but the small slugs did not slow his rush. The knife drawn back, he came down at the prostrate doctor.

There was no chance to fire again. Still lying on his side, Adams jabbed with the rifle, stuck the muzzle full into the falling man's throat.

Behind him he heard Wilson's gun blast again. Heard the banker scream furiously, a wild, horrible cry of terror.

The breed above Tom Adams swayed on the rifle muzzle. Adams squeezed the trigger of the gun again. The report was muffled, softer than the thud of the body striking the floor . . .

He saw the girl's wide eyes staring beyond him, and turned. It was a slow, agonized movement. He kept waiting to hear Wilson's gun once more, to feel the bullet crash into him. His body seemed to move like a slow-motion picture, endlessly.

The banker screamed again. His gun roared.

Adams stopped his movement. "Great God!" he whispered.

The banker's head and shoulders were inside the crematory and the half-breed Prune was shoving, cramming in his body. It seemed incredible that Wilson could have missed his shots at that range, but even in the long second that Adams watched, Prune made one last heave. The banker cried again, a cry that turned Adams' stomach and that suddenly burned short. The body slid out of sight inside the square door.

Slowly Lem Prune turned. Adams tried to bring up the gun but it was heavy . . . heavy. The room was spinning. He saw Prune take one step toward him. Adams tried to center the rifle but the muzzle wouldn't move.

The room kept spinning and Prune seemed to waver with it. The rifle muzzle wouldn't follow him. The half-breed was almost on Adams now. Too late to use the gun. The man was pitching down at him. Down . . .

For a long while Adams lay staring, dazed, at the man beside him, at the blood oozing from Prune's chest and belly.

Bob Wilson had not missed his last shots . . .

The things that followed seemed to Adams as though they were happening in a dream. He somehow forced himself to his knees, crawled and cut the ropes from Ann Meadows. He remembered the abrupt appearance of Sam Mason, and heard the faraway sound of the man's voice as he explained that he had just returned from driving Marie to York. Later, Dorothy Harkins had entered.

Next, he remembered Ann telling him to be quiet as they drove toward a hospital. She was explaining that she had recognized Wilson as the man outside her window by the way he held his head. "Edith must have recognized him, too," Ann said. "That's what frightened her. Maybe he wouldn't have hurt me if I hadn't recognized him. He only wanted me to leave town."

"I know," Adams whispered. "All the property around this town has oil. I saw the government report. But the townspeople didn't know about the oil. Wilson's bank must have had mortgages on nearly all the property, but the government is making it difficult to foreclose. He figured if he could make everybody leave town, they'd all be glad to get what they could, stay—"

"Hush!" Ann said. She cradled his bloody head in her left arm. Put her right hand to his lips.

It was the next day before Adams learned what had happened to Ben Larkin and to Dorothy Harkins. Larkin, too, had recognized Wilson, Ann said. Then Wilson had killed him, cremated the body. Dorothy had been kidnapped during the morning, held prisoner in the swamp village until she was carried to the shack where her captor found and released Prune.

"Wilson told me about the explosion that happened when we were first coming here," Ann said. "He had fixed it up, had the idiot set it off. Then he ran his car into the shallow ditch on purpose. If Larkin hadn't come by they would have killed me then."

"What about Dr. McGregor?" Adams asked. "Was that a mask?"

"Yes. He told me he'd killed McGregor because the doctor suspected him. He drugged Mason's liquor, slipped McGregor's body into the crematory instead of old John Perkins'. He threw Perkins' body into the half-breed village where you found it, thinking that would throw suspicion on Sam, who claimed he'd burned the body. He made the mask using the doctor's actual face after he'd killed him." Ann shuddered.

Adams raised a hand to his bandaged cheek. "They nearly made a mask of me," he said. "And a damn ugly one."

Ann leaned forward, stopped. "I can't kiss you, there're so many bandages."

"Take 'em off," Adams said. "No need to save my life if I can't use it."

MODELS FOR MADNESS

CHAPTER ONE

THE GREAT TOMORROW

TIME PASSES VERY SLOWLY in the narrow cell of the death house. There is no clock, no way to judge the creeping minutes except by the occasional meals which the guards bring, by the slow crawl of the sunlight through the barred windows and across the cement floor. During the long hours of the night I lie awake and hear time drag past with a cruel and terrific slowness. Four more days and four more nights I must stay here; then they will lead me down the short corridor that stretches into eternity.

The big, blank-faced chair, the electrodes on leg and head, the furious hum of the current and my body lunging against the straps that hold it. Another murderer gone . . . I shall be glad, glad when those four days and nights are over. For even here, alone, barred off from the world, I am afraid.

I am not trying to beg for mercy. I don't want to live—now. This will not be read until after my death. It is partially to help pass the time that I write, and also because I want those whom I leave behind to understand as much as is possible. God knows, I don't understand fully, but I do know that I didn't commit these murders wilfully, and that no matter what horrors I performed with my hands I never wanted to do them.

More than this no one will be able to understand. That's why I would not help the lawyer which the court forced me to have at my trial; that's why I pleaded guilty and refused to answer questions. I didn't want to kill those persons, and yet . . . Now it is best that I walk down that short corridor into the small room with the large chair—and into eternity.

You will comprehend more fully if I start with the dream. It is a dream which has haunted me and torn at my nerves until I was half mad with terror, has held me trembling through long fear-whipped hours of darkness. It haunts me even now, in this cell where I can reach no one. My hands are big and strong enough to take a human throat and rip the windpipe from it, but they cannot shake these bars through which the sunlight streams in slanting, mote-filled beams. And I am glad . . .

The dream came to me the night before the first murder. It was too horribly real to be a dream and I sat up in bed suddenly, my body wet with perspiration. For a moment I couldn't breathe because of the terror that cut into my chest like an icy wire. That couldn't have been a dream, I thought. It couldn't! It was like a picture flashed in the darkness. It was like . . . And then, although I have never understood how, I knew what it was. I never meant to say the words, but I heard my own voice muttering them into the darkness.

It was as if the night had split for one moment letting me see into the future!

I can't explain that feeling. I have never put much faith in dreams, but in the first instant I *knew* I had looked into the Great Tomorrow. This was what added so much to the sickening terror of the dream itself. I can't explain *how* I knew it, but I want anybody who reads this to understand that I *did* know it. The truth simply was in my mind from the first, though for days I tried to tell myself that I was being absurd. But all the time I *knew*.

I can see the dream now as plainly as I did when I sat bolt upright in my bed, cold and shaking. I can see my own face, distorted almost into bestial savageness and with the eyes so squint as to be like those of an Oriental; I can see my big body hunched over Neta Phillips, her slender waist cradled in my left arm, her dark hair flowing loose. And I can see my right hand tearing her throat like a steel claw, ripping out the windpipe, see the wild spurt of the blood and the savage, scarlet rivulets flowing down toward her breasts.

In the second while the dream lasted I was aware also of a peculiar odor. Perhaps I use the wrong word when I say "odor," because it wasn't actually a smell; but it more nearly touched on that than any other sense. It was the sensation, the feeling that a person gets on entering a home in China where one family has lived for hundreds of years, where, within the very walls of the house, and in the air you breathe, you become aware of history, of the quiet ghosts of unforgotten ages. Somehow, in the first horrible moment of dreaming, I became aware of such an odor.

"It was just a dream," I told myself, and I lay back. But I couldn't sleep. It seemed absurd that I should be so afraid of a dream. I tried to laugh at the idea of my harming Neta Phillips. I believed then that I was going to marry Neta; that there was nothing on God's earth that I wanted so much. Even now it shakes me to remember how I loved her. There were times while she stood spotlighted in front of the orchestra and sang, that I had to grip my table to keep from getting up and catching her in my arms and shouting to the world that I loved her, loved her! So you can understand how absurd the idea of killing her would seem.

But I couldn't forget it. I kept lying there thinking about the dream, and about the way my eyes had looked. Not like my own at all, but slant and terrible as those of a Chinese demon. And I remembered the peculiar Oriental odor which had come with the dream, and I got to thinking about Tai Ming.

A year before, at the university where I was doing some graduate art work on a scholarship—and Neta was finishing her senior year—we had known Tai. A quiet, studious young man with all the education the West could give him, and with the exquisite politeness of the Orient, he had amused Foster Duncan and me by the seriousness with which he worshipped his ancestors. Foster had suggested that I draw the caricatures of Tai and all his family. Neta had urged me not to, but I did anyway.

We were in Tai's apartment when I showed them to him. I shall never forget the change which came over his face. One moment it was bland, smiling, almost Occidental. The next it was contorted in savage and terrible fury and his eyes were those of a Chinese fiend. But the snarl had lasted only a moment. After that his face was quiet, and passive, and utterly without expression. His voice was as smooth as silk, and flat. He was coldly, silently furious at the humorous drawings of the members of his family.

"You have insulted a thing more precious than life, not only to me, but to my entire family; to those who have not yet been born and to those who have been dead for thousands of years. It is an insult that we do not forget." And in that same flat, silky voice he went on to swear in words that were beyond retracting.

I had tried to apologize then, seeing how seriously he took the joke. He had only bowed and held open his door. I remember that last glance of his room as I went out. It was the average room of an American college boy, strictly Occidental; and yet, in the very air which pervaded the place, there was something weird and Oriental and inescapable.

That was a few days before commencement, and I never saw him again. I hadn't thought of him for several months until the night of the dream. For a long while I lay there thinking of him and of Neta and of the way Foster Duncan had laughed at the joke. I tried to keep thinking of them so that I could shut the dream from my mind. But I couldn't.

Finally I got up and switched on the lights. "A deep drink of bourbon will put me to sleep," I thought. When I reached for the bottle I saw the faint blue lines on the back of my hand, blinked against the light and looked at them more closely. They were barely visible and tangled, almost like a Chinese letter. "Must have been sleeping, with my hand pushed against a wrinkle in the sheet," I thought. Then I took a stiff drink of the whiskey and forgot about it.

It was the next night at the club called Death's Roadhouse that the whole thing was recalled, horrible and unforgettable, to my mind.

My uncle, Wade Farlan, owns and operates the roadhouse. It hadn't been doing so well under the name of The Silver Moon when he bought it. He had changed the name to Death's Roadhouse, and filled the place with wax models of famous murders. I think the only reason he bought the place was to have a chance to out-do the Dead Rat Cabaret in Paris, a place which held a strange fascination for him. The idea had appealed to the tired and wealthy of the city. They flocked there nightly, partially for the weird atmosphere, partially to hear Neta Phillips sing. I had agreed to do the gruesome decorations and the models, and help him with the roadhouse, simply because my work as a sculptor hadn't proved as good as I thought it would—and I wasn't earning a living.

The lights in Death's Roadhouse are a dim and ghastly green that flickers constantly. The orchestra is hidden behind palms, and makes a specialty of weird, wailing music. Around the walls, scattered among the tables, even on the dance floor, are the wax statues; and I think I did a good job on them. For they were terrible enough by daylight, and in the dim, ever wavering illumination of the place they seemed to move, to be in the very act of murdering one another. A man splitting a woman's head with a hatchet; another ripping his wife's throat with a razor; a nude woman on her hands and knees, with a knife still seeming to quiver in her back . . .

The night after the dream I was sitting at a corner table with Neta when Foster Duncan dropped in and joined us. It was several minutes before Neta's specialty number was to begin—a wailing, gruesome song that packed the roadhouse nightly. I have always wondered how Neta could sing that number, it was so entirely different from her quiet, lovable nature. While we were waiting the conversation got around to college somehow, and Neta said, "I had a letter from Tai Ming today. He's gone back to China."

At first I didn't know why the mention of Tai's name should frighten me so. Then I remembered I had been thinking of him the night before; and the dream came back to me like thunder. I had to fight my nerves to steadiness before I asked, "What did he have to say?"

Neta looked at me curiously, her level, dark eyes opening wide. For a moment she glanced at Foster, then back to me. "What's the trouble with both of you? You look as if you had seen a ghost."

I turned to Foster, who is a lanky, rather gaunt man with a sense of humor that is liable to take a cruel turn. His mouth was twitching slightly, but as I looked at him he controlled it and began to laugh. "I've never quite got over the way he cursed us about those pictures you drew. He said he was going to have revenge, and he meant it."

Whenever Neta smiled there was a sudden light in her dark eyes. "You don't have to worry about that any more. That's why he wrote me. He said he was sorry about the rumpus he raised; that he should have known that neither of you meant any insult. It was a very polite, nice letter."

"That's bad," Foster said. "A Chinaman apologizes for stepping behind you just before he sticks a knife in your back." He tried to make his voice sound as if he were joking, but there was a nervous, jagged edge to it.

I opened my mouth to say that I had been thinking about Tai the night before, but stopped when I saw Roger Swanson coming between the tables and scattered statues. It was too dim in the place to distinguish his features, but I recognized him by the sleek cut of his clothes and the gliding way he moved.

He paused beside our table, scowling at me. In the glow from the green lamps, his blond hair took on a sickening color and his thin, rather handsome face seemed to twist with the wavering of other lights, "You might get up and see if there is any work for you to do," he said. "And it's about time for Neta's number. The orchestra leader was asking for her." He wheeled and walked away from us, a slim, too-immaculate figure among the statues of death.

Foster turned his gaunt head and looked after him. "The collar ad doesn't seem to care for either of you," he remarked.

I said, "He's my cousin, but there's little love between us. He took law at school, though my Uncle Paul—the eccentric old millionaire who lives with one servant out on Woodley Road—knew he'd never be able to win a case, and took mercy on him, made him his secretary or something. It must be hell on Uncle Paul. He hates everybody, except maybe Neta; and he hates Roger worse than all the others put together. But blood's blood in my family, and so he gave Roger the job. And Uncle Wade lets him do some publicity work for the roadhouse."

"How is your Uncle Paul?" Foster asked. "I haven't heard you mention him in more than a year."

"I haven't been to see him in two or more. He lives shut up with his books and one servant. Roger is his only connection with the world, and I don't envy him that one. He doesn't want visitors."

"I knew an old duck like that once. He . . ." But suddenly I did not hear Foster's voice; I did not hear the muted wailing of the orchestra or the dulled murmur of voices from other tables. I was conscious of no sound at all, of nothing except an odor that was more a *feeling* than an odor—the feeling of ancient, Chinese homes heavy with history and ancestry worship . . .

It was the smell I had sensed last night, just before I dreamed I had murdered Neta. All at once that picture flashed horribly clear in my mind. I could see her black hair swaying about her face, see my big hand at her torn throat, almost feel the fingers wet with blood.

And in that same instant I saw it!

The statue was not twenty feet from us, close to the wall, and half hidden by banked palms. Somehow I hadn't noticed it before, but then, all at once, I was staring at it. Slowly my mouth began to open, muscle began to ache along my jaw and my eyes grew wide with terror.

I felt Neta's hands on my arm, shaking me, heard her voice thin and shrill. "Jim! What is it? What's wrong?" But I never looked at her. I couldn't take my eyes from the statue.

The shifting green lights flickered on it through the palms so that it seemed to quiver with heavy breathing. But it was not that which held me. It was the horror of the figures themselves.

It was the statue of a large, wide-shouldered fellow holding a smaller man with his left arm, while with his right hand he ripped out the man's throat. And in the long, furious instant that I stared, I knew that the contorted face of the killer was my own face!

I didn't hear anything then, didn't feel anything except the cold terror starting deep in me and rising like a black flood. The wild, unexplainable sensation of looking into the future struck me, froze my veins into jagged icicles. I came half erect, gripping the table, shaking it. My eyes bulged, fixed on the face which was a horrible mask of my own face.

"It's only wax," I thought. "Someone is playing a joke on me. That's all. A . . ." But then the dream was clear in my mind again: the picture of Neta held exactly as this man was held, her throat torn open as his was, and my own face, with the eyes of a Chinese demon, exactly the same.

My gaze shifted to the face of the victim. There was something familiar about that face, though it was twisted with unbearable agony—the mouth open so that I had the wild impression that it didn't scream, only because the sound had been torn from its throat a second before.

And then, at a table just to the left of the statue, I saw the man who was modeled as the victim!

He was in dinner clothes, seated opposite a pretty blonde girl who was leaning toward him, grasping his arm. But his eyes were on the statue, wide and terrified, he was unmoving as the wax images, and his face was ghastly under the lights.

I don't remember getting up from the table. From that time on the whole thing was like a black dream; I can never be sure how much of it I remember and how much a furious and terrified imagination has created since. I only know that I was going toward the wax models, my hands stretched out in front of me, thinking: "I'll touch them; I'll prove they are only wax, and then . . ."

When the lights went out I don't know. I didn't hear any of the confusion, the wisecracks shouted into the dark, the women giggling hysterically. It seemed to me that I was gradually being absorbed by the darkness as I pushed my way through it. And I knew that I was swerving toward the table where the man in dinner clothes sat with the blonde. Something was pulling me toward him while I fought to keep away, to go toward the statues, instead. I struggled with every fading ounce of my strength, but somehow I swerved more and more toward the table.

Perhaps I screamed then; perhaps it was the man or the girl he was with who screamed. All I remember is the high and terrible cry jangling in the darkness . . .

CHAPTER TWO

HANDS OF BLOOD

THE LIGHT SEEMED TO HAVE BEEN AROUND ME a long time before I became aware of it. I was standing erect, doing something with my hands that I didn't understand, and there was a steady, liquid sound in my ears. Then, with a slow, sure rush, consciousness came back to me.

I was in the lavatory of the roadhouse, scrubbing my hands. A steady stream of water splashed into the marble washbowl and gurgled down the drain. It was in the water that I first saw the faint red coloring. And then I looked at my hands . . .

For a long while I stood there staring at them. I didn't breath, because my lungs were cold and rock-hard against my ribs; my mouth was open, but I didn't make any sound. I could feel my eyes aching against their sockets, and in my mind was the picture of those statues, of the blood gushing from a torn throat, of myself swerving in the dark toward the table where the living image of one of those statues sat.

What happened after that I could not remember. But thick between my fingers was the dark smear of blood! And underneath the blood the blue lines that were like a Chinese letter showed plainly!

I must have stood there a full minute before I became aware of the chaos bursting in the dining room. Men were shouting, women screaming, tables crashing over. And then, suddenly, above it all, I heard the voice of my Uncle Wade sound like thunder. "Be calm! No one's going to leave here before the police come!"

Somehow I finished washing my hands, quickly and thoroughly—but the blue lines would not come off. Somehow I forced myself to go back into the dining room, where I didn't know what I would find. I tried to keep my mind blank, but pictures burst like shells in my brain so that I staggered as I walked. Why had that blood been on my hands? How did I get in the washroom? Why was the whole roadhouse in such a terrified uproar? I didn't want to guess at the answers, and yet I couldn't keep from it. What had happened in those seconds of blackness I didn't know.

The green, wavering lights were on when I slid past the palms into the dining room. In the nasty glow the wax statues seemed more alive than the human beings, but I was not interested in any statue but one. Between me and the place it stood, every person in the roadhouse had gathered in a circle. They were all looking at something on the floor, and none of them saw me.

Over the heads of the crowd I could gee my Uncle Wade in the center, his mane of white hair pushed back from his forehead, his dark eyes burning. All the men in my family are large, but Uncle Wade is the biggest of the lot, and the hardest, despite his fifty years. He was bellowing orders to his men, and waiters were jumping toward exits. His voice rode high over the hysterical sobbing of the women. A man in front of me turned away quickly, his hand over his mouth, as though he were about to get sick. Beyond him, I could see the floor in the middle of the circle.

I didn't cry out because I couldn't. All the while I had known what would be there, though I had tried not to admit it even to myself. Now the sight struck me like a fist in my stomach, and I rocked backward, my mouth open as though there were not enough air in the room for me; and yet I could not breathe.

Flat on his back at my uncle's feet was the man toward whose table I had swerved in the dark. The green light twitched across him, but he was still, horribly still except for the slow-widening blood under his face.

His whole throat was gone, as though the windpipe had been ripped out with a gigantic hand! The torn flesh hung in jagged ribbons, and the blood drooled from it in unceasing streams!

For what seemed ages I stood there, sick with a terror that was beyond comprehension. And starting deep inside me, rising into my brain with the slow, furious pressure of my blood, came the dream. I had seen a statue of this man and of me ripping out his throat. Now he was dead. *And I had dreamed of murdering Neta!*

Fear was a cold agony crushing my mind. Through it came the sound of muffled voices that I heard without understanding. Uncle Wade was bellowing, "Every one go back to their tables and wait for the police."

A woman was saying over and over, "Oh, God. It's real. He's really dead. He's really dead."

A man asked, "Who is he? I saw him sitting there, and then the lights went out and when they came on, he . . ."

Another voice said, "It's John McDavid. He's the fellow who's been doing the stories the critics all rant about."

The deep voice of my uncle boomed, "Go to your tables!" The command crashed into my brain like a whip-lash and I turned, reeling, toward the corner where I had been sitting with Neta and Foster Duncan.

Persons were passing on all sides, but no one noticed when I stopped. I couldn't go any farther. Every muscle in my body shook with terror and wild impulses slashed counterwise through my brain. A long while I stood there, gaping at the spot where the statue had been.

"God!" I whispered. "Great . . ." I couldn't say any more because there was no air in my longs, and my ribs were crushing inward.

The statues, with my face and the face of John McDavid had vanished. In its place was one of the wax figures I had modeled.

I turned slowly, staring about the room. There was no doubt of it—this was the place. But the statue I had seen a short while ago was not there. I had the eerie feeling that it had never been there, except in my imagination. It had been no more real than the dream, a brief rent in the curtain of the future! And if one of them had come true, then the other . . . . Oh God! I put both hands over my eyes and stood there, swaying.

Something plucked at my arm and I turned to face Neta. "Jim, where have you been? What was wrong when—" She stopped, staring into my eyes.

Looking at her I felt terror like a living agony inside me. My gaze took in her full, soft mouth, the dark hair that framed her face, her slender, curving figure—and seeing her I saw the dream like a wall of flame and horror between us.

"Let's go to the table," I said huskily, and went toward it. I was unconscious of the room about me, of the noises, of everything except this horror which had taken place, and of the terrible picture which lived in my imagination: Neta, her throat torn as McDavid's had been, the dark blood streaming dawn onto her breasts.

Foster Duncan was not at the table.

Neta pulled her chair close to me, took my big hands in her small ones. "Now tell me," she whispered. "What happened to you? You're not hurt, not . . . ?"

I looked at her, and felt love roll over me like a great wave. And there was courage in knowing I loved her so much. Surely I couldn't harm her. I tried to tell myself that the whole thing was crazy.

After the lights went out something or somebody had killed McDavid and struck me in passing, knocking me momentarily unconscious. At college I had played a whole quarter of a football game and never been able to remember it. That was what had happened tonight.

Then I thought of the statue. How in God's name could I explain it?

"Neta,"—the words hurt my throat when I spoke—"did you notice . . ." I turned my eyes away from her, afraid for her to see the terror jerking in my face. "Did you notice that statue? Did you see anything . . .?"

Her hands tightened on mine, tried to pull me around—but I kept looking away from her. "Which one?" she asked. "I haven't noticed any new ones. Why?"

I swung to face her then, my jaw set hard. "There was one near the table where McDavid sat. Did you . . .?"

A new look came into her eyes now, a slow, growing shadow of wonder and doubt and fear. It was a long moment before she turned to glance at the statue I indicated. "It's been there all evening," she said. "What's wrong with it?"

I didn't answer her. I don't think my face had changed; for her words had frozen me, stopped the very beating of my heart until it hung cold as a stone inside me. No one had seen the statue, with my face and the face of the dead man—except he and I. Now he was dead with his throat ripped apart. *And there had been blood on my hands!*

"It was never there," I thought. "Never there except in my mind and his. We were seeing into the future, and the dream I had of Neta . . ."

It was several minutes later that Foster Duncan came back to the table. I don't remember anything he had to say, and the police investigation is a vague, blur in my mind. What had happened in those moments of darkness? How had the blood got on my hands, and why had I slipped away to wash it off? The questions thundered over and over through my brain.

The police, I remember vaguely, went over the roadhouse from end to end. They reenacted the crime, keeping us in our former seats. But neither Foster Duncan nor Neta mentioned the fact that I had been out of my chair, going in the direction of McDavid, when the lights went out. No one else seemed to have noticed. So the police learned nothing, and at last they let us go home.

I didn't sleep that night. It seemed to me that if I shut my eyes, the dream would come crashing back into my mind—and I was afraid. I tried to tell myself that there was no connection between the statue and the dream. I tried to believe I had been working too hard; that I was beginning to imagine things. I thought of a thousand excuses. But I must have known the truth, though I would not admit it even to myself.

The next morning I was up and shaving earlier than I am usually awake. In the mirror I could see the steady dread that showed in my eyes and the dark, sleepless lines rimming my cheekbones. My fingers were trembling when I raised my hand to look at the blue lines etched on the back of it, and when the doorbell rang I jumped and cut myself with the razor.

It was my Uncle Wade.

He stormed in, his white mane of hair blowing back from his forehead, his dark eyes glittering. He waved a newspaper under my face and bellowed, "Look at that! Look, damn it!"

It was a lurid account of the murder, describing the weird atmosphere of the roadhouse and all the gruesome details of the crime. The police claimed that McDavid had been killed by an animal of some kind, saying that no human being could have torn his throat apart as had been done. The fact that the lights were out at the moment was merely a coincidence, they said, which gave the beast courage to attack. Already a reporter had found two persons who remembered having seen strange animals near the roadhouse. One of them was supposed to have noticed a monstrous dog, while the other said that what he had seen was an apelike thing.

"Perhaps that's what it was." I almost whispered the words. "Perhaps it was an animal after all, and—"

"What the devil do I care what it was?" Uncle Wade yelled. "These damn newspapers will frighten everybody in the city! There won't be a person in Death's Roadhouse for weeks. If it happened anywhere else it would be a murder and that's all, but with those damn statues . . .!" He began to curse the whole idea and me for having made the models.

"But it was your scheme," I told him. "You asked me to model them."

"I don't give a damn who asked you!" he bellowed. "You made them, and they'll ruin my business." He stormed out of the place, still cursing.

I was supposed to have a date with Neta that afternoon, but I phoned and told her I was feeling ill and would meet her later at the roadhouse. I was afraid to see her, afraid to be alone with her because of the dream crouched like some great cat in the back of my mind, ready to spring.

For more than an hour I walked up and down my small apartment, reading the paper Uncle Wade had left. I read the story until I knew it by heart, and gradually the idea that it was a beast which had killed McDavid took root in my mind. "That's what it was," I kept telling myself. "It couldn't have been anything else. In escaping it brushed against me, got blood on me and knocked me unconscious. It was some beast that . . ." I shuddered, looking down at my hands, with the corded muscles and the queer blue lines on the right one.

Once more I began to think of Tai Ming and the satin smoothness of his voice as he had sworn vengeance. But that was absurd. He couldn't have done this, and anyway he was in China. He had written Neta that he realized we meant no insult. I also thought of Foster Duncan saying, "A Chinaman apologizes for stepping behind you just before he sticks a knife in your back."

About four o'clock I walked down to the corner for the afternoon papers. I wanted to go out, I wanted to quit thinking the terrible thoughts that were gnawing through my brain; and somehow I was almost afraid to leave the apartment. I didn't want to read any more about what had happened last night, and yet I could scarcely wait for the papers to appear on the newsstands.

Seeking a new lead for their stones. the afternoon sheets had played up the wild beast angle. Perhaps the reporters were purposely exaggerating; perhaps hysteria had struck the fanners who lived near Death's Roadhouse. Anyway there were four new reports of persons who had seen some monstrous creature nearby, though none of them had seen it clearly. They told of some great, hairy, ape-like thing which showed for a moment between the trees—and vanished.

It doesn't seem strange now that I felt better when I read of the creature. "Those persons have actually seen it." I thought. "It's the thing that killed John McDavid last night. It's not just the imagination of some frightened persons."

But that night when it was time to go back to the roadhouse, terror returned to me. I could feel it as close to me as the darkness itself, feel it tightening around me, stopping my breath and the very flow of my blood.

If Uncle Wade expected his business to be ruined by the publicity, he was wrong. The place was packed to the walls, though a strange, taut quietness hung over the crowd. Every person there was thinking of last night's tragedy, and they were conscious of the weird influence of the roadhouse. They did not dance close to the wax figures which seemed to writhe under the green lights; and the last tables to fill were those near the statues.

Purposely I avoided Neta. She was sitting at the same table where we had been the night before, and both Foster Duncan and Roger Swanson were with her. I paused once and looked at them, feeling love for the girl rise even with the black terror that surged through me, even with the sudden striking of the dream into my mind—the picture of my hand tearing at her throat . . .

It was about midnight when Roger Swanson came into the office where I was sitting with Uncle Wade. His thin, handsome face was as sullen as ever beneath his blond curls. "Why are you avoiding Neta?" he asked. "You know she's been trying to speak to you all night."

"I've been busy," I replied. "I haven't had time."

Swanson said, "You're lying. You've been avoiding her, and she knows it."

I don't know what made me lose my temper then. Perhaps the fear had been eating at my brain so long that suddenly it broke through—because for the next few seconds I was a madman. I had my fingers in Swanson's coat and was shaking him, yelling: "Damn it! I'll see her when I want to, and you keep the hell out of it!" I flung him to one side, hurled myself at the door.

Behind me Uncle Wade's deep voice was saying, "Well, I'll be—!"

It was that sudden outburst that made me realize how frightened I was. My whole body was trembling, and ice was crushing the breath from my lungs. "I'm going insane," I thought. "Insane with fear of something I don't understand, something that's eating into me. But I can't see it, and I can't touch it."

I stood for a long moment, in the semi-darkness near the wall, and looked at the dance floor. My nails dug into my palms until they brought blood. My whole body was rigid. "I've got to face it," I thought. "I can't hide any longer, or I'll go mad. I've *got* to find out, tonight." My knees were stiff, my body cold as I went toward the table where Neta was sitting with Foster Duncan.

"Hello," Foster said when I came up. "Where have you been all night?"

"Working." I sat down, trying to keep my face blank, to fight down the fear that was like a terrific spring coiled inside me, ready to break loose. But Neta's dark eyes were on mine, and I could feel the worry and the hurt in her gaze. And I felt more than ever my terrific love for her.

"This story about the beast is growing into quite a yarn," Foster remarked. "I've heard several persons claim they saw, or even touched, it—last night. Funny they didn't think to tell the police right after McDavid was killed."

"But it must have been some kind of animal." My voice got suddenly high, shrill. "It *must* have been!"

Foster's dark eyes squinted. "Maybe, maybe not," he said.

A few minutes later Neta got up to sing, and after her act was over, Foster left. When she came back to the table I thought she was going to start asking questions, but she didn't. She just sat there and looked at me with the worry and the hurt showing darkly in her eyes, trying to give me courage by the quiet beauty of her nature. I wanted to tell her what had happened, tell her why I was afraid; yet when I opened my mouth there were no words I could say. It was only a dream and a trick of my imagination which had frightened me, I thought, and to explain that would sound absurd.

But I was afraid to sit here alone with her. I was afraid that looking at her would cause the whole horrific vision to stab like a sword into my brain; that I would start out of my chair, as I had done the night before, lunge toward her, my hands reaching for her throat. And then . . . So I sat there, my hands gripping the edge of the table, my face turned from hers—though I could feel her eyes watching me.

Whenever I saw acquaintances, I called them over to sit with us, and I talked loudly, nervously. My eyes kept creeping toward the particular statue I had made last night that had changed into an image of myself.

But tonight nothing happened. At about 2:30 most of the crowd began to leave, and at 3:00 the roadhouse was closed.

I knew then what I had to do—because another day of constant dread, of fear ceaselessly gnawing into my mind, would drive me insane. It was the fact that I didn't *know* anything which hurt the most. And I had to know! I had to stay here tonight alone. I had to find out!

Neta, Roger Swanson, Uncle Wade and I gathered in the parking lot after the roadhouse was closed. "Damn bunch of morbid-minded thrill searchers," Uncle Wade yelled. "They'll storm the place for a night or two and then when nothing happens they'll all quit coming."

"They haven't quit coming yet," Swanson said. "I'm getting you fifty thousand dollars worth of free advertising out of this."

"Damn you and your advertising! Damn Jim and his wax models! A man would be better born without a family." Uncle Wade crawled into his automobile, slammed the door. I saw his white hair gleam in the dashlight. Then his car tore out of the lot.

I turned to Neta. "I've got to stay and do a little work. Roger will drive you home, and I'll see you in the morning."

She faced me squarely, her face tilted up to look into mine, her dark eyes defiant. "I'm not sleepy," she said flatly. "I'll stay until you finish your work."

I tried to argue with her. I even lost my temper and screamed that I didn't want her, but she only stood there straight and slim. "I'm staying," she said.

Swanson said, "I'll be glad to drive you home, but you'll have to come along now. I'm not going to stand here all night and listen to a lover's quarrel."

Neta said, "I'll wait for Jim." She turned and went toward the dark roadhouse.

"Well, that's that." Swanson kicked his motor into action, swung his car out of the parking lot.

Neta was leaning against the door when I reached her. I opened the door with my key, reached through and switched on the light. Without speaking I went down the corridor which led to the large dining room. My fingers fumbled along the wall, found the switch, and the wavering green light smeared out over the empty dance floor, the deserted tables, and over the ghastly wax statues which seemed to tremble and pulse with the eerie light.

I stood there, motionless, while the weird spell of the place began to tighten about me. My eyes strained against the semi-gloom as I sought the statue—which last night had pictured my hands ripping the throat of John McDavid.

Neta's fingers tightened on my arm, pulled me around to face her. In the green light her skin took on a horrible corpse-like appearance. Fear showed plainly in her dark eyes, but her chin was firm. "All right," she said. "Now tell me what's happened. What's made you act this way? Why did you look like you did, just before McDavid was killed last night?"

I didn't answer. I just stood there staring at her, feeling an agony of cold terror crush in against my ribs.

"What is it?" she asked again. "Tell me."

What could I say? I couldn't tell her the truth. I didn't know what the truth was. I loved Neta with every muscle and fiber in me; I didn't want her to believe me insane. Looking at her I could feel the dream gathering furiously in my mind, swelling like a great spring that must snap free at any moment. What if it came again while we were here alone? What if I saw a vision of my hand at her throat?

"Get out of here," I screamed. "Take my car and drive to the city. Get out, damn it!"

She recoiled a half-step, and I saw her eyes widen and her mouth jerk. Then she was close to me again, her hands on my chest. "You've got to tell me what's wrong, Jim. I love you."

"Listen," I said. "I want you to go home. I've got an idea about what killed McDavid last night, and I want to investigate it. It won't be safe for you here."

"You mean you saw—somebody?"

"No. I don't know what it was. But I want to find out and you—"

"I'm staying," she cut in. "It's as safe for me as it is for you. If it's what the papers say—some kind of a beast—it may be miles away from here by now." There was a strange light in her eyes as she looked at me. I couldn't tell how much she believed. But I knew that she loved me, and though she was small and quiet and modest there was an indomitable courage inside her.

"I'm going to look at the statues." I turned on my heel and began to walk around the room, pausing at each wax image, thumping it with my fingers to make sure it was exactly as I had originally made it.

I was half-way around when it happened.

Neta's voice called out suddenly, sharp with terror, "Jim, what—!"

I spun to face her.

She was near the edge of the dance floor. Just in front of her were wax figures representing Peter Caroway, the man who murdered four wives by slashing their throats with a razor, and one of the women he had killed. In eerie, moving light it seemed that the blood was seeping down the woman's throat. Beyond Neta was the model of a man splitting a woman's head with a hatchet, and close behind her was a huge wax Chinese, his long finger nails glittering in the light, his hands almost circling Neta's throat.

"What is it?" I called to her. "What's happened?"

Slowly her face lost its expression of terror, but when she smiled her lips were still quivering. "Nothing. I thought I heard somebody. It's just that this place has got on my nerves."

"It would—" I started to say it would get on anybody's nerves, but I never finished. I began to lean forward, body stiff, eyes bulging. There was something about the wax face of the Chinese, the color it took as the lights flickered over it, and the eyes which seemed to be glaring down at Neta.

"Good God," I whispered. I couldn't say any more. My breath was like jagged ice in my throat and nostrils, and my lips were suddenly stiff with terror. *For the Chinese bending above Neta had the eyes and mouth of Tai Ming!* The whole face had a terrible, horrific resemblance to that of the man who had sworn revenge. It was contorted with unbelievable savageness. It was old without showing age, like the face of a demon who has lived through eternity.

And in that same terrifying instant I knew that I had never made this statue!

I don't know what made Neta take that half-step backward. Perhaps it was the look on my face from which she recoiled instinctively. Perhaps she cried out. But I heard no sound, because the very air of the room seemed to have congealed about me, holding me cold and utterly still. I only know that she did step backward so that her throat was within an inch of the Chinese's hands—and it was in that instant that I knew he was not a wax figure!

I saw the light gleam on his fingernails as they moved. I saw his eyes widen and the savage light in them leap like a flame. I tried to scream at Neta, tried to hurl my body in a mad rush toward her, but I made no sound and did not move. It was as if I had become one of my own statues, though inside me terror was a black cyclone bursting against my ribs.

The light glittered like green flame along the Chinese's fingernails again—and they were at Neta's throat.

I moved then. It was a sudden leap, as if the spring of terror, which had been coiling in me for two days, had abruptly snapped. I heard the loud, jangling scream that slashed the air, the machine-gun beat of my shoes. I was racing toward her across the dance floor, arms flailing, a man gone mad with terror.

I think she screamed too. She half spun, her hands coming up in front her breasts, then lunged backward to strike against the pedestal on which the Chinese stood. Together they went over, with a crash.

I tried to swerve and stop running, but I was going too hard. My right foot hit the overturned pedestal, and suddenly I was in the air, seeming to hang there like a feather. Then the dance floor tilted upward and I struck it, hard. The green lights flickered into a black, quivering darkness through which I tried time and again to fight my way back to consciousness.

I couldn't have been stunned for more than ten seconds. I could feel Neta's hands on my shoulders and hear her voice, before I could see her, saying: "Jim, Jim, what is it?" Then I was on my feet stumbling toward the overturned pedestal and the still figure of the Chinese beyond it. He was lying face downward, bent from the waist, his claw-like hands holding his body from the floor.

I caught him by the shoulders and jerked with all my strength. "Damn you!" I yelled. "I—"

It was a figure of wax, one I had fashioned with my own hands, not a month before. And staring into its face I could see absolutely no resemblance to Tai Ming!

CHAPTER THREE

BLOOD—AND THE SYMBOL AGAIN!

HOW LONG I STOOD THERE without moving I don't know. My eyes had swollen until they ached against the sockets. My mouth was open, but there was no air in my lungs, and a cord of ice was cutting into my ribs. Perhaps it was only my imagination, I thought. Perhaps the figure had never had any resemblance to Tai Ming. The flickering lights might have made it seem to, move, reflected in its glass eyes—and I might have imagined the fury and murder which I saw there. But if all this were imagination, then . . .

There was only one answer. I was going insane.

But insanity couldn't have put those lines on my right hand. They were tangible evidence I actually had. Suddenly I was glad because of them—and I raised my right hand, tilting my eyes downward to find the blue lines. I wanted to see them, make sure they were really there.

Abruptly, Neta screamed!

The cry shot high and terrible, jerking at my fear-cold muscles, turning them slowly. I was half-way around when a man's voice said: "Hell! There's more yelling going on here this time of morning, than there is while the place is running."

At the far edge of the dance floor, barely visible through the dim light a man was standing. Even in the semi-darkness I could see the high, sharp angles of his face, the arched brows and the way his eyes glittered in the flickering lights. His whole face was Satanic, and his mouth curled with the savage humor of the Devil.

Neta cowered against me. Her hands were tugging at my arms, and she was making small whimpering sounds, deep in her throat. But courage began to come back to me. Here, at last, was something definite, something I would put my hands on and fight.

"Who the hell are you?" I called out.

He crossed the dance floor with a lanky, loose jointed stride. The smile on his face was confident, disdainful. "I go by the plain name of Bill Jones," he said. "You can believe it or not, but it's true. And like a good newspaper reporter I already know who you are, and don't need to ask."

I recognized him now from pictures I had seen in the *Times Democrat*. He was a man in his early thirties, but fast gaining a national reputation. Only a few months before, he had published a book of savagely humorous essays, and a year ago, he had won the Pulitzer Prize for reporting.

"What was that big crash I heard?" he asked. "Did you find the ape, or the werewolf—or any of the other things persons have been seeing since last night?"

"No. I just stumbled over one of the statues and upset it." I could feel Neta's eyes on me, could feel the terror and the question in them, but I wouldn't look at her.

"What are you doing here this time of night?" Jones asked. "You got any idea about the killing?"

For a moment I looked at him. He was lank but there was an indication of strength in his tall body, and his face was completely without fear. It would be good to have him with us, I thought. If the stories of the beast were true and we found the thing, he could help with the fight which would follow. If it were not a beast which had killed McDavid . . . The dream, crouched in the black portions of my mind, was constantly gathering strength, growing larger and larger. If it struck suddenly, then Jones would be there to protect Neta.

"I had an idea about that killing, and I stayed to investigate," I replied. "Miss Phillips stayed with me, though I tried to get her to go home."

There was a sudden tightening of his gaunt body. The angles of his face seemed to grow more sharp, his dark eyes glittered. "Yes?" he said.

"It's about the statues," I explained. "Last night, just before McDavid was killed, I thought I saw a statue which I hadn't made. I was too far away to be certain and, before I could investigate, the lights went out."

He grinned. "I'd been wondering about these statues. That's one reason I came out tonight. Let's get started."

We didn't find anything after going over the entire room carefully, tapping on every statue, making absolutely certain that they were the same wax figures I had modeled. And all the while fear crawled like some horrible worm inside me, eating its way toward my brain. Somehow I knew that we would not find the figures which I had seen, and I tried to make myself believe that there were no such figures—except in my half crazed imagination.

But I kept telling myself that those statues had to exist; and I thought of the beast which persons claimed to have seen. What if we found it—a thing which could rip open a throat and vanish again during a few moment of darkness? I wanted to keep Neta close to me, with my arm around her, and protect her with my body ... And I was afraid of the dream lurking like a storm inside me, afraid of the picture in the back of my mind, of my own bloody hands at Neta's torn throat.

"Well." Jones said, when we had finished searching the dining room, "is that all?"

"There are a few in the attic," I answered. "I've been using it for a studio, but there are no lights up there."

Jones shrugged. "There should be candles—somewhere."

We found some in the kitchen, and he and I each took one. "Come on," he said. "How do we get up there?"

The stairway winds up from the back hallway. The steps haven't been painted in years and are soft with decay, so that our shoes made dull, hollow sounds as we went up them. I led, Neta followed, and Jones came last. The light of the candles flickered like a yellow wave over the narrow walls, licked into the blackness in front of me, and faded.

I reached the top and stopped until they came abreast of me. The candle light flickered out across the floor, touched on the ghastly face of a statue lying on its back, and oozed into darkness beyond. Through the great sky-light overhead I could see tiny, white stars deep sunken in a black sky.

Jones took a half-step forward, swinging his candle so that the light rippled out into the darkness. For an instant a bestial face, long lips snarled back from yellow teeth, an up-raised hand clutching a gleaming knife-blade, were visible. Neta made a choked cry and flung herself against me.

"It's one of my statues," I said. "I haven't finished it yet."

Jones swung the candle back so that the light fell on the wax figure again. "Very neat," he said. "This whole place would fit in with a good bloody murder."

I didn't answer him. Perhaps I already knew what was coming, or maybe the strain was beginning to tell, for my nerves were drawn to the cracking point. But certainly fear was in me as it had never been before, starting deep in my stomach, storming upward. And with it the dream was crowding closer against my brain.

I said, "Stay here, Neta, with him. I want to look around." I moved ahead, the candle light wavering ahead of me and shimmering over the wax figure stretched on the floor. I stooped beside it, ran my hand over its cold, contorted face. I knew that it was wax, and I knew that I had made it, but I wanted to spend as much time as possible before I moved farther into the darkness.

I felt that there was something gruesome and horrible beyond bearing hidden in that black sea; and I wanted to avoid it. I wanted to leap to my feet and run screaming from the attic, go plunging down the rotting stairs, away from Death's Roadhouse, to find bright lights and crowds. But somehow I fought my muscles to steadiness and stood up, facing into the darkness beyond the candle light. It was there and I knew it, crouched like a black panther, waiting for me. My mind was already tottering on the edge of insanity, but I had to face this thing and find out what it was.

I stepped forward, and the light flowed ahead while darkness closed in thickly behind me. At that moment there was not even the sound of breathing—nothing except the dull thud of my steps. One, two, three, I took . . .

Then I smelted the thing which was something of an odor, but more the feeling of ancient Chinese walls, heavy with history!

I knew it was going to happen. I knew that I couldn't stop it; it was too late to run now, too late even to scream out to warn Neta. I was like a man in a dream who sees himself walking toward death and is unable to stop; like a bird looking into a snake's eyes, seeing the snake come toward him and unable even to flutter his wings.

I don't know how I raised the candle and held it farther in front of me. Perhaps I didn't really move at all, and it was only the light which stretched into the darkness, to touch faintly on the waxen image. The thing was almost completely hidden in darkness and I never saw it clearly, but in that first shuddering instant I knew what it was. It was a statue of myself holding a man with my left arm while my right hand ripped out windpipe and jugular vein. And the man held was the reporter, Bill Jones!

For a second that hung poised and, separated from all time, I stood there.

Then, inside me, the cyclone of terror and madness burst.

I can still hear in my mind's sound-memory the scream that shot upward and reverberated under the vaulted walls of the attic; that slashed and beat at the darkness. I recall the candle falling from my hand as I turned, and the way its flame sputtered and went out as it fell. I remember the yellow circle of light that Jones' candle made and my body hurdling through the blackness toward it, but I don't think I ever saw the reporter's face. Headlong I struck him, and we were both crashing over and his candle was out, so that darkness seemed almost to hurtle through the huge attic . . .

I fought something that fought with me. My hands were deep-buried in a part of it, jerking and tearing. Then, slowly, the darkness oozed into my mind, and there was no sensation or memory left.

I was on my knees and had been there a long time, it seemed. The darkness was like a wet blanket held flat against my eyes. There was no sound except the dull beat of my heart, the whisper of air through my open mouth. I blinked hard at the darkness, strained my eyelids wide open, in an effort to see. I slid my right hand across the floor in front of me—and then I touched it!

In that first instant I knew what it was. I felt the blood damp on my palm, oozing between my fingers, and I felt the flesh that was still warm and horribly slimy. It was a human body, with its throat torn wide-open!

Somehow I kept from screaming. Perhaps I couldn't have screamed, for at first I was numb, and there was no thought, no emotion in my brain. Then memory crawled back into my brain and I recalled the statue and the struggle on the floor and the screams that had beat like furious wings in the darkness.

Then I heard the sounds, like claws slowly raking the floor, and a husky, labored breathing. And into my mind crashed the picture of the ape-thing, which persons claimed to have seen.

I was lost in the pitch blackness of the attic with the thing which ripped the throats from its victims!

I tried to stop breathing then, to still the very beating of my heart, for fear the sound would give me away. I had no idea where I was in the attic, or in which direction I faced. I was afraid to move, afraid to make any attempt to escape, lest the floor creak under me.

And then another thought began to form in my brain. What had happened to Neta? Was she alive in the attic? Had she escaped, or—Good God! Suppose the torn throat I had touched, the blood that smeared my hand, were hers!

I think I stopped breathing. Every muscle in my body began to contract upon itself, while there was a lump in my throat that was like fingers digging at my own windpipe. Somehow I started my right hand across the floor toward the body which I knew was there, although I could not see it. The blood smeared out under my fingers as they moved.

It was that oozing blood which brought full consciousness and realization bursting into my mind. My hand was thick with blood, and I could feel it congealing over my wrist and forearm. It was impossible to have got that much on me from merely touching the body! How had the blood got there?

There was only one answer—and I fought it with every fiber of my brain. I hadn't killed the reporter! I *couldn't* have! I had heard a sound in the darkness that must be the beast. It had to be—because if there were no beast, then I . . . And if there *was* a beast here in the darkness, then what had happened to Neta?

I wanted to call her, to hear her voice so that I would know she was alive. But what if she didn't answer, if the figure blotted out by the darkness was hers? And if she did answer and the beast were in the room, what would happen then? Again I thought of my hands and the sticky blood smeared over them, and in my mind there was a picture of the statue I had seen; a vision of myself ripping the throat from Bill Jones.

How long I crouched there staring into the darkness I don't know. Abruptly I heard the sound again, a claw scratching on the dank flooring. I couldn't stand it any longer then. I had to know!

Suddenly my voice was screaming into the darkness, shouting with wild, maniacal fury: "Neta, Neta, where are you, what's happened?" My left hand plunged into my coat pocket, came out with a match. Even as the yellow flame spurted I heard Neta's short cry, the frantic tap of her heels on the floor. All at once, she was in my arms, sobbing.

I remember the moments that followed only as a horrible agony through which I went, knowing already what had happened. I found the candle, lit it, and gazed down at the mutilated body of Bill Jones, at the black pool of blood under his torn throat. I circled the attic, praying to find some beast that could have killed him, praying that it would attack me—and knowing all the time that no such thing existed. I looked at every wax figure in the place, but there was none I hadn't sculptured. The statues with my face and lace of Bill Jones did not exist.

Finally I turned to look at Neta; and in her eyes knowledge was a quivering and horrible certainty. She backed away from me, cringing.

I couldn't let her look at me that way.

"Neta," I whispered, "don't look at me like that. I didn't kill—" I reached out toward her, the candle light flickering brightly across my bloody hands.

I think she screamed then and leaped from me. But I had ceased to notice her. I could feel my eyelids stretching wide, eyes bulging as I looked at the back of my hand.

Beneath the congealing blood, the blue lines had become viciously dear as though they were etched there with blue flame.

There was no doubting now that it was some kind of Chinese symbol!

CHAPTER FOUR

THE VENGEANCE OF THE GODS

A GREEN SHADED LIGHT threw a bright cone of illumination over the desk and the square-faced police sergeant seated behind it. Neta was in a chair to the left, her face strangely pale in contrast to her black hair. In the semi-darkness behind me I could feel the eyes of the detectives who stood watching, near the wall.

"All right," the sergeant said. Hw voice was low and brittle, his eyes as lusterless as buttons as he looked into mine. "Let's hear your story again, and make sure you are telling the truth."

I leaned forward, put both hands on the edge of his desk. When I did the blue Chinese lines gleamed on the back of my right hand. I clenched it suddenly, thrust it deep into my pocket, shuddering. "I've told you what happened," I said. "Why do I have to go through it again?"

Neta leaned forward, deathly pale. For a moment I thought she would faint, but she steadied herself. "Please, Sergeant, we are so tired. Can't you let us go now? We've told you everything."

The sergeant turned his black eyes on her. In the back of the room I heard the restless movement of a detective's foot, heard one of them whispering to another.

The sergeant said, "I'll let you go very soon, miss. I want to hear Mr. Farlan's story again just to get it straight." His eyes came back to me, dull, expressionless and yet seeming to reach through my eyes to the very terror that was in me. "All right," he said, "let's hear it."

I told him about meeting Bill Jones while we were searching the roadhouse, but I did not tell him of the statue which I had seen come to life. "We went into the attic," I told him, "Jones and I carrying candles. It's dark there. You saw how dark it was. I stepped away from Jones and Miss Phillips and then I—I saw something and—"

"You saw *what?*" The detective's voice was never loud but it was hard and brittle as pig-iron.

"I—" My voice began to get hysterical. My hands were gripping the edge of the desk again, shaking it. "I—I don't know what it was! It was in the dark and I just—"

"What did it look like? If you saw it you've got to have some idea."

"I tell you I don't know," I yelled. "Perhaps it wasn't anything—and I just imagined It. Perhaps it was a statue, and because of the candle light I thought it moved. But it—it—" I knew I had to tell them something—anything but the truth. "It looked big and black, and shapeless, but I thought it had eyes. It frightened me. I staggered back against Jones, and both our candles went out. Then something struck me—and I don't remember what happened after that. When I came to, Miss Phillips, and—the reporter and I were there—alone. That's when we telephoned to you."

"There's blood on your coat," the sergeant said, utterly without expression. "And there was a little on your wrist, though your hands were very clean, when we reached there."

I could feel Neta's eyes on me, and the eyes of all the detectives hidden in the semi-darkness of the room. Across the desk the sergeant sat, quiet and blank-faced as a graven image. But the very dullness of his gaze set new terror grasping at my throat.

"I know," I had to swallow before I could make the words coherent. "In the dark I touched Jones and got his blood on me. I couldn't stand it—and I washed my hands before you came."

For a minute that dragged into years, the sergeant watched me. Then he said, "And what are those funny blue lines on the back of your hand? The ones that look like a Chinese laundry mark?"

I couldn't keep the fear out of my eyes then, and my mouth began to jerk. "I don't know what they are. They have been on there for a week or more."

It was an hour later that they let us go. If it hadn't been for Neta they might have held me, though there was very little evidence. But Neta corroborated my story on every statement, and though I could feel the horror and the dread in her eyes when she looked at me, she never mentioned my wild charge at the Chinese statue or the way I had whirled and leaped into Bill Jones. But when we came out of the police station into the early morning sunlight, she said, avoiding my gaze: "I'll take a cab and go home. It's out of your way; you don't need to drive me." There was a taut, trembling sound to her voice.

"But I want to take you home. It's no trouble and—" I stopped, seeing the wild dread in her face, the way she instinctively cringed from me. And there was love in her eyes, too, a love that struggled against the horror inside her.

My voice was a dead pain in my throat when I said, "All right, I'll call a cab for you." One was passing and I hailed it, stood flat-footed on the curb watching as she got in and rode off.

It was when I turned toward my own car that I saw the police sergeant standing in the doorway, watching me. His face was as expressionless as ever, his eyes lusterless as buttons. I almost ran toward my car then, and my hands were shaking so that the gears clashed badly when I started.

It was almost two full days since I had been asleep. Yet I paced nervously up and down for hours after reaching my apartment. Time and again I would throw myself on the bed and lie there, face buried in the pillow, hands gripping the cover, trembling. But even then I kept my eyes open. I was afraid, if I shut them, that a black flood of sleep would come over me . . .

It was about noon when Foster Duncan came in. His gaunt, dark face looked more hollow than ever, more strangely in contrast to the odd sense of humor which always marked his conversation. Fear showed plainly in his sunken eyes.

"I read in the afternoon papers about what happened," he said. "I came right on over here to talk to you." He dropped into a chair, dug out a cigarette. When he lit it, I saw that his fingers were trembling.

"Listen," he said, "what do you make of all this? Have you any ideas about it'"

I turned toward him slowly. "What do you mean?"

For a moment he puffed on his cigarette, then flicked off the ash. "I know it sounds crazy. but I've been thinking about this thing, and I can't get over the idea that Tai Ming is behind it. He swore to have revenge on us. You drew the pictures, and you'd be the one he'd start on. The other night we were talking about him, and you looked so damned odd just before the lights went out and McDavid got killed. And then last night . . . Even from the news-paper story I could tell that the police suspect you. This morning I got one of these break-my-back-bowing-to-be-polite-letters from Tai. He was too doggone apologetic about having lost his temper with us. A Chink will brush your clothes with a whisk-broom so that when he stabs you in the back he won't get his knife dirty.

And then that funny looking Chinese thing on the back of your hand. Where did it come from?"

Instinctively I jerked backward, and my hand came up rigidly before my face. "What—! How did you know about that?"

"I can see it on your hand now, and I saw it last night, and night before last, just after McDavid was killed. It was never there before. What caused it?"

"I—I don't know." I stared at the thing without breathing, without seeing it almost, though every tiny part of it was etched indelibly in my mind. Somehow it began to take on a new and terrible fascination as I looked, and in my mind the low, silky voice of Tai Ming swearing revenge sounded again. But Tai was in China now. How could he have anything to do with the horrors taking place thousands of miles away from him? He had written Neta and Foster that he no longer held any grudge. But why hadn't he written me?

After Foster had gone I sat for more than an hour staring blankly at the lines on the back of my hand. Where *had* they come from? Perhaps it was only a bruise, and its curious Chinese shape was only a coincidence. But I couldn't make myself believe that, and the longer I looked at it the more convinced I became that it had some secret meaning, some weird and horrific significance.

"I've got to know," I said aloud. "It doesn't really mean anything, but I've *got* to know."

I was halfway to the door before I began to wonder whom I could ask. I only knew one Chinese in the city personally, a young man taking his doctor's degree at the university, but I didn't want to ask him. Suppose these marks did have some meaning? Suppose they told the story of what had happened these past two nights at Death's Roadhouse? Would Lee Sung go to the police and tell them what he had read on the back of my hand? I didn't know, but I didn't want to take the chance. "It will be better to ask someone who doesn't know me," I thought.

I left my automobile and took a street car to China Town. At the first Chinese restaurant I passed I got off the car and went in. It was a small dark place, heavy with the odor of food. A waiter, seated at a small table in the back, was talking with two other Chinese. The shrill babble of their voices sounded eerie and strange in the semi-darkness.

I went straight up to them, moving stiff-kneed, face rigid. "Do any of you speak English?"

They all three stood up. "Yes," two of them began at once, "speak vellee well!"

"All right," I said. "Can any of you tell me what this means?" I pulled my right hand from my pocket, held it palm-down before them. In the dim light the blue lines were dully visible.

Two of the men looked at it blankly, then at me, shaking their heads. But all at once the third man was taut, rigid, bending over my hand, his own yellow fingers coming upward, quivering. Then he was backing away from me, shrilling terrified words in Chinese. The other two swung toward him for one half instant, and the yellow masks of their faces broke into trembling horror. They backed away from me, half crouching, toward the rear of the restaurant

For a long moment I stared after them looking from one face to another. Then terror seized me. "What is it?" I yelled. "What does it mean?" I started forward, hands raised to shake the truth from them.

The waiter screamed, an unbelievably high, piercing shriek. Then, like a trained dance chorus, all three turned and leaped for the door. For a moment they blocked the portal, pawing, jibbering at one another—and were gone.

I found Lee Sung in his apartment on Greensboro Avenue. He is a small man from the south of China with the bland imperturbable face, the polished manners of the well-bred Oriental. "What is it?" he asked me in English that held no trace of accent. "You look worried."

"I am." I lighted a cigarette and began to smoke nervously. He watched me with dark, unfathomable eyes.

"Several days ago," I said slowly, "some lines began to show up on the back of my right hand. They looked like a Chinese letter, and I didn't know where they came from. I don't mean to trouble you, but I was down in Chinatown today for lunch, and some Chinese saw the lines and jumped up and ran away. That got me interested. I showed the waiter my hand. He ran, too, I was frightened, and wanted to know . . ."

His expression never changed. "Perhaps I can tell you. Let me see."

I put out my right hand and caught the arm of his chair. Through an open window, afternoon sunlight fluttered in a golden stream over my sunburned skin, making the blue lines come brilliantly alive. Lee Sung leaned over and peered at them.

There was no perceptible change in his face. Suddenly, however, it was stiff and mask-like, and his expression might have been modeled in wax. After a moment he raised his slant eyes to mine.

"Well?" I said huskily.

"This is going to sound strange to you because you are not acquainted with Chinese customs and beliefs. Not all of as believe it ourselves. It is what you refer to as a superstition in English. And yet it is so well-founded—it has been confirmed by history so often—that it is impossible for the most educated of us to disbelieve entirely."

"What are you trying to tell me?" My voice was tense, edged with hysteria.

"You are acquainted with the ancient Roman custom of household gods, minor deities who look after the welfare and the safety of the home. The Chinese household gods are not so well known, perhaps because they differ in one major respect from those of the Romans, whose gods were deities who protected the home by keeping the fires burning, the members of the family healthy and other similar services. The Chinese gods do not protect the home. They are jealous, demon-like creatures who revenge insults to the family honor. Sometimes they are represented as a kind of half beast and half man, sometimes as the most powerful and bloodthirsty of the family's ancestors. But always they are terrible supernatural creatures who exist only to destroy those who have insulted the family they protect."

I was half out of my chair now, fingers digging into its arms, my weight resting on the balls of my feet, body drawn taut. "And this—this mark on my arm?"

Lee Sung said, "That is the seal by which one of these demons would mark his victim."

I slumped back into my chair, limp and not even trembling. In that first moment I accepted without reservation what he had said. At first my mind did not even struggle for hope and I *knew* the truth—that there was no escape.

But a man cannot cease to hope and to fight for existence very long. I was standing up pacing the floor, my hands clenching and unclenching nervously. "But that's absurd," I said. "You know such things can't exist. That's an old folk-tale."

"Yes?" He said the one word flatly.

I whirled on him. *"You* don't believe it! You can't believe that sort of thing!"

He made a gesture with his fragile, yellow fingers. "No. I don't believe it. And I don't disbelieve it. I have seen this mark before and . . ." He gestured with his thin hands again. "I don't want to see it on me. Probably I would commit suicide."

"No!" I hurled the word at him. "Why would you do that? How do these demons revenge themselves?"

"There are many ways. Their victims have been found frozen in the ice of rivers. They have been driven mad. They have died of disease—some very bad disease."

I don't remember leaving Lee Sung's apartment. I don't remember the next few hours. I only know that it was twilight when I came, and that there was one thing in my mind, dominating every thought and action, driving me like a whip-lash. I had to get away. I had to escape. During those hours of blankness the dream had moved into the front of my brain, and there was never a moment now when I was not conscious of it. At every step I took the picture of Neta, her head thrown back across my left arm, her throat torn and bloody, moved before me. I had to get away before I saw her again.

Instinctively, terribly, I knew that the next time it would be Neta who was killed.

I was going up the steps of my apartment when I saw the man standing on the sidewalk about forty yards away. For a half instant I paused, looking at him. And then, sick at heart, I crossed the porch, pulled open the door and went into the house. For I had seen that same man several times today without paying any attention to him, but now I knew who he was—a detective! As long as he watched me, there would be no chance to escape.

I didn't give up hope of getting away. I took all the money that was in my apartment, dropped a few small valuables into my pockets, and slipped out the back door. I had gone a block and a half when I saw the other man following me. I knew that he, too, was a detective. I stopped in the drug store, bought another pack of cigarettes and went back to my place. I tried once more, just after dark fell, but it was no use. I couldn't slip away from them.

It was then that I decided to go to Death's Roadhouse. I knew that if the detective became too suspicious about me, I would be carried to police headquarters for questioning. Somehow I couldn't face the sergeant's eyes again.

Almost everyone knows what happened at the roadhouse that night. Papers from one end of the country to the other made big stories of it. But I am the only one who knows why it happened, although the whole country wondered, and, during my trial, the court made an effort to force me to confess. I didn't want to tell, and I refused. But after I'm electrocuted, Friday night, I want Neta to know. That is one reason I'm writing this.

I kept away from Neta all the early part of that night. I wouldn't even go near the table where we generally sat. Whenever I saw Roger or Foster Duncan coming toward me, I ran from them. Once I met Neta's gaze full on me, but she did not call and I turned quickly away.

It happened shortly after midnight.

I was seated across the room from Neta, drinking heavily; but the liquor hadn't seemed to have any effect on me. I was so nervous that twice my drinks sloshed over as I raised the glass to my mouth.

From where I sat I could see Neta at a table with Roger and Uncle Wade, but I tried to keep from looking at her. I don't know what force it was that turned my eyes toward her time and again. I could see only her profile, a gruesome, greenish shade under the flickering lights. She was wearing her black hair differently tonight, combed back from her forehead and fluffy and loose around her neck. It was like this that I had seen her in the dream. Every time that I glanced at her, now, the vision came storming back into my mind with a new and mounting horror.

"It's going to happen tonight," I thought. "It will happen tonight and I can't stop it. I can't even run from it, because it has already reached across thousands of miles and there is no avoiding it." I shook myself the way a dog shakes water from his coat, and I gripped the edge of the table until my nails and knuckles were a sickly white.

"I won't really hurt Neta," I promised myself. "I couldn't hurt her because I love her more than I do my own life. I *couldn't* hurt her." Yet I knew even then that it was coming.

I asked the waiter to bring me another drink, waving at him furiously with my whole arm. "Listen," I told him, "I want a bottle of Scotch, and I want it quickly. You don't need to worry about the soda."

He looked at me curiously. "You are doing a lot of drinking tonight, Mr. Farlan. Do you think—?"

"Damn it," I yelled at him, "bring me the bottle. I don't need to think."

"Yes sir," he said, and turned away.

But the liquor did no good. It didn't dull the terror that was gathering inside any chest, and it didn't wipe out the vision of Neta's torn throat. Instead it seemed that with every swallow I took, the knowledge came clearer and clearer inside me. "It's going to happen tonight," I whispered aloud. "I can't stop it." I glanced toward Neta. Her face was almost lurid under the green wavering lights. Almost viciously I jerked my gaze away.

And then I saw it!

In the dull shadows near the wall not twenty feet from me, was a statue identically like the others. But this time it was Neta's contorted face which stared up into mine—And from her throat the blood gushed horribly.

I don't recall getting to my feet. I heard the crash of the whiskey bottle and then the heavier boom of the overturned table. There was a startled cry from persons near me, then abrupt silence crashing through the crowded roadhouse. Somehow I was walking toward the statue, wavering from side to side, my big hands clawlike in front of me. Even as the darkness started sliding into my brain, I knew that I was not going toward the statue at all—but toward Neta!

The vision of her torn throat and spilling blood burst like a shell under my skull. At the same instant from deep inside me there came the choked scream of my emotions, saying: "You love her. You love her more than your own life. You can't hurt her." I heard my own voice shouting insanely over and over: "I killed them. I killed them—and I'll kill her. You've got to stop me."

There were hands on me, hurling me down and I got one brief glimpse of the detective's face. After that there was nothing, not even memory.

And now, so help me God, I have written the entire truth as I know it. The detectives caught me before I could reach Neta. They used my shouted confession to convict me of the other two murders. At the trial, I asked for no defense because I wanted none. I wanted to be locked in this small death cell from which there is no escaping, except down the short corridor which leads into eternity.

And here, back of these barred windows through which even the sunlight comes dimly, I am still afraid that if I were released the thing would happen again. This time they might not be able to save Neta. It is better that I should die, and I am glad that it is only a short while now before they come for me.

~ ~ ~ ~ ~

When I stipulated that this account should not be read until after my execution I didn't realize the horrible consequence which might result. I believed that I would be in the death cell, alone, until the guards came for me; that it would be impossible for me to do any harm. I had told the prison authorities that I wanted no visitors. It didn't seem possible to me that I would ever again come face to face with Neta Phillips.

She must have exerted a great deal of political pull or even bribery to reach me. It was late at right and the curious, death-like silence that hangs over prisons had stilled the very air in my cell.

Through the barred door a dim grey light spilled, leaving the corners of the cell and the steel bunk in deep shadows. I sat on the bunk, shoulders hunched, and stared at the black bars of the window against a blue-black sky.

There was the hushed whisper of a guard's shoes in the corridor, the louder *tap-tap* of other steps. I didn't even turn. Perhaps it is only now that I realize that I heard those steps, for I was never aware of the door opening, or of the sound of it closing again. I just sat there, shoulders hunched, my mind as blank as the window at which I stared.

"Jim," Neta's voice was very soft, and I thought at first that I was dreaming. Then she said, "Jim!" again, and all at once I was on my feet, spinning to face her.

She and Roger Swanson stood just inside the barred door. Her slim figure showed plainly against the lighted corridor, but her face was in the shadows. I saw her hands, like small white birds as she raised them to reach for me. "Darling," she said, "I've wanted to see you for so long. I had to come." She stepped toward me.

With one great leap I went backward and struck against the far wall of the cell. "Keep away from me," I shouted. "Don't come any closer."

She paused, one foot still in front of the other, her hands raised. "Jim!" There was a terrible hurt in her voice. "What have I done? Why did you avoid me all during the trial? Why are you acting like this?" Her words were very low, as though the deep silence of the prison had affected her so that she whispered unconsciously. During all the time that she was there none of us spoke loudly. Even when I shouted at her the sound was scarcely above a hoarse whisper.

I had to swallow the terror mounting in my throat before I could answer her question. "It's nothing you've done. It's me. I've gone insane. You've got to keep away from me or—or—" I couldn't say she would be murdered as the men had been. I couldn't force the words out of my throat.

In the utter stillness of the cell I could hear her breathing as she looked at me, silent, pleading with her eyes. Roger Swanson was standing near the door watching us quietly. "You're not insane," Neta said finally. "But you're in some kind of trouble. You've got to tell me what it is. Perhaps I can help you. If you had let me see you during the trial—"

"I don't want to see you." I hurled the words at her in that queer whispered scream which the prison had forced on me. "I told them not to let you in here. And I wish to God you'd get out while there's time. I don't ever want to see you again."

She made a choked, gasping cry and stepped backwards. Then all at once she had slumped on the bunk and terrible, racked sobs shook her body.

"God, I can't stand this," Roger Swanson said hoarsely. He pulled a flask from his pocket, unscrewed the top with one twist and raised it to his lips.

With two long strides I passed Neta and reached him, snatched the flask from his hands. "I need it!" I turned it up and gulped at it until it was dry, then handed it back to him. In all the prison there was no sound except Neta's racked sobbing and the rasping of my own breath.

Abruptly I swung toward her. "Get out," I said softly. "Please get out, quickly. You've got to go, because soon . . ."

I was still speaking when I smelled that odor which was not an odor at all, but rather the feeling of ancient Chinese walls. And in that instant I knew what was coming.

"Oh God!" I tried to cry aloud, but the words choked in my throat. I tried to scream at her, to scream for the guards to come and hold me. My mouth jerked with the terrible and searing effort to cry out, but there was no sound.

I was wavering toward her and though I tried to stop myself I could not. It was as if I were off balance, and instinctively I stumbled forward to keep from falling. I could feel my hands coming up, the big fingers hooked, claw-like, reaching toward her throat.

Neta was on her feet now, her face white, her eyes wild with terror. "Jim," she whispered, "Jim!" I could see her whole body trembling as she tried to break the ropes of terror that held her. "Jim," she said again.

But already the darkness was sliding into my head I seemed to lose my balance and stumble forward again. My hands were already at her throat. Then with a last terrific struggle of consciousness I dived at Roger Swanson.

"Hold me," I yelled at him. "Keep me away from her." My arms were already around him when I saw the light gleam on his right hand and a new, unbearable terror smashed into me,

For his right hand was blade of steel, the fingers long and hooked. In that instant I knew who had killed McDavid and Bill Jones!

The heavy steel hand swung up, at my head. But I was close to him and the blow landed glancingly on the back of my neck. Then my left hand closed on the steel.

I had five inches more height and forty pounds more weight than Roger Swanson. I tore at his arm, snatched it from behind my neck and jabbed it at his own throat—forced it against his gullet, with all my superior strength. Instinctively, he tried to snatch his hand away. The steel fingers struck like a hawk's claw, buried themselves in his throat. With the last blind reeling of my consciousness, I tried to tear the hand from his neck. I saw the flesh burst, the wild gush of blood.

I heard Neta's shrill, hysterical scream smashing against the cell, and I felt the rush of warm blood over my face. After that there was nothing but oblivion . . .

Because of Roger Swanson's death, the whole thing was never explained as clearly as it might have been. The police, however, brought out all the necessary details. For a long time after the investigation, which resulted in the killings being pinned on Roger, and subsequently in my release from prison, even the police were baffled by Roger's motive. It was not until after they had sought out my uncle, Paul Farlan—the wealthy and eccentric recluse—for whom Roger acted as secretary, that his purpose became clear.

Kinship is close in my family, so Uncle Paid had willed Roger enough money for him to live on. But Roger, the police learned, already owed that much. My uncle had divided the rest of his estate into three equal portions, One part was to come to me. The rest was to go to the two men whom Uncle Paul had decided were winning the most promising literary careers of anyone in the state and who needed the money. Because he never read the newspapers it is not likely that he would ever have been aware of their deaths. The old man spent most of his time reading books, but he would not allow a newspaper or magazine into his home.

He did, however, hear of my conviction as a murderer, because Uncle Wade told him. It was then that he changed his will, leaving my share to Neta, who was the only person that he really cared for. And while he was making this change, it occurred to him that the other two beneficiaries might die; and he inserted a clause leaving their share to charity under such conditions.

This meant that Roger would get nothing at all except his own share unless Neta were killed. And so Roger tried that last desperate attempt in the jail. When he first originated his plans, the will was so phrased that by eliminating the beneficiaries the entire estate would have been divided between Roger and my Uncle Wade who were the only living relatives. Uncle Wade was an old man and could not have lived much longer.

We never learned just what kind of knockout drops he was using on me. I am sure, however, that they were administered earlier, and that the odor immediately preceding each attack was some kind of catalytic agent which speeded up the reaction. The last dose he gave me must have been in the flask from which he only pretended to drink. I don't know when he administered the others, but a man drinks plenty in a roadhouse.

Concerning the dream, I have never been certain. I had probably been doped before going to sleep and then, during those half stupefied moments when I was coming out from the effects of the drugs, a picture of the statue which I was to see later may have been flashed against the dark wall of the room.

The steel glove which Roger used had fingers which worked on the same principle as ice tongs; the harder he pulled away, the deeper the fingers dug in. It was because of this that he was killed when I tried to pull the hand from his throat.

We were never able to locate the Chinese whom he had hired to help him, though the police are still working on the idea that it was the Chinese who modeled the wax statues with my face and the faces of the victims. They did find, however, the trap doors by which he caused the statues to appear and disappear, and the electric wires which he had rigged up so that from several places inside the dining room he could disconnect the entire light service.

The blue marks are still on the back of my hand. They must have been stamped there by tiny tattoo needles, probably set in a rubber stamp, during the brief moments when I was unconscious. I don't know. But I do know that now, whenever I look at them and then look up to see my wife's eyes watching me, I feel the swift surge of terror, the cold fear sweeping along my spine. And I shall never forget these things. I cannot look at those blue lines and at Neta's white throat without shuddering . . .

RAMBLE HOUSE's

HARRY STEPHEN KEELER WEBWORK MYSTERIES

(RH) indicates the title is available ONLY in the RAMBLE HOUSE edition

The Ace of Spades Murder
The Affair of the Bottled Deuce (RH)
The Amazing Web
The Barking Clock
Behind That Mask
The Book with the Orange Leaves
The Bottle with the Green Wax Seal
The Box from Japan
The Case of the Canny Killer
The Case of the Crazy Corpse (RH)
The Case of the Flying Hands (RH)
The Case of the Ivory Arrow
The Case of the Jeweled Ragpicker
The Case of the Lavender Gripsack
The Case of the Mysterious Moll
The Case of the 16 Beans
The Case of the Transparent Nude (RH)
The Case of the Transposed Legs
The Case of the Two-Headed Idiot (RH)
The Case of the Two Strange Ladies
The Circus Stealers (RH)
Cleopatra's Tears
A Copy of Beowulf (RH)
The Crimson Cube (RH)
The Face of the Man From Saturn
Find the Clock
The Five Silver Buddhas
The 4th King
The Gallows Waits, My Lord! (RH)
The Green Jade Hand
Finger! Finger!
Hangman's Nights (RH)
I, Chameleon (RH)
I Killed Lincoln at 10:13! (RH)
The Iron Ring
The Man Who Changed His Skin (RH)
The Man with the Crimson Box
The Man with the Magic Eardrums
The Man with the Wooden Spectacles
The Marceau Case
The Matilda Hunter Murder
The Monocled Monster

The Murder of London Lew
The Murdered Mathematician
The Mysterious Card (RH)
The Mysterious Ivory Ball of Wong Shing Li (RH)
The Mystery of the Fiddling Cracksman
The Peacock Fan
The Photo of Lady X (RH)
The Portrait of Jirjohn Cobb
Report on Vanessa Hewstone (RH)
Riddle of the Travelling Skull
Riddle of the Wooden Parrakeet (RH)
The Scarlet Mummy (RH)
The Search for X-Y-Z
The Sharkskin Book
Sing Sing Nights
The Six From Nowhere (RH)
The Skull of the Waltzing Clown
The Spectacles of Mr. Cagliostro
Stand By—London Calling!
The Steeltown Strangler
The Stolen Gravestone (RH)
Strange Journey (RH)
The Strange Will
The Straw Hat Murders (RH)
The Street of 1000 Eyes (RH)
Thieves' Nights
Three Novellos (RH)
The Tiger Snake
The Trap (RH)
Vagabond Nights (Defrauded Yeggman)
Vagabond Nights 2 (10 Hours)
The Vanishing Gold Truck
The Voice of the Seven Sparrows
The Washington Square Enigma
When Thief Meets Thief
The White Circle (RH)
The Wonderful Scheme of Mr. Christopher Thorne
X. Jones—of Scotland Yard
Y. Cheung, Business Detective

Keeler Related Works

A To Izzard: A Harry Stephen Keeler Companion by Fender Tucker — Articles and stories about Harry, by Harry, and in his style. Included is a compleat bibliography.

Wild About Harry: Reviews of Keeler Novels — Edited by Richard Polt & Fender Tucker — 22 reviews of works by Harry Stephen Keeler from *Keeler News*. A perfect introduction to the author.

The Keeler Keyhole Collection: Annotated newsletter rants from Harry Stephen Keeler, edited by Francis M. Nevins. Over 400 pages of incredibly personal Keeleriana.

Fakealoo — Pastiches of the style of Harry Stephen Keeler by selected demented members of the HSK Society. Updated every year with the new winner.

Strands of the Web: Short Stories of Harry Stephen Keeler — Edited and Introduced by Fred Cleaver

RAMBLE HOUSE's OTHER LOONS

Alexander Laing Novels — *The Motives of Nicholas Holtz* and *Dr. Scarlett*, stories of medical mayhem and intrigue from the 30s.

Amorous Intrigues & Adventures of Aaron Burr, The — by Anonymous — Hot historical action.

Angel in the Street, An — Modern hardboiled noir by Peter Genovese.

Anthony Boucher Chronicles, The — edited by Francis M. Nevins Book reviews by Anthony Boucher written for the *San Francisco Chronicle*, 1942 – 1947. Essential and fascinating reading.

Automaton — Brilliant treatise on robotics: 1928-style! By H. Stafford Hatfield

Best of 10-Story Book, The — edited by Chris Mikul, over 35 stories from the literary magazine Harry Stephen Keeler edited.

Black Dark Murders, The — Vintage 50s college murder yarn by Milt Ozaki, writing as Robert O. Saber.

Black Hogan Strikes Again — Australia's Peter Renwick pens a tale of the outback.

Black River Falls — Suspense from the master, Ed Gorman

Blood in a Snap — The *Finnegan's Wake* of the 21st century, by Jim Weiler

Blood Moon — The first of the Robert Payne series by Ed Gorman

Case of the Little Green Men, The — Mack Reynolds wrote this love song to sci-fi fans back in 1951 and it's now back in print.

Case of the Withered Hand, The — 1936 potboiler by John G. Brandon

Charlie Chaplin Murder Mystery, The — Movie hijinks by Wes D. Gehring

Chelsea Quinn Yarbro Novels featuring Charlie Moon — *Ogilvie, Tallant and Moon, Music When the Sweet Voice Dies, Poisonous Fruit* and *Dead Mice*

Chinese Jar Mystery, The — Murder in the manor by John Stephen Strange, 1934

Clear Path to Cross, A — Sharon Knowles short mystery stories by Ed Lynskey

Compleat Calhoon, The — All of Fender Tucker's works: Includes *Totah Six-Pack, Weed, Women and Song* and *Tales from the Tower*, plus a CD of all of his songs.

Compleat Ova Hamlet, The — Parodies of SF authors by Richard A. Lupoff – A brand new edition with more stories and more illustrations by Trina Robbins.

Contested Earth and Other SF Stories, The — A never-before published space opera and seven short stories by Jim Harmon.

Cornucopia of Crime, A — Memoirs and Summations of 30 years in the crime fiction game by Francis M. Nevins

Crimson Clown Novels — By Johnston McCulley, author of the Zorro novels, *The Crimson Clown* and *The Crimson Clown Again*.

Crimson Query, The — A supervillain from the 20s by Arlton Eadie.

Dago Red — 22 tales of dark suspense by Bill Pronzini

Dancing Tuatara Press Books — *Beast or Man?* by Sean M'Guire; *The Whistling Ancestors* by Richard E. Goddard; *The Shadow on the House, Sorcerer's Chessmen, The Wizard of Berner's Abbey, The Ghost of Gaston Revere*, and *Master of Souls* by Mark Hansom, *The Trail of the Cloven Hoof* by Arlton Eadie and *The Border Line* by Walter S. Masterman, and *Reunion in Hell* by John H. Knox, and *The Tongueless Horror* by Wyatt Blassingame. With introductions by John Pelan. Many more to come!

David Hume Novels — *Corpses Never Argue, Cemetery First Stop, Make Way for the Mourners, Eternity Here I Come*, and more to come.

Day Keene Short Stories — League of the Grateful Dead, We Are the Dead and *Death March of the Dancing Dolls*. Collections from the pulps by a master writer. Introductions by John Pelan.

Dead Man Talks Too Much — Hollywood boozer by Weed Dickenson

Death Leaves No Card — One of the most unusual murdered-in-the-tub mysteries you'll ever read. By Miles Burton.

Deep Space and other Stories — A collection of SF gems by Richard A. Lupoff

Detective Duff Unravels It — Episodic mysteries by Harvey O'Higgins

Devil Drives, The — A prison and lost treasure novel by Virgil Markham

Devil's Mistress, The — Scottish gothic tale by J. W. Brodie-Innes.

Dime Novels: Ramble House's 10-Cent Books — *Knife in the Dark* by Robert Leslie Bellem, *Hot Lead* and *Song of Death* by Ed Earl Repp, *A Hashish House in New York* by H.H. Kane, and five more.

Don Diablo: Book of a Lost Film — Two-volume treatment of a western by Paul Landres, with diagrams. Intro by Francis M. Nevins.

Dope Tales #1 — Two dope-riddled classics; *Dope Runners* by Gerald Grantham and *Death Takes the Joystick* by Phillip Condé.

Dope Tales #2 — Two more narco-classics; *The Invisible Hand* by Rex Dark and *The Smokers of Hashish* by Norman Berrow.

Dope Tales #3 — Two enchanting novels of opium by the master, Sax Rohmer. *Dope* and *The Yellow Claw*.

Dr. Odin — Douglas Newton's 1933 potboiler comes back to life.

Dumpling, The — Political murder from 1907 by Coulson Kernahan

Edmund Snell Novels — *The Sign of the Scorpion, The White Owl* and *Dope and Swastikas* (*The Dope Dealer* and *The Crimson Swastika*)

End of It All and Other Stories — Ed Gorman's latest short story collection

Evidence in Blue — 1938 mystery by E. Charles Vivian

Fatal Accident — Murder by automobile, a 1936 mystery by Cecil M. Wills

Finger-prints Never Lie — A 1939 classic detective novel by John G. Brandon

Freaks and Fantasies — Eerie tales by Tod Robbins, collaborator of Tod Browning on the film FREAKS.

Gadsby — A lipogram (a novel without the letter E). Ernest Vincent Wright's last work, published in 1939 right before his death.

Gelett Burgess Novels — *The Master of Mysteries, The White Cat, Two O'Clock Courage, Ladies in Boxes, Find the Woman, The Heart Line, The Picaroons* and *Lady Mechante*

Geronimo — S. M. Barrett's 1905 autobiography of a noble American.

Gold Star Line, The — Seaboard adventure from L.T. Reade and Robert Eustace.

Golden Dagger, The — 1951 Scotland Yard yarn by E. R. Punshon

Hake Talbot Novels — *Rim of the Pit, The Hangman's Handyman.* Classic locked room mysteries.

Hell Fire and **Savage Highway** — Two new hard-boiled novels by Jack Moskovitz, who developed his style writing sleaze back in the 70s. No one writes like Jack.

Hollywood Dreams — A novel of the Depression by Richard O'Brien

House of the Vampire, The — 1907 poetic thriller by George S. Viereck.

I Stole $16,000,000 — A true story by cracksman Herbert E. Wilson.

Inclination to Murder — 1966 thriller by New Zealand's Harriet Hunter

Incredible Adventures of Rowland Hern, The — 1928 impossible crimes by Nicholas Olde.

Invaders from the Dark — Classic werewolf tale from Greye La Spina

Jack Mann Novels — Strange murder in the English countryside. *Gees' First Case, Nightmare Farm, Grey Shapes, The Ninth Life, The Glass Too Many.*

Jim Harmon Double Novels — *Vixen Hollow/Celluloid Scandal, The Man Who Made Maniacs/Silent Siren, Ape Rape/Wanton Witch, Sex Burns Like Fire/Twist Session, Sudden Lust/Passion Strip, Sin Unlimited/Harlot Master, Twilight Girls/Sex Institution.* Written in the early 60s.

Joel Townsley Rogers Novels — By the author of *The Red Right Hand: Once In a Red Moon, Lady With the Dice, The Stopped Clock, Never Leave My Bed*

Joel Townsley Rogers Story Collections — *Night of Horror* and *Killing Time*

Joseph Shallit Novels — *The Case of the Billion Dollar Body, Lady Don't Die on My Doorstep, Kiss the Killer, Yell Bloody Murder, Take Your Last Look.* One of America's best 50's authors.

Jvlivs Caesar Mvrder Case, The — A classic 1935 re-telling of the assassination by Wallace Irwin that's much more fun than the Shakespeare version

Keller Memento — 500 pages of short stories by David H. Keller.

Killer's Caress — Cary Moran's 1936 hardboiled thriller

Koky Comics, The — A collection of all of the 1978-1981 Sunday and daily comic strips by Richard O'Brien and Mort Gerberg, in two volumes.

Lady of the Terraces, The — 1925 adventure by E. Charles Vivian.

Lord of Terror, The — 1925 mystery with master-criminal, Fantômas.

Marblehead: A Novel of H.P. Lovecraft — A long-lost masterpiece from Richard A. Lupoff. Published for the first time!

Max Afford Novels — *Owl of Darkness, Death's Mannikins, Blood on His Hands, The Dead Are Blind, The Sheep and the Wolves, Sinners in Paradise* and *Two Locked Room Mysteries and a Ripping Yarn* by one of Australia's finest novelists.

Muddled Mind: Complete Works of Ed Wood, Jr. — David Hayes and Hayden Davis deconstruct the life and works of a mad genius.

Murder in Black and White — 1931 classic tennis whodunit by Evelyn Elder

Murder in Shawnee — Novels of the Alleghenies by John Douglas: *Shawnee Alley Fire* and *Haunts.*

Murder in Silk — A 1937 Yellow Peril novel of the silk trade by Ralph Trevor

My Deadly Angel — 1955 Cold War drama by John Chelton

My First Time: The One Experience You Never Forget — Michael Birchwood — 64 true first-person narratives of how they lost it.

Mysterious Martin, the Master of Murder — Two versions of a strange 1912 novel by Tod Robbins about a man who writes books that can kill.

N. R. De Mexico Novels — Robert Bragg presents *Marijuana Girl, Madman on a Drum, Private Chauffeur* in one volume.

Night Remembers, The — A 1991 Jack Walsh mystery from Ed Gorman

Norman Berrow Novels — *The Bishop's Sword, Ghost House, Don't Go Out After Dark, Claws of the Cougar, The Smokers of Hashish, The Secret Dancer, Don't Jump Mr. Boland!, The Footprints of Satan, Fingers for Ransom, The Three Tiers of Fantasy, The Spaniard's Thumb, The Eleventh Plague, Words Have Wings, One Thrilling Night, The Lady's in Danger, It Howls at Night, The Terror in the Fog, Oil Under the Window, Murder in the Melody, The Singing Room*

Old Times' Sake — Short stories by James Reasoner from Mike Shayne Magazine

One After Snelling, The — Kickass modern noir from Richard O'Brien.

Organ Reader, The — A huge compilation of just about everything published in the 1971-1972 radical bay-area newspaper, THE ORGAN.

Poker Club, The — The short story, the novel and the screenplay of the seminal thriller by Ed Gorman

Private Journal & Diary of John H. Surratt, The — The memoirs of the man who conspired to assassinate President Lincoln.

Prose Bowl — Futuristic satire — Bill Pronzini & Barry N. Malzberg .

Red Light — History of legal prostitution in Shreveport Louisiana by Eric Brock. Includes wonderful photos of the houses and the ladies.

Researching American-Made Toy Soldiers — A 276-page collection of a lifetime of articles by toy soldier expert Richard O'Brien

Ripped from the Headlines! — The Jack the Ripper story as told in the newspaper articles in the *New York* and *London Times.*

Robert Randisi Novels — *No Exit to Brooklyn* and *The Dead of Brooklyn.* The first two Nick Delvecchio novels.

Roland Daniel Double: The Signal and The Return of Wu Fang — Classic thrillers from the 30s

Rough Cut & New, Improved Murder — Ed Gorman's first two novels

Ruled By Radio — 1925 futuristic novel by Robert L. Hadfield & Frank E. Farncombe

Rupert Penny Novels — *Policeman's Holiday, Policeman's Evidence, Lucky Policeman, Policeman in Armour, Sealed Room Murder, Sweet Poison, The Talkative Policeman, She had to Have Gas* and *Cut and Run* (by Martin Tanner.) This is the complete Rupert Penny library of novels.

Sam McCain Novels — Ed Gorman's terrific series includes *The Day the Music Died, Wake Up Little Susie*

Sand's Game — A selection of the best of Ennis Willie, including a complete novel.

Satan's Den Exposed — True crime in Truth or Consequences New Mexico — Award-winning journalism by the *Desert Journal.*

Secret Adventures of Sherlock Holmes, The — Three Sherlockian pastiches by the Brooklyn author/publisher, Gary Lovisi.

Sex Slave — Potboiler of lust in the days of Cleopatra — Dion Leclerq.

Shadows' Edge — Two early novels by Wade Wright: *Shadows Don't Bleed* and *The Sharp Edge.*

Shot Rang Out, A — Three decades of reviews from Jon Breen

Sideslip — 1968 SF masterpiece by Ted White and Dave Van Arnam

Singular Problem of the Stygian House-Boat, The — Two classic tales by John Kendrick Bangs about the denizens of Hades.

Slammer Days — Two full-length prison memoirs: *Men into Beasts* (1952) by George Sylvester Viereck and *Home Away From Home* (1962) by Jack Woodford

Smell of Smoke, A — 1951 English countryside thriller by Miles Burton

Snark Selection, A — Lewis Carroll's *The Hunting of the Snark* with two Snarkian chapters by Harry Stephen Keeler — Illustrated by Gavin L. O'Keefe.

Stakeout on Millennium Drive — Award-winning Indianapolis Noir — Ian Woollen.

Suzy — Another collection of comic strips from Richard O'Brien and Bob Vojtko

Tales of the Macabre and Ordinary — Modern twisted horror by Chris Mikul, author of the *Bizarrism* series.

Tenebrae — Ernest G. Henham's 1898 horror tale brought back.

Through the Looking Glass — Lewis Carroll wrote it; Gavin L. O'Keefe illustrated it.

Time Armada, The — Fox B. Holden's 1953 SF gem.

Tiresias — Psychotic modern horror novel by Jonathan M. Sweet.

Totah Six-Pack — Fender Tucker's six tales about Farmington in one sleek volume.

Triune Man, The — Mindscrambling science fiction from Richard A. Lupoff

Ultra-Boiled — 23 gut-wrenching tales by our Man in Brooklyn, Gary Lovisi. Yow!

Universal Holmes, The — Richard A. Lupoff's 2007 collection of five Holmesian pastiches and a recipe for giant rat stew.

Victims & Villains — Intriguing Sherlockiana from Derham Groves

Wade Wright Novels — *Echo of Fear, Death At Nostalgia Street* and *It Leads to Murder,* with more to come!

Walter S. Masterman Mysteries — *The Green Toad, The Flying Beast, The Yellow Mistletoe, The Wrong Verdict* and *The Perjured Alibi, The Border Line, The Curse of Cantire.* Fantastic impossible plots.

Werewolf vs the Vampire Woman, The — Hard to believe ultraviolence by either Arthur M. Scarm or Arthur M. Scram.

West Texas War and Other Western Stories — by Gary Lovisi

Whip Dodge: Manhunter — A modern western from the pen of Wesley Tallant

White Peril in the Far East, The — Sidney Lewis Gulick's 1905 indictment of the West and assurance that Japan would never attack the U.S.

You'll Die Laughing — Bruce Elliott's 1945 novel of murder at a practical joker's English countryside manor.

Young Man's Heart, A — A forgotten early classic by Cornell Woolrich

RAMBLE HOUSE

Fender Tucker, Prop.   Gavin L. O'Keefe, Graphics

www.ramblehouse.com   fender@ramblehouse.com

228-826-1783   10329 Sheephead Drive, Vancleave MS 39565

18313341R00154

Made in the USA
Lexington, KY
26 October 2012